FOR THE LOVE OF A SOLDIER

It's 1943 and Maggie Evans is living with her parents when the GIs arrive. Southampton is transformed and Maggie's not the only girl to fall for an American soldier. She's never met anyone like Steve Rossi, but when he pulls a knife during a fight, Maggie begins to wonder what other secrets he's concealing. Then Maggie is seen chatting to another GI, Joshua Lewis. Joshua is kind, considerate – and black. Steve's a bigot – not the only one in Southampton – and he warns Joshua off. But are Maggie's feelings for Joshua as platonic as she says...

FOR THE LOVE OF A SOLDIER

FOR THE LOVE OF A SOLDIER

by

June Tate

Magna Large Print Books
Long Preston, North Yorkshire,
BD23 4ND, England.

British Library Cataloguing in Publication Data.

Tate, June
     For the love of a soldier.

     A catalogue record of this book is
     available from the British Library

     ISBN   0-7505-1681-X

First published in Great Britain in 1999
by Headline Book Publishing

Copyright © 1999 June Tate

Cover illustration © Nigel Chamberlain by arrangement with
Headline Book Publishing

Published in Large Print 2001 by arrangement with
Headline Book Publishing Ltd.

Magna Large Print is an imprint of Library Magna Books Ltd.

Printed and bound in Great Britain by
T.J. (International) Ltd., Cornwall, PL28 8RW

With love to my younger daughter, Maxine, who several years ago urged me to join an evening class for Creative Writing, instead of talking about it, and was therefore responsible for starting me on this wondrous journey. How can I ever repay her?

With thanks to my older daughter, Beverley, who brings so much laughter into my life, and to Alan, my husband, my friend ... my love.

Chapter One

Southampton, 1944

Jack Evans glared balefully across the breakfast table at his daughter. 'I suppose you and your mate are off to the dance at the Guildhall again tonight?'

'Now don't start, Dad,' Maggie protested, sipping her tea.

'Start, I haven't even begun! You know what I think about you and that Ivy, swanning around the town with the Yanks. They're here today and gone tomorrow. These men are only after one thing. People will say you're no better than a tart!'

Maggie's cheeks flushed with anger. 'Thanks a lot. You speak to me as if I'm some loose woman off the streets instead of your daughter. Have I ever brought any disgrace to this house? To you or Mum?'

His tone softened a fraction. 'No you haven't, but I don't want you getting a bad reputation, that's all.'

'For God's sake! We only go to dance.'

His mouth tightened. 'That's what they all say. But I've seen the women pushing prams with their Yankee bastards in them. No doubt before too long we'll see prams full of babies as black as the ace of spades. I don't want that for you.

13

They've got no shame these women, and most of them have husbands in the forces, fighting for their country. I think it's disgusting. Your friend Ivy, for one, should be ashamed of herself,' he continued. 'Her man is with Monty's army. He'd bloody kill her if he knew she was fraternizing with them soldiers.'

Maggie's temper rose in defence of her friend. 'What Ivy does is her business and none of yours!'

He banged the table with his fist. 'It is my business when you're mixing with the likes of her. People will think you're cheap, like she is.'

Rising to her feet, her face white with rage, her green eyes flashing, Maggie snapped at him. 'How dare you speak to me like that! I'm a good girl, and you sitting there all sanctimonious with your preaching, just shows what a hypocrite you are.'

He was furious. 'What do you mean?'

'You think Mum and I don't know what goes on here? You think we don't know that your front room, the one you keep under lock and key, isn't filled with black market gear? Most of it American! But that's a different story, I suppose.' She walked away. 'You make me sick!' she cried as she opened the kitchen door.

Jack was puce. 'What I do is none of your business.'

'And what *I* do is none of yours!'

'Whilst you're living under my roof it is,' he called after her retreating figure.

Maggie slammed shut the front door of the Bricklayer's Arms in College Street and strode

14

off, seething with indignation. She was sick and tired of her father's constant tirades about the American soldiers. It made a change to have fellows in the town that were a bit different, who had a bit of life in them.

Southampton had suffered greatly from the Blitz in 1940. Buildings had been cleared, one-storey shops had been erected, but all around there were still signs of the devastation caused by the constant bombing. Three years later, the arrival of the American Army, billeted around the town in camps, had somehow lifted the spirits of the town. The natural exuberance of these men was welcomed by many, but as they were better dressed than their British counterparts and much better paid, it also caused a great deal of conflict. But the biggest scandal of all was the arrival of a company of two hundred black American soldiers. For many of the townsfolk it was the first time they'd encountered men with black skins and they were horrified when they blatantly walked around the streets of Southampton with white girls on their arms.

Arriving at the entrance of the munitions factory where she worked, Maggie took a scarf out of the pocket of her dungarees and tied it around her auburn hair, turban fashion. As she clocked on she was greeted by Bill the foreman.

'Going out tonight are we?' he asked with a grin. Maggie's love of dancing was well known among her workmates.

'Why, William? Are you asking me for a date?'

'What would my Nellie have to say about that?'

15

She patted his face. 'What would she say if I told her how you flirted with all the girls?'

'You cheeky tyke! I ought to tan your bottom.'

'Promises, promises,' she teased.

'Now you behave, Maggie Evans. Here. You know what they say about utility knickers, don't you?'

'No, what?'

'One Yank and they're off!' He walked away laughing loudly at his own joke.

Maggie made her way to her machine, shaking her head in mock despair.

In the canteen at midday, listening to *Workers' Playtime,* she was joined by her great friend, Ivy.

'What's up, love?' Ivy asked. 'You're looking a bit down in the mouth.'

'I had another run-in with my father this morning. For God's sake, I'm twenty-one. Old enough to take care of myself.'

'Don't be too harsh with him,' reasoned Ivy. 'If I had a daughter our age, I'd be worried about her virginity too. These Yanks are like bloody octopuses, hands everywhere. All jeeps and genitals they are. It's something they put in their coffee if you ask me.'

Maggie chuckled. 'Well that's something *you* don't have to worry about, losing your virginity. You being a married woman.'

'I don't feel married. Me and Len were only together six months when he was sent overseas. He's been away almost a year now.'

'Have you heard from him lately?'

'I had a letter this morning. He'd been in some place called Tripoli.'

16

Thinking of her father's remarks, Maggie said, 'Would he mind you going dancing, having a good time?'

'What! He'd go mad. A jealous bugger, my Len. Not that I give a toss. Look, a passionate little sod he is. He used to get the hump when I had the curse. He'll be off having it away with some woman, somewhere. He'd need his oats, wouldn't be able to help himself, of that I'm sure!'

'That's a dreadful thing to say.'

Ivy looked calmly at her friend. 'Look, Maggie, I know my old man, he'll be having a good time all right. It won't mean anything, and let's face it, there's a war on, he could be killed and I'd have missed all this fun for nothing.'

Maggie was shocked. 'You don't even sound upset by the idea.'

Ivy's eyes clouded. 'To be honest, I can't remember what he looks like unless I look at his picture, and then it's like a stranger staring back at me.' She smiled suddenly. 'When he comes home, it'll be all right. We'll start all over again, it'll be like a honeymoon. I doubt I'll be able to walk by the time he's finished with me!'

Maggie smothered a grin. Ivy was quite outrageous, and although she didn't agree with her cavalier attitude to marriage, their friendship was strong. She worried, though, that when her husband came home, he might learn of Ivy's adventures and she was fearful of the consequences.

She supposed her own parents were happy in their way. She adored Moira, her mother, but her father was a difficult man to love. He had been

17

born with one leg shorter than the other and she knew that at times this made him feel less than a man. Yet he was able to clear a bar of awkward customers when there was any trouble, and fights did break out now and again in his pub in the docklands of Southampton. For a cripple, he was able to move surprisingly quickly. He was wiry in build and very strong.

It was because of the love she felt for her mother that she had elected to stay in Southampton and work in a factory, as opposed to joining one of the women's forces and getting away, tasting a bit of freedom. Her father gave her mother a hard time on occasion with his sharp tongue, although Moira, a spirited woman of Irish stock, only took so much, then she let rip.

Behind her husband's back, Moira encouraged Maggie to enjoy herself.

'You have a good time, darlin',' she would tell her. 'You're only young once and sometimes life can turn out to be disappointing. None of us knows what's before us.'

It made Maggie wonder just how happy her mother was with her chosen mate. Yet she never said a word against her husband and when she felt he was right, she stood by him against her daughter; but this didn't happen often.

Jack Evans limped to the side door of the pub in answer to the urgent knocking. On the doorstep stood Sonny Taylor, a local spiv, wearing his wide-shouldered camelhair coat, with the usual silk tie. His blond hair was sleeked back with Brylcreem.

18

He handed a heavy box to Jack then picked up another, pushing his way inside. 'Close the bloody door then,' he ordered sharply. 'Don't want any of your neighbours poking their noses in, do we?'

Unlocking the door of the front room, Jack ushered the man inside. 'What you got this time?' he asked, his eyes bright with greed and anticipation.

Sonny grinned at him. 'Nice little haul,' he said. 'Cartons of Camel and Lucky Strike cigarettes, nylon stockings, large tins of pineapple chunks and a dozen bottles of bourbon. Know anyone who needs petrol? I've got a contact that's very well placed.'

'I can get rid of anything you can find,' said Jack. 'Put that down there and come into the bar. We'll have a drink and I'll pay you.'

They sat on the wooden bench against one of the walls in the horseshoe-shaped bar. Jack poured them each a scotch from a bottle hidden beneath the counter. 'I keep it here because if the bloody Yanks see it on the shelf they want to buy the whole bleedin' bottle!'

They had the place to themselves as it was too early for opening. Sonny Taylor was well pleased. He'd make a nice little pile from this haul. It didn't bother him that Jack would make more. He was the one storing the stuff, taking the risk. The police could come to Sonny's gaff at any time, they wouldn't find a thing, he'd always made sure of that, but Jack Evans stood to lose a great deal if ever his haul was discovered.

'Got a buyer for that lot?' asked Sonny.

Jack tapped his nose, knowingly. 'Now then, I don't ask where you got the gear and you don't ask where I sells it. OK?'

'Fair enough.' He downed the last of his scotch. 'I'll be on my way. I'll probably see you next week.'

The landlord let him out of the pub and, opening the door to his room, went inside, locking it carefully behind him. The room was stacked with cardboard boxes. He looked around with glee. This should earn him a small fortune.

He took a cigarette from a packet of Gold Flake and lit it. This was better than earning a pittance being in the armed forces any day! He had a nice little business going with the pub as well. Sometimes beer was short, but he knew a few of the draymen from the brewers and he helped them out with stuff now and again. The odd barrel of beer came his way often enough to keep things ticking over nicely.

Being in the heart of the docklands, his pub was busy. Not only with the locals, those who lived in the two-up-two-down council houses that lined the shabby street, but many merchant seamen knew they could always get a beer at the Bricklayer's, and he had a steady stream of regular American soldiers too. They paid over the odds for a shot of the bourbon that he carefully rationed out. He couldn't abide the brash buggers, but Moira found them attractive: their unusual accents, their flattering ways with the ladies. It used to sicken him hearing them paying compliments to his wife, but it made her happy.

He puffed on his cigarette and frowned. Deep

down he knew she was disappointed with her lot. She had been a sparky Irish colleen when first they met, full of life, but the years had dimmed her happiness. It was only when she was serving in the bar, flirting with the punters, she really came to life and was like the young girl he'd wed.

Maggie had inherited her spirit and that worried him. She loved to dance, to have a good time. That in itself was no bad thing, but now it was wartime. He'd watched the thousands of troops marching through the dock gates in preparation for D-Day, earlier this month. Behind all the cheerful faces he'd seen the look of fear in their eyes. Servicemen, of any nationality, didn't know what was before them and that led to a kind of madness. Live for today and to hell with tomorrow. That was fine for them, but not for his daughter. Despite their continuous haranguing matches, he loved her and worried about her.

Later that evening, Maggie and Ivy queued to get into the Guildhall. They paid their three-shilling entrance fee and rushed to the cloakroom to hang up their coats and gas masks. They preferred the Guildhall to any other dance hall as the floor was sprung and the ballroom large, although by the end of the evening they knew that the floor would be full with heaving bodies, jitterbugging away to the music of Bert Osborne and his band.

The girls stood near the edge of the dance floor. They never sat in the row of plush seats and waited to be asked to dance. As Ivy said, 'Some shortarse may ask you, then when you stand up you tower over them. It's just too embarrassing!'

There were representatives from all the armed forces in the hall, but before very long they saw two American soldiers making their way towards them.

'Don't like the look of yours,' Ivy joked, but in fact both the young men were good looking.

One of them headed straight for Maggie. He was tall, with an olive complexion, a shock of dark hair, neatly cut, and large blue almond-shaped eyes. He smiled as he swaggered confidently to her side.

'Hi, Red,' he said. 'I saw you as soon as you arrived. Did anyone tell you you look just like Rita Hayworth?'

Maggie burst out laughing. These Yanks, they were all full of bull.

'And I suppose you could get me into films as soon as the war is over!' she retorted.

He looked knowingly at her. 'Nah! You're too smart for that old line. I'm Staff Sergeant Steve Rossi, and this is my buddy, Bob Hanson.'

'Maggie Evans,' she responded, and turning to Ivy she introduced her.

'Like to dance?' asked Steve as the band started to play Glenn Miller's 'American Patrol'.

She held out her hand. 'That's what I came for.' They moved towards the dance floor.

Steve was very adept on his feet. He had a natural rhythm and they matched each other's steps without any trouble. The petticoat under her skirt swirled, showing her long slender legs off as he twisted her about. They were both breathless at the end of the number but as the poignant strains of 'Moonlight in Vermont' started, he drew her into his arms, holding her firmly, looking into her eyes.

'This is much better,' he said softly into her ear as he put his cheek next to hers.

Maggie could feel his strong arms about her, the broad shoulders, the taut muscles, the pungent smell of his cologne. Maleness exuded from him as strongly as his personality. This was a real man, she felt. Someone who knew his way around.

He talked softly to her. 'You move real well, Maggie,' he said. 'You're a natural dancer and what's more you really enjoy it, don't you?'

Her eyes shone as she said, 'I do. I just love to dance ... I've not seen you here before,' she added.

'I've been here a couple of times,' he answered. 'But I'm sure glad I came tonight.' He drew her closer.

When at last the music stopped, he led her to the bar and bought her a gin and tonic. They sat at a small table. He moved his chair next to hers and put his arm along the back of her seat.

'How long have you been in Southampton?' she asked.

'I came last year,' he told her, 'with the 14th Major Port Transportation Corps.'

'And what exactly does a staff sergeant do?'

'I'll have you know, young lady, I'm a mighty important guy. Our role is to coordinate the shipment of our troops, military equipment, and stores throughout the port. I run the stores. I'm in charge of all the victuals. The food – eggs, bacon, meat, fruit, vegetables – cigarettes and booze. Without me, the army couldn't function!'

Maggie found herself liking this man. He was full of himself all right, but he had great charm and charisma.

He put his arm around her shoulder, leaned forward and added, 'I'm also in charge of ladies' perfume, nylon stockings, candy and gum. Whatever you want I can get it.' He stared at her with his deep blue eyes that twinkled and with a slow smile asked, 'Do you want it, Maggie?'

'Are you trying to bribe me, by any chance?' she asked.

'Damn right I am. You stick with me kid, you won't want for anything.'

The band struck up another slow number and again they danced. Steve didn't speak and they both took pleasure in matching their steps, gliding around the floor to the slow foxtrot, her favourite dance. Maggie thoroughly enjoyed it. Too often she'd be asked to dance by someone who spent most of the time stepping on her toes, or being marched around the ballroom by a man who didn't know how to turn, so it added to her enjoyment immensely to be in the arms of such an expert.

When the music stopped, Steve didn't release her at once, but just gazed into her eyes, his brashness gone. Not a word did he utter and for a moment Maggie was thrown. It was as if she was with another person. The confidence was still in his posture but suddenly she felt the power of the man and wondered just what was beneath the façade.

The moment passed as quickly as it came and Steve returned her to her seat. She watched him swagger to the bar, his broad shoulders straight, his uniform pristine and his forage cap tucked neatly in one epaulette. Whilst he was waiting to be served, another soldier came up to him and Maggie watched the encounter with interest. There was a quiet but heated exchange, and Steve kept poking the other man in the chest with his index finger, the expression on his face grim and menacing, until the soldier produced some money and handed it over. Steve took a wad of notes from his own pocket, and added the other man's contribution to it.

When he returned to the table he was as jovial as before. Maggie was curious and wondered what the confrontation had been about. 'That man at the bar, was he a friend of yours?'

'No, he owed me some money and he didn't want to settle his dues.' He smiled at her. 'But now it's all been sorted.'

'Oh, I see. Tell me, what did you do for a living before you joined the army? Did you work in a shop or in an office?'

'Jeez, no!' he laughed. 'A nine-to-five job would drive me crazy. I dealt in merchandise. If people wanted something, I found it for them. Wheeling and dealing, we call it. Now I do it for the army and get paid for it.'

'Where are you from?' she asked, her curiosity growing.

'New York City. Or a small part of it called Little Italy.' At her puzzled expression he explained. 'Within the city there are various sectors that are inhabited by certain nationalities. In German Town, the residents are of German extraction, Chinatown, the Chinese, Harlem, the coloureds. I'm from Italian stock. Third generation. My grandfather was an immigrant who came over from the old country.'

'Tell me about New York,' urged Maggie. 'I've seen it in the films of course, it looks an exciting place.'

'It's wonderful, you'd love it. The tall skyscrapers, the stores. You wouldn't need any clothing coupons there. You'd have a great time in Macy's store; it's the largest one in the world, you know. Then there's Broadway with all its theatres and bright lights. Times Square. The place buzzes, it's fascinating. But what about you?'

'There's not much to tell. I was born here, went to school of course, then I worked in an office for a while. Now I work in a munitions factory, doing my bit for the war effort. All very dull.'

'And your parents?'

'Dad and Mum run a pub.'

'Really? Where?'

'In the docklands. The Bricklayer's Arms in College Street.'

'I'll have to find it and come and have a drink. Taste some of your warm beer.' His tone was teasing. 'You limeys always drink warm beer and your coffee stinks!'

She burst out laughing. 'I've heard it all before. Some of the Yanks use our place and they always say the same. What about your family?' she asked.

There was a sudden change in his expression and his jaw tightened for a moment, then he smiled. 'My old man's Italian, Momma too. I have several brothers and sisters but I don't see much of them. We live different lives.'

'Does your mother write to you? I know that letters from home are important.'

The smile faded. 'No. Momma's not into writing much. I send her a card now and then. How about we get some air, Maggie? It's very hot in here.'

It was obvious that he didn't want to continue the conversation and Maggie wondered why. But it was very warm in the ballroom and she'd welcome some air.

Carefully pulling back the blackout drapes, they made their way outside. There was a chill in the June night and Steve put his arm around her. 'We should have brought your coat,' he said. But she was warm within the fold of his arm.

They leaned against a wall and he pulled her to him. His mouth covered hers and he kissed her without hesitation; at first gently, moving his lips over hers, then more deeply and she felt the tip of his tongue softly probing the warm cavern of her mouth. It was enjoyable and she returned his kisses. His arms enclosed her and his hands expertly undid the back of her bra through her dress, releasing her firm full breasts, but she stopped him as he moved to caress them.

'That's far enough, sergeant,' she said firmly.

'Oh gee, honey. Don't stop me now,' he entreated.

But she could feel his erection against her body

and knew this could only continue one way, unless she put a stop to it. 'No, Steve. I'm not a pushover. I didn't come here for sex. I came to dance.'

He reluctantly released her. 'You don't mean that.'

'I certainly do. Besides, we've only just met.'

He stroked her cheek gently. 'What happens if we get to know each other better? Does that change anything?'

'I don't know.'

'Will you let me see you again, Maggie?'

'Maybe, but only if you keep your hands to yourself!'

In the darkness, she heard him chuckle. 'That I can't promise.' But as he drew her closer once more, he just held her, gently caressing the back of her neck as his mouth moved sensuously over hers.

Feeling the hunger in his kisses, she knew this was different. He was not a man to dismiss lightly – and he attracted her like no other man had done before. There was a drive about him, a certain magnetism, a hint of danger ... and she knew she was hooked. She badly wanted to know him better.

When they returned to the dance a few moments later, they were joined by Bob and Ivy. 'I've been looking for you,' accused her friend.

'We stepped outside for a breath of air,' explained Steve. 'Come on,' he said to his buddy. 'Let's get the girls a drink.'

As the two men left, Ivy said, 'A breath of air, eh! That's one way of putting it, I suppose.'

'It was stifling in here,' Maggie protested.

'Of course it was, love,' Ivy grinned. 'You seeing this bloke again?'

'Yes, probably.'

'He'll make sure you do. I saw the way he was looking at you. I'm going out with Bob some time next week. It's all arranged.'

Maggie frowned. 'Do you think you should?'

'Now don't start getting all righteous on me,' snapped her friend.

Putting a hand over Ivy's, Maggie said, 'I know it must be hard for you with Len away for so long, but do be careful. If you start to see Bob on a regular basis and Len finds out ... what then?'

'How will he know? Unless you tell him.'

'Of course I won't! How could you think of such a thing?' Maggie was outraged.

'All right. Keep your hair on.' Ivy gave a sly smile. 'I know you wouldn't.' She leaned forward and confided, 'This Bob is so nice, not like my Len. He's been telling me all about his home town in Idaho. Some place called Zanesville.' There was a dreamy look in her eye as she gazed into space. 'They live a different kind of life there.' She sighed deeply. 'It sounds wonderful.' She looked at Maggie. 'He isn't married, you know.'

With an anxious expression, Maggie snapped, 'But you are. Or had you forgotten!'

The two men returned and so stopped any further confrontation between the two girls.

When the dance was over, the four of them met up outside after the girls had collected their coats. Steve put his arm around Maggie. 'I've a pass for next Saturday, how about we take in a movie?'

'Yes, I'd like that,' she agreed.

'Fine. I'll meet you outside the Odeon cinema at six thirty. After, we'll go for a meal some-where.' He drew her to him and gave her a long lingering kiss. He cupped her face in his hands and stared into her eyes. 'We're going to have such a good time together in the future, Maggie.'

'We are?'

He kissed the tip of her nose. 'I promise,' he said. As the two girls walked home through the darkened streets, clutching their torches to show the way, their gas masks over their shoulders, Maggie knew that her father's fears for her were well founded, for if she continued to see Steve Rossi, she wouldn't be a virgin for much longer. He was a man with a man's desires, no boy to be kept at arm's length. Somehow it didn't worry her a bit. In fact she even found the idea exciting. Thank goodness her father couldn't read her thoughts. He'd kill her.

Chapter Two

Corporal Joshua Lewis of the 552nd Port Com-pany sat beside the driver, looking through the windscreen of the American Army truck with its easily distinguishable white star painted on the side, as it headed out of the army camp towards Fair Oak. As the truck left the environs of the town, he looked around the now verdant countryside, the cows chewing the cud in one field, sheep in another, and thought of home.

If he had been driving through his own state of Mississippi, the scene would have been very different. Those fields would be full of growing cotton, picked by negroes like himself, overseen by white men. He smiled wryly. Nothing had changed. All the officers in his company were white. They still reigned supreme.

There was a smile of affection on his face as he thought of his father, the pastor of the local Baptist church, a leading light in his community, fighting for the rights of his people against insurmountable odds. Joshua closed his eyes and let his mind fill with the sound of the choir that used to sing there every Sunday. The spirituals came from the very soul of every man, woman and child in the congregation; dirt-poor people, but with love and God in their hearts. He started to hum the melody of a spiritual to himself.

'Here we are, corp.' The voice of the driver broke through his reverie and he opened his eyes as the truck turned into an unmade road, leading to Willows Farm.

The vehicle was brought to a halt and they both alighted and walked around the back, ready to unload the scraps from the camp kitchen – the potato peelings, bits of cabbage and other discarded vegetables.

Arnold Biggs came striding over in his wellington boots with his old trousers tucked inside, and torn sweater stretching over his broad frame. He peered inside one of the three bins of waste and cursed.

'I told you before it ain't no good putting coffee grains amongst this lot, it upsets my pigs!'

Joshua apologized. 'Sorry, sir. I gave strict instructions that they were to be dispersed separately.' He looked inside the other two bins. 'These are all right though. I'll take the other one back with me.'

Farmer Biggs, thus mollified, mumbled beneath his breath for a moment and then conceded. 'Fine. Only I can't use it. Upsets them something chronic.'

Joshua put his hand in the pocket of his tunic and handed the farmer a packet of pipe tobacco. 'I got this from the PX stores for you, sir.'

Biggs's face broke into a wide grin. 'Thanks, son. Appreciate it. You going to the dance on Saturday at the village hall? I heard your company was invited.'

'I'm not much into dancing,' Joshua confessed.

The farmer looked surprised. 'Thought you darkies were born with a natural rhythm. You know, being used to dancing to the beat of the jungle drums!'

Joshua felt his companion beside him stiffen with indignation, but he just smiled at Arnold. 'We came out of the jungle a while back, sir. And Uncle Sam prefers to see us march as we go into battle. He don't care much for fancy dancin'.'

There was an uncomfortable flush on the farmer's face as he said, 'Right then. See you tomorrow.' He turned on his heel and walked away.

The two soldiers climbed into the truck and

headed back to camp, the driver shaking his head. 'The only jungle I've ever seen, man, is the one in *Tarzan* movies!'

'Don't blame the old guy,' Joshua reasoned. 'It's the first time most of these folk have ever seen a black man.'

His colleague laughed. 'Next time I'll bring some jungle drums!'

A day later, Steve Rossi leaned against the bonnet of his jeep in the New Docks as he checked the list of stores due to be unloaded from the ship that had anchored half an hour earlier from the United States. Waiting near him were several of the company of black soldiers who were to help with the task. He looked over at the laughing group with an expression of extreme distaste.

'Uppity niggers!' he muttered. 'Take them out of the cotton fields, the plantations, put them in a uniform and they think they're somebody.' Although he was a Yankee, and not from the south, he'd an inbred dislike of them. He remembered how although you could walk through Harlem, in New York City, during the day with relative safety, no white person would venture through the district at night without fear of mortal danger.

If he were honest, it was much the same in German town, the Hispanic area and other ghettos. The rivalry between the different ethnic groups was fierce and most times fraught with danger, but he'd learned how to take care of himself. It usually started with exchanged insults.

As soon as anyone called him a dirty wop, he'd feel duty bound to defend his culture and himself, for to turn away from such a jibe marked you a coward. It had caused him to fall foul of the law on more than one occasion and his proud Italian father had been angry and ashamed of him until eventually it had caused a family rift when once again his father had had to stand bail for him.

'You think I work all hours to keep you outta trouble?' the old boy asked. 'You take the bread from the mouths of your family, you break your momma's heart. Why don't you get a proper job like your brothers?' He didn't wait for an answer but continued, 'No, you think you're too smart to do an honest day's work. This is the last time, you hear? From now on, you get in trouble, I let you rot! You go and live your own life, you leave my house tomorrow. I don't help you no more. You bring too much trouble to us, to our name.'

Steve had moved out of the family home, despite the tears and entreaties from his mother who gesticulated wildly at her husband as she begged him to change his mind.

'He is our son, our own flesh and blood. Families stick together, that's what you've always taught our children.'

But Mr Rossi remained firm. 'He don't stick with no one, Momma, only himself is he interested in. He don't bring the family down no more. Now he learns how to be a man.'

Steve had left and lived by his wits, wheeling and dealing until he decided that joining the army would be his safety net.

These painful memories were brought to an end when at last he got the signal from on board to start unloading, and as the cranes lifted the goods in a large net from the hold and swung them over the side of the ship, he yelled to the negroes to 'Step lively! Move your black arses and get to work.'

They handled the forklift trucks with speed and dexterity. When this equipment had first arrived from the States, it caused great interest among the English dockers who'd never seen the like before. It took a long time to load all the goods onto the waiting trucks. As one was filled it took off to the main camp to be stored. There was one final load and Steve was getting impatient.

'Come on, Rastus. You ain't picking cotton now. Move it!'

Joshua Lewis looked at him coldly. 'Corporal Lewis is my name,' he said quietly but in a firm voice.

Rossi looked at him in astonishment. 'I don't give a fuck what your name is! To me you're just another black bastard in a uniform.'

Joshua looked at him with contempt. 'And you are just a bit of white trash. There were plenty of them in the cotton fields too. Your uniform doesn't make a man of you. You're still white trash.'

The disgust in the tone of the negro enraged Rossi, but before he could reply, one of the military police walked over, wearing his smart white tin hat with MP emblazoned on it, an armband declaring the same and a baton tucked in his belt. 'You nearly through here, soldier?'

'Yes,' said Steve. He glared at Joshua. 'Get your men onto the truck and get the stuff back to the stores.' He climbed into the jeep and drove off at speed, his wheels squealing as he made a rapid U-turn.

The negro grinned broadly as he climbed into his vehicle.

'Having trouble with the staff sergeant?' asked the driver, who'd heard the exchange.

Shaking his head, Joshua said, 'No. He's just a white boy with a big mouth.'

When he arrived back at headquarters, Steve commandeered the various crates and boxes into different sections, with a separate section of his own. He smiled as the last box containing bottles of bourbon was placed there.

Joshua watched him from a distance, knowing exactly what was going on. He'd caught on to the devious ways of Rossi a long time ago. How long did this man think he was going to get away with his little scam? He shrugged. He supposed it could be for the duration of the time that they were here. Who was going to check? Rossi was in charge and, he had to admit, the man was efficient at his job, even if he was a pain in the butt. He turned away. It was no concern of his anyway. Joshua, having finished his duty, climbed into a jeep with three of his men and returned to camp.

His own negro company were in segregated units and, in many cases, separate work details, billets and recreational facilities. They had their own Red Cross Club too, but when they went into Southampton, to the various pubs, it wasn't possible to keep the different companies apart. This often led to fights.

For the most part the townsfolk found the negroes quieter, and more polite than the other brash soldiers, but they still found their colour strange and treated them as a curiosity.

Joshua made his way to the mess hall, queued up with his tin plate and mug, collected his food, a mug of strong coffee, sat at the end of a long table and took out a book to read as he ate his food. His father had instilled in him his love of reading as a young boy, recognizing his son's studious nature, and had introduced him to great writers as well as the Good Book. Over the years, through such a medium, Joshua had educated himself.

Alone in his office, Steve made a long distance call to London and in hushed tones said, 'The next shipment is in. It'll take me a few days to get it to the place we agreed. I'll call you again. Make sure you've enough money with you and don't mess me around. I can easily find another buyer. Remember that!' He put the receiver down, took a cigar from a box in the drawer, bit off the end, spat it onto the floor, moistened the length of cigar with his mouth, then lit it. He blew the smoke out slowly, making a large smoke ring in the air.

He watched it float across the room before it disintegrated, and thought of the redhead he had a date with that weekend. Feisty little thing, she was. A great body, beautiful full breasts and slender legs. They'd have a good time, he'd see to that. A slow smile spread across his face. He bet she'd be a great lay. He'd take her some nylon stockings, a box of candy, some perfume. That ought to do the trick. Although he'd been frustrated when she'd stopped him fondling her at the dance, he'd admired her for it. Too many women were only too pleased to open their legs just for a drink and a night at the movies. Well, that was fine with him. There was no need for any Yank to go without a woman in Southampton. Apart from the local girls wanting a good time, the town was full of prostitutes. Not that he ever paid for sex. He didn't want a dose of the clap, but with so many women being grateful to his comrades, you could never be too careful. That's why he always kept a supply of condoms. He wasn't going to get caught. Not him.

He stretched, yawned, and decided to grab a bite to eat, then have an early night and save all his energy for Miss Maggie Evans.

It was Friday night and the locals had been paid, so the Bricklayer's Arms was busy. The air was filled with lusty voices singing 'Roll out the Barrel', accompanied by the pianist hired at weekends to play in one corner of the bar.

In another, four men were playing darts. Nobby Clarke took his place on the oche and raised his arm, ready to throw his first arrow, grinning at the barracking from his opponents.

'Go on then, Nobby,' encouraged his partner. 'We just need double top and we've won. Then these two buggers have to buy the beer.'

'Don't be daft,' said his opponent, 'he couldn't hit the side of a house with a bloody great gun, not even one of them Big Berthas!'

Nobby kissed the point of his dart and said, 'Come on, darling. Win for Daddy.' He threw it and grinned broadly as it found its target. Turning he said, 'Mine's a pint of bitter.'

At that moment the bar door flew open and a woman stormed in carrying a plate with sausages and mashed potatoes on it. She marched up to Nobby and yelled at him, 'You told me you'd be home early. Well *here's* your bloody supper.' She tipped it over his head and walked out.

There was a roar of laughter from all the customers as they watched him wipe the potatoes and gravy from his head, his face and his working clothes. He looked at Maggie, who always worked behind the bar on a Friday, and said, 'This gentleman owes me a pint of bitter. Be a good girl and get it for me.'

She put it on the counter in front of him, struggling hard not to laugh. Nobby drank it down in one go, then with an expression of thunder on his face, he walked out of the pub.

'Oh dear,' said Moira quietly to her daughter, 'Grace's in for another black eye, I fear. But she did ask for trouble making her man look a fool like that, especially knowing his temper.' She walked towards the door. 'I'd best go and clear up the mess before someone slips on it.'

As she returned with a mop and bucket, one of the American soldiers in the bar stepped forward and in a deep Southern accent said, 'Let me do that for you, ma'am. A good-looking lady like you shouldn't be doing stuff like that.'

She beamed at him. 'My, but you've a silver tongue in your head. But here you are.' She handed him the mop, aware that Jack was listening and watching with a sour expression.

When the soldier had finished he looked at Moira and asked, 'Shall I take this outside in the back yard for you, ma'am?'

Jack stepped forward and snapped, 'No. Give it here, I'll do it.'

Maggie moved over to her mother's side as her father left the bar. 'Go on like that and you'll end up with a black eye too.

Moira glared at her. 'The day your father raises his hand to me will be the last one he remembers and he knows it!' Picking up a glass cloth she turned away and started to wash glasses in the small sink beneath the counter.

Maggie chuckled to herself, knowing that her mother spoke the truth. Her parents often exchanged angry words, but that was all. Her father, for all his difficult ways, loved his wife, and even if he was able to throw a punch in the bar if it was absolutely necessary to calm a fight, and she had seen him do it on occasion, he would never raise a hand to Moira.

Later in the evening two of the local prostitutes arrived with two black soldiers. One came to the counter and asked Maggie politely for two pints of beer and two gin and tonics. There was a sudden feeling of hostility amongst the small group of white Americans, led by the Southerner who'd mopped up. He walked over to the lad

40

who was waiting for the drinks.

'You're in the wrong place, ain't you, *boy?*'

The negro looked at him and answered softly, 'No, I don't think so.'

Jack stepped forward at once. 'All right, Yank,' he said, addressing the white man. 'We don't want any trouble here.'

The soldier looked at him. 'You let these no count niggers drink with decent folk?'

Quietly Jack said, 'Look, son, one war's enough, don't you think?'

One of the locals, already in his cups, joined in. 'His money's as good as yours, mate. On the field of battle he bleeds the same as you do and it's the same colour. Funny that, ain't it?'

The Southerner was getting annoyed. 'Well, you limeys would know about bleeding, wouldn't you? Especially after that fiasco at Dunkirk!'

The mood of the bar turned ugly. Someone else called out, 'Bloody cheek you've got, you only came into the war because you was caught with your trousers down at Pearl Harbor!'

Suddenly the soldier was faced with a room filled with irate Englishmen. Jack leaned over the counter and said grimly, 'I think you and your mates had better leave, don't you?'

One of his companions pulled the soldier's sleeve. 'Come on, Hank. It's time we were going.'

'I wouldn't stay in this flea pit if you paid me,' he snapped. 'You prefer niggers, you have them!' He turned on his heel and left, followed by his two buddies.

Jack turned to another GI drinking alone. 'Do you feel the same way as your friends?'

He grinned. 'Not me, Pops. I got my own troubles.'

'Whew,' said Maggie to her father. 'I thought we were in for a free-for-all for a minute.'

Jack shook his head in disgust. 'Why the bloody hell they have to fight amongst themselves beats me. Why don't they take all their frustration out on the bleedin' Germans!' He lit a cigarette and turned away to serve someone.

Maggie walked over to the lone GI and asked, 'Have you been over here long?'

'No, I arrived last week, soon to be shipped out I guess.' His brow furrowed. 'It wasn't until we landed in England most of us realized just how bad things had been for you. You folk must have had a pretty rough time.'

It had been bad of course, and frightening. The docks had been a prime target in the Blitz and there was many a night when Maggie, huddled in their leaking Anderson shelter with her family, wondered if they would all live to see the next day.

'You soon forget,' she said.

The evening passed quickly. One of the negroes had a word with the pianist, slipped him a couple of pounds, and took to the ivories, playing boogie woogie and jazz. Everyone's feet were tapping to the beat. Jack stopped a few as they started to jive.

'Enough of that, you lot! I only have a licence for music, not for dancing. You want to dance, go to the bloody Guildhall.'

Eventually it was time to close the bar. Last orders had already been called and Jack started with the same spiel as he did every night.

He clanged a small bell hanging behind the bar. 'Time, ladies and gentlemen, please! If you haven't got a home to go to we've got an air raid shelter. Now come along, I don't want to lose my licence. Drink up and bugger off home.'

They closed the bar, swept the floor, emptied the ashtrays and washed the dirty glasses, then went into the back room for a cup of cocoa before bed. Moira and her mother sat together chatting about the night's events.

'Those Southern boys really hate the darkies, don't they, Mum? I can't understand it. The ones that have come in here have always been polite and no trouble.'

A line creased her mother's brow. 'I don't understand either, darlin', but I have to say it doesn't look right them being with white women. Even prostitutes. They should stick to their own kind.'

'That would be a bit difficult,' Maggie retorted. 'How many black women have you seen around?'

'You know what I mean. If a white woman fell in love with one of them, think of the trouble it would cause in the future. The blacks in their home town wouldn't like it.'

Maggie rose from her seat, kissed Moira good-night and went to her room. The two bedrooms were over the front entrance of the pub. Maggie turned off the light, opened the blackout curtains, pulled down the top window, leaned out and look around the darkened street. Raised voices could be heard from the Clarke residence. Oh dear, she thought, they're really at it tonight. The arguments of Grace and Nobby were legendary in the street, but the couple had been married for many years, nevertheless.

She heard the sound of a car's engine and watched as a vehicle drove slowly up the street, stopping outside the pub, its lights faint between the narrow slits of the covered headlamps. Two men got out. She saw the tips of their lighted cigarettes and was surprised when she heard one knock softly on the side door of her place. She recognized her father's voice and leaned forward, peering into the darkness.

There was a lot of to-ing and fro-ing and she guessed that whatever goods he had stashed away in the front room were being moved. Shortly after, the side door closed, and the car was driven away. She heard the sound of the bolt being put across. Then she heard her father's footsteps as he came up the stairs to bed.

She frowned. He was playing a dangerous game. What would happen if the police caught him in his illegal activities? What would happen to her mother? She was angry with him, putting everything at risk: his future, her mother's. But she knew whatever she said to him, he'd go his own way.

She undressed and climbed into bed. Tomorrow she had her first date with Steve Rossi. She snuggled under the blankets and pictured the sexy Italian in her mind. He would be hard to handle, of that she was sure, and with a frisson of excitement she wondered if she had bitten off more than she could chew. She wasn't going to give her virginity away easily, but she wondered just how long she could make him wait. It was a dilemma, but one she felt she was going to enjoy. She would know tomorrow how much of a problem she had. One thing was for sure, she wasn't going to end up with an illegitimate child. She had plans for after the war. She wanted to get away from the docklands of Southampton. Work in London perhaps, see a bit of life. Many of her school chums had married far too young; this was not for her. She wanted much more, and maybe her first step into real womanhood would be with Steve Rossi.

She turned over, closed her eyes, and was soon asleep, but she was beset with confused dreams: her mother sitting outside the Bricklayer's Arms surrounded by her furniture, and herself pushing a pram with twin babies – one white and one black.

Chapter Three

Sitting in front of the dressing table, Maggie swept her hair up at the back, securing it with kirby grips and combs. She twisted the ends into curls on the top of her head, and paused to look at her reflection, turning her head first one way, then the other. It certainly made her look older and more sophisticated. She'd seen Betty Grable wear her hair this way in one of her films and liked it, and as Steve Rossi had appeared so much more a man of the world than other young men she'd encountered, she wanted to impress him. She dabbed Coty's L'Aimant perfume behind her ears then rose from her seat, grabbed her coat and walked downstairs.

Her mother was alone in the bar. She looked at the new hairstyle. 'Very chic,' she said with a knowing smile. 'Going out on a date?'

'Just to the pictures, and maybe after for a meal,' said Maggie. 'I won't be late.' She kissed her mother's cheek.

'Have a good time,' said Moira. 'But take care,' she added.

'I'll be fine, don't you worry about me,' Maggie assured her.

Walking down to Bernard Street she waited for a tram to take her to Above Bar. She was looking forward to the film. She liked Gary Cooper and this time he was teamed with George Raft. *Souls at Sea* sounded exciting, and the second feature with Joel McCrea looked good too.

Alighting from the tram, she thought how nice it would be when the war was over and the vehicles could once again be painted in their vibrant red, instead of the awful gunship grey of wartime. She peered along the road and saw Steve Rossi leaning casually against the wall of the cinema, smoking a cigarette. Her stomach tightened with anticipation and nerves.

'Hi, honey!' he greeted her as she walked up to him. He looked appreciatively at her hair. 'My! Very Miss Hollywood,' he said as he took her arm and led her into the cinema. He handed her a box of American candy. 'Here, I hope you like it.'

Her eyes lit up with delight. 'Thank you. What a treat.'

'There's plenty more where that came from.'

Upstairs in the circle, the usherette showed them to their seats. Maggie was glad that Steve hadn't asked for seats in the back row. Many a time she'd had to struggle with the groping hands of some young man, when all she'd wanted was to look at the screen. As the lights went down and the programme began, Steve put his arm around her, but that was all he did, and she was greatly relieved.

After the main feature, the newsreel came on, and Steve watched closely as it showed American troops in the Pacific, storming ashore on the Japanese-held island of Saipan. Then there was footage of the storm, the worst for forty years, that destroyed the Mulberry Harbours off Omaha Beach. She heard Steve curse under his breath as he lit a cigarette and she realized that one day he and his company may well be over there too and she was aware, more than ever, that life was full of uncertainty.

When the programme finished, everyone stood as the national anthem was played, then, taking her arm, Steve escorted her down the stairs. Outside he said, 'Come on. Tonight you'll eat some really good Italian food.'

He took her to a small restaurant in a back street and was greeted warmly by the owner. She was faintly amused as the men chattered away in a foreign tongue and kissed each other on both cheeks. She smothered a smile as she pictured her father's reactions if that was to happen to him!

'Was that Italian you were speaking?' she asked.

47

'Si, signorina. My family only speak Italian at home, so I grew up to be bilingual.'

She was impressed. 'I never knew this place existed,' she said. 'Is that man a friend of yours?'

Steve laughed. 'No. But I was told about this place.' He shrugged. 'We Italians stick together. The owner cooks Italian food if you ask for it. If you lived abroad and you found an English restaurant, you'd be the same. You'd be asking for roast beef and Yorkshire pudding.'

'You're probably right, but we would shake hands formally. The men would think it sissy to kiss one another!'

'That's because you're born in this cold and wet climate. We have hot Latin blood in us. We are a passionate race, as you'll soon find out,' he said with a cheeky grin.

The owner brought a bottle of wine to the table and poured it into the glasses. 'This is Chianti,' Steve said. 'The life blood of an Italian.'

She took a sip and liked it. Although she worked in a pub, there was not a bottle of wine in the cellar and this was a new experience. As was the spaghetti Bolognese. The homemade pasta was delicious, but Steve had to show her how to twist it round her fork.

'*You* have to be in charge, Maggie,' he laughed. 'Not the pasta!'

In the background soft music of Italy was playing. Pictures on the walls were of Rome, the Bay of Naples, palm trees, sunlit beaches and vineyards.

'Have you ever been to Italy, Steve?'

He shook his head. 'Not yet. But it's inbred in

me. One day I'll go and visit the old country.' He looked at her with his almond-shaped eyes, leaned across the table, took her hand and said, 'Maybe I'll take you there.'

Maggie was no fool, she knew that such remarks had no real significance in wartime, but it was a pleasant thought. 'I'd like to travel,' she said. 'When the war is over there's a lot I want to do.'

Steve looked at her, his eyes full of mischief 'Live for today, Maggie. Life is here, now. Take it in both hands and enjoy it!' He held her with his gaze. 'Don't be scared of taking a chance. This isn't a dress rehearsal, you know. You only get one bite of the cherry!'

She laughed. 'You don't understand the British. We are a nation full of reserve.'

'I've learned that already.' He poured her another glass of wine, then he stared intently at her. 'It's time you learned to let your hair down. I have an all-night pass,' he said softly. 'Come and spend it with me. I've booked a room at the Dolphin Hotel. The Star Hotel is full of the US Navy.' He smoothed her cheek. 'Let's really get to know one another.'

She was taken aback by his brashness. She didn't know whether to be flattered or insulted. 'You've got a bloody cheek!'

He wasn't fazed. 'No I haven't. You're a desirable woman. I want to hold you in my arms, make passionate love to you. What's wrong with that?'

'For one thing we've only just met, and you've taken for granted that I leap into bed with anyone. That's what's wrong!'

'Not at all,' he protested. 'I didn't think that for a moment. But don't you see, war doesn't give you the time for niceties. I could be shipped out tomorrow, next week, any day. Let's not waste a moment of the time we have together.'

'All the more reason to be sensible,' she retorted. 'I sleep with you, and then you're gone. I'll be just another conquest to add to your list. No thanks!'

He caught hold of both her hands. The feel of his flesh against hers as he stroked the back of one hand with his thumb, sent her pulses racing. 'Oh, Maggie honey, don't you see? If I wanted just another conquest as you call it, all I have to do is walk down the street. I want much more. I want you. I want you to be my girl.'

'Why me?'

'Because you're beautiful, intelligent. You're not like the others, good-time girls. That makes you very special.'

She was flattered of course; nevertheless, she wasn't going to give in for a lot of sweet talk. 'Then if I'm that special, you'll wait.'

He shook his head. 'What are you afraid of?'

'I'm not afraid,' she declared. 'But I'm not easy either. If that's all you bought me dinner for, I might as well leave now!'

'Hey! Calm down. There's no need to get mad with me. OK, I'll wait ... but only if that means you'll be my girl and that eventually, you'll let me love you as I want to. I'll take care of you, Maggie. I won't make you pregnant, I promise.'

Her senses were reeling. Yes, she'd had to cope

with young men who took her out and tried to get fresh with her, but no one had ever put into words what exactly they wanted, until now. And to talk about pregnancy. This was all too real and she knew that Steve meant every word. He would expect to sleep with her and soon. How brave was she? It had been drummed into her by her mother that men expected to marry a virgin, that they wouldn't want secondhand goods.

'What do you mean by being your girl?' she asked.

He burst out laughing. 'I would have thought that was very clear. You don't go out with other men.'

'And what about the times when you'd be on duty? I'm not sitting at home, if that's what you think. I like to go dancing and I'm not giving that up for anyone.'

He didn't look particularly happy about this, but after a moment's consideration he said, 'OK. But you don't let anyone take you home. I don't want some other guy smooching with my girl.'

It was her turn to be amused. 'You make a lot of rules, don't you?'

He gave her a cheeky grin. 'It's best if we both know what's expected of each other.' He kissed the palm of her hand. 'You won't regret it, Maggie. We'll have such fun together. I'll spoil you. Italians know how to appreciate a woman.' He took a small package from inside his tunic and handed it to her. 'This is for you, honey.'

She opened the package with barely concealed excitement. Inside was a small bottle of Chanel No 5 perfume and two pairs of nylon stockings.

51

This was indeed manna from heaven. She opened the bottle of perfume and smelt it. She'd heard of Chanel of course, but the scent was so different from her own, or Californian Poppy or Evening in Paris, which was the favourite of the moment.

'Thank you,' she said shyly. 'That's very kind of you.'

He grinned broadly at her. 'Nothing's too good for my girl. You'll learn in time, what it's like to go out with a real man.'

As she looked at him, the firm cut of his jaw, the strong arms, broad frame, she wondered just what it would be like to be in bed with him. Being touched by him. She knew about sex, but as yet hadn't experienced it first hand. It was a daunting thought, now she was really faced with it, and there was no doubt that Steve Rossi was everything he said. A real man. Inside her there were flutterings of fear. What if her father found out? Although she was twenty-one and had railed at him for treating her like a child, she still wanted his approval. And now she was playing with fire.

Steve called a taxi and took her home. He looked at the frontage of the Bricklayer's Arms and said, 'I'll call in one night soon and have a drink. Meet your folks.'

Maggie wasn't sure that was a good idea. 'Let's leave that for a while,' she suggested. 'Let me get to know you better first.'

He pulled her to him and kissed her. 'I'm all for that,' he whispered into her ear. 'Don't make me wait too long. I'm Italian. I've got a lot of hormones in my body!'

She chuckled. 'You'd better start drinking tea. That'll calm you down!'

'To hell with that! I'll call you soon.' His mouth covered hers again and she felt the passion in his kiss. 'Remember, Maggie. You're my girl now.'

She got out of the taxi, relieved that the pub was in darkness. Her parents would be in bed and she would be spared any inquisition from her father. She was much later than she had intended, but obviously her mother had persuaded him that she was fine. She'd given Steve her telephone number. The public telephone, used by the customers as well as themselves, was situated in the small hallway where at least there would be a modicum of privacy. She didn't want either of her parents to know about Steve Rossi. Not yet.

It was Sunday. In the small council house in Marsh Lane, Ivy put a spoonful of Camp coffee into two mugs, added milk and a meagre portion of sugar, apologizing to Maggie as she did so.

'I had Bob round here and he's got such a sweet tooth, my weekly ration's all but gone.' She grinned broadly. 'But it was worth it!' Maggie shook her head in despair. 'You're looking for trouble,' she warned her friend.

But Ivy was not to be daunted. She sat at the table and told Maggie all about the new man in her life. 'His family have a general store with one of those soda fountains in it. You know, you've seen it in the films, where the kids sit around with all those fancy ice-cream drinks. It was in one of these places that Lana Turner was discovered!' She sat back in the chair with a satisfied smile.

'So now you're telling me you're going to America after the war to be discovered.' Maggie thought it was hilarious, but her smile faded as her friend became serious.

'Well, I did think I could. Not to be discovered, that's being silly, but it's not an impossibility, you know. American soldiers do get married.'

Maggie's eyes widened with alarm. 'But you're already married!' Seeing the flush of guilt on Ivy's face she said, 'You haven't told him, have you?'

Ivy wriggled with discomfort, then she looked at Maggie and pleaded, 'Please don't tell him. I don't want to spoil it all. He's so different to Len. He treats me so nice. And in bed,' she flushed, 'he is wonderful. I didn't know sex could be like that. He makes sure that I enjoy it as much as he does.'

'Oh, Ivy!' Maggie didn't know what to say. 'But surely you must love Len, or else why did you marry him?'

'I married him to have sex! Yes I liked him, of course I did, but I didn't want to get up the spout and I kept saying no when he tried it on... So we got married.'

'But it'll take years to get a divorce!' exclaimed Maggie. 'This whole idea is crazy. Anyway, aren't you jumping the gun a bit? How do you know that Bob is thinking about the future? You know what these servicemen are like, full of promises. For all you know he may have a wife back home!'

'No,' protested Ivy. 'Bob's not like that! He

54

showed me pictures of his family, the store. Oh Maggie, it's huge. When he goes home after the war, he's going to manage it for his father.'

'That's hardly a proposal!' Maggie snapped.

'Bob's told me that above the store is an apartment, a flat, and that's where he'll live.' Her eyes pleaded for understanding. 'I know he likes me, Mags. I'm sure if we keep seeing each other he'll eventually ask me to marry him.'

'Oh my God!' Maggie covered her face with her hands. This was far worse than she had imagined. She stared hard at Ivy. 'You have to stop this now, you know you do.'

'Why the bloody hell should I? I have a chance to get away from all this.' She gesticulated around the small room. 'I can have a new life, a better life, in a different country, away from this whole shabby area.' She caught hold of Maggie's hand. 'Len doesn't earn much money as a carpenter and he hasn't any ambition. We'll go through life scrimping and scraping. He'll spend his nights in the pub and where does that leave me? In America, it all sounds so wonderful, so different.' She sat up straight. 'And I want to be part of it.'

'Living above a general store in a small town doesn't sound very wonderful to me. For God's sake, Ivy! You're living in a dream world.' She looked at her friend's left hand. 'Where's your wedding ring?'

'In the drawer,' said Ivy with an unabashed stare. 'I want a new start and I'm going to get it!'

'So what are you going to do?'

Ivy's eyes clouded. 'I don't know, to tell you the truth, but I'll think of something.' She looked hopefully across at Maggie. 'You might want to go to America after the war, with Steve. We could go together.'

But somehow Maggie wasn't at all sure about this. Steve fascinated her, but the future was very uncertain for everyone with a war still raging. She changed the subject. 'Come on, let's go to Bedford Place. I need to take some stockings to be mended. Let's look around the shops, try on a few dresses, forget about men for a while. I think you're mad, but I won't let on about you being married.' It was against her better judgement but hopefully Ivy would come to her senses, once the novelty of her new relationship wore off. God, she hoped so, because she saw nothing but trouble ahead if she didn't.

Staff Sergeant Rossi drove his jeep through the dark of The Avenue, slowed down at a military checkpoint, showed his papers to the sentry and was sent on his way. He smiled to himself. It was all too easy for him to get the necessary documentation. He had a ready supply in his office to cover all his needs: an official stamp which he used for his legitimate dealings and his own personal ones.

Southampton Common was now a military camp, with camouflage nets strewn across the trees to avoid detection from enemy aircraft. Civilians were not allowed access here any more. He drove on to the small village of Otterbourne and turned off by the green, doused his lights and parked. He took a pack of Lucky Strike from his pocket and lit a cigarette, then waited.

He had great plans for after the war. He was making big money, thanks to the shortages, and he had a ready market for all he could lay his hands on. When he returned to New York City, he'd really be somebody. He'd set himself up in business dealing with commodities and he'd show his father just what a man of importance he'd become.

He sensed the arrival of the Rover Saloon before he saw it. Over the years he'd acquired an uncanny sixth sense, and in the ghettos of New York it had saved his skin on more than one occasion. He got out of the jeep.

Two men approached and shook him by the hand. They spoke with the unmistakable accents of the East End of London. 'Got the gear then?' asked one.

Steve led them to the back of the jeep and looked around. All the houses were in darkness, not a light showed with the blackout regulations, and apart from the distant sound of a dog barking, nothing stirred. He unstrapped the bands of leather on the canvas covering and threw them back. Then together they went through a list with the aid of a torch held inside the vehicle to avoid detection. There were boxes stacked with goods and three large jerry cans filled with petrol.

'Did you get the other?' one man asked in a gruff voice.

'Yeah,' said Steve, and from inside his jacket he produced something wrapped in a piece of cloth. He removed the cloth to reveal a military pistol. 'A Colt 45 with three clips,' he said. 'That's all I could get this time, but it'll cost you.'

''Ow much?'

There was a great deal of grumbling when they were told.

Steve didn't hesitate, but wrapped the pistol and made to put it away. 'That's all right, gents,' he said. 'You either pay or you don't. I can sell it elsewhere.'

The two men eventually agreed his price and he smirked to himself as they counted out a wad of notes into his hand. 'You won't mind if I don't give you a receipt,' he laughed.

But they weren't amused. They hurriedly removed the goods from the jeep with his help, and drove away.

Steve unwrapped a piece of chewing gum, threw the wrapper on the ground, put the gum in his mouth, got into the jeep and drove away singing lustily, 'This is the Army, Mr Jones.' Yes, and the army was going to pay through the nose and build his future for him.

Chapter Four

Sonny Taylor was getting ready to go for a morning pint at his local boozer when there was a knock at the door. Wiping his hands on a towel, he opened it. On the doorstep stood two local detectives.

'Morning, Sonny,' said the first. 'We were just passing and thought we'd call.'

'Oh yeah,' said the spiv. 'Well, gents, I'm just on my way out. Sorry.'

They pushed past him. 'You won't mind if I use your lav, will you?' said the second man and walked through the scullery to the outside privy.

His companion grinned. 'Sid can't hold his water these days.' He sat down on the sofa and looked around the room. 'Well, I'll say this for you, Sonny. You're a tidy man.'

Taylor wasn't fooled for a moment. The tecs were just sniffing round. They were probably making another concerted effort to curb the black marketeering. It happened fairly regularly, which was why he never kept any goods in his home.

He picked up his jacket and put it on. 'I'm not a bleedin' public toilet! There's one just down the road, why doesn't he use that?'

The detective got up and started to look round, picking up a book here, turning papers over there. He went to pick up a bill lying on the sideboard but Sonny put his hand over it. 'You got a search warrant?' he asked.

The detective grinned back at him. 'Bit touchy, aren't you? Why would I need a warrant? This is just a friendly call.'

'My arse!' exclaimed Sonny and as Sid returned, he opened the front door. 'Time to go, gents.'

The two men left, grinning all over their faces. 'Keep your nose clean, won't you,' they said as they walked away.

Sonny made his way to his local and ordered a pint of beer, then sat and waited. This seedy pub in the dock area was like his office. It was here that all the people with something dodgy to sell knew they could find him. His gaze swept the bar, but there was just the usual punters there. He knew every plain-clothed policeman and he was very careful, always making sure the coast was clear before he did any business.

A shabbily dressed man sauntered over clutching a half-pint glass of beer and sat next to him. 'Want to buy some clothing coupons?' he asked.

'How many?'

'I've got six books,' he muttered.

Sonny looked at the man's poor attire. He himself took great personal pride in his appearance. He knew an excellent tailor who was only too pleased to accommodate him, charging extra for the lack of his customer's coupons, of course. With an expression of distaste, he said to the man, 'I'm surprised you don't use some yourself!'

'No need to get personal!' was the angry retort. 'Do you want them or don't you?'

'Keep your hair on,' said the spiv. 'Yes I'll take them. Usual rates.' He put his hand inside his jacket pocket, took out several notes and handed them over. 'You get any more, you know where to find me.'

Taylor drank up, left the pub and made for a telephone box. He put his pennies in the slot and dialled, then he pressed button A and spoke quickly. 'Jack! A couple of the Old Bill called on me an hour ago. Watch your step.' He replaced the receiver and pressed button B, but nothing came out. It was a habit of his and very often

60

coins came tumbling down the chute. It was like a bonus for using the public facilities.

Jack Evans replaced the receiver with a sigh of relief. Thank God he'd cleared all the stuff from the front room, because he knew he'd get a visit fairly soon. The local uniformed police called during opening time as it was, making sure there was no trouble. This was part of their regular duties and never bothered him. They would stand in the hallway near the hatch where he served those with a jug who wanted a pint to take out. The police always had a glass of beer on the house. He never ever offered them anything else, believing that a copper was never off duty.

Sure enough the same two detectives called on him later in the day, asking questions. Had he been offered any dodgy gear? Jack denied it vehemently. 'Not in my place, gents,' he told them. 'I've got a business to take care of and the missus would half kill me! Mind you, some of the GIs that use the place sometimes give her a tin of fruit or some chocolate. She particularly likes Hershey bars. But that's all.'

When the men had left, Jack smirked as he wiped a few glasses and put them on the shelf. If only they knew! He had a separate bank account for the money made from his dodgy dealings. It was a fair amount already. His retirement would be comfortable, he'd see to that. He fancied a small bungalow beside the sea somewhere. Bournemouth perhaps, or the Isle of Wight. He'd be able to make it up to Moira for the disappointments in her life. She could be the queen bee in her own home. He gave a smile of satisfaction at the thought. He was forty-five now; with a bit of luck he ought to be able to retire when he was still a young man. It would depend how long the war lasted of course. As far as he was concerned, the longer the better.

He had no compunction about such thoughts. Being born a cripple had given him a twisted opinion of right and wrong. He would have given anything to be normal and younger, a man who was physically perfect. If the truth were known, and he'd never confessed this to anyone, he'd have been thrilled to be able to enlist in one of the armed forces, do his bit for his country. But he was too old now anyway and, feeling less than a man at times, he'd decided to make as much money as he could from the situation. He felt it compensated him for the freak of nature that had been his lot. He was still amazed that Moira had consented to be his wife so many years ago. But of course then he was a relatively happy young man. It was only as the years progressed, when he felt he'd lost out on so much, that he became embittered.

At work, Maggie removed her turban, shook out her hair, which had become plastered to her head, clocked off and walked out of the factory, where to her surprise she saw Steve Rossi standing beside his jeep.

'What on earth are you doing here?' she asked. 'And how did you know where I worked?'

He grinned at her. 'So many questions,' he chided. 'Aren't you pleased to see me?'

Several of her workmates walked by, making ribald remarks. Her cheeks flushed with embarrassment. 'Don't take any notice of them,' she said.

He offered her a cigarette. 'Ivy told Bob where you worked and what shift you were on.'

'Oh, I see. Ivy's not on until later,' she said.

'I know,' said Steve. 'It was you I came to see, you silly goose, not her. Look, I've got a couple of hours off this afternoon, why don't we do something?'

'Like what?'

He held her hand. 'It's a lovely day, why don't we take a walk through the park? I want to get to know you better, and what's more important I want you to get to know me, to trust me.' He stared into her eyes, his gaze intense. 'When you learn to trust me, then you'll let me make love to you.'

She quickly looked about her to see if anyone had heard his remark, but most of the people on her shift had gone. 'You don't mince your words, do you!'

He laughed at her consternation. 'Oh you British with your quaint ways.' He stroked her cheek gently. 'Your shyness is very cute. Well, what do you say?'

As soon as he touched her, her heart began to race. This man was outrageous, but that only made him the more exciting. 'I'll have to go home and change,' she said.

'That's fine. I have to go back to camp anyway. Where shall I meet you, or would you like me to pick you up at home?'

Maggie shook her head. 'Meet me at the Bargate, near the American Red Cross Club, at two o'clock. Is that all right?'

'That's fine with me, honey.' He kissed her swiftly, climbed into the jeep and drove away.

Bill the foreman walked over to her, having observed the scene. 'You watch that young bugger,' he warned. 'He'll have your drawers off before you can say knife!'

'Don't be disgusting!' she retorted.

He looked at her with raised eyebrows. 'I know men, my dear, and I know that look in his eye. You be careful is all I'm saying. Now get off home and don't be late in the morning.'

The mid-July day was warm as Maggie walked to her rendezvous. Despite the constant reminders of war, the comings and goings of troops through the docks, companies moving out, the wounded being shipped in, today in the full sun and almost clear skies there was no feeling of doom and gloom. People went their own way. Life carried on. Maggie thanked her lucky stars that she wasn't living in London. The city had been suffering from attacks from the flying bombs and a massive evacuation plan had been under way. But here, all seemed well.

Steve arrived at the same time as she did. He jumped from the jeep that delivered him, saluted the driver and walked over to her.

He put his arms around her and kissed her heartily. 'Hi, honey! My, but you look good enough to eat.'

Though pleased at his flattery, she was finding

64

it hard to handle his natural exuberance. Americans were so uninhibited and it took some getting used to. He tucked his arm through hers and they walked past Hanover Buildings to the park.

All the railings had been taken away for the war effort, of course, and in several places deep trenches had been dug, but the flowerbeds were a blaze of glory and it was pleasant just strolling along. They sat on a bench and watched a bunch of American negroes throwing a ball, catching it in their large baseball mitts.

'They're practising for a match next week. Have you ever seen baseball played?' he asked.

She shook her head.

'Then we'll go. It's next Sunday afternoon. I'll tell you the rules as we watch. It's one thing the niggers are good at,' he conceded.

'You don't like the darkies, do you?' Maggie said. 'Why not?'

He lit a cigarette and tried to explain. 'It's something you limeys will never understand. For years the niggers were slaves on the cotton plantations in the South, then Lincoln did away with slavery, declaring everyone equal.' His mouth tightened in an angry line. 'These people will never be equal. They're ignorant, lazy and good for nothing. Put them in a uniform and they get full of themselves. It isn't right.'

Maggie was horrified at his attitude. 'If they're good enough to join the army, fight for their country, die on a battlefield, they are surely due some respect!'

He gave a snort of derision. 'Respect? You've

65

got to be kidding!'

His dismissive attitude began to annoy her. 'No I'm not! What gives you the right to be so superior?'

He looked at her in amazement. 'Because I am.' He saw the anger shining in her eyes and put his arm around her. 'Maggie, honey, don't let's fight. This whole thing is strictly an American thing. You Brits have your problems too, you know.'

But she was still up in arms. 'Really!'

There was a smile of amusement on his face. 'Yes. I mean it. What about the troubles in Ireland between the Catholics and the Protestants? We all have our sore spots, you know.'

With her natural good humour she could see the sense of his argument, and laughed. 'I suppose you're right.'

'Come on,' he said. 'I'll take you out to tea.'

In a small tea shop they sat down and when the waitress brought the tray over, Maggie couldn't help teasing him. 'I imagined you would have ordered coffee.'

He grinned. 'I'm no fool. No one over here knows how to make it. Besides, I'm trying to integrate my ways to yours. If I understand you better, then it'll bring us even closer.'

She burst out laughing. 'I don't believe that for one minute.'

He shrugged. 'Christ, Maggie, I've got to find some way to creep beneath that reserve of yours or I'm going to go crazy.'

She looked sceptically at him. 'I bet you say that to all the girls.'

'No I don't!' He caught hold of her wrist. 'Let's

66

get one thing straight. I don't go round picking up any woman. OK, I'm no saint, but I am particular. From the first moment I saw you, I wanted you, real bad. I'm not some stupid kid in a uniform away from home for the first time. I'm a man. I know what I want ... and I'll wait.'

She found his steady gaze and the intensity of his words disconcerting and for once was lost for a reply.

'If you want me to go and not bother you any more,' he continued, 'all you have to do is tell me. I just hoped you wanted the same as I did. The decision is yours.'

As she studied his face, the large blue eyes staring into hers, the full passionate mouth, the long sensitive fingers, she knew she didn't want him to leave. But she knew the consequences of telling him so. He'd made that very clear.

'No,' she said softly. 'I don't want you to go.'

He smiled at her. 'You had me worried for a minute there,' he said. He held her hand to his mouth and kissed the palm. 'You won't regret it, honey. I promise you.'

Maggie saw one or two people watching them, but she didn't care. She had taken her first step into the unknown. And it was both exciting and frightening.

During the following three weeks, Steve met her whenever he was able to. He took her to the baseball match and explained the intricacies of the game. She was amused at the enthusiasm showed by the mainly American onlookers. There were a few locals watching, with bemused ex-

pressions. 'Just like a glorified game of rounders!'
one was heard to remark.

They went dancing, which Maggie really
enjoyed, visited the various cinemas, met for a
drink, and during this time she grew to know him
better. He was excellent company. She liked his
sharp sense of humour and admired his air of
confidence. He made her feel special, and if they
met any of his buddies he introduced her as his
girl. His embraces became slowly more intimate,
but Maggie tried to keep his willing hands in
check. He would complain as he kissed her.

'Christ, Maggie, you're driving me wild. I'm
trying hard not to go too far, but the feel of you
in my arms, your soft breasts pressed against me,
what do you expect from a full-blooded man?'

One evening after a meal at their now favourite
Italian restaurant, Steve poured her a glass of
wine and said, 'Next weekend I have a forty-
eight-hour pass. I have to go to London on
business, but that won't take long. Come with
me, Maggie.'

'Isn't it dangerous there now with the doodlebugs?' she asked.

'It's not so bad now as it was,' he said. 'They've
strengthened the coastal fortifications and are
shooting them down as they come over the
Channel. You'll be quite safe with me, I'll take
care of you.'

It wasn't really the bombs that were worrying
her. She knew if she said yes, then she'd be
expected to sleep with him. 'When are you
thinking of going?' she asked.

'We can catch a train on Friday evening and

come back late on Sunday night.' He looked longingly at her. 'Please say yes. London is an exciting city, we can have such a good time.' At her hesitation, he continued to plead his case. 'You're a great girl, Maggie honey. We've really enjoyed being together these past weeks, please come with me. I know you don't give yourself to a man easily, but I desperately want to hold you, love you. I'm not such a bad guy, am I?'

She studied his strong masculine features. He was a very good-looking man and there was this strong chemistry between them that she could no longer deny. Taking a deep breath, she agreed. 'All right.'

As they walked back through the park she wondered just what excuse she could give to her parents. Her father would go mad if he thought she was going to London, let alone with a Yank.

It was in Ivy's house, the following evening, that Maggie voiced her concerns.

'Tell him you're staying with me,' said her friend. 'After all it's not the first time you've done so.'

'But this will be two nights. What excuse can I give?'

'Why do you need an excuse!' exclaimed Ivy. 'Blimey! You're always saying you're old enough to take care of yourself, but listen to you, you sound like a child.'

'You don't know my father!'

'Oh yes I do. Just say you're keeping me company because I'm a bit down. Monty's army has been having a tough time in Italy. Tell him I'm worried about Len.'

Maggie looked immediately concerned. 'Oh Ivy, I'm sorry. I didn't realize.'

'It's all right. I'm sure he's fine. I'm bound to worry of course.' She looked at Maggie. 'Yes, I know I'm having a good time, but naturally when you read the papers about the fighting, you wonder.'

Maggie put her arm around Ivy's shoulders. 'Of course you do, it's only natural.' Secretly she was delighted to see the concern being shown by her friend. Perhaps the novelty of Bob and his general store was dying a natural death.

'I'm sure you'll hear from Len very soon,' she said, trying to reassure her.

Ivy frowned. 'It takes a time for the mail to get through, but then I sometimes get two letters together.'

'Do you write to him?'

'Of course I do.' She gave a wicked grin. 'I don't tell him what I've been up to of course, but I know that letters are important. I'm not that bad a wife.'

'No of course you aren't. Come on, let's go to the pictures and forget about it all.'

The film, *Hollywood Canteen*, cheered them, but the newsreel showed French women having their heads shaved for collaborating with the enemy. The humiliation was hard to watch.

'Poor bitches,' muttered Ivy. 'Probably some of them were only doing it to survive or get food for their kids. No one knows what they'd do in that situation. War changes everybody one way or another.'

70

But they put such thoughts behind them as in the interval the theatre organ rose from the depths in all its glory and the organist played a selection of the popular songs of the day.

At the end of the second feature Ivy and Maggie walked home with the aid of their torches, Maggie planning mentally what she was going to say to her father before the next weekend.

The following evening after closing time, as she helped her father to clear away the dirty glasses, Maggie took a deep breath and said, 'I'm going to stay with Ivy over the weekend, Dad, so I won't be able to help in the bar on Friday night.'

He looked at her and scowled. 'But you know how busy we get. I need you here.'

She felt a moment of panic. She'd told Steve she was going and nothing was going to stop her. 'Ivy is in a bit of a state, you see. She hasn't heard from Len and she's worried.'

'Not enough to stop her having a good time!' he replied scornfully.

Maggie leapt to Ivy's defence. 'What is she expected to do? Her husband's been away from home for ages. She can't just sit around at night and worry. It would drive her crazy.'

'Lots of other women do it!'

'Look, Dad. Ivy works hard at the factory. She's doing her bit for the war effort.'

'In more ways than one!'

'Well I'm sorry, but I'm going to stay with her. She's my friend and she needs me.' She walked out of the bar and went upstairs to her room.

As she sat on her bed she saw that her hands were trembling. She didn't like lying, but she really was determined to go to London ... and now she would.

In the privacy of his room, Steve Rossi lay on his bed in his singlet and underpants, a glass of bourbon beside him and a smile of satisfaction on his face. Maggie had given in to his demands much sooner than he expected.

Wherever he was based for any length of time, he liked to choose one woman to go out with. It suited him better. It saved all the trouble of picking up a girl when he felt like company or sex. With one woman, she was usually content to wait for his call. All he had to do was pick up the phone. Although Maggie Evans was different. She made that clear. She wasn't content to wait at home, she insisted on still going dancing. Well, that was all right by him. He'd told her that she wasn't to leave with a man and she'd agreed. Again his Italian charm had worked.

He was looking forward to going to London. He'd got to know the city well since he'd arrived in England. He'd made many contacts there through nefarious ways and he was on to a big deal. It should make him a lot of money.

He'd show Maggie a good time too. After all, she was his girl now and he did like to spoil his women, as he had told her. He didn't think she would make ridiculous demands on him either. She was much too independent for that, and he was thankful. Some women got so possessive. He'd even promised one or two that after the war they'd go to New York and become his wife. But he only did that if it was really necessary. Usually he just dumped them. But Maggie really did fascinate him. She was different. He wondered how different she would be between the sheets. It would be very interesting and enjoyable finding out and he could hardly wait.

Chapter Five

The following Friday evening, Maggie made her way to the station entrance clutching a small case and her gas mask. Her heart was pounding with excitement and tension. She questioned her decision to go with Steve, every step of the way.

She was filled with trepidation at the thought of a man seeing her naked, touching her, making love to her. What would it be like? Would she enjoy it? Would she be disappointed? Would she disappoint him? So many thoughts filled her mind, but she kept walking towards the entrance, her head held high.

Steve was already there, waiting. His face lit up with a broad smile as he hurried towards her and greeted her with a kiss.

'I was afraid you'd change your mind,' he said as he took her case.

Maggie's cheeks flushed; she'd been so overcome with guilt earlier in the day, she almost didn't go, but the urge to prove to herself that she was a woman and not a child had spurred her on.

'Of course not,' she said. 'Why would I?'

'Never mind, you're here and our train is due in shortly.'

When the train arrived, he ushered her into a crowded carriage and placed their cases on the luggage rack before sitting beside her. As he put his arm around her, Maggie was aware of the hostile glances from their fellow travellers at his open show of affection. The British reserve had been severely shaken at the arrival of the GIs. Their natural exuberance had caused a lot of people to be embarrassed, which had aggravated their feelings of hostility towards the men from overseas.

Maggie was incensed by their judgemental attitude which they made no attempt to hide. She deliberately smiled warmly at her companion and said in a steady voice, 'I'm really looking forward to this weekend.'

He pulled her closer and kissed her cheek. 'So am I, honey. I can hardly wait until I can get you alone.'

Maggie could almost hear the tutting of disapproval from two elderly women sitting opposite. It made her smile mischievously. When did they last share a bed with a man, she wondered. She grinned across at them and was amused when they looked quickly away.

The train eventually arrived at Waterloo Station and as they started to walk, Maggie was shocked at how battered, dirty, worn and scarred was the city of London, which was swarming with people dressed in so many different uniforms.

She looked around her in amazement. This was

a different London to the one she remembered visiting with her mother, before the Blitz. Strange languages assailed her ears: French, Polish, an American twang; the occasional British voice, a Cockney taxi driver asking, 'Where to, guv?' London had become a Mecca for all the nationalities who were now part of the war.

ARP wardens mingled with the crowds, their gas masks slung over their shoulders. Barrage balloons floated above. Mountains of sandbags barricaded important buildings as they did in Southampton, but here it was more noticeable somehow, with so many buildings so close together. Yet despite all the trappings of war, there was such an air of excitement about the place. It was like getting a sudden shot of adrenalin.

Steve put his arm around her shoulders. 'Happy, honey?'

She beamed at him. 'This is super. The place is so full of life, especially after Southampton. Where on earth has everybody come from?'

'London's the place to be,' he told her. 'All servicemen and women come here when they can. This is where it's all happening.'

They stopped outside a small but comfortable hotel. 'Here we are,' said Steve. 'A buddy of mine recommended it. He said the rooms were comfortable and it wasn't too noisy.' With a cheeky grin he added, 'And the beds are comfortable.'

Maggie felt her cheeks colour.

They entered the hotel and made their way to the reception desk where Steve signed the register and was given a key. As they made their way to the lift he said, 'How does it feel to be Mrs

Steve Rossi for the weekend?'

She laughed and held out her left hand. 'Without a wedding ring? I don't suppose we fooled anyone. Do you?'

'Hell no, but who cares anyway! There's a war on and anything goes.'

The bedroom was comfortable and adequately furnished. Ugly blackout curtains covered the chintz drapes at the windows. A matching chintz cover was on the double bed. Maggie felt a nervous fluttering in her stomach as she looked at Steve.

Putting down their cases he said softly, 'Come here.'

She went willingly to his arms, her lips open to receive his kiss.

As he held her he said, 'I can't tell you how often since we first met I've longed for this moment. I promise you'll enjoy it too.'

He slowly undressed her, smoothing her soft skin with his long fingers. Kissing her eyes, her neck, her mouth. Murmuring words of seduction, promising her delight after delight, sending her senses reeling.

She couldn't believe this was happening to her. Here she was, standing naked in a hotel bedroom, with an American who was undressing in front of her as she watched. As he slipped out of his uniform, she ran her hands across his broad chest, covering him with kisses. She felt the strength of his muscular arms as he lifted her naked body and carried her over to the bed. To Maggie it seemed surreal, like a scene in a romantic novel where the hero rides up on a white horse, but this time he'd arrived by train.

She felt Steve running his fingers through her hair, cradling her head, his mouth exploring the contours of her face. She could feel the warmth of his skin next to hers, his bare body against hers. Her own body was behaving strangely.

'Jeez, Maggie. You're so beautiful.' His warm breath against her skin made her quiver with anticipation. He pushed back her auburn tresses and kissed her slim neck.

She felt the rising tide of desire sweeping through her at his every touch and tenderly ran a finger across his full sensuous mouth. All her feelings of guilt, of nerves, were swept aside, dispelled by the sensations of her body.

Never in her wildest dreams had she thought that sex could be like this: this feeling of abandonment, the thrill of feeling Steve covering her body with his kisses, until she thought she'd lose all sense of reason. She felt his arousal as he lay on top of her and she was slowly filled with an intensity deep inside her she'd never experienced before.

As his hand slipped between her thighs, she felt a throb of desire engulf her. It was almost more than she could bear. It didn't lessen for a moment as he slipped on a condom.

Her lover took possession of her slowly; even so, she felt a sharp pain, but it was one of pleasure and she cried out until her passion was unleashed.

They lay together after, exhausted, in each other's arms.

Steve stroked her cheek and looked tenderly into her eyes. 'You didn't tell me this was your first time,' he said softly.

Unable to speak, she just shook her head.

'You know what they say, don't you?'

Her eyes opened wide. 'No. What?'

'When a man takes a woman's virginity, she belongs to him for ever.'

She traced a finger down his nose. 'I don't belong to anyone but myself.'

He chuckled. 'You're a strange woman, Maggie. But wonderful. We're going to have a great time together, you and I. You have a warm passionate nature and I love that.'

'You're not so bad yourself, sergeant.'

'Staff sergeant, if you please!'

She laughed. 'I'm sorry. This certainly isn't the moment to demote you! You should be wearing at least one gold star after that performance.'

He nuzzled her neck. 'Before this weekend is over, honey, I aim to be a five-star general.'

She lay in his arms and thanked her lucky stars she'd given away her innocence to a man who was as experienced as Steve. With him she'd felt cosseted, desired... A woman.

Steve stretched and said, 'I don't know about you, but I feel like a drink.' He slipped off the bed and disappeared into the bathroom for a while. On his return he took a bottle of bourbon from his case and poured drinks into the glasses on the side table. 'No ice, I'm afraid.'

Maggie pulled a face as she sipped the sweet spirit.

'Don't you like it?' he asked.

She shook her head and, caressing his bare chest, whispered, 'I'd rather have you.'

Putting down his glass, he leaned forward and kissed her gently. 'You're insatiable. But now we've got to get dressed. I've an appointment to keep, then we'll go for a meal, have a few drinks ... and then we can start all over again. OK?'

Reluctantly she agreed.

It was just after nine o'clock at night when they emerged from their hotel. Maggie was amazed as Steve led her around the streets with the certainty of a tour guide.

'You've obviously been here before,' she remarked, as they stopped in front of a door marked with a sign that read The Ace of Clubs.

'After arriving in Scotland on the *Queen Mary*, I spent my first leave here,' he explained. 'I get up as often as I can so I know it pretty well. It's a fascinating city. So many old buildings. In New York the oldest is probably only a hundred years old.' He banged on the door of the club.

To Maggie's surprise, someone slid open a hidden panel, spoke a few words to Steve, then opened the door.

They walked down some steps to a basement bar with small booths around the wall and tables in the centre. The only illumination was from small table lamps. A pianist played softly. Despite the cosy glow from the lamps, the place was decidedly sleazy. The air was filled with the odour of stale beer, cigarette smoke and cheap perfume.

Maggie shivered with apprehension as she sat at the table in a small booth. She looked around furtively as Steve went to the bar. She sensed an air of menace in the place and wanted to leave – now.

There were a few American soldiers sitting at the bar with girls who were obviously prostitutes, a small group of civilians in city suits, three matelots in their bell-bottomed trousers and wide sailor collars, and a couple of English soldiers from the Royal Engineers. But there were two other characters who, although well dressed, looked as if they'd stepped right out of an American gangster movie. To her surprise, Steve went over and sat with them.

A waiter set two glasses on the table in front of her. 'The gentleman said he would only be a moment, miss.'

She thanked him and waited, nervously fingering her glass. The conversation between Steve and the two men was earnest. There was no idle banter being exchanged here. The usual bonhomie that seemed to be Steve's style was now replaced by a tough exterior. He was talking fast and forcibly. Then he produced a small bag that he'd taken from his case in the hotel, and handed it to one of the men. His companion offered a large envelope to Steve, who nodded and pocketed it.

Maggie began to feel uncomfortable as the two soldiers stared across the room at her. They grinned and, to her horror, came over to the booth.

'Hello love,' said one.

'Fancy that bloody Yank bringing a nice girl like you to a place like this. He should be ashamed of himself,' said the other. 'Come along with us, girl, we'll give you a good time, won't we?' he said turning to his mate.

80

The other man leered at Maggie. 'Yes we will. We'll show you what real men are like.'

Maggie's eyes flashed angrily. 'On your bike!'

The first soldier got annoyed. He leaned over the table until his face was only inches away from hers, breathing fumes of stale beer over her. 'You're just like all the rest – lift your skirts for a pair of nylons!'

Scared by the angry curl of his lips, she clutched her glass tightly.

Suddenly Steve was behind the soldier. He pulled him away and sent him flying across the bar. 'You leave my girl alone, buddy!'

The other soldier stepped towards Steve with a raised fist. 'He's not your buddy, mate!' He swung a punch at Steve, who ducked expertly and slammed his own fist into the other man's face. The man staggered backwards, blood pouring from his nose.

Maggie looked on in horror. She watched, her senses alert, as the bar became silent. The sailors were all for stepping in to defend their country-men, but the American soldiers at the bar warned them to stay out of it. The mood of the place was ugly and dangerous. The two men Steve had been doing business with watched the scene with interest and didn't move.

The two soldiers made for the GI, a united force of strength. Maggie felt the blood drain from her face as Steve produced a knife from his boot and held it out, blade first. 'I don't advise it, you guys,' he said, as he crouched, ready for their onslaught. 'But if you must, which one of you is going to be first?'

The other Americans moved forward, menacing the soldiers who looked around and saw they were outnumbered.

'All right, Yank! You win this time, but if we see you again, we'll bloody have you!' They turned and walked towards the exit.

Heart pounding, Maggie was stunned as Steve put away the knife, sat beside her and in a perfectly normal voice said, 'I'm sorry about that, honey. Drink up and we'll be off.'

She rounded on him. 'Is that all you have to say?'

He looked at her with surprise. 'I'm sorry, I didn't realize you were so upset. Barman, bring the young lady a brandy!'

'Of course I'm upset!' She glared at him and felt her cheeks flush with rage. 'This may be a daily occurrence in your life, it certainly isn't in mine.'

Putting an arm around her he said, 'Of course this isn't a normal occurrence, don't be so silly. But there is a lot of resentment towards us from the Brits. We get paid more than them, we're better dressed and we take all the women. They hate us.'

'But you had a knife!'

'Oh I see, that's what worried you.' He caught hold of her hand. 'I was brought up in New York City. Believe me it's tough for a kid. If you don't learn to take care of yourself at a very early age, you never get to grow up. I learnt to survive, and no two limey soldiers would ever get the better of me.'

She saw the anger in his eyes. 'Would you have

used it?' she asked.

He stared at her intently. 'We'll never know, will we? Now let's drink up and get the hell out of this place.'

As they left the club, Maggie asked, 'Who were your friends? The two men at the table you spoke to?'

'Just a couple of guys I met one day. We help each other out from time to time.'

'They looked as if they'd cut your throat as soon as look at you.'

'You're right. They probably would,' was the sharp reply.

No more was said about the incident as they wined and dined before returning to the hotel, and Maggie decided, as Steve kissed and caressed her, to dismiss the whole incident from her mind. Nothing was going to spoil this week-end for her.

The two days passed in a whirl of activity. On Saturday they shopped at the PX store in Great Audley Street, where Steve purchased his ration of chocolate, razorblades and cigarettes. He also bought toothpaste and shaving cream. 'You can take this all home to your folks,' he said. 'I've got more than I need back at the base.'

They dined in a fashionable restaurant, then Steve took her to an American servicemen's club, called Rainbow Corner,

Maggie was enthralled at the place. It was like being in America. Juke boxes pumped out such favourites as 'Don't Sit Under the Apple Tree' and 'Deep in the Heart of Texas' by the Andrews

Sisters. On one wall was a big map of the United States. Steve led her over to it and pointed out New York. 'Maybe one day you'll see it for yourself,' he said.

'What are all the little flags stuck in it for?' she asked.

'When you come in here, you put one in your home town. See? There's obviously lots of guys from my area.'

He took her downstairs to the basement where she ate American doughnuts and drank a glass of Coke. He apologized. 'Sorry, they don't serve anything stronger here.'

But she didn't mind a bit, she was fascinated with the place and was amazed at how well organized everything was. A barber was installed, there was even a lady willing to do mending or sew on stripes.

During their last night, Maggie lay in Steve's arms after they had made love. 'What are we going to do when we get back to Southampton?' he said. 'I'm going to go crazy if I can't make love to you.'

She moved even closer to him. 'I don't know,' she said. She sighed. She didn't want to go back to just holding hands. Not now. She had walked around during the day hugging the secret of their intimacy to her. She found herself smiling constantly. She was glowing in her newly awakened womanhood. She kept putting her hand out to touch her lover. It was such a strange feeling, this closeness.

'I'll think of something,' he murmured. He yawned and apologized in a weary voice. 'You've worn me out, young lady,' he teased.

She watched his eyes close, then he was asleep. But she was wide awake. Despite the thrill of this new and wonderful experience, she couldn't dismiss from her mind the fracas at the club. She'd had a glimpse of a brutal side to the cocky American and it disturbed her. When he made love to her, he was gentle and thoughtful of her needs as well as his own. Yet as he made love to her, she couldn't help remembering the grim expression on his face as he threatened the two soldiers with his knife. Would he have used it had he been pressed? She had no doubt that he would have done.

She tried to analyse her feelings for him. It wasn't love, she knew that. Was it infatuation? No, that was for teenagers. He was fun to be around, and as a lover he was wonderful. He gave her a good time. She felt a tremor of guilt. Was that all she was, a good-time girl? She dismissed the idea at once. She went out with Steve because she liked him, was fascinated by him, not for what he could give her. This was wartime after all, and who knew what was ahead of them. She would grab each moment as it came.

Outside Southampton railway station, Maggie dissuaded Steve from taking her home. Before putting her in a taxi, he drew her into his arms. 'Jeez, honey, I don't want to let you go.'

'I know,' she said as she kissed him.

'I'll be in touch, real soon,' he said as he helped her into the waiting vehicle.

Maggie gave the driver Ivy's address.

When she arrived at her destination and knocked on the door after paying off the taxi, Ivy ushered her into the living room.

As she sat beside Maggie she asked, 'Well. How was your dirty weekend?'

Maggie glared at her. 'It wasn't like that!'

'Oh, sorry!' quipped Ivy with a mischievous grin. 'Don't tell me you spent a weekend with that horny bastard and there was no sex, because I won't believe it.'

Maggie couldn't help laughing. 'I had a great time.'

Stirring her tea, her friend asked, 'What was he like in bed?

'You don't honestly expect me to give you every detail!'

With a laugh Ivy said, 'Why not? I want a blow-by-blow description.'

'Well you're not going to get one!' declared Maggie.

With a sly nudge Ivy asked, 'Was he hot stuff? Did he wear you out?'

'Ivy! Will you behave.' Despite her indignation, Maggie couldn't keep a broad smile from spreading across her features.

'You don't have to say a word. You look just like the cat who ate the cream. You're absolutely glowing. It's not every day a woman loses her virginity, you know. You'd better wipe that satisfied grin off your face when you get home,' warned Ivy, 'or your dad will catch on straight away. Then the shit *will* fly. Men like their daughters to remain pure and untouched, surrounded by their children.'

Maggie looked thoughtful. 'Strange, isn't it. Sex is wonderful, but I can't picture my mum and dad doing it at all.'

'I know what you mean,' said Ivy.

'Steve's going to call me as soon as he has some free time,' said Maggie. 'I hope it's soon.'

'You won't hear this week, love ... of course, Steve wouldn't know until he got back! They leave early tomorrow morning on manoeuvres. Bob told me last night.' At the look of despondency on Maggie's face she said, 'Don't worry, they're only away for five days. Look, there's a dance on in Fair Oak tomorrow night for the company of darkies. Let's go.'

'How will we get there?'

'A couple of trucks are picking up the girls at the Guildhall at seven o'clock, bringing us back at eleven.' At Maggie's hesitation she added, 'These blokes are meant to be great dancers. Come on, come with me. It'll cheer us up whilst the boys are away.'

'All right. Call for me and we'll go to the Guildhall together.'

'I'll meet you outside the pub,' said Ivy 'If I come in your dad will have a go at me about having a good time with Len away fighting, you know how he goes on, and he might start asking awkward questions about the weekend.'

With a worried frown Maggie agreed. 'Yes, we don't want that. I'll say we stayed in and listened to the wireless because you didn't feel like doing anything else.'

It was only a short walk from Ivy's place to the

pub, and Maggie made her way home. She slipped in by the side door. She couldn't face her father after the lies she'd told. She couldn't possibly behave as if nothing had happened and she was sure he'd see the guilt written in her eyes. She needed time to pull herself together.

She made her way upstairs and started to unpack. As she took out the goods from the PX store, she wondered just how she was going to explain them away. Shaking her head she thought, you start with one lie and that just leads to another. She would put the stuff in a drawer for another time, then she'd think of something.

There was a tap on the door. She hastily covered the goods with a dress as her mother walked in.

'Hello, love. How's Ivy? I expect she was glad of your company.'

'Oh yes, she was,' Maggie said hurriedly.

'What did you do?'

'Nothing much. Sat and talked, listened to the wireless. Just had a quiet time, really.'

'I'm just going down to help your father close the bar and clear up. I'll see you in the morning.'

Maggie walked over to her, held her close and kissed her cheek. 'Goodnight, Mum. I love you lots. God bless.'

She breathed a sigh of relief as she was left alone. She was so worried about being caught out! She'd have to be very careful what she said. It would be all too easy to give the game away. She hated lying to her mother, but how could she tell her she'd been to London to lose her virginity!

As she undressed and washed, she wondered what Steve was doing. He'd said he'd ring her as soon as he was free. She couldn't wait to see him again, to be held in his arms. But where could they go to be together, alone, in Southampton? Living at home made things very difficult. And now that she'd given herself to him, Steve wouldn't be content with just going to the pictures and out for a meal. He had booked a room at the Dolphin Hotel at one time in the hope that she would stay the night, but if he did that again and she went with him, how long would it be before their relationship was discovered? Oh she was playing with fire all right, but she didn't regret her weekend for one moment. She enjoyed being a woman!

Climbing into bed, she hugged her pillow to her, pretending it was the attractive Italian she was cuddling, and fell asleep.

Chapter Six

Jack Evans was much too occupied at the pub to worry about his daughter and her friend. Late the previous night, when his wife and Maggie were in bed, he'd taken in a load of black market goods. His small room was stocked to the ceiling and he was worried about how long he'd have to keep them. His usual punters were away for two weeks and the police were becoming especially vigilant. For once he was feeling nervous about the chances he was taking. Apart from the tinned goods and cigarettes, the nylons and petrol coupons, he had six large jerry cans filled with petrol from Sonny Taylor. If there was a raid or a fire, the pub would go up in a cloud of smoke. Consequently he was very edgy and bad tempered.

Moira had had enough of his waspish tongue, and as Maggie arrived home, she could hear raised voices coming from the kitchen.

'Don't you use that tone of voice to me, Jack Evans!' she heard her mother say. She knew she was angry because when Moira was excited or in a temper, her Irish brogue broadened.

'I've put up with you snapping my head off all day, so I have, and I'll not put up with it any longer.'

Maggie walked into the room. 'What's going on?' she asked.

'Your father's got a cob on. Something's on his mind and I'm bearing the brunt of it.'

Maggie looked angrily at her father. 'What's up, Dad? Got another load of goods in, have you?'

He glared at her. 'What on earth are you talking about?'

'It's always the same. You take a load of stolen goods and then you're so twitchy about it you take it out on Mum.'

'Don't be ridiculous.'

'I'm not the one being ridiculous.' She sat opposite him. 'Don't you care what happens to us, to Mum and me?'

He looked startled. 'Whatever do you mean?'

She tried to reason with him. 'If the police

catch you, you'll lose your licence after all these years. What'll happen to Mum then?'

His face was flushed with anger and guilt. 'I'm only doing it for your mother.'

Maggie's anger exploded. 'Don't give me that old crap. Men always lay the blame at someone else's door. You're doing it for yourself, to make money. It's greed, that's all.'

He tried to justify himself. 'I'm saving for our retirement. Then we can have a nice bungalow somewhere.'

'And what good will that be if you're in prison?'

Moira was looking anxious. 'She's right, Jack. I don't know exactly what you've got in the front room, but every time you get stuff in, you're like a bear with a sore head until you shift it. It's too dangerous. I don't want a bungalow anywhere! Stop taking these chances. Please.'

'Now don't you start.' He rose to his feet. 'I know exactly what I'm about.' He glared at his daughter. 'Do you take me for a complete fool?'

'Frankly, yes. Whilst you continue to defy the law this way, you are being a complete idiot.'

'You'll speak to me with a little more respect, my girl. Instead of having a go at me, you'd be better sorting your own way of life out instead of running after the Yanks the way you do!'

Maggie's eyes flashed with anger. 'That's right! Change the subject. At least what I do is legal and above board.'

He stormed out of the room.

Moira sat down and buried her face in her hands.

Maggie went over to her and put a comforting

arm about her. 'Don't worry, Mum,' she urged.

'But I do,' said Moira. 'And you're right, if we lose the pub, how could I live?'

Maggie hugged her mother. 'Whilst I'm alive, you'll never have to worry,' she said.

'Ah but you're a fine girl,' said Moira, 'but you have your own life to lead. You shouldn't be concerning yourself with mine.'

'But of course I'm concerned! I love you and I hate to see you unhappy. Look, Mum, if the worst ever happens, you and I will always be together. I'll always take care of you.'

Moira gazed at her with tear-filled eyes. 'You're a darlin' child. What would my life be without you around to cheer my day.'

In the bar later that evening, seeing her mother's drawn features, Maggie insisted she relieve her behind the counter. 'Go and have a nice hot bath. Listen to the wireless. Try and relax. I'll work in the bar.'

Moira gratefully complied.

Maggie went over to her father who was changing a barrel of beer. 'You're worrying Mum to death, you know. Why don't you give it all up. She'll be happier and so will I.'

'And what about *my* happiness?' he snapped. 'This is the one time in my life I can make a load of money. You think I'll throw away such an opportunity? Never. I'd be a fool.'

Seeing the determined set of his mouth, Maggie gave up. Nothing she could say would dissuade him. She was wasting her time.

The following evening, Maggie and Ivy climbed into one of the American trucks that had been sent by the base and were driven to Fair Oak village hall. They beamed with delight as they were given corsages to wear on their arrival.

'These Yanks certainly know how to put things over,' enthused Ivy. 'Look at the stage.'

The humble village hall was bedecked with flags. On the stage was a large Union Jack draped on one side and a Stars and Stripes on the other. In front of them sat an American service band. The army captain in charge of the soldiers came over and thanked them for coming.

The two girls danced until they were worn out.

'Blimey!' exclaimed Ivy as she collapsed into a seat. 'These darkies certainly know how to move, don't they?'

Halfway through the evening the band took a break and the officer announced that a corporal from the company would play the piano for their entertainment.

A tall soldier took a seat and started to run his hands over the keys, playing boogie woogie and jazz. Maggie was fascinated and walked nearer the stage to listen, her foot tapping to the music as she stood. Some people danced but the majority gathered round, clapping their hands, bodies swaying with the music. Once or twice the soldier looked around at his audience and caught Maggie's gaze. He smiled at her and played on.

When the band eventually returned, the applause from the dancers was filled with enthusiastic appreciation.

To her great surprise the man walked over to

her. 'Hi there! You were really swinging to the music.'

She smiled at him. 'Where did you ever learn to play like that?' she asked.

'No one taught me, ma'am. I picked it up myself using the piano in my daddy's church.'

'They play music like that in church?'

He chuckled. 'Well as a matter of fact, no they don't, only gospel music. I played that every Sunday, but I'd sneak in and play jazz whenever I could. But if he caught me at it, he used to be mighty angry.'

'I suppose it isn't quite the thing for such a place.'

He shrugged. 'Who can say for certain? If jazz was around in the Lord's day, I'm sure he'd have liked it.'

His reasoning amused Maggie. 'We'll never know, will we?'

'I guess not. Say, can I get you a drink, only I'm really thirsty.'

'Do you have American Coke?'

He grinned broadly. 'Well that's a surprise.'

'I tasted it for the first time recently,' she told him, 'and I liked it.'

He went to the bar, returning with two glasses. 'Here you are. Let's sit at a table, shall we?' When they had settled he asked, 'What's your name?'

'Maggie, short for Margaret ... and yours?'

'Joshua. Joshua Lewis.' He held out his large hand, and Maggie took it in hers.

'That's a name from the bible, isn't it?' she asked.

He smiled softly. 'Sure is. My daddy is a

preacher. All the family have biblical names. I've a brother Abraham, another called Matthew and two sisters, Ruth and Jemima.'

'I don't remember a Jemima in the bible!'

'It was the name of one of Job's daughters in the Old Testament. She hates it,' he added, 'and insists on calling herself Delilah. She says if she must have a name from the Good Book, then she'll be somebody interesting!'

Maggie was highly amused. 'She sounds quite a character.'

'She gives my poor momma many a sleepless night, but she's a good girl at heart, just spirited.' He looked at Maggie. 'Not unlike you, I imagine.'

'Now why would you think that?' she asked, intrigued by his remark.

The corners of his mouth twitched as he tried to suppress a smile. 'It's the way you hold your head, I guess. The way you walk. Almost in defiance. Who do you defy, Maggie?'

She smiled ruefully. 'Mostly my father.'

His laugh was so melodic, she felt she could sit and listen to it for hours. There was something about Joshua Lewis that was unusual, but she couldn't put her finger on it.

'So what do you do to amuse yourself when you're not working?' she asked.

'I play jazz,' he said with a broad grin. 'Music is my life. What kind of music do you like, Maggie?'

'I like Glenn Miller,' she said, 'but Frank Sinatra is my favourite.'

'What about Billie Holliday and Ella Fitzgerald? Do you like them?'

'I don't know much about them,' she admitted.

'Have you ever heard of Count Basie and Duke Ellington? Louis Armstrong?'

'Well I have heard of them, but that's all.'

'Oh my, Maggie. Your musical education has been sadly neglected,' he teased. 'If you haven't heard the golden tones tinged with sadness of Louis Armstrong's trumpet playing, you've missed a real treat. An experience.'

The band struck up a slow number and he asked, 'Would you like to dance?'

'Yes, thank you.' She got up and, walking to the dance floor, turned and felt his arms about her. He was quite a bit taller than her and of slender build but his shoulders were broad and he had a presence about him that was indefinable.

His movements were fluid as they traversed the floor and she felt as light as a feather in his arms. Looking up into his dark brown eyes she said, 'For a pianist, you dance very well.'

'Why thank you,' was all he said.

As the music continued, Maggie couldn't help comparing this stranger with Steve. Whereas Steve would have been talking rapidly, joking with her, teasing her, flirting with her, trying to seduce her, Joshua was quiet. Yet it wasn't an uncomfortable or awkward silence, it was restful, enjoyable, relaxing.

At the end of the dance they returned to their seats. 'Do you like being in England?' she asked.

He beamed at her. 'It's beautiful around here. Not that I've seen much more than Southampton and the docks, and a little of the New Forest, but I've read books about it. The history is mighty interesting.'

'What are you doing here?'

'Our company is here to help unload the goods from the ships that dock, bringing food and equipment for the US Army stationed in your country.'

The band started to play a fast number and Joshua looked at Maggie and said, 'Would you like to jive?'

When she said she would, he led her onto the floor. The pace was fast and furious and Joshua held her firmly as he spun her around and his eyes sparkled as she followed his steps until the end of the number.

'You're quite a mover, Maggie,' he said with a grin.

'You don't exactly stand still,' she said, breathless from the dance.

They stayed on the floor as the last waltz began. He held her close and said, 'I've really enjoyed talking to you, Maggie.'

'I've enjoyed it too,' she replied.

And she had. She wished they'd met earlier in the evening because she was intrigued by this man. But as the number finished, he said, 'You take care now, and don't upset your father too much.'

She saw the mischievous glint in his eye and grinned at him. 'I'm afraid I can't promise that. My dad and me were born to fight with each other.'

He touched her arm gently. 'That's a great pity,' he said.

At that moment Ivy appeared holding their

coats. 'Come on, Maggie. The truck's ready to take us home.'

'Goodnight, Joshua,' said Maggie. 'Take care.'

'And you too,' he said as he walked them to the door.

When they were settled in the back of the truck Ivy asked, 'Who was your friend?'

'A man called Joshua, the son of a preacher,' she explained.

'Blimey! Did he give you a lecture on the sins of the flesh?' joked Ivy.

'No, not at all. He talked to me about music. He likes jazz, that was different from the usual line of bull.'

'Don't be bloody daft,' said her friend, 'all men are the same if you ask me.'

'Well I'm not asking you!' snapped Maggie, annoyed at the generality.

'Sorry I opened my big mouth!' retorted Ivy.

Maggie apologized. 'No, I'm sorry, but he really was nice.'

'Did he ask to see you again?'

Shaking her head Maggie said, 'No, of course he didn't.' And she knew that she wished he had.

'Just as well,' said Ivy. 'Steve would blow a gasket. Never mind, love, only another few days and the boys will be back at camp. Ooh! I can hardly wait! I used my precious coupons on some new underwear.' She nudged Maggie. 'Not that Bob needs any encouragement.'

But Maggie didn't want to talk, all she wanted to do was be quiet. Silent, as she'd been when she was dancing with Joshua Lewis.

Chapter Seven

When Steve returned from his manoeuvres, he rang the Bricklayer's Arms to arrange a date with Maggie, who fortunately answered the telephone. She was pleased to hear his cheerful voice and realized how she'd missed him.

They met that evening and went to the Red Lion for a drink.

When he returned from the bar with their order, they sat close together and Steve put his arm around her and kissed her cheek.

'Let me look at you,' he said. 'That was the longest week of my life. I couldn't wait to get back.

'I've missed you too.'

He stroked her face. 'We had such a good time in London, didn't we?'

'Yes,' she agreed. 'Except for that bit of trouble in the club.'

He frowned as he said, 'You're not still worrying about that, surely?'

She stared steadily at him. 'All I could think about was what would have happened if those tommies hadn't left.'

'When we were in London, I was taking care of you, protecting you.' He smiled confidently. 'At the sign of a knife most guys back off.'

'And what happens if they don't?'

'Believe me, they always do.'

'Have you ever had to use it?' she persisted.

'Look, Maggie, when I was growing up I was in the middle of gang wars every day of my young life ... and yes, sometimes I had to use it or go under.'

She was horrified.

At the look on her face, Steve defended himself. 'It's all very well for you, honey, living here in cosy old-fashioned England. I've seen pictures of kids with their skipping ropes, boys with catapults. Believe me it's all very tame in comparison.'

'I don't believe it!' she protested. 'Kids are kids, the world over.'

'It all depends on their environment, honey. All right, let me put this to you. If you were a teenager and five young men from another gang came at you, what would you do?'

She hesitated.

'I'll tell you what you'd do. You'd use whatever was at hand. A metal bar, a chunk of wood ... a knife.'

There was a sick feeling in the pit of her stomach. 'Did you ever kill anyone?' she asked.

'No of course not! I may have nicked someone, cut their jacket. It was them or me. Don't you understand?'

It didn't sound so unreasonable, as she thought about it. Just because things didn't happen like that in her own country, should she condemn him for it? And looking into the smiling eyes of the good-looking Italian, she didn't think she should. 'I'm sorry,' she said.

He squeezed her hand. 'That's my girl.' He

kissed her cheek and said softly, 'I've got to be back at camp by midnight, but on Saturday night I've got an all-night pass.' He pushed a stray strand of her hair away and caressed her ear. 'Shall I book us a room in a hotel?'

At his touch she knew she couldn't refuse him. 'Yes,' she said. 'I want to be with you, too.'

As Maggie was getting in deeper with her relationship with Steve Rossi, her friend Ivy was plotting and scheming while she listened to the whispered words of love from Bob Hanson as they lay together in bed.

'Tell me again about your home,' she pleaded.

Bob chuckled. 'You're just like a child, wanting the same story every night.'

She snuggled even closer. 'It just sounds so wonderful. So different from this dead and alive country.'

'What a terrible thing to say,' he chided. 'You should be proud of your heritage!'

With a sigh she said, 'I am really, I just want to see other things, other places.'

He looked at her with affection and caressed her. 'You are a real cute woman, you know that? My folks would love you, I'm sure.'

Ivy held her breath.

Bob rolled over and taking her into his arms said softly, 'Would you like to meet them?'

She looked at him wide-eyed. 'How on earth could I possibly do that?'

'You could if we were married.'

She let out a squeal of joy. 'Are you proposing to me?'

His laughter filled the small room. 'Of course I am. Will you marry me, Ivy?'

She flung her arms about him. 'Oh, yes please.' She pushed him on his back and sat her naked form astride him. 'Mrs Ivy Hanson,' she said with a broad grin. 'I love you, you crazy Yank!' She smothered him with kisses as she moved sensually over him. Feeling his erection beneath her she said, 'I'll show you just how good a wife I'll be. You'll never want to go to work.'

'If I don't, how will I be able to buy food, keep you?' he asked with a chuckle.

But as Ivy nibbled his ear he said, 'Who the hell wants to eat anyway!'

Two days later, Ivy sidled up to Maggie at the factory and held out her left hand, waving it under her friend's nose. 'What do you think?' she asked.

Maggie was appalled as she looked down at the engagement ring. 'I think you've lost your marbles. That's what I think!'

But Ivy was not to be deterred. 'You can say what you like, but I'm going to live in America!' She turned on her heel and stormed off.

Maggie went to the ladies room and lit a cigarette. Now what could she do? Ivy was crazy thinking she could get away with this. Was she going to commit bigamy? She couldn't get a divorce just like that, it would take ages. And anyway, Bob didn't even know she was married! And what about Len? What would he have to say about all this? She would have to try and knock some sense into her somehow.

But it was to no avail.

When the shift was over, she waited for her friend. She tucked her arm through Ivy's and said, 'For God's sake, be realistic. You can't possibly marry Bob Hanson.'

'He's going to find out all the necessary details,' Ivy declared. 'Then I'll know exactly what I'm up against.' She glared at Maggie. 'I'm going to America somehow and nobody is going to stop me. If you want to walk away from our friendship, that's fine with me!'

'Oh Ivy!' The two walked side by side in silence. Maggie had no intention of leaving her friend, because she felt that soon enough Ivy was going to need her. This stupid idea of hers would only lead to trouble and she couldn't leave her to face it alone.

When she returned home she was met with her own kind of trouble. Her father was waiting in the kitchen for her. 'You were seen in the Red Lion with a Yank the other night, despite what I said,' he accused.

She wearily took the turban off her head and shook loose her hair. She looked straight at her father. 'That's right. His name is Steve and I've been seeing him for some time.'

His thin cheeks puffed up with anger. 'How dare you defy me this way!'

She sat down at the table and faced her father. 'Look, Dad. You made it perfectly clear you intend to go your own way with your black market dealings without any regard to Mum and me, so I don't feel you have any right to dictate to me how to run my life.'

She thought he was going to have a fit. 'Whilst you live under my roof I certainly have the right to tell you what to do,' he yelled.

Maggie felt her anger beginning to rise. 'I pay for my keep. You don't give me anything for nothing.'

He leaned on the table and put his face near to hers. 'Whether you pay or not, you do as I say – or you get out!'

Suddenly she'd had enough. 'If that's the way you feel, I'll leave as soon as I find somewhere else to live,' she said. 'By the end of the week if at all possible. That suit you?' She got up, walked out of the room and went upstairs.

A short while later there was an urgent knocking on her door and a distraught Moira came in. 'What's this your father tells me? You're leaving home?'

Maggie put her arms around her and held her close. 'That's right. I won't have him dictate to me any longer.' She felt her mother tremble as she began to cry. 'It's the only way, Mum. I must be free to live my life. I'll still come and see you.'

Moira looked up, her face wet with tears. 'What if he won't let you?'

'Huh! I'd like to see him try and stop me!' she exclaimed. 'I'll tell him I'll shop him to the police if he doesn't.'

Her mother looked horrified. 'You wouldn't do that, would you?'

Maggie grinned. 'Of course not, but the miserable devil doesn't know that, does he? Now I've got to get changed, I want to see about a flat somewhere.' She tried to smile. 'Imagine ... if I have my own place you can come and stay when the old bugger gets on your nerves.'

Moira took out a handkerchief from her sleeve and wiped her eyes, smiling bravely. 'That would be nice.' Then with an anxious look she said, 'You will take care of yourself, won't you?'

'Of course I will,' Maggie said gently. 'I'm not moving miles away after all, and I promise I'll see you very often.' The two women clung together.

As she held her mother she thought, Well, I've taken that first step. I'm free. Now I'm in charge of my own destiny. And she wondered just what was before her.

A while later, downstairs, Moira was thinking about her daughter with a sinking heart. So young, so vulnerable. So innocent ... or was she still? She prayed to God she was. What could she say to her to warn her of the pitfalls of life? She loved Maggie so much and she didn't want to see her get hurt. From the moment the nurse had placed her daughter in her arms she'd adored her. Through the difficult years with Jack, here in the pub, Maggie had been her salvation. Without her, what would she have done? She was filled with despair at the thought of her leaving, but she knew that it was time to let go. It didn't ease the pain she felt deep within her heart.

It was with feelings of both excitement and trepidation that Maggie made her way to an estate agent later that day. She was sad to leave her mother behind, but she felt that things would only get worse between herself and her father if she stayed. This way she could continue to meet Steve and live her own life without any fuss. She would certainly keep a close eye on her mother's welfare, though.

She stopped in front of an agent's window and looked at the flats advertised to let. She frowned as she saw the asking price of some of them. She'd deliberately gone to an up-market agent in the High Street, thinking to get away from the docklands, but she realized that to survive, she would have to lower her sights.

She made her way to an office near Holy Rood, advertising the poorer area of the town, and saw that there was a small selection that suited her pocket. She was about to go inside when a low, deep voice said, 'Hello, Maggie. How are you?'

She turned and looked into the smiling eyes of Joshua Lewis. 'Joshua! What a surprise.'

He beamed at her, his eyes lighting up with pleasure. 'I wasn't sure you'd remember me.'

'The man who played the piano so well ... how could I forget!'

His melodic laughter flowed. 'What are you doing here?'

He looked a mite perplexed when she said, 'I'm leaving home and am looking for a place to rent.'

His dark eyes twinkled. 'Don't tell me ... you've fallen foul of your father again.'

She burst out laughing. 'Yes, you could say that. Didn't you ever have any family rows?'

'What, with two brothers and two sisters? We certainly did! All the time.'

'And what did your father do?'

He chuckled. 'He took his slipper to us.'

Maggie started to laugh as she pictured this. 'Did it hurt?'

'Not much. We boys used to put something down the back of our trousers. He didn't do this to the girls, of course, which used to make us mad. But we never left home because of it,' he said with a grin.

'Maybe you didn't, but I've made up my mind.'

'Would you like a cup of tea somewhere?' he asked. 'I have the rest of the afternoon free. We could catch up on the short conversation we had at the dance.'

'I'd like that very much,' she answered, 'but first I'll just pop in here. Come with me if you like.' She opened the door and walked inside.

The middle-aged man behind the desk looked up at his customer with a welcoming smile which disappeared very quickly as he saw her companion.

'Can I help you?' he asked coldly.

Maggie felt the hairs on her neck prickle at the veiled hostility of the man. 'I'm looking for a small, one-bedroom flat,' she said.

'I'm not at all sure that I have anything suitable,' he answered, without making any attempt to assist her.

'Now look here,' she began.

But Joshua stepped forward and with a smile said softly, 'I think you may have jumped to the wrong conclusion, sir. This lovely young lady is just showing me around your town. You folks have all been so kind to us GIs, away from home, and we really appreciate it.'

The man looked slightly abashed and coughed. 'Humph, well I may have something, miss.' He looked through his books and offered her three addresses. 'If you like to take a look at the properties from the outside and if you're interested, come back and see me.'

'Thank you,' she said coldly. 'I'll look at these details and think about it.' She stalked angrily out of the office.

Outside Joshua caught hold of her. 'Hey there! Cool down. My word, you're as fiery as your beautiful red hair.'

She turned to him. 'It just makes me so angry the way other people make judgements about things that don't concern them!'

There was a note of resignation in his voice as he said, 'I've been living with prejudice all my life. You learn to be tolerant.'

She gave him a glance filled with curiosity. 'Why don't we go for that cup of tea and you can tell me all about it.'

The long conversation that followed over several cups of tea was most enlightening and horrifying to Maggie's ears.

'What do you mean, negroes are only allowed to sit in the back of the bus?'

'Because the front is reserved for the white folk,' he said quietly. 'And if all the seats are full, we have to give ours up to them. We even have separate schools. Back home in Mississippi, I wouldn't be allowed to sit in the same place as you to eat.' He chuckled softly. 'Back home if I was caught sitting at the same table as a white woman, as we are now, I could be lynched!'

'You're kidding!'

He shook his head. 'No, Maggie, I can assure you I'm not. That night at the dance was the first time ever that I had held a white woman in my arms. At home if I'd done that I'd be a dead man.' He looked at her expression of horror and said, 'Now perhaps you'll understand why the white GIs hate us so much. Here it's all so different. Here we have so much freedom to mix and it drives them crazy. To them we're just no count niggers, coons. Worse than the dirt beneath their feet. They want to keep us in our place – as they see it!'

But whilst they'd been chatting, Maggie had become aware of angry glances and low mutterings from some of the other patrons of the tea room. She looked around and caught many a hostile look. She straightened her back, defiantly.

It was as if Joshua could read her mind. 'Let it go,' he said firmly, but quietly. 'How about we take a look at these properties that guy gave you?'

She nodded her agreement and waited as he paid the bill, outstaring any who dared to glance their way.

The first two flats were in the Chapel area; Maggie just looked at the addresses and turned them down out of hand. The area had been devastated during the bombing and it was one of the poorest districts. College Street wasn't anything special, but she didn't want to lower her sights that much. The final address was in Bugle Street, and the two of them made their way to the Old Walls.

Joshua was fascinated by the history of the place. 'You can just picture it, can't you,' he said, his eyes shining with excitement. 'The knights of old, the soldiers walking the battlements, protecting the town from marauding forces.'

'You have been reading too many books,' she teased.

He turned to her with a grin and said, 'Well I know all about Robin Hood and King Arthur.'

'But that's all fairy stories.'

'Aw, Maggie don't tell me that! They're some of my favourite characters. Old Henry the Eighth was for real, though. I know that much.'

She knew he was teasing her but she didn't mind a bit.

Before they found the address the estate agent had given them, Maggie took Joshua to look at St Michael's church. As they entered the doorway, he removed his hat. They walked quietly around the church, enjoying the tranquillity of the place. Here, Joshua seemed at home, she thought. She sat in a pew and left him to wander. She watched as he stood in front of the altar, saw him lower his head in silent prayer, and waited patiently until he came and sat beside her.

He looked at her with a soft smile and said, 'Here, in God's house, everyone really is equal.'

They sat in companionable silence until he said, 'Perhaps we'd better find this flat you want to see.'

With some reluctance, she got up and made her way to the door.

The row of flats looked all right and she

decided to return to the office and ask the agent to show her around. When she told Joshua her intention he said, 'Fine. I'll leave you now.' At the surprised expression on her face he said, 'It's best, I think, if I'm not around.'

She was immediately defensive. 'It makes no difference to me,' she declared.

'Maybe, but it makes a difference to the guy in the office. It's better this way.'

'I've really enjoyed being with you,' said Maggie.

His face lit up as he smiled. 'It's been my pleasure. I'm glad we ran into each other again.' They stood gazing at one another, reluctant to part.

'Will I see you again? I'd really like to hear more about your family.' As soon as the words were out of her mouth, Maggie wondered why she'd uttered them. She wasn't usually that forward, but she didn't want this unusual man just to walk away.

The pleasure her words gave him showed in his expression. 'I'd be mighty happy to see you again, Maggie.' But suddenly he looked concerned.

'What's the matter?' she asked.

'You saw the effect today, of us being together. It could be the cause of some embarrassment to you, and I wouldn't like that.'

Her green eyes flashed angrily. 'Look, Joshua!' she declared. 'I'm leaving home because I won't be dictated to. When people pay my bills and keep me, then they have the right to have a say in my life. If I won't let my own father do that, I certainly won't let a stranger!'

111

He burst out laughing. 'Oh, Maggie. All those years ago, all the people of the town would have had to do was have you walking the Old Walls. No one would have dared try to enter the town.'

She too started to laugh. 'I'm not that bad! 'Don't you *ever* get angry?' she asked.

'Only when I really have to,' he said. 'I try to stay out of trouble.'

They made an arrangement to meet again the following week and Maggie bade him goodbye, then made her way back to the estate agent's office.

Chapter Eight

The agent sent his assistant to accompany Maggie to the flat in Bugle Street. As soon as she stepped inside she knew she would take it. The bedroom had a double bed in it, a wardrobe, and in front of the window stood a dressing table. The sitting room was adequate, with a three-piece suite that had seen better days, but with a bit of spit and polish, a couple of cushions and a vase of flowers to brighten it, it would be fine.

The bathroom was small, as was the kitchen, but the cooker was clean and there was a selection of cheap china and a few saucepans. It would be hers. When she locked the door behind her, she would be in her own home. What a thrill!

She walked over to the sitting-room window

and looked out. To her right was the New Docks and straight ahead, in between other buildings, in the distance, was Southampton Water. But what appealed to her most of all was the quiet. College Street and the pub with its comings and goings was a noisy, busy place, but here, behind the Old Walls, it was a sort of haven.

'The usual tenant is away in the army,' volunteered the agent, 'and the wife has gone to stay with her mother. That's why we're able to offer it,' he explained.

Maggie quickly calculated that she had enough savings in the bank to cover the expense, and at least, unlike with hire purchase, she didn't require a guarantor. Turning to him she said, 'I'll take it. When can I move in?'

He smiled his approval and said, 'If we go back to the office, sign the necessary papers, and you give me a month's rent in advance, you could move in this weekend if you wanted to.'

'That's super,' she said. 'Let's go.'

Having completed the necessary business, Maggie walked out of the office clutching the key to her new abode. She hugged it to her chest and walked home, a smile of satisfaction on her face which faded quickly as she wondered how she was going to break the news. Her mother would be upset, she knew, but she wondered if her father had really believed her when she said she would leave. He wouldn't let her go with a good grace, of that she was certain, and she still had two days before she moved.

Jack Evans was sitting at the kitchen table eating chips and a mushroom omelette made from dried egg when Maggie walked in. He completely ignored her, which under the circumstances suited her fine.

Moira gave her a worried glance and asked, 'Are you ready to eat?'

'Give me time to have a wash, Mum, will you?'

'There's no hurry I'll just put some chips on,' answered her mother with an uncertain smile.

By the time Maggie returned, Jack had left the room to prepare the bar for opening that evening. When her mother put her meal before her, Maggie said, 'Sit down, Mum. I've something to tell you.'

'You've found a place,' said Moira.

She caught hold of her hand. 'Yes, I have. I move in on Saturday.'

'So soon? Well, darlin', you know I'll miss you, don't you?'

Maggie felt a lump in her throat, but she managed to smile. 'Of course I do, but I intend to come back and work in the bar as usual. So we'll still see lots of each other. And you can come to my place. But you know, don't you, I don't have a choice?'

Moira nodded. 'Tell me about the flat.'

Maggie could barely keep the excitement from her voice as she described it to her.

'And what about this American you told your father you've been seeing?'

The question surprised her. She'd forgotten she'd told her father about Steve. 'He's a staff sergeant. He's really nice,' she said, desperately wanting her mother's approval. 'He's from New York City.'

114

'I'm glad you've met someone nice,' Moira said. 'But I do hope you'll be careful. War destroys people. Life is so unreal. These men are sent over to the war zones and they don't know if they are going to live or die. Because of this they take every advantage of a good time. They live for today and to hell with tomorrow, and who can blame them. But they leave, and the women stay behind to face everything on their own. Be careful, Maggie. Enjoy yourself, certainly, but for God's sake, don't mess up your life.'

She could see the anxiety in her mother's eyes. 'I promise,' she said. 'You're not telling me anything I don't already know. Steve is nice and I enjoy his company but I know it's only for a short time. He's bound to leave, and who knows when? There's too much I want to do with my life after the war to mess it up whilst the war is on. There's nothing to worry about, I promise.'

Moira took both Maggie's hands in hers and stared at her. 'You know don't you, that if anything should go wrong, and in this life, nothing is certain, you could come to me, no matter what your father says?'

Feeling the tears well in her eyes, Maggie said, 'Who else would I go to?'

'Right,' said Moira, blinking away her own tears. 'I think I'd better put the kettle on.' She got up from the table and asked, 'When are you going to tell your father?'

With a grimace she said, 'I don't know. I'm dreading it.'

'I suggest you start packing when he's busy in the bar and when you're ready to leave, you tell

115

him then. You do it before and he'll be hell to live with.'

Maggie knew her mother was right. She nodded her agreement. 'That's what I'll do then,' she said.

On Friday night, she worked in the bar as usual, trying her best to behave naturally. It was difficult, as Jack only spoke to her when it was necessary. Moira and she tried to make up for the lack of conversation by chattering.

Jack was griping to his customers about all the Yanks in town, digging slyly at his daughter. That started a heated discussion about the war and the necessity of gathering as many troops as possible to fight on their side, no matter what their nationality.

Maggie was grateful to hear her father call time. She cleared the empty glasses and made her escape to the sanctuary of her bedroom, knowing that come tomorrow, she would have to face him.

The following morning, Moira insisted that Maggie eat some breakfast before she left. She handed her ration book over to her. 'Here,' she said. 'You'll be needing this.' She also gave her a small bag with bread, milk, a small amount of tea and a bottle of Camp coffee, a tin of fruit and a small tin of condensed milk. She slipped in a piece of cheese too. As Maggie started to protest she said, 'Don't worry, I managed to get a little extra. I swapped a couple of tins of fruit one of the GIs gave me.'

'You watch yourself,' Maggie warned.

'Now remember,' said Moira, 'you're only allowed one-and-tenpence-worth of meat a week, but chicken, rabbit, sausages and offal are off rationing. Just watch the butter and sugar, it doesn't stretch very far. Buy fish when you can get it, too. You don't need coupons for that.'

Maggie looked at her in admiration. 'I honestly don't know how you managed.'

Her mother looked at her archly. 'The butcher fancies me!'

'Mother!' She handed Moira a slip of paper. 'Here's my address. Are you sure you'll be all right?'

'Don't you worry about me,' said Moira. 'You just take care of yourself. I'll ring for a taxi, then you'd better get your cases ... and then tell your father.'

Maggie's heart was thumping as she walked into the bar where Jack was polishing the beer pumps. 'Dad,' she said. 'I need to talk to you for a moment.'

He looked up and stared coldly at her. 'Well?'

'I'm waiting for a taxi. I'm leaving.'

A frown creased his forehead. 'What do you mean, you're leaving?'

'I've got a small flat and I'm moving in this morning. I think it's for the best.'

He exploded. 'You think it's for the best, do you? The best for who? You break your mother's heart and it's for the best! What about helping in the bar? You're walking out on all your responsibilities!'

Maggie felt the heat of anger burning her

117

cheeks. 'I'm not the one breaking Mum's heart, you are, with your black market dealings. But it's easy for you to put the blame on somebody else. You always do anyway. And I'm not leaving you in the lurch as far as the bar is concerned. I'll come and work as usual.' She moved towards the door.

'You walk out of here, you don't come back. Understand?'

She whirled around and walked back until she was facing him. 'Wrong! I'll come back to work in the bar to ease Mum's load and I'll come to visit her too and you won't stop me. And by God you'd better treat her right or I'll shop you to the Old Bill!'

The blood drained from his face as he looked at her in disbelief. 'You wouldn't dare.'

She glared at him. 'Let's hope we never have to find out.'

At that moment there was a knock on the side door. Moira called, 'Maggie, your taxi's here.'

She walked out of the bar, hugged her mother, picked up her cases and left the Bricklayer's Arms.

Moira watched the taxi drive away then quietly closed the door. She glared at Jack who was standing behind the bar. 'I hope you're satisfied!' She spat the words at him and walked into the kitchen.

Maggie paid the taxi driver, put the key in the lock of her new abode and walked in, placing the cases just inside the door. She went immediately to the kitchen, found a small vase, filled it with water and unwrapped the bunch of flowers she'd purchased on the way. She placed the vase on a small table, stood back and smiled. That's better, she thought, that makes it look more homely. She sat on the settee, pushed herself back into it and spread her arms. It was really quite comfortable. Then she turned and lay on it. Her feet dangled over the end, but she smiled as she thought that she and Steve would be quite comfortable curled up here together.

Oh my God! She sat bolt upright. In all the excitement, she'd forgotten that she was to meet him this evening. He'd booked a room at the Court Royal for them as he had an overnight pass. She looked around. No, she wouldn't bring him here tonight; first she needed to get it just right. The first thing to do was to unpack, then she'd make a cup of tea, do a bit of shopping, have something to eat, then a bath and meet Steve. At least she didn't have to worry about her father's recriminations any more. It gave her a wonderful sense of freedom. Yes, she would enjoy living alone.

Back at the Bricklayer's Arms the atmosphere was tense. Jack was trying to appease his angry wife, without success. Moira stood in front of him, her Irish temper at its height.

'So, now I suppose you're happy, having driven your only daughter away!' she accused.

'Now, Moira, it wasn't like that at all. I didn't want her to leave. That was her decision.'

'You're a selfish man, Jack Evans. You go your own way without regard to anyone. Why I ever married you in the first place I'll never know. I should have listened to my mother.'

Jack knew that Moira's mother had never liked him and that bit deeply. 'She said I'd never amount to anything. Well she was wrong. Haven't we a fine pub, money in the bank, aren't we making a good living?'

'That's all you think about, is making money. You have no heart, no feelings. Well you can take yourself off to Maggie's room and sleep there for I don't want you in my bed!' She stormed out of the kitchen.

Jack knew that he was in deep trouble. Never in all the years they'd been married had they ever spent a night apart. Whatever cross words had passed during the day, they had always been swept away by an arm across his wife's body. Sometimes it had led to sex. They'd often had their best sex after a row. But now... God how he hated the Yanks. Without them this situation would never have occurred, he told himself, but in his heart he knew that it would have happened anyway. Maggie was a woman now, not a girl to be ordered about any more. He shrugged. Well what's done is done. Perhaps a taste of life outside the family wouldn't be everything she hoped for. After all, although she paid her mother for her keep, alone, she'd have to cope with electricity bills, rates, food. He gave a slow smile. Moira might keep on about money, but you needed it to live. Yes, Maggie wouldn't find it quite that easy, then maybe she'd come home. This way he managed to smother his feelings of guilt. He could always find a way to do that.

Later that evening, Maggie walked into the bar of the Court Royal Hotel to meet Steve. She saw him standing at the counter talking to the barman.

'Hiya, honey!' He put an arm around her and kissed her cheek. 'What'll you have to drink? The usual gin and tonic?'

'Thank you, that's fine.'

'Right. Sit yourself at a table and I'll bring it over.'

She watched as he ordered. He really was a handsome man, and when he smiled across at her she felt a fluttering of excitement and desire inside at the thought that, later, she would be lying naked in his arms.

He sat beside her. 'What's new?' he asked.

'I've rented a flat,' she said with barely concealed excitement. 'I've left home!'

He whistled quietly. 'Wow! What brought that on?'

Oh dear, she thought. I can't tell him it's because of him, can I? 'My dad and I don't see eye to eye,' she said. 'I want to be free to live my life. After all, I'm not a child any more.'

He slipped his arm around her shoulders and caressed the back of her slender neck. In a low husky voice he said softly, 'No, you're very much a woman. I can vouch for that.' His gaze lowered to the soft swell of her breasts and she felt herself blush. 'So tell me about this place ... and why the hell are we here instead of there?'

'I only moved in a few hours ago!' she protested. 'I want to have it just right before I show it to you.'

'And that's it?'

She gave a mischievous grin. 'That's it. I want it to be a surprise. I'll cook you dinner the next time you're off duty.'

'Gee, honey, that'll be just great. I'll get a couple of steaks from the cookhouse. Get another key cut, then if I'm free I can come by and leave some things for you. I can supply you with a few stores to help out with the rationing.'

Her enthusiasm waned. She wasn't going to give anyone a key. This was her very own piece of heaven. No one but her had the right to enter it, without invitation. Oh no, that wouldn't do at all. But how could she tell him without seeming ungrateful? She changed the subject. 'Anyway, how are you?' she asked.

'Fine. I can't wait to hold you in my arms,' he said softly. 'It seems ages since we were together in London. By the way, have you eaten?' he asked.

She confessed to having had just a sandwich.

'Right, then,' he said. 'We'll go into the restaurant, have something to eat, then...' He kissed her forehead. 'Then I'll take you to bed.'

As they entered the dining room, she thought, Thank heavens I have a place of my own, because much as she wanted to be with Steve, she felt cheapened at staying with him in the hotel. In London it didn't matter, but here in her home town she felt differently. She guessed that the staff would gossip about the Americans and the women they brought here for the night. She didn't think she could face having breakfast in the dining room the following morning. To have dinner was fine, she reasoned, because anyone could walk in off the street for that, but breakfast announced to all and sundry that she'd stayed the night.

She was able to put these feelings of guilt behind her for a while once they were together in their bedroom and Steve took her into his arms. He was as passionate as he'd been in London and Maggie revelled in their lovemaking. He whispered to her in Italian. She didn't know what he was saying but it sounded to her like a language of love.

Neither of them got much sleep that night and she smiled to herself, now knowing what Ivy meant about not being able to walk after her husband came home. But she was happy and content. What did it matter if this was just a passing thing? Steve was her first man and because of this she felt really close to him, even knowing it was a transient liaison.

The following morning, at her reluctance to eat in the dining room, Steve ordered two breakfasts from room service. 'I have to be back at camp by ten thirty,' he said, 'I wish we could spend the day together.'

She too was reluctant to say goodbye. She studied the smiling eyes of her lover, his broad shoulders beneath his open shirt, the dark curls of the hair on his chest peeping out at the top of his olive green vest, the long fingers that had given her so much pleasure. 'Next time you can come to my flat,' she said proudly.

He reached for his jacket and took out a pen

and small notebook. 'You'd better give me the address,' he said with a cheeky grin. 'I don't want to lose you now, do I? And don't forget to have a spare key cut for me, because I can't contact you by telephone. I should be free on Tuesday from the late afternoon. What shift are you working next week?'

'The early one,' she told him. She gave him the address but made no mention of the key.

He held her close as they said their goodbyes in their room. 'I'll see you on Tuesday next,' he whispered in her ear as he nuzzled her neck. 'You behave now. You're my girl, remember.' He delved into his jacket pocket and pushed some notes into her hand. 'Here, honey. Buy some things for your new home.'

Maggie looked at the money and then at him. 'I don't want this!'

He was surprised at the hostile note in her voice. 'Jesus! Whatever's the matter? I don't know what you need or I'd get it myself.'

She felt embarrassed. Now she realized that Steve was just being generous, but for a moment it had felt to her that he was paying for the sex they'd had and she felt demeaned. 'It's nothing,' she said hurriedly.

He shook his head. 'Women! As long as I live I'll never understand them!'

She stuffed the notes in her pocket and made for the door. 'I'll see you on Tuesday,' she said.

'Come back here, Maggie,' he said and caught hold of her. 'What did I do that upset you?'

'Nothing,' she said. 'I misunderstood, that's all.' She kissed him on the cheek and left him to pay the bill.

She walked back to her flat feeling deflated. She'd been happy to be with Steve, but as soon as he'd given her the money, the happiness faded. For one moment she'd felt no better than a whore. And he was becoming too possessive, wanting a key to her flat. What right had he to ask such a thing? Next he'd be offering to pay the rent!

She opened the door of her flat, walked in, sat down and lit a cigarette. She might be his girl but that didn't mean she'd give up her freedom just when she'd found it. She was free to invite whoever she wanted here. Just imagine if she had a visitor who didn't know about her relationship with Steve and he walked in. Oh no, she was entirely independent and the sooner he knew it the better. When next they met, she wouldn't mess around, she'd tell him that he couldn't come and go as he pleased and there would be no spare key for anyone!

Whilst she was making a cup of tea she thought how much she would like to invite Joshua to her new home. After all he'd been the one to help her find it. She frowned. Steve had better not find out about him. Knowing the way he felt about negroes she knew he'd be furious. But it was only friendship. She wasn't being unfaithful. She knew, though, that Steve Rossi wouldn't see it that way. Nevertheless, she was determined to meet with the gentle Southerner, as planned.

As Steve made his way back to camp, he was feeling very pleased with himself. The night spent with Maggie had been great and now that she had her own apartment, that would make things even better. For him it would be a Godsend. He badly needed a place to stash his stuff. His London connections were urging him to sell them more of his goods, but he couldn't take too much out of the stores at once without causing suspicion. With a place to put it, however, he could take it out little and often. He was making a great deal of money at the moment and if he played his cards right, by the time the war was over he would have enough money behind him to start a business in a big way.

With a frown he wondered just what had triggered Maggie's sudden anger when he gave her money. How strange, usually his women were only too pleased to accept it, but of course Miss Maggie Evans was quite different from his usual conquests. He shook his head. Women!

Maggie of course was in complete ignorance of Steve's plans to use her place for his illegal dealings and, having decided to put him in the picture about her newfound independence, she pottered about happily, preparing lunch for Ivy. She'd previously arranged this, ringing her friend at the factory, guessing that Steve would have to return to camp early after his overnight pass.

Ivy had been very curious about the move, and Maggie had said she would explain when she saw her. Maggie was also anxious to find out what was happening to her friend's crazy plans to marry Bob Hanson and live in America.

She listened to the Forces request programme,

and concentrated intently as they played an Ella Fitzgerald number, remembering that she was an artist that Joshua liked. As the record finished, she could see why. The voice was rich and deep and the music had a beat of its own.

An hour later there was a knock on the door. Ivy had arrived.

She bustled in, full of beans as usual, but as Maggie took her coat she saw that she was still wearing Bob's ring.

She walked around the flat inspecting every room. In the bedroom she sat on the bed and started bouncing on it. 'Well, love, the springs are all right,' she said archly.

'Now behave,' scolded Maggie. 'I'll put the kettle on.'

'Then you can tell me whatever made you move out of the pub,' urged her friend. 'Have another row with your old man, did you?'

She regaled her with the news.

'Your poor mum must be upset, I bet she gives your dad a hard time.'

With a grimace Maggie said, 'Yes, you're probably right.' There was a hint of sadness in her voice as she confessed, 'I really hated to leave her, but I'll still be working in the bar on Fridays and I'll call and see her often, in between.'

Ivy settled on the settee and drank her coffee. 'Some of my neighbours had a go at me for taking Bob home,' she said. 'Bloody cheek! Who are they to tell me how to live my life? I gave them what for I can tell you!'

Maggie grinned to herself. She could just imagine it and she bet the language hadn't been

127

too choice either. 'So what's happening about you and Bob?'

With a sigh her friend said, 'The captain is under orders from his commanding officer to put a hold on marriage applications for the time being. It seems there have been quite a lot of requests and they want the men to take their time and consider what it entails. You know, what with the war, some of the boys may be sent to France to fight very soon. Are you doing the right thing, taking an English girl away from her folks? What about the girl you left behind? All that sort of stuff ... Bob's furious.'

'If that makes him angry think how he'd react if he discovered you were already married!'

To her surprise Ivy didn't jump down her throat. 'Oh Maggie, I don't know what to do. I've grown to love that crazy Yank. At first it was just lust, and a way of getting out of here, but he's a good man. Kind, thoughtful, he wouldn't harm a fly. He'd make such a wonderful husband and I really want to be his wife. I thought I was happy before, but now I know what real happiness is. I don't want Len any more. He's rough and ready in comparison. You know, all he's interested in is sex, the pub, and his meal on the table when he walks in. My dad was like that and Mum didn't have much of a life. I don't want to be like her, and now I've got the chance of something better.' She looked at Maggie, her eyes reflecting the anguish of her situation. 'If I lose Bob, I've lost everything.'

'Oh Ivy.' Maggie put a comforting arm around her. 'What a mess. I don't know what to say. What if you were honest with Bob and told him the truth?'

Ivy looked horrified at the idea. 'I couldn't do that. What if he walked out on me?' She shook her head. 'Oh no. I can't take that chance. I'll just have to bluff it out. When it comes to filling in the forms, I'll lie!'

Maggie looked at her aghast. 'You'll be committing bigamy! You can go to gaol for that.'

'Who's going to find out? As soon as we're married I'll be shipped to the States.'

'When Len comes home, they'll find out! He's not going to sit quietly after discovering what you've done. If he reports it to the police, then you'll really be in the shit.'

The old Ivy surfaced. 'They'd have to find me first!'

At that point, Maggie gave up. There was nothing she could say to change the situation and make Ivy see sense.

The following day, Steve Rossi took a telephone call in his office. His expression changed on hearing the voice on the other end. 'I told you not to call me here. I'll be in touch when I have something for you. In an emergency you can contact me at–' He took a small notebook from his uniform pocket. 'Flat 2, 14 Bugle Street. But only in an emergency. If I'm not there, leave a message with my girl. And don't call me here again!' He slammed the telephone down. Shmucks! Didn't they realize how dangerous a call to his office was? They could blow the whole deal.

129

Chapter Nine

Doug Freeman, or the ice man as he was known by the underworld fraternity, due to his predilection for ice picks, slammed down the receiver of his telephone. 'Cocky little bastard! That bloody wop gets right up my nose, telling me where and when to call him. He's getting far too big for his American boots.'

Charlie his trusty helper tried to calm him. 'They're all like that, guv. Don't take no notice. We want what he's got and he bloody well knows it.'

Doug frowned. 'I just don't trust him, he's far too sharp for my liking. The trouble with him is he doesn't know who he's dealing with. Perhaps we should teach him a lesson?' He looked enquiringly at his companion.

Shaking his head Charlie said, 'I don't think we should rock the boat just yet. It would be a pity to lose that connection. Where else could we get such a steady supply of goods? Not to mention the artillery.'

But Doug was not so easily persuaded. 'No one talks to me like that and gets away with it.'

And it was true. Doug Freeman was a hard man. All his life he'd been on the wrong side of the law. He'd spent time in Borstal as a young tearaway, had done a stretch in Wandsworth for grievous bodily harm, and only missed a charge of murder by a hair's breadth, through lack of evidence. He was a person that few ever crossed and if they did, it was usually the last time. Occasionally a body floated along the Thames to be discovered washed up on some muddy bank by the River Patrol.

Doug's hero was George Raft. He would go to the cinema and see all his films. He particularly liked the ones co-starring James Cagney, but he thought Cagney was a tough little bugger, whereas George Raft had an air of sophistication about him that Doug envied. He was also a dapper man, which Doug tried to emulate with his bespoke suits, his black shirts and ties, trilby hat. But where the film star could carry this off, Doug couldn't. He had no class. He was a big chap with ginger hair and a temper to match – with two left feet. He liked to watch the films where his hero would dance the tango with the leading lady, usually a glamorous blonde, but he knew that on a dance floor he was a failure.

He was a big-time villain. The East India docks was on his patch, the Isle of Dogs. Here he ran a string of prostitutes, a protection racket, and was up to his neck in black market racketeering. He was a man to be feared.

He lit a large cigar. 'So he's got a bird, has he?' He stored that piece of information away for future reference. 'Well at least now we have a way of contacting him. I'm not prepared to hang around waiting for his call. He's got half my bloody money up front – he was quick enough to take that, I notice. It's time he showed me a bit of respect! When he delivers his next load, I'll have a word.'

Seeing the menacing smile on his boss's face, Charlie knew that if he wasn't very careful, Steve Rossi would be taught a lesson he wouldn't forget.

Against the might of Doug Freeman, Jack Evans was small potatoes. He didn't consider himself a racketeer, just a bloke trying to take advantage of a situation and make a bit of money for his retirement. But things weren't panning out as he'd hoped.

Sonny Taylor had gone cold on him. Whereas he used to be always popping into the Bricklayer's Arms with a bit of news of another load of stuff, now he was evasive, saying to Jack that things were tightening up. The police were becoming too vigilant. 'Just be patient,' he said. 'When I get some goods, I'll let you know.'

What the landlord didn't know was that Sonny had had a visit from Charlie, advising the spiv that it would be in his best interests to sell any goods he had to Doug Freeman. Unlike Steve, Sonny knew of Doug's reputation and was only too pleased to comply. What the hell! It didn't matter to him who he sold the stuff to, as long as he got the money. The only thing was that now he had to put himself in jeopardy by finding an old lock-up garage to store his ill-gotten gains instead of letting Jack do it, thereby putting himself in danger from the law. He scowled. That sod Freeman didn't pay as much as Jack, but at least, Sonny told himself, he was keeping out of trouble. And if he was clever, eventually he could still put some stuff Jack's way.

Jack had emptied his front room of goods at long last, but now it had been empty for a while and he was frustrated. He stood inside the room with the door open. What was the point of closing it, he thought angrily. There was nothing for anyone to see.

And Moira was still insisting that he stay in Maggie's room. She cooked his meals, did his washing and ironing, but there was little conversation between them as she'd not forgiven him for the departure of her loving daughter. All in all, he was not a happy man.

Maggie, however was in her element. She came home from the factory every day, and with sheer delight put her key into the door of her very own home. It never ceased to give her great pleasure. She'd bought a few things to brighten it with the money Steve had given her, and now as she stood and looked around her she was like a cat with a saucer of cream.

She had been back to the Bricklayer's Arms the night before to do her stint in the bar. Her mother had been delighted to see her, as were the regulars, who had been dismayed to hear of her leaving. She'd taken a bit of stick over that.

'Getting too good for the likes of us, girl?' Nobby had quipped.

'I'm here, aren't I?' she retorted. 'I've got to keep an eye on you,' she said with a broad grin.

'You sound just like the bloody missus,' he grumbled.

She turned to her mother. 'I've got a day off

tomorrow, Mum. Why don't you come and see the flat? We can have a cuppa and a long chat.'

Moira's eyes lit up with delight. She was very curious to see where Maggie was living and it would do her good to get out of the pub for a bit. 'I'd love to.'

'Come about eleven,' she said, knowing her father wouldn't be busy and moan at Moira for leaving him alone behind the bar.

The following morning, Maggie was rushing around with a duster, plumping a cushion here and there. She so wanted her mother to approve of her first home.

At long last there was a knock on the door.

Maggie ushered her inside.

Looking around the living room, Moira smiled and said, 'But this is lovely, and so cosy.' She looked at Maggie. 'I'm sure you'll be very happy here ... and it's so quiet!'

'I know, isn't it great? After College Street it seemed strange at first, but I love it. Come and see the bedroom.'

Moira walked over to the window looking at the water in the distance, wondering if Maggie had shared her bed with a man, praying that she hadn't. But she didn't show any of these anxieties as she turned back.

'I wouldn't mind living here myself,' she said.

The two of them spent a couple of hours chatting before Moira rose from her chair.

'I must get back, love, and prepare a meal for your father. You take care of yourself. If you want anything, you let me know.'

'I can always call you from the telephone box down the road,' Maggie said. She walked Moira to the door, kissed her goodbye and said, 'I'll see you next Friday evening.'

Maggie was really pleased that her mother approved of the flat and this evening Steve was coming round for dinner. She wondered just what his reaction would be.

Just as Maggie stepped out of the bath later that afternoon there was a knock at the door. She answered it, wrapped in a towel, with another around her freshly washed hair.

Steve stepped inside and with a lustful gleam in his eyes said, 'Well, it looks as if I've arrived at just the right moment.' He closed the door behind him and slowly pulled the towel away from her body.

'Steve!' she protested.

'Now don't give me that,' he said as he pulled her to him. His mouth covered hers, his hands explored her naked form. 'Where's the bedroom? You'd better tell me quickly or I'll take you here in the hall.'

'What would the neighbours think?' she asked with a chuckle.

'Who the hell cares.' He lowered her to the ground, and quickly removed his jacket and trousers.

She undid his tie and shirt, removing them swiftly, running her hands over his broad shoulders, his chest, returning his hungry kisses with a fervour. They couldn't get enough of each other. It was like a wonderful spread of delicacies

135

laid before a starving man. Their lovemaking was frantic and exciting, both of them reaching a climax very quickly. They lay puffing and panting, exhausted, on the slightly threadbare carpet. It was only then that Maggie realized that Steve hadn't used any contraception. Oh my God! she thought. I could get pregnant.

He saw the sudden look of anxiety in her eyes.

'What's the matter?' he asked.

She told him.

'Christ!' he exclaimed. 'Gee, honey, I'm sorry. I'm usually so careful. It was the unexpected sight of you half undressed.' He pulled her to him and held her. What a damned fool I am, he thought. Oh well, if the worst came to the worst, I'd pay for an abortion. He helped her up. 'Come on sweetheart,' he urged. 'It'll probably be all right.'

'And if it isn't?'

He held her hand. 'Let's not worry about that until the time comes. When is your next period due?'

'In about a week's time,' she answered.

'Then we don't have long to wait. Come on now, go and get dressed and then you can show me this new place.' He picked up a bag he'd hastily dropped on the carpet. 'I've got two steaks here for us and a bottle of wine.' He kissed the tip of her nose. 'Go along now.' He patted her bottom as she passed him. 'I'll put the kettle on,' he said. 'I've brought you some tea and a few other things as well.'

Whilst she dressed, Maggie tried not to worry, but try as she would she couldn't rid herself of the possible consequences of their reckless passion.

That would be the end of her freedom. An unwanted pregnancy was the last thing she needed. Oh how stupid they had been. But she knew she'd been as much at fault as Steve. She slipped into a fresh pair of french knickers, and a floral dress, then made her way to the kitchen.

To her surprise, Steve was already cooking. He'd also brought a lettuce, tomatoes, and a cucumber. He was mixing a salad in a bowl he'd found in the cupboard. There were some slices of a strange-looking meat on a plate.

'What's that?' she asked.

'Italian salami. Try it,' he said with a grin.

She did. The taste was unusual, as was the texture. She wasn't sure if she liked it or not.

He raised an eyebrow. 'What do you think?'

'To be honest, I don't know. It's a bit chewy.'

'Before long I'll have you appreciating everything Italian,' he promised.

She smiled as she watched him. He was completely at home in the kitchen. Around his waist he'd tied a tea towel. 'To keep any grease marks off my uniform,' he explained.

He opened the bottle of wine and when the steaks were cooked they sat at the table.

The meat was delicious, but there was a flavour about it that was alien to Maggie. She asked what it was.

'Garlic. No Italian would cook without it. It does make your breath smell but as we are both eating it, then it won't notice.' He produced some American chewing gum. 'Put this into your mouth tomorrow before you go to work,' he said. 'It'll disguise it.'

Later, they sat in a tight huddle on the settee, drinking the remains of the wine.

'Gee, honey, this is really great,' he said. 'I have to be back by midnight though.'

'Just like Cinderella,' she said.

'Who the hell is Cinderella?'

With a chuckle she told him.

'Yes, very quaint. Very English. But I'm not into glass slippers.' He drew her nearer and kissed her. 'Let's go to bed,' he suggested. 'I promise to be careful.'

They did ... and he was.

As they sat having a cup of tea together before he departed, he looked around the room. 'This really is a neat place you've got here. Is there much storage place?'

'There's an empty cupboard in the hall,' she said.

'Did you get the key cut for me?' he asked.

She felt her nerves tense. Well, here goes, she thought. 'No,' she replied.

'I guess you've been busy,' he said.

'No it's not that, Steve. I don't want anyone else to have access to my place. It's private. Mine.'

He looked at her with an expression of astonishment. 'What's that supposed to mean?'

She tried to explain. 'This place marks my first step into independence. Having left home, for the first time I'm free. Free to come and go, have my friends to stay, with no one to answer to. Just imagine if I had a friend here for a cup of tea, or my mother, perhaps, and you walked in with your own key. Think how embarrassing it would be.'

She saw the anger reflected in his eyes. 'Are you

138

saying our relationship is an embarrassment to you?'

'No of course not.' She knew now he wouldn't understand, but she wasn't going to change her mind. 'This place to me is absolutely private. No one is going to have the right just to walk in when they want, but me.' She held her breath. There, now she'd said exactly how she felt.

'I'm damned if I understand!' he exclaimed. 'Aren't you my girl? I know every inch of your body. There isn't a part of it I haven't kissed or tasted. You give me that freedom, but I'm not allowed the freedom of your home. Your bed, yes – but that's it?'

She was a little alarmed at the anger and indignation pouring forth from her lover, but she was angry herself and she was adamant.

'I wouldn't put it quite like that, but yes.'

He was furious. 'I don't understand you. I was delighted that you had your own place. It would give us somewhere private. I was going to suggest that I pay the rent, but I guess that would invade your privacy too.'

That was the last straw. Her temper flared. 'I don't want you to pay my rent, thank you. I'm not a kept woman. This flat is mine. I pay all the bills ... and you can come when I invite you.'

'When you want a good screw! Is that it?'

'Don't you dare to talk to me like that. You make me sound like some cheap tramp. You of all people know that's not the case.'

This comment stemmed his anger. He knew that she'd been a virgin and he had no reason to believe that she'd been with another man. 'I'm

139

sorry, Maggie, but this doesn't make a lot of sense to me.'

She put her hand out to touch him. 'I don't expect you to understand,' she said, 'but my father tried to rule my life for so long and I must be able to please myself now, or it's all been for nothing.' She looked at him, hoping to make him see reason. 'It wasn't easy for me to leave my mother. My father can be difficult to live with.'

This struck a familiar chord with the American and he studied her face, putting out a hand to caress the worried features. 'OK. If that's how you want it.'

There was such a look of relief on her face that he took her into his arms.

'Hey! You know what? We've just had our first fight. How about that?' He looked at his watch. 'I'd better be going. I don't know when I'll be free. Probably not until the weekend and maybe not even then. There's a lot of movement in the docks during the next few days and I'll be on duty.' He frowned. 'I wish you had a telephone. It would be more convenient. I'll put a note through your door as soon as I know anything. All right?'

She nodded. 'That'll be fine.'

He kissed her goodnight and left.

She collapsed on the settee and lit a cigarette. That had been a bit nasty for a while, and at one time she had thought Steve was going to walk out, he was so angry. It was the second time she'd seen that side of him and she didn't like it. But then, as she admitted to herself, she'd become very heated also. Never mind, at least now he knew where he stood. And tomorrow she had to meet with

Joshua. She was sure that he wouldn't have made such demands, but then she couldn't have found two men who were so different.

She went to bed, completely exhausted, praying to God that she wasn't pregnant, telling herself that one week before a period wasn't the most fertile time of a woman's cycle and hoping the book she'd read was correct.

Steve on the other hand was furious. It was essential that he have a key to Maggie's place. He wanted to be able to come and go whenever he slipped goods out of the camp. He'd taken a sneaky look at the cupboard in the hall and found it adequate for his needs. Fortunately, Maggie didn't have a lot of stuff of her own and probably wouldn't require it. He rubbed his chin in contemplation. He'd have to find a way round it somehow.

The following day, Maggie met Joshua outside the bombed remains of Holy Rood church. As she approached she saw him studying what was left of the once beautiful building. She walked up behind him.

'Hello, soldier. Need some company?'

He turned and gave his broad smile as he saw her. 'Maggie. How nice you look. I like the new hairstyle.'

She flushed at the unexpected compliment and marvelled at his observation. She usually wound her auburn tresses up into a Victory roll, but when she'd washed it last time she'd turned the ends under into a smooth pageboy.

141

'Thank you. Flattery will get you anything,' she quipped.

He chuckled. 'Really? Is there anything special you want to do?'

This in itself was a change. Steve usually told her where they were going, and as she thought about it, all she wanted to do was talk to this man. 'No, not really.'

'It's such a nice day, why don't we go and sit in the park?' he suggested and that was exactly what they did.

Once again Maggie felt calm and comfortable in the company of the Southerner as they walked. She ignored the pointed glares from some of the passers by, but smiled as several children danced around Joshua, chanting, 'Got any gum, chum?'

He just laughed and handed out a couple of packets from his trouser pocket. He didn't take her arm, simply walked alongside her.

They found a quiet spot beneath a tree to shade them from the warm summer sun. 'Is the climate in your home like this?' she asked.

He shook his head. 'Hell no! In the summer it's hot and steamy, perspiration drips off you before you even move. But you get used to it.' He began to tell her about his home; about the Mississippi Delta, an impenetrable wilderness of cypress and gum trees; about the plagues of mosquitoes. 'And of course there are gators.'

She looked puzzled.

'Alligators.' He saw her eyes widen in horror. 'Yes, we have plenty of those. You catch a young one, they cook up real well.'

'You eat them?'

He grinned broadly. 'Sure we do, and catfish, so called because they have whiskers. Then there's the poverty and the music of course. Apart from our spirituals, there's the Delta Blues.'

'What on earth is that?' she asked.

In a low deep voice, he began to sing a song called 'Crossroads Blues', which spoke of a stranded night in the chilling emptiness of the Delta. The poignancy of the words touched her deeply as did the soulful yet melodic tune, but she marvelled at the beautiful voice of the man sitting beside her.

He began to tell her how slaves were brought into America from the African continent to work the plantations. 'They were the property of the plantation owner,' he said. 'They lived in shacks. There they jumped over the broom and had their children.'

'What do you mean, jumped over the broom?'

He laughed, his eyes bright with amusement. 'A man and a woman literally jumped over a broom on the ground and that meant they were married.'

'As easy as that?'

The smile faded. 'Nothing was easy about being a slave, Maggie. Life was hard, the overseers were harsh and the owners left the discipline in their hands.'

'I saw a film about that once. I thought it was so cruel.'

'That was the way it was,' he said. 'Abraham Lincoln of course freed the slaves which certainly didn't please the white bosses. Mind you, some of them did good. They made their way to Oklahoma at the time of the landrush and staked out a claim for themselves.'

'And now?'

'There's still great poverty in the South. The white man is still king ... But to sit and watch a paddle steamer sail down the Mississippi river is such a pretty sight. You can hear the swish of the water as the paddle turns. And if you're real lucky, you can hear the music of the jazz band on board.'

There was no note of censure in his voice and she admired his acceptance of the whole situation.

'If there was such poverty where you came from, how did you make a living?' she asked.

Joshua smiled at her. 'I escaped and went to New Orleans.'

'What did you do there?'

'Why, played the piano in a jazz band. New Orleans breathes jazz,' he said, his eyes shining with enthusiasm. 'I was truly among my own there. You know, whenever there is a funeral, a band leads the procession.' He grinned at her look of surprise.

'Playing music?' asked Maggie, incredulous at such a thing.

'Certainly, playing! Why not? I can't think of a better way to start your journey to the pearly gates.'

'Well, it's not like any funeral I've ever seen.'

He laughed at her dismay. 'It sure is the way that I want to go, although my daddy may not agree. In his church it's all gospel singing. Beautiful – but not my style.'

'What are you going to do after the war?' she asked.

144

'I'm heading for New York. I can always find work there.' He leaned towards her. 'Music is my life, Maggie.'

She'd noticed he was carrying a small book and was curious. 'What are you reading?' she asked.

'It's a book of poems.'

'A jazz musician who reads poetry? You are a constant surprise,' she said.

'I don't know why you find that so odd,' he argued. 'Music is a kind of poetry, isn't it? Art too.'

'I've never thought of it that way.'

'Music, words, pictures, they all tell you something in their own way.'

She thought for a moment. 'Yes, I suppose they do.'

He began to recite.

Maggie lay back on the grass and listened. She didn't know when she'd experienced such a sense of peace as she did at this time. For the first time she really listened to the words of Shakespeare's sonnets and wondered why at school they had sounded so different.

A while later, she invited Joshua back to her flat for tea.

He was delighted.

When they arrived, he looked around and admired it. 'Is this better than living with your family?' he asked.

As she poured the boiled water into the teapot, she frowned. 'Well, my father can be a difficult man, and even though I love him, there comes a time when you can't take the arguments any more. I miss my mother a lot. I see her every

Friday when I work in the bar. Apart from that, I love my independence.'

They sat side by side on the settee.

'Don't you have a young man, Maggie? A good-looking girl like you would have fellows queuing at the door I would think?'

She didn't feel she had to lie. 'I am going out with an American staff sergeant,' she said. 'He's with the 14th Major Port. Steve Rossi is his name.' She knew that something was wrong as soon as she mentioned Steve's name.

'Have you known him for long?' Joshua asked.

'Not really. Just a few months. Do you know him?'

With a wry smile he said, 'Well, we don't exactly socialize, but yes, I know him.'

'And you don't like him, do you?' she asked.

'Who I like and don't like doesn't matter, Maggie, but I have to tell you that he is trouble.'

'He's very nice,' she argued.

'I'm glad he treats you right,' he said. 'But, Maggie, watch your step, that's all.' He looked at his watch, drank his tea and stood up. 'I really have to go.' He shook her hand. 'Thanks for the company.'

They walked towards the door. 'I would like to ask you out to a movie or something, but your boyfriend wouldn't approve.'

'We can be friends, Joshua, can't we? I'd like to go to the cinema with you.'

'He won't like it.'

'I'm free to choose my own friends,' she said angrily.

He chuckled. 'Keep your cool, girl. If that's fine

146

by you, then it's fine by me. How about Monday evening at six thirty? I'll see you outside the Regal cinema. If we don't like the movie showing there we can go elsewhere.'

'That suits me.' She let him out of the door and closed it.

Now she really was playing with fire. Steve hated negroes with a vengeance. He was also very possessive. Joshua said he was trouble, but he couldn't be right, surely? And in what way was Steve trouble? She hadn't seen anything of it, only that incident in London, but then he was protecting her. When they were together, there was no reason to believe Steve was anything but a charmer. His friends seemed OK – those that she'd met when they were out together. Joshua must be mistaken.

Having convinced herself that Joshua was wrong about Steve, Maggie decided it was too nice a day to stay in. She'd walk along the water-front and take her mother some flowers. Picking up her handbag, she left the flat.

Chapter Ten

As Maggie turned the corner into College Street, she saw the local children swinging on a rope slung over an exposed beam in the remains of a bombed house. There was a huge knot tied at the bottom of the rope which acted as a seat; they jumped on it and swung across the building, yelling and screaming. She smiled to herself. Nothing's changed.

She stopped at the side entrance to the Bricklayer's Arms and walked in, making her way down the narrow hallway to the kitchen. Through the open door she could see her mother sitting at the table, lost in thought.

'Hello, Mum. How are you?'

Moira leapt from her chair and hugged her daughter. 'What a lovely surprise. Sure and it's wonderful to see you again so soon.'

Maggie handed her the flowers she'd purchased on the way. 'These are for you,' she said.

Moira bustled about filling a vase with water, and arranging the summer blooms. 'So what have you been doing?'

'I met a friend and we walked in the park.'

'Anyone I know?'

'He's a GI I met at a dance.'

'But I thought you were already going out with a GI?'

'I am.' She grew impatient. 'He's just a friend. His father's a preacher and he plays jazz.'

'What, the father?'

'No, Mum. Joshua.'

Moira looked at her. 'Joshua? That's an unusual name.'

'He's from the company of black soldiers.'

Her mother spun round and stared at her. 'You go where angels fear to tread, Maggie. You know how folks look down on girls who go out with the darkies!'

'Negroes, Mother. Negroes! Joshua isn't ashamed of who he is. He's a nice man ... a negro, not a darkie or a nigger!'

'You have no idea what you're getting into, have you? Don't you care what people think?'

'Frankly, no. I care what you think.'

'You know how I feel about it.'

'I don't want to fall out with you, Mum, so let's leave it, shall we!'

Her mother gave her a hard look. 'You'll go your own way whatever I say. You're stubborn, just like your father!'

Maggie changed the subject. 'How is Dad, when he's not raging at me?'

Moira shrugged. 'The same as ever. He'll never change. Although his front room is empty at the moment and has been for a while.'

Maggie was surprised. 'Has he given all the black market stuff up, then?' she asked hopefully.

'Is it a miracle you're expecting? Of course not, but that Sonny Taylor hasn't been round lately. It's driving your father barmy. He's losing precious money, isn't he? Nothing else is important.'

The bitterness in her mother's voice hurt her and she asked, 'Have you two been rowing?'

Moira shook her head. 'No, not at all.' She lit a cigarette. 'How's the flat?'

It's obvious that things aren't going well, thought Maggie and felt guilty at having left the family home, but she wasn't going to lie to her mother. 'It's just fine,' she said. 'I can't tell you how lovely it is to be independent. Not to have anyone telling me how to run my life. It's such a pity you can't come and live with me. I miss you.'

Moira forced a smile. 'Now that wouldn't do at all,' she said. 'That would spoil the whole point of

149

being a free person.' But oh, how she wished that she was able to do the same. As she looked at her daughter, however, she sensed that she had something else on her mind, yet knew better than to probe. If Maggie had something to tell her, she would do so in her own time.

Maggie would have loved to unburden her worries that she might be pregnant to her mother, but she didn't dare.

An hour later Moira let her out of the side door. Nobby Clarke saw her and called to her. 'Hello, Maggie girl. How are you?'

'I'm fine, Nobby, and you?'

He grinned at her. 'When are you coming home to live, lass? I'm sick of that old bugger's face! We need someone behind the bar who's good-looking and with a bit of life.'

'You should try for the job of barman then,' she said with a broad grin.

Nobby burst out laughing. 'Flatterer! You take care, young lady,' he said.

'I will. Give my love to Grace.'

At the door she hugged her mother. 'You look after yourself. When I know what shift I'm on next week, I'll give you a ring and you come round to the flat again.'

Moira's face lit up. 'I'd love to.'

Maggie told her, 'I'll give you a call in a few days.'

Moira gazed affectionately at her. 'You take good care, you hear?' With a heavy heart she watched her daughter walk down the street, wondering just what it was that the girl had on her mind. *I miss you more than you'll ever know,* thought Moira. Since Maggie had gone, she'd been really lonely. The girl was the light of her life and her husband was no substitute at all.

When the pub closed that night, Jack walked into the kitchen and said to his wife, 'Now that our Maggie's settled, isn't it time you and I stopped this nonsense and got back to a normal way of life?'

She glared at him. 'You're not the man I married, Jack Evans. Then you were happy, carefree. It didn't matter a toss to me that you were crippled because your spirit was strong and healthy, but now you're an embittered old man. I'll tell you one thing, if I was in a position to leave here like Maggie, you wouldn't see me for dust!' She walked out of the kitchen and seconds later he heard the door of her bedroom slam.

He was shattered by his wife's words. He had expected her to be upset when Maggie had left, but he had been sure now that their daughter saw Moira fairly regularly, she'd be fine, even if he and Maggie had had words. Never ever had he expected to hear her say she'd like to leave him. He went into the bar and poured himself half a pint of bitter. You could never tell with women which way they'd turn. He'd buy her something nice, try to sweeten her up. Perhaps if he didn't get in any more black market stuff she'd come round. He'd think about it, because Moira was his life, if only she realized it.

But when Sonny Taylor came knocking on his door with news of books of clothing coupons, and a promise of more goods in the near future, he

151

forgot all about his good intentions in his eagerness to make some more money.

Later that evening, Maggie had an unexpected caller. When she opened the door, Steve was standing there with a cardboard box, filled with stores. He grinned broadly at her. 'Hi, gorgeous. Santa Claus has called early.' He walked in and deposited the box in the kitchen. 'I can't stop for long,' he said, 'but I thought this would help.'

He unpacked some tea, a bag of sugar, coffee, a couple of tins of ham, a carton of American cigarettes, a tin of sliced peaches and some Hershey bars, chewing gum and American magazines.

Maggie was thrilled with such bounty. She hugged him. 'Thanks, thanks a lot.'

He caught hold of her and kissed her. 'I told you I'd take care of you, didn't I? Look, I have a few things on the jeep, I wonder if I could store them in your cupboard for a couple of days?'

How could she refuse? But as he made several journeys to and fro, she wondered just what was going on here. 'What is all this?' she asked.

'Just a few gifts for some folk who have been good to me, and there is to be a kids' party in a month's time, so I'm collecting a few things. Look, honey, I have to fly. I hope to see you for much longer very soon.' He kissed her briefly and left.

Maggie frowned. She was thrilled with the goods he'd given her but... She opened the door of the cupboard and looked inside. There were cartons of cigarettes, nylon stockings, bottles of whisky, gin, bourbon. Tinned goods. She wasn't a fool, this wasn't for any children's party, this was contraband, and she had it in her flat. She was absolutely furious.

She stomped around the sitting room. She had railed at her father for storing such things, putting his livelihood in jeopardy, and now she was in the same position. How dare Steve do this to her! What if the police found out and came round?

She was even more incensed when she got home from the factory the following day to find a note from Steve saying some friends of his would be collecting the stuff.

Two men arrived later in a private car and knocked on her door. A couple of rough diamonds with broad smiles. 'Hello, darlin', got some stuff for us? The Yank told us to pick it up.'

She barely spoke to them as they took the goods, but as they drove away she thought, I suppose the car is filled with black market petrol too! She remembered Joshua's warning. How much did he know of Steve's activities, she wondered. A hell of a lot more than she did, that was for sure. She thought back to the two men in the seedy club in London. How stupid she was not to have put two and two together then!

She made a cup of tea and sat down, trying to think of what to do. What a liberty this man had, not only using her place as a drop but then to send two strangers to collect it. Who did he think he was? She would never be put into this situation again and if Steve didn't like it, he could go to hell! She prayed, fervently, that her period wouldn't be late. That would just about be the last straw. Carrying the child of a black

153

marketeer. How her father would crow.

As Steve made his way to Maggie's flat a couple of days later, he wondered what sort of a greeting he'd receive. Maggie was a bright girl, she would no doubt have realized that something was going on. But he'd been desperate. He'd lost a lot of the money Doug Freeman had given him in a crap game and he knew they'd be getting restless if he didn't come across with the goods. He'd had an opportunity to take a load out of the camp, but with no place to store it he was in trouble and the only way to save his hide was to use Maggie. He knocked on her door. He was sure he'd be able to talk his way out of it.

'Hello, honey,' he said with a broad smile, and stepped inside. He went to take her into his arms, but she pushed him away.

'You bastard!' she said. 'How dare you take advantage of me and send your thugs around here?'

'Aw, come on, Maggie. It was only for a couple of days. I didn't think you'd mind helping me out.'

'You lied to me, Steve Rossi. Kids' party, my arse! Do you think I'm stupid?'

He went to catch hold of her arm. 'Now don't be like that, babe.'

'Don't you babe me!' She threw off his hold and walked into the kitchen.

He followed, trying to placate her.

She turned on him, her fury reflected in her eyes, as she spoke. 'You bring me a few stores to sweeten me up then you fill my cupboard with

154

stolen goods. Not content with putting me in this dangerous position, you send someone to collect it. You gave out my address to strangers! How dare you?'

'Come and sit down,' he entreated, 'let me try and explain.'

She reluctantly followed him into her sitting room.

'In wartime,' he began, 'everyone is into some kind of scam, or fiddle, as you limeys call it. I'm only doing what everyone else is doing. Making a few bucks on the side.'

'What if you're caught?' she demanded. 'You'd be court-martialled, sent home.'

He gave a confident smile. 'Me, get caught? You've got to be kidding!'

She looked at him and shook her head. 'You didn't even consider that I might have been in trouble if the police had called and discovered your haul. I could go to prison! You're so arrogant. So cocksure of yourself. If you want to take those kinds of risks, fine. But leave me out of your schemes. I don't want anything to do with them.'

'Gee, honey, I'm sorry, but I was really stuck. And why on earth would the police call here?' He put an arm around her shoulders. 'I promise it won't happen again, OK? Come on, don't be mad at me. I only have a few hours, let's not fight.' He stroked the back of her neck.

But Maggie was still seething. She glared at him. 'I don't know you at all,' she said. 'This charming front you put on is all a sham. You used me, and now you come round here all sweetness and light expecting to take me to bed, no doubt!'

He was not deterred by her attitude. With a slow smile he said, 'Of course I was hoping for a few moments of love with my girl, I wouldn't be human if I wasn't, but if you're not in the mood, then that's fine.'

She glared at him. 'You can't use people like this, Steve. It isn't right. It isn't being responsible. You tell me I'm your girl as if I'm supposed to be special and you treat me like this... Well, I won't put up with it!'

He gazed into her eyes. 'You know, when you're angry, your eyes go a deeper shade of green and your nostrils flare. It's very sexy. And I can assure you that I am charming.' He caught hold of her hand and kissed her palm. 'Don't be cross, honey. We get so little time together.' He pulled her closer and kissed her gently. 'I really do think a lot of you, you know. That's why you're my girl. I wouldn't do anything to put you in any kind of danger. Honest. I think far too much of you to do such a thing.'

'But you bloody well did!' She was exasperated.

He looked shamefaced and said softly, 'I promise I won't ever do such a thing again. You are my girl and you are special.'

She saw the beguiling look in his eyes and for a moment her anger faded.

Being so well schooled in the art of seduction, Steve knew that he was going to win her round. He kissed her again, at first gently then gradually with more passion. He was relieved and delighted when he felt Maggie beginning to respond, but as he went to slip his hand beneath her skirt, she stopped him.

'That's as far as you go,' she said firmly.

He didn't persist but was content to have over-come her anger. She obviously wouldn't let him use her flat again, he'd have to find somewhere else. Or someone else with some spare room. These guys were prepared to spend a lot of money and he wasn't going to miss the oppor-tunity of making a killing, not for any woman.

After he'd left the flat, Maggie was angry with herself for giving in so easily to Steve's advances. He thought he could twist her around his little finger. It was about time he learned that she was no pushover.

Still wary of Steve and his antics, she began to question Joshua about him when they were sitting in the cinema, during the interval, a few days later.

'Why did you warn me about Steve Rossi?' she asked. 'Why do you think he's trouble to be around?'

Joshua gazed at her with an anxious expression. 'Has he treated you bad?' he asked.

'No, nothing like that,' she said, reluctant at this stage to tell him anything.

'Rossi is a man who makes a fast buck wherever he can,' he started. 'Being in charge of the stores puts him in a mighty useful position. I know that he's selling army goods outside the camp.'

'You do? How?'

'I've been on many a detail to collect stores when they dock. He has them stored away, but he has his own stash put separately. It's so obvious that I'm surprised no one has spotted it yet.'

'Are you certain?'

'Oh, yes. I have a buddy who works as a clerk. He's been keeping an eye on him, but he don't want to be involved. Rossi is clever and my buddy is black. You don't go looking for trouble in this army.' He gave her a sideways glance. 'You make sure you don't get mixed up in his mess, Maggie, because he's involved with dangerous men. Some heavy dudes from London, so I hear.' He paused. 'I know he can pour on the charm, but believe me, he'd sell his mother and his soul for a good price.'

Maggie felt her stomach lurch when she thought of the two men who came to her flat. Were they part of some London mob? She guessed that they were. Well anyway, she'd have nothing more to worry about. Steve would have no reason for them to call again. But she thought how ironic was the situation. She had left home to get away from her father and his bad ways, but here she was going out with someone just like him, if what Joshua said was true. But apart from that one time, Steve had been good to her and she still felt drawn to him, however much he'd annoyed her.

She sat back and enjoyed the film. Somehow she always felt at ease when she was with Joshua.

Joshua walked her home, but refused the invitation to go to Maggie's flat for a cup of coffee. 'No I don't think that's wise, do you?'

'Why ever not?'

He took hold of her hand. 'I really like being with you, Maggie. You're a wonderful girl. But what would happen if Rossi came knocking on the door?'

She didn't answer because she knew that would be a dire thing to happen. Steve would be furious. 'Perhaps you're right,' she said.

He smiled at her, his dark eyes crinkling at the corners. 'But that doesn't stop me from taking you out for a drink, does it?'

She grinned back at him. 'No, I don't see that it does. I'll meet you at the end of the road. When?'

'How about tomorrow, seven thirty. I've arranged to swop my duty with a buddy.'

'Until tomorrow then.'

She went into her flat, but she couldn't put aside Joshua's warnings about Steve. If Steve was in deep with the black market, she was taking a chance being involved with him. Her period was due tomorrow; she'd wait and see what happened then, before she made up her mind what to do about her lover.

Chapter Eleven

Maggie didn't sleep at all well, and when she met up with Ivy in the factory canteen the following day, her friend looked at her and said, 'Blimey! You look a bit rough.' With a sly smile she asked, 'That Steve round last night, was he?'

'No, I went to the pictures with Joshua.'

Ivy looked astonished. 'You mean the coloured bloke you met at Fair Oak?'

Maggie nodded.

'Bloody hell! Does Steve know about this?'

'It's none of his business,' snapped Maggie. 'I'm a free agent.'

Ivy gave her an anxious look. 'I don't know Steve Rossi as well as you do, love, but I can tell you this, if he finds out he won't like it. He's the possessive type.' She sipped her tea. 'You sleeping with this Joshua?'

'No of course not! What do you take me for? We're just friends, that's all.'

'Oh yeah? Listen, Maggie, there's no such thing as friendship between a man and a woman. It may start out that way, but it doesn't end there. They always want more. You either give in or bye bye baby.' She paused. 'Pity really. I've met a few blokes I would have liked purely as friends, that I didn't fancy physically, but their ego and sex drive always got in the way.'

'Well Joshua is different. He hasn't attempted to lay a finger on me.'

'What is he then, some bloody saint?'

'No of course not, just a nice man.'

Ivy didn't press the subject, but knowing Maggie as well as she did, she knew that something was bothering her. 'What's wrong? You've got something on your mind.'

Maggie felt the need to confide her troubles, they were weighing mightily upon her. 'I'm afraid I may be pregnant.'

'Oh, Christ!' Ivy took a cigarette out of her overalls. 'How late are you?'

'My period is due today, but we made love once without using a french letter.'

'You're panicking a bit soon, aren't you? My period is often a couple of days adrift.'

Maggie shook her head. 'Not mine. I could almost set the clock by it and I don't even feel as if I'm due on.'

'Well there's no point in getting in a state about it yet. You start worrying and that in itself might mess things up.'

'Whatever will I do if I am?'

'We'll sort that one out when we have to ... if we have to. Got any gin at home?' she asked.

Maggie looked puzzled. 'No, why?'

'Buy a half-bottle when you leave here, run a hot bath and sit in it, and drink a hefty slug of gin.'

'What the hell will that do?'

'Damned if I know. It's just an old wives' tale, but it's worth a try.'

That night, Maggie did as her friend suggested. She started running the water and sat in the bath until it was as hot as she could bear, sipping the gin. The taste of the neat spirit turned her stomach and after a time she felt faint. Her head began to swim, and she quickly ran the cold water, soaked a flannel and put it on her forehead, pulling out the bath plug at the same time. She felt desperately ill.

Staggering into the bedroom, wrapped in a towel, she lay on the bed. The ceiling seemed to be in a spin and she knew she was going to be sick. She rushed to the bathroom and threw up.

When the next day Ivy enquired after her health, she glared at her friend. 'All it did for me was make me ill and give me a bloody hangover!'

'Sorry,' said Ivy. 'I was only trying to help. Here, someone once told me about some stuff called slippery elm.'

'Oh for goodness' sake, keep your witch's brews to yourself, will you! You're likely to kill me off with your damned cures.' She walked angrily away.

Afterwards she felt guilty at her outburst; after all, Ivy was only trying to help her. At the end of the shift, she waited for her to clock off.

'Sorry. I shouldn't have bitten your head off like that.'

Ivy caught hold of her arm. 'It's all right. It's only because you're worried.'

A frown creased Maggie's brow. 'How ever would I tell my mother? And as for Dad ... it doesn't bear thinking about.'

'Well, should the worst come to the worst, you could always have an abortion.'

Maggie looked both appalled and frightened. 'Oh my God! But that's so dangerous.'

With a shrug Ivy said, 'It depends who does it.'

Maggie shot her a suspicious look. 'You seem to know a lot about it.'

'Now don't get clever! I had a mate who had one, that's all.'

'Was it successful?'

'Oh yes, but it was bloody painful.'

Maggie felt her stomach turn at the thought. 'Thanks a lot!'

'Steve Rossi could always marry you, then you'd have no need to worry ... if you did get caught I mean.'

'No!' The word was out of her mouth before she even thought about it.

The vehement tone surprised Ivy. 'Well it might be better than having a bastard child.'

'Oh, great!'

Ivy looked a bit shamefaced at her lack of diplomacy. 'Sorry, Mags. I always did call a spade a spade and not a bloody shovel.'

'I don't want to be Mrs Steve Rossi, that's all.'

Ivy looked puzzled. 'Whyever not? A good-looking bloke like him, I'd have thought he would be quite a catch.'

But she wouldn't be drawn. 'Have you any more news from Len?' she asked, to change the subject.

Shaking her head Ivy said, 'No, except he's in Italy somewhere. I read in the *Daily Mail* that the Eighth Army were advancing on the Gothic Line, whatever that is. All I can say is that it's a pity the attempt to top old Adolf a couple of months ago wasn't successful. The war might be over if it had worked.'

'And then Len would be on his way home ... and where would that leave you?'

Ivy gave a cheeky grin. 'Up the bloody creek without a paddle, that's where!'

That evening, Maggie washed and changed, then walked down the road to meet Joshua. It was a balmy September evening as they strolled down Bugle Street to the waterfront. Along Western Esplanade, convoys of American trucks were parked, waiting embarkation to the shores of France. Troops sat about chatting to each other,

163

lolling against their vehicles. Waiting, as so many had done before them. Children clambered around in their search for American chewing gum, candy, and bits of the troops' K rations which they gave away. American Red Cross women were handing out hot coffee and doughnuts.

On the other side of the road, soldiers were being marched towards the docks, packs on their backs, rifles slung over their shoulders. They ambled more than they marched, which in the beginning had made many of the local residents compare them most unfavourably to the more precise march of the British tommy. But by now it was an everyday occurrence. Millions of troops had passed through Southampton and no one noticed the difference any more.

It was the same with the German prisoners of war, who arrived, housed behind barbed wire in the transit area outside the gates of the New Docks. At first they too were the centre of everyone's attention, and it was the pastime of many to go and take a look at the enemy. Now they were part of the norm.

Maggie watched the passing troops and, turning to Joshua, asked, 'Will you be one of them one day?'

'I guess. At the moment we're here to assist with the arrivals of the ships' cargoes, but no one knows for how long.'

'Does it worry you, the thought of going to war?'

'What's the point?' he said philosophically. 'If my number's up, there isn't a great deal I can do about it.' He turned towards her, the corners of his mouth twitching with amusement. 'I'll just get them angel trumpets playing my kind of music.'

'Oh, Joshua!' She paused and with a mischievous grin asked, 'What happens if you go to hell?'

'Maggie! How could you think of such a thing, me a good clean-living boy all my life.'

'But have you been? How am I to know?'

He raised his eyebrows. 'And I'm not going to tell you. You'll just have to take my word for it.'

She found herself wondering about his past. Was there a girl somewhere ... had there been other women? He was a nice-looking man, with a sense of fun about him. Surely somewhere there had to be someone. Yet she hesitated to ask and find out that there was.

They walked along to the High Street, until they came to the American Red Cross Club used by the negro soldiers. They sat at a table with some of his friends, and as they laughed and teased one another, she was taken by the warmth and camaraderie of the men.

'How about a song, Joshua?' asked one.

He looked at Maggie and refused, saying he was entertaining a lady, but she said she didn't mind, that she'd really like to hear him sing.

He ambled over to the piano and sat down. He sang a couple of popular tunes in a deep melodious voice: 'The Banks of the Wabash', 'Old Man River' and then a rousing rendition of 'Joshua and the Battle of Jericho', where the walls came tumbling down, and others. His comrades sang along with him, and for the first time Maggie heard the haunting music of the negro spirituals.

It moved her deeply. Then the mood changed as he began to play his own kind of music and she realized how talented he was.

She told Joshua so, when he came over and sat beside her.

'Next week we're giving a concert at the Guild-hall,' he said. 'Will you come? It's on Sunday evening.'

'I'd love to, I'll bring my mother, she'd really enjoy it.' She was thoughtful for a moment and then said, 'I'm surprised you haven't gone into the church like your father.'

Joshua shook his head. 'The church isn't for me, Maggie. Yes, I suppose you could say I'm religious; being a son of a preacher I was bound to be, but I don't have what it takes to dedicate my life to the Lord. Not like my father. But he's an open-minded guy. He knows what music means to me.' He sipped his drink and then asked, 'Tell me, you still seeing the sergeant?'

She felt her cheeks flush. 'Yes. Yes I am.'

He shook his head. 'A pity. You're worth far better than Steve Rossi.'

'It's not serious,' she told him. 'He's only going to be here for a while.'

'Then why bother?'

His straightforward question threw her for a moment and his steady gaze was more than a little disconcerting. 'He's fun to be with, that's all.'

'And dangerous. I guess that adds to the attraction.'

Maggie felt she had to defend herself. 'I don't think of him as dangerous. He's just good company.'

'He has to be more than that, Maggie. Rossi doesn't go in for pure friendship.'

It was as if this man was looking into her soul. She held his gaze and said, 'That's right. He's also my lover.'

'This darned war changes everything,' he said with a note of sadness in his voice.

'What do you mean?'

There was no expression of condemnation on his face as he said, 'Normally a girl like you wouldn't give herself to a man like Rossi. You'd save yourself for the man you plan to marry. But in wartime, things change and that's a pity.'

She looked at him sceptically. 'Are you telling me that you've never made love to a woman?'

He grinned broadly and his eyes were full of mischief. 'What a crazy question. I'm a man after all.'

'You didn't answer me,' she persisted with a smile of amusement, filled now with curiosity.

He shrugged. 'Well there have been a few, here and there. We country boys grow up fast.'

'And is there anyone waiting for you?' She held her breath waiting for an answer.

Shaking his head, he said, 'No, Maggie. No one.'

She thought, how strange. He was a man who was experienced and yet he'd never even tried to kiss her. 'Joshua Lewis, I don't think I've ever met a man quite like you!'

His laughter rang out and one or two people looked over at the table to see what had amused him so.

'I don't know whether to take that as a compliment or not,' he said.

'It certainly was not meant as an insult,' she assured him.

'Thank heavens for that!'

At the end of the evening he walked her home.

'Won't you come in?' she asked.

'If I did, what would you do if Rossi knocked on the door?'

'He won't,' she explained. 'He's on duty.'

He cast a wry glance in her direction. 'When the cat's away...'

'It's not like that at all,' she protested. 'I've had such a good time, I thought it would be nice to give you a cup of coffee before you walk back to camp, that's all.'

He thought for a moment, smiled slowly and said, 'That would be real nice.'

Whilst Maggie was entertaining Joshua, Ivy was curled up on the settee in her house with her fiancé, Bob Hanson.

'Once we get the all clear from the CO,' said Bob with a broad smile, 'we'll make a date for the wedding. What about the members of your family?' he asked. 'I've yet to meet any of them.'

'I told you, Mum and Dad have both gone,' said Ivy hastily. 'All the rest are spread about the country. We don't keep in touch.'

'But surely, honey, you want some of them there on your big day?'

She snuggled closer and kissed him. 'All I want is you, you big lug.'

'What about Maggie? At least ask her. I've a lot of my buddies that want to come.'

'Oh, have you?' This was not what she wanted to hear at all. The fewer people that knew about it the better. 'I just want a small ceremony at the registrar's office. Nothing fancy, a nice quiet affair with a couple of witnesses.'

He looked at her in amazement. 'I don't believe I'm hearing this! I thought a bride longed for a big splash. I want to give you a wedding day you'll remember for the rest of your life.'

'But I'll remember a small intimate one as much as a big affair.'

He looked at her tenderly. 'You're a great girl, Ivy, that's why I love you so much. Let me do this one thing for you, it will give me so much pleasure.'

What could she say? 'If you really insist.'

He gathered her into her arms and kissed her passionately. 'We're going to have such a good life together,' he murmured into her ear. He softly caressed her breast. 'And we're going to have lots of kids to look after us in our old age.'

They lay side by side, locked in an embrace, their passion so intense that they didn't hear the key put into the lock of the front door.

'What the bloody hell's going on here?' an angry voice demanded.

Ivy shot up to a sitting position. 'Oh my God, it's Len! He must have got leave!'

Bob got to his feet. 'Who the devil are you?' he asked.

Len glared at him. 'I'm the one who should be asking that. What do you think you're doing with my wife?'

'Your wife?' Bob looked astounded. 'This young

lady is my fiancée.'

'Fiancée, my arse! I certainly don't remember having divorced her.'

Bob turned towards Ivy, his face devoid of colour. 'What's this all about? I think you owe me some kind of explanation.'

She got to her feet, her voice trembling. 'I meant to tell you,' she said, 'but I didn't want to lose you. I love you! I want to be your wife, I want to go to America and live with you.'

Hanson was shaken to the core. He looked at Len, who was as stunned as he was. 'Gee, I'm sorry, buddy,' he said. 'I had no idea.' He picked up his jacket and put it on. Turning to Ivy he asked, 'How could you do this to me?'

'Don't go, please don't go,' she pleaded.

He just stared at her in disbelief. 'I have no place here,' he said quietly and walked towards the door.

She ran to him and clutched at his arm. 'I'll get a divorce!' she cried.

But Bob Hanson looked coldly at her. 'How could I ever trust you again?' He opened the front door and left.

Ivy stood with her back against it and faced her husband, tears streaming down her cheeks.

Len's anger began to surface now that he was recovering from the shock she'd given him. 'You bloody slut! There I am, fighting for my country, facing death day after bloody day and you're here having it off with a fucking Yank!' He slapped her across the face. 'I'll teach you a lesson you won't forget in a hurry.' He lunged at her, but Ivy swiftly ran around the table in the middle of the room out of his reach.

'Don't you give me that!' she yelled at him. 'You've been having a bloody good time while you were away and don't you tell me any different. I know you, Len Brooks. You wouldn't go without your oats for very long.'

He glared at her. 'And what if I have? It's different for a man, away at war. It's expected. A bit of pussy here and there don't mean a thing. I was always coming home to you, you're my wife. Something you seem to have forgotten! Were you really going to marry that Yank?'

'Yes, I bloody well was!'

'That would have been committing bigamy,' he said incredulously.

'So what? He was worth it.'

That was it. Len stretched across the table and caught hold of her arm, dragging her round to where he could reach her. He looked down at her engagement ring. 'You couldn't wear my wedding ring, but you could wear his.' He tore it off her finger. Then he hit her.

Back at Bugle Street, Maggie and Joshua were sitting drinking coffee and chatting when there was a frantic knocking on the door. Maggie felt suddenly sick inside, but Joshua, seeing the stricken expression on her face, stood up. 'I'll answer it,' he said, and went to the door.

He was appalled at the sight that met his eyes. 'Maggie! Come quickly,' he called.

She ran down the hallway, just in time to catch Ivy, as she slipped to the floor in a faint. 'Oh my God! Lift her, Joshua, and bring her inside.'

They lay her down on the settee and propped up her head with cushions. Her face was covered in blood. Her eyes were swollen and her mouth. Her clothes had been ripped and her nails broken from trying to fight off her attacker.

Joshua went to the kitchen and returned with a bowl of warm water. 'Get me some cotton wool,' he demanded. Then he proceeded to gently bathe Ivy's face. 'Who on earth would do such a thing to a defenceless woman?' he asked.

Maggie could guess who the culprit was, but she said nothing.

Eventually Ivy came round. She opened her eyes as much as the swelling allowed. 'Maggie?' she whispered.

'I'm here, Ivy. It's only me and Joshua. You're quite safe.'

'It was Len. He came back and found me with Bob.'

'I thought as much.'

'Who's Len?' asked Joshua.

'Her husband.'

'Bob's gone for good,' Ivy wailed. 'I've lost him, I'll never be happy now.' She held out her hand. 'Len even took his ring. What am I going to do?'

'We're going to carry you into my bedroom and you'll rest,' said Maggie. 'I'll call the doctor to take a look at you.'

'No, I don't want a doctor.'

Maggie looked at Joshua and raised her eyebrows in question.

'I think it wise that you get her looked at,' he advised.

172

'Will you stay with her whilst I go to the telephone?'

He nodded and continued to bathe Ivy's wounds.

On her return, Joshua carried Ivy into the bedroom where he left the two women alone. Maggie carefully undressed her friend, put her in one of her nightdresses and made her comfortable. 'You try and rest,' she said. 'I'll leave the door open, then you can call if you want anything.' She picked up a glass from the bedside table, went to the bathroom to wash it and fill it with fresh water. Back in the room she urged Ivy to take a sip. It was difficult for her, as her mouth was so swollen. Maggie bit her lip as she watched Ivy's suffering. She settled her, then went back to Joshua.

'How is she?' he asked.

'In a bad way. You were right about the doctor.'

He shook his head, his expression one of sadness. 'This is no way to carry on,' he said.

'It was always going to end like this,' she explained. 'Ivy got engaged to a GI without telling him she was already married. Then her husband came home unexpectedly, and found them.'

'I see,' he said. 'It was very foolish of her, but even so, no woman deserves that.' He looked at Maggie. 'You two are quite a pair, aren't you?'

She smiled wryly. 'We have no one to blame but ourselves.'

The doctor came and examined Ivy. 'She has sustained bruising to her ribs,' he said, 'but they're not broken. The bruising will be worse before it's better, I'm afraid. Just keep bathing

173

with cold water to try and keep the swelling down. Keep her quiet, try to get her to eat something. Soup, porridge, scrambled eggs. Something she doesn't have to chew. If you want me again, give me a call, but it's just a matter of time, really.'

'Thank you,' said Maggie as she showed him to the door.

Joshua walked towards her. 'I have to go, Maggie. Will you be all right?'

'Yes. Honestly, I don't know what I would have done without you.'

He smiled at her. 'I'm glad I was here to help,' he said. He kissed her on the cheek. 'I'll be in touch, OK?'

'OK,' she replied and shut the door behind him, locking it, just in case Len found out where she lived and came looking for his wife. Then she went to see how Ivy was.

Chapter Twelve

Maggie was wondering how she was going to manage to look after Ivy and still go to work. Her friend wasn't well enough to be left alone, she felt, so, quickly slipping to the call box down the street whilst Ivy slept, she rang her mother, explaining her predicament.

'What shift are you on?' asked Moira.

'Eight 'til two.'

'I'll be there at seven thirty tomorrow morning,' she said.

'But what about Dad?'

'He can manage,' said Moira sharply. 'I'll tell him a friend needs me. What he doesn't know won't hurt him.'

'Thanks a lot, Mum. I didn't know who else to ask. See you in the morning.'

She spent the evening bathing Ivy's face with cold flannels, and even managed to get her to eat some scrambled egg.

Ivy didn't say much, but it broke Maggie's heart to see her in such an unhappy state.

The following morning, Moira arrived promptly. She took one look at the sleeping form of Ivy and muttered angrily to herself, 'What a silly girl to put herself in such a position.'

'Yes, I agree,' said Maggie, 'but she thought she'd found happiness at last. She just wanted to better herself with the man she loved.'

'That's as maybe,' retorted her mother, 'but she went the wrong way about it.' She sighed. 'There's many of us would like to change our way of life, but we have the good sense to know when we're beaten!' She looked at Maggie. 'Off you go or you'll be late for work. I'll take care of this wounded soldier. I'll have something for you to eat when you come home.'

Maggie made an excuse to the factory supervisor that Ivy had the flu to explain her absence from work, but later, at her own machine, she couldn't help wondering what her friend would do when she was better. Would she return to Len? Would he have her back? So many problems. But at least she had company for a while, and Ivy could stay with her for as long as it took to make up her mind what her next move was to be. And if her period didn't start soon, she'd have a few decisions to make herself.

And where was Steve? He should be with her, worrying as she was. After all it was as much his fault as hers.

When she returned home, it was to find that her mother had prepared a meal, washed Ivy and brushed her hair, which made her look better. She was sitting up in bed, sipping homemade soup.

'Hello, Mags,' she said through swollen lips. 'What a bloody turn-up for the books. I've really burnt my boats this time.'

'Don't you worry,' Maggie said. 'I'm glad to see you looking a bit brighter I'm just going to see Mum, and have a bite to eat; then I'll come back and we'll have a chat.'

Moira had made a fish pie, having slipped out to the fishmonger when Ivy woke. She sat with Maggie as they ate. 'You're looking a bit pale,' she remarked.

'I'm just tired, that's all. How's Dad these days?' she asked.

'The same as always, but when he rids himself of his latest haul he'll be happy, no doubt, counting his money.'

'Oh, Mum. I'd hoped that was all behind him.'

'Yes, well, so did I for a time, but Sonny Taylor came round again, didn't he? If he gets caught...'

'It's no good worrying,' said Maggie. 'If he does, then we'll face up to it together, but don't get yourself in a state now.'

Moira gave a wry smile. 'And you, Maggie. How about you? Are you happy?'

'Yes, why wouldn't I be?'

'And Joshua? Do you still see him?'

'Yes, Mum. I do.' She looked straight at her mother. 'He's a good friend.'

Moira made no comment.

Maggie placed her hand over her mother's. 'I'm worried about you,' she said softly. 'You seem so very unhappy.'

Moira forced a smile. 'I'm all right, really. Just going through the change, that's all.'

'No, Mum. It's more than that. Perhaps I shouldn't have left home. If I'd stayed, you wouldn't be like this.'

'Now you listen to me, darlin'. You have your own life to lead. You're a woman now, not a child. I made my choice years ago.' With a sad smile she said, 'Your father wasn't always like this. When this damned war is over, perhaps we can get back to the old ways again. War unsettles everyone, not just me.' She nodded in the direction of the bedroom. 'Take Ivy for instance. In normal times that would never have happened to her. Well, I'd better be off. Shall I come again tomorrow?'

'Ivy looks so much better. If I leave her a flask of tea and a snack to see her through the morning, she'll be all right. And Dad might start asking questions if you disappear again. I'll call you in a couple of days though.' She hugged her mother. 'Thanks, Mum. Don't get upset about Dad. It really isn't worth it.'

'No, you're probably right. As long as you're fine, that's all I care about.'

After seeing her mother on her way, Maggie went into the bedroom. 'How are you feeling?' she asked.

'Like shit!' said Ivy. She shook her head slowly. 'It's all gone wrong, Mags. Bob doesn't want me and I don't want Len. What a mess, eh?'

'What are you going to do?'

'Get back on my feet, get back to work, find a flat somewhere and start all over again. I've got a bit of money saved.'

'What about Len?'

'What about him? Yes, all right, what I did was wrong, but he'd been having a bit on the side, he admitted as much.'

'He did?' Maggie was surprised.

'Didn't I tell you he would? Well now he can have as many women as he likes ... but he can count me out!'

Maggie caught hold of her hand. 'You know you can stay here as long as you like, don't you?'

'Thanks, Mags. You're a real friend.' She wrinkled her nose. 'Do you think I could have a bath?'

'Of course. Can you manage?'

'I think so,' said Ivy getting stiffly out of bed, clutching her bruised ribs. 'You might have to help me,' she said, plaintively.

Maggie ran the water and gently lowered Ivy into it. She washed her back, then left her to see to herself. 'Give me a call when you're ready,' she said, 'and I'll help you out.'

Between them, they managed.

Ivy sat on the settee, snug in Maggie's dressing gown, drinking the ever-welcome tea. 'That

Joshua is a really nice chap,' she said. 'Very gentle, very kind. I can see why you like him so much.'

With a smile Maggie said, 'Yes, he's a gentleman in every sense of the word.'

'Still just friends then?'

Maggie gave her a sharp look, but Ivy chipped in quickly. 'You don't need to look at me that way, Maggie. You may not be aware of it, but that bloke thinks the world of you and you know my theory about friendship between a man and a woman.'

'Well this time you're wrong.'

'We'll see,' was all her friend said. 'But where does Steve fit in to all this? I'm worried that he'll find out about Joshua. Then all hell will break loose.'

'Well, so far he hasn't.'

Steve Rossi had his own problems and the fact that he might have got his girlfriend pregnant was far from his mind. Doug Freeman was getting angry that he hadn't come up with the rest of the goods for which he had paid a lot of money and Steve was in London trying to keep his own head above water, trying to explain to the gang boss that the situation was beyond his control.

They were sitting in a seedy pub alongside the East India Docks and Freeman was glaring at the GI.

'You took my fucking money and I want what I paid for!'

'It's not as simple as that,' argued the American. 'I can't just get the stuff out of the camp when I like. I have to watch my butt. I'm taking one hell of a chance, you must know that.'

Freeman grabbed the front of Steve's uniform jacket and hauled him closer. 'You listen to me, you jumped-up wop. Nobody plays fast and loose with Doug Freeman. You don't seem to realize who you're dealing with, sonny.'

Rossi hadn't been brought up in the back streets and ghettos of New York for nothing. He knew this man was dangerous; he just had to look into his eyes to recognize the cold steely glare of a man who was completely ruthless. He knew he was in real trouble and he was getting desperate.

'There's another big shipment coming in from the States in a couple of days' time,' he said. 'I'll divert the last truck and if you can meet it at a destination that I'll give you, you can switch the cargo from one vehicle to another, but it will have to be something that won't be a cause for curiosity.'

Freeman grinned. 'How about a furniture removal van?'

'Yeah, that should do it,' agreed Steve.

Doug Freeman's smile faded. 'You'd better be on the level, my son, because if you try to be clever, then my boys will be after you and your uniform won't save you, I can promise you that.'

With an expansive smile Steve said, 'Why on earth should I do that? We're in business together.'

'It had better not be monkey business. I want the goods or I want my money back ... do I make myself clear?'

'Very.' Steve rose from his seat. 'Nice dealing with you guys. I'll be in touch.'

'When?' snapped the Londoner.

'The day after tomorrow.'

Freeman got to his feet too. His big powerful frame towered over the American. 'If I don't hear I'll be down to Southampton myself. Remember that, Yank.'

'There's no need for all these threats, Mr Freeman. It was just a hiccup, that's all.'

'With your throat cut that's one thing you wouldn't suffer from, Sergeant Rossi. Get my drift?'

'Sure thing,' said Steve. 'I must go, I've a train to catch.' He saluted jauntily and left the bar.

Once outside the pub, Steve loosened his tie and undid the top button of his shirt, which felt as if it was choking him. Christ! That was close, he thought. He was in no doubt that Freeman was a man who would carry out his threats. It was no use Freeman asking for his money back, he didn't have it all any more. He'd lost most of it in that crap game. Now he had to work out a plan to get this truck to Freeman. How he was going to do that without being discovered he didn't know, not yet. But he would have to keep his word if he wanted to remain healthy.

He made his way to the station racking his brains trying to formulate a plan.

As he walked through the gates of his camp one of the guards greeted him. 'Hi there, Steve. Haven't seen you around.'

'No,' he answered. 'I had a forty-eight-hour pass. I went up to London for a break.'

'That explains it then,' said the soldier.

'Explains what?'

'I was in Southampton last night. I saw your girl

181

walking along with another GI.'

'You must be mistaken.'

The soldier grinned. 'No sir! You can't mistake that red hair and that figure.' He gave a sly grin. 'I see she fancies dark meat now.'

Steve frowned. 'What the hell are you talking about?'

'She was with one of them niggers.' His grin broadened as he saw the look of fury on Rossi's face.

'Where was this?' Steve demanded.

'Walking down the High Street towards the waterfront. Large as life. Maybe you'd better black your face next time you see her! Perhaps you're a mite too pale for her now.' Steve glared at him and walked through the gates towards his quarters.

It was a further three days until Ivy felt able to go back to work, and then only because she needed to keep the money coming in. She and Maggie had come to an arrangement and decided to work on separate shifts; this way they wouldn't be with each other all the time. It would make the sharing of such a small flat much easier.

When she arrived at the factory, she told Bill she'd fallen down the stairs, being so weak after the flu.

He gave her a jaundiced look and said, 'Of course you did.' He'd had a visitation from Len looking for his wife and had put two and two together. But when Len had asked if he had any idea where he could find Ivy, he'd said no.

'Your old man's been looking for you,' he

warned. 'If he comes again, what shall I tell him?'

Ivy hesitated. If she saw Len outside the factory she'd be fairly safe from his temper, she reasoned. 'I'll see him,' she said. 'But do me a favour, keep an eye on me, will you?'

'You women! You play with fire and wonder why you get burnt!' But seeing the stricken look on Ivy's face his tone softened. 'All right, don't worry, I won't be far away. Now get off back to your machine.'

The following day, Len arrived outside the factory and Ivy was summoned.

She walked outside and faced her husband. 'What do you want?' she asked. 'Come to look at the damage you did, have you?'

He looked at her bruised face. 'You asked for it, girl. Going behind my back like that. What man would put up with it?'

'Do as I say but not as I do! Is that it? You can dip your cock anywhere, but I'm not allowed to have any fun.'

He did have the grace to look a little shame-faced. 'Look, Ivy, I've got to go back to camp today and I want to know what's going to happen.'

She frowned. 'I don't follow you.'

'When are you coming home?'

She looked at him in astonishment. 'You can't be serious! You think I'm going to forget what you did to me and come crawling back?'

'You're still my wife!'

'In name only! When you have your next leave you'll find all my stuff gone. I never want to see you again, Len Brooks.' She turned on her heel

183

and went back inside the building.

Len went to follow her but Bill stepped out of his office. 'Hey! Where do you think you're going? This is government property!'

'I want to talk to my wife.'

'She's said all she wants to, now on your bike!' For one moment he thought the irate soldier was going to argue, but he obviously thought better of it. He scowled at Bill and walked away.

As Maggie was walking home alone from work the following day, Steve Rossi, with a squeal of brakes, drew up in his jeep alongside her. Her smile of welcome died on her lips as he glared at her and said, 'Get in!'

'But you're not allowed to give civilians lifts,' she protested.

'Get in, Maggie, or so help me God I'll come round there and put you in this damned vehicle myself!'

Not wanting to cause a scene and feed the curiosity of the few passers-by who had slowed to watch, she did as he asked. They drove in silence to her flat. He jumped down from the driving seat, came around to her, dragged her from the passenger's side and pushed her towards her front door. 'Open it!' he demanded.

'What the hell do you think you're doing?' she asked as she took her key from her bag.

He snatched it from her, opened the door and pushed her inside, slamming the door behind him. 'What sort of game have you been playing behind my back, Maggie?'

She saw the anger blazing in his eyes and was at

a loss to know what she'd done to deserve such treatment. 'What on earth are you talking about?'

'Where were you last Tuesday evening?' he asked.

Then she knew. She glared at him, her back straight, her nostrils flared. 'I was out with a friend, someone who certainly would never treat me as you have just done.'

'You were out with a nigger! Go on deny it.' His face was taut with fury.

'I was out with a gentleman.' She stood defiant.

'I told you if you were going to be my girl you were not to go out with anyone else.'

'I'm not *going out* as you put it. Joshua is just a friend. There's nothing more to it than that. It's all quite innocent.'

He stormed into the sitting room. 'How do you think I feel when one of my company tells me he's seen my girl walking along the street with another GI, then tells me it was with one of the coons?'

She flew at him. 'Don't you dare use that expression. It's disgusting. You have no respect for anyone. Not even me.'

'Now you're talking nonsense.'

'Am I?' She stood in front of him, her anger blazing now. 'You force me into your jeep, push me in through the door of my own home. You don't even ask how I am, or whether I'm carrying your child. All you can think about is your bloody pride.'

He was too enraged to consider her feelings. 'Well, are you pregnant or not?'

She was horrified by his coldness. 'My period hasn't started, but don't let that worry you.'

'I don't see the problem. If you are pregnant, I'll pay for an abortion. It's as simple as that.'

She slapped him around the face. 'You callous bastard! That's all it means to you, isn't it?'

He caught hold of her wrist in a vice-like grip. 'These slip-ups happen, it's a fact of life. It's nothing that can't be solved.'

'Like your black market stuff? You've used me all along, Steve Rossi, and I was dumb enough to fall for your line. I don't mean anything to you. I'm just a convenience. A good lay, isn't that what you Yanks say?'

'That's not how I think of you, you crazy woman. You're my girl, mine. I told you the rules in the beginning.'

'Rules!' she laughed harshly. 'You don't play by any rules but your own. You bend the rules to suit yourself. You tempt fate, my friend, selling off army supplies to London villains. I'm the stupid one for staying with you. Especially now that I realize you don't care for anyone but yourself.'

He grabbed her by the arms. 'I do care about you, Maggie, but I won't have you mixing with trash. And what's more I'm going to put a stop to it.' He let go of her and walked towards the door.

'What are you going to do?' she asked, afraid that his anger could put Joshua in danger.

At the door he paused. 'I'm going to find that black son of a bitch. That's what I'm going to do!' The door slammed behind him and within seconds she heard the jeep being driven away.

Now Maggie was really worried, not for herself but for Joshua. She remembered with horror seeing Steve in London when he was threatened.

What on earth could she do? Picking up her handbag, she rushed to the telephone box down the road, and quickly leafed through her notebook until she found the number of Joshua's camp, put her money in the machine and dialled. Her heart pounded as she waited for an answer.

The soldier on duty told her that it wasn't possible to get Joshua to the phone, and could she leave a message? She hesitated. What could she say that would warn him without giving too much away? She racked her brains.

'Tell him that our mutual friend is looking for him,' she said, 'and to be careful.' She put the receiver down and walked back to her flat, beside herself with worry. She reasoned that she'd not given Steve Joshua's surname. Surely amongst the negroes in the camp there had to be more than one with the same Christian name? She was going crazy, wondering if Steve would discover her friend's identity; and if he did, what would he do then? She would never forgive herself if anything happened to that lovely gentle man.

Rossi was getting nowhere with his enquiries at the negro camp. If any of the GIs knew anything they were keeping quiet. He racked his brains. Where would this man have taken Maggie? He enquired in a few pubs near the High Street where they were seen, without success, and eventually made his way to the Red Cross Club, using the excuse that he was only checking to see if they were getting enough stores delivered for their use. Then he casually asked about a red-haired girl who might have been there last night.

187

The soldier on duty grinned. 'Yeah I remember her. What a sight! That hair. A real looker.'

'Who was she with?' asked Steve.

'Corporal Lewis, a real nice guy. Great jazz musician.'

'Lewis, eh? Thanks. Give me a call if you need anything.' He made his way outside. He remembered Lewis, the preacher's son. He'd been on duty with him several times in the docks. He recalled the man pulling him up when he referred to him as Rastus. Well he'd teach him a lesson he wouldn't forget. Put him in his place. It was time these guys realized they couldn't get away with everything just because they were in this country.

He made his way to the 552nd Port Company camp. At the gate the guard let him pass once again. It was not unusual for Steve to visit the camp to discuss requirements with the quarter-master there, so the guard didn't question his presence. He parked the jeep and asked one of the men where he could find Corporal Lewis.

Chapter Thirteen

In the East End of London, Doug Freeman was gathering some of his boys in preparation for the removal of the army supplies in Southampton. The large furniture van was all ready, parked out of sight in a warehouse in the docks.

'When we hear from the Yank we'll know where

the meeting place is,' he said. 'Then it will have to be swift and efficient. We don't want the Old Bill on our tail. There will be some furniture already on the van so you pack the stuff behind it, just in case. You'll carry shooters, but only use them in an emergency. Understand?'

The men nodded.

'Right, as soon as I hear from Rossi, I'll let you know.'

He and Charlie left the warehouse and made their way to their local for a quiet drink. They sat at a table in the corner where they knew no one would disturb them. 'I'm still not happy with that cocky bastard,' said Doug. 'He'd better come across, that's all.'

Charlie frowned and said anxiously, 'You don't think he's going to be a problem do you, guv?'

Doug's eyes narrowed. 'I've got a funny feeling about him, that's all. I hope I'm wrong because if he crosses me, he's in real trouble.'

'I'm sure he wouldn't be that stupid,' said Charlie.

'Let's hope you're right,' growled Freeman. 'If he lets me down I want my money back and then I want his bloody hide! One less soldier among the Yanks won't be missed. There's too many of the bleeders around anyway.'

'At least they pay good money for the toms, guv.'

Doug Freeman grinned. 'Yeah, that's right. Well it's swings and roundabouts, I suppose, but I should really invest in one of them VD clinics. They're the ones doing the most business if you ask me!'

The two men laughed heartily and drank their beer.

Joshua Lewis was in the latrines washing his hands when Steve found him. The staff sergeant slammed the door shut behind him. And locked it.

'What you trying to do, Rastus? Wash the black off your hands?'

Joshua looked up. 'I stand as much chance of doing that as you do of cleansing your black soul,' he said evenly, wiping his hands on a roller towel attached to the wall. He stared at Rossi. 'I've been expecting you, sergeant. What can I do for you? I presume this isn't a social call?'

'The hell it isn't! I heard you were seen out with my girl.'

'And so?'

Steve took a step forward and in a voice full of menace he said, 'I'm here to tell you to keep away from her. Understand?'

Joshua grinned at him. 'Sticks in your craw, doesn't it, man? Maggie is a wonderful young woman, much too good for you. She doesn't look down on us negroes like you do, Rossi. She sees us as real people. But you wouldn't understand that.'

Steve's temper was rising rapidly. He was incensed by the calm attitude of this man. Who the hell did he think he was? 'The trouble with you niggers is that over here the British don't understand. You're jumped up with your own importance, knowing damned well that at home you wouldn't dare speak to a white woman, let

190

alone date her. It's time you were put in your place.'

Joshua's laughter echoed around the small area. 'And you think you're the man to do that, do you?'

Steve bent down quickly and removed a knife from his boot. He gripped it firmly and pointed the blade at the other man. With an evil grin he said, 'Oh yes. I'm going to teach you a lesson you won't forget.'

Ripping the roller towel from the wall and winding it around his arm, Joshua moved away from the basin into the centre of the room and said, 'Come on then, sergeant. What are you waiting for?'

Filled with rage, Steve circled Joshua several times, then lunged at his opponent; Joshua quickly swiped at Steve's hand with his covered arm, knocking it up into the air. But Rossi hadn't been in street fights all his life for nothing. The two men continued to circle each other, stooped, ready to strike.

Joshua smiled at him. 'Maybe you thought, as a son of a preacher, I'd turn the other cheek. Well, think again.'

Again Steve jabbed at him with the pointed blade but the negro was light and fast on his feet, stepping out of danger. Steve came back at him, slicing the fold of the towel. He laughed triumphantly and went for Joshua again, this time nicking his shirt at the shoulder, drawing blood. He jabbed again, but this time the negro took him by surprise and with a fast flick of his foot he caught the hand that was holding the knife and

Steve Rossi saw it fly through the air.

'Now,' said Joshua, as he quickly unwound the towel, casting it aside, 'we're on equal terms.'

'You'll never be equal!' snapped Steve and with his hands balled into fists he threw a punch at his opponent catching him on the chin, sending him reeling. Joshua recovered quickly and pushed him in the chest, then as Steve once again flew at him he sent him flying to the floor with a hard punch to the jaw. But as he went to lean over him, Steve pulled his legs up and pushed Joshua in the stomach with his feet. He went backwards, losing his balance.

Rossi leapt to his feet, threw himself on top of Joshua and started to pummel him. They rolled around exchanging blows. Lewis was surprisingly strong. He caught hold of the other mans throat and squeezed until Steve was gasping for breath, then he punched him in the face. Steve collapsed on the floor.

Getting to his feet, Joshua stood over his adversary and said, 'Be grateful I don't finish you off, soldier. And if I hear you've been mistreating Maggie, *I'll* come after *you*. You hear?' He unlocked the door and walked away.

Steve Rossi got slowly to his feet and staggered over to the basin. He looked at his reflection in the mirror. Already he could see his eye was swelling and his lip was split. He was going to look a sight by tomorrow. He bathed his mouth, swilled his face, picking up the towel from the floor to wipe it dry. Inside he was seething.

When he arrived at the gate, the sentry looked at his bruised face in astonishment but made no comment. He lifted the bar and let the driver through, but as he watched the back of the jeep disappearing into the distance he grinned broadly to himself.

'My oh my! Looks like that white boy just got himself a lesson!'

The following day Steve's commanding officer sent for him.

As he stood to attention in front of his CO Rossi felt a flush of embarrassment as the officer stared at him.

'I've heard rumours, Rossi, that you were over at the 552nd Port Company yesterday. Is that right?'

'Yes, sir. I was just checking on their store situation.'

'I suppose you're going to tell me you walked into a door whilst you were there.'

'Yes, sir!'

'Don't give me that crap, soldier! We have enough trouble in the town between the blacks and the white soldiers already. I don't expect this of my sergeants. You're supposed to set the men an example.'

'Yes, sir.'

'Go pack your kitbag. I'm sending you up to Norfolk with Lieutenant Cowalski to go around our camps up there. I want a detailed report on their stocks. It seems some are not getting through. I want to put a stop to this pilfering.

'But, sir, tomorrow we have a big shipment coming into the docks!'

'That's all right, sergeant. I'll have you covered. There's a jeep waiting to take you both to the station and at the other end someone will meet you. You've got ten minutes.'

'But, sir!' Steve protested.

'Don't argue, Rossi. That's an order!'

'Yes, sir.' Rossi saluted, turned smartly on his heel and left the room. Outside he cursed loudly. What the hell was he going to do now? Doug Freeman was expecting a call from him today to give him the meeting place. Now he wouldn't be here. Jesus! He knew he was in deep trouble.

He quickly packed a few things and carrying his kitbag he headed for his office, thinking to call Freeman, but Cowalski was just walking out of the door.

'Come on, sergeant,' he said firmly. 'We'll miss our train if we don't make a move now.'

Steve followed him, his mouth in a tight line. There was nothing he could do for the moment.

The following day at the factory, Ivy cornered her friend as they were about to swop shifts. 'I've got something to tell you,' she said. 'This morning I went into the paper shop and met one of Steve's mates. He says that Rossi has been in a fight and his face is in a mess, but that was all he knew.'

Maggie then told her what had transpired between her and Steve. 'He was awful,' she said. 'Making me get into his jeep. But I was really worried about Joshua.'

With a grin Ivy said, 'Well if he was the one involved with Steve, he really put up a good fight. And if it was him, I don't know what state he's in of course, but he didn't do bad for the son of a preacher.'

'It's all my fault,' said Maggie. 'I should never have gone out with him, knowing how Steve feels about the negroes. But Joshua is such a sweet man.'

'This guy said that Steve's been sent up to Norfolk,' said Ivy. 'He won't be back for a few days anyway. Got your period yet?' she asked.

'Still late. I'm three days overdue. I'm really worried.'

'Look, love. Three days is nothing. Sometimes it happens. After all, you left home, that was distressing for you. Such things can upset the workings of a woman.'

'God, I hope you're right.'

When she arrived home, Maggie saw Joshua waiting, leaning against the wall of her building. She rushed up to him. 'Are you all right?' she asked anxiously. 'I heard about the fight.'

He smiled, his eyes twinkling. 'One of the good things about being black is that the bruises don't show!'

'Oh, Joshua! I'm so sorry, really I am. Look, come in and I'll make you a cup of tea.'

'OK, Maggie. I think you and I need to talk.'

She fussed about making a pot of tea, casting worried glances in her friend's direction, but he just smiled at her. 'I'm OK, honestly.'

She sat beside him. 'I really feel it's all my fault,' she said. 'I should have known what the outcome would be if Steve found out.' She placed a hand on the negro's arm. 'I'm so sorry.'

He chuckled softly. 'I quite enjoyed teaching him a lesson,' he said. 'It was time somebody did.'

195

She shook her head, and with a sad note to her voice said, 'I don't really believe that. I think of you as a man of peace, not someone mixed up in a brawl.'

He burst out laughing. 'I don't quite know where you got that idea from, Maggie. I have as much anger in me as the next man. I've had to fight my corner as I grew up. I'm no different to anyone else. I have the same emotions, the same needs.'

'But you control them.'

He stared intently into her eyes and in his rich low voice said softly, 'Maybe, but it ain't always easy.'

There was something in the way he looked at her that threw Maggie for a moment. 'What do you mean?'

'I think it's best we leave it at that. What I want to know is, what are you going to do about Rossi? Are you still going to see him?'

She shook her head. 'No. I've decided that I've had enough. I don't want to be involved with him any longer.' Even if I am carrying his child, she thought. 'After all, as I told you, it's only a passing thing. He's bound to be shipped out at some stage and all I want is a quiet life. I don't want Steve Rossi bullying me, telling me who I can see and who I can't.'

He caught hold of her hand. 'You don't know just how happy that makes me, Maggie. He's no good and I don't want to see you involved with the likes of him.'

'Why should you care?' she asked.

'How could I not?' He frowned. 'He's not going

196

to like it, though.'

'That's too bad!' she said. 'I'm in charge of my own destiny, not Steve Rossi.'

'That's my girl,' he said. He drank the rest of his tea. 'Give me a piece of paper and a pencil. I'll leave you a number where I can be reached when I'm in camp. There's a telephone in my corridor.'

'Why do you want to do that?' she asked.

'Well, you never know,' he said. 'If there's trouble of any kind, you give me a call, you hear?'

'Yes, all right.' If only she'd had this number the other night, she thought, all this trouble could have been avoided.

After he'd written down the number, he rose from his chair and said, 'I've got to get back. I'll come and see you real soon. That's if you want me to. I don't want to complicate your life any more.'

'Of course I want to see you again,' she retorted. 'Why wouldn't I?'

He gazed earnestly at her. 'Going around with a coloured man has its own problems, Maggie. You already know that. I'll understand if you say no. The last thing I want is to bring you any trouble.'

She walked with him to the door. 'I'll see you at the concert on Sunday,' she said.

As he walked back to the camp, Joshua could feel his anger growing inside at the thought of Steve Rossi treating Maggie so badly. She was such a wonderful woman. It was a great shame she'd ever met the staff sergeant, who had no principles and no respect for anyone, let alone a woman. It riled him to think of Rossi making love to her, and knew that was because he longed to take her into his arms himself. But there was

197

nothing he could do about it.

When she was alone, Maggie poured another cup of tea and sat ruminating. Joshua wasn't kidding when he said that Steve wouldn't like it when she told him she didn't want to see him any more. He was an arrogant man who wouldn't take rejection lightly. Well, that was tough. She knew now that he was trouble and that he had a violent side. She didn't want to see any more of that. She'd seen plenty in the bar of the Bricklayers Arms often enough, when some of the punters had turned nasty. She didn't like violence. It frightened her. Bugger all men! she thought. Except for Joshua, he was different.

She got up and walked into the kitchen, and was suddenly aware of that heavy, dragging feeling low down in her stomach and prayed that her period might start. Then her troubles would really be over.

How wrong she was. They were only just beginning.

Chapter Fourteen

Doug Freeman was pacing the floor of his office, his face puce with rage. 'So that bloody Yank hasn't called then?'

Charlie shook his head. 'No, guv. We haven't heard a word.'

'I damn well knew it! I had a feeling about him

all along. Right, we'll give him another twenty-four hours and then if we've heard nothing, you and I are off to Southampton for a couple of days. We'll see what that bastard's up to. He's still holding half of my money and I want it – or the goods.'

'Where do you reckon on staying?'

'I know the landlord of the Horse and Groom, in East Street. He'll put us up.'

Charlie grinned to himself. Trust his boss to pick that particular pub. It was notorious, and, being near the docks, was just the place to pick up information. It was full of prostitutes who brought in the foreign troops and a large number of American GIs. All the local villains and spivs used it too. It was a tough place. Many a time he'd seen a fight both inside and out of the pub. The police and military police were constant visitors.

Once there, they'd soon find out where the missing Yank was. He himself disliked Steve Rossi and his bumptious ways. He'd take great delight in roughing him up, teaching him a lesson. It was about time someone took him down a peg or two, and he was just the man for the job. Oh yes, he was going to enjoy himself all right.

Two days later, Doug Freeman and his sidekick were drinking in the Horse and Groom and the place was filling up with people. There were several British tommies, French sailors with their cheeky red pompoms on the tops of their hats, merchant seamen, Canadians and American GIs. At the far end of the bar, in an alcove, were two full-sized, stuffed brown bears, standing on hind legs, towering over six feet tall. Some of the tommies were playing at stabbing them with pretend bayonets.

'Christ!' said one. 'I hope the bleedin' Hun isn't as big as this bugger!'

'Well if he looks as hairy as Bruin here,' said his mate, 'at least we can skin him after we kill him and have a fur coat for the missus.'

Doug and Charlie sat quietly surveying the scene. Charlie suddenly nudged his boss as Sonny Taylor walked in and stood at the bar. Freeman rose from his seat and walked over to him.

'Hello, Sonny. How's business?'

Taylor looked around. His face paled as he looked into the cold eyes of the London villain. He'd been sending him black market stock but had held back on quite a bit which was now sitting in Jack Evans's front room, behind locked doors.

'Mr Freeman,' he said with a forced laugh. 'How the devil are you?' He held out his hand which Doug ignored.

'I'm looking for Staff Sergeant Steve Rossi of the 14th Port. He's a friend of mine. Do you know him, by any chance?'

Sonny shook his head. 'Never heard of him. What makes you think I'd know him?'

'You usually know everyone and everything that's dodgy.' He gripped Sonny's arm in a tight hold, making the spiv wince. 'You hear anything, you let me know. I'll be around for a few days.' Freeman walked away.

'Bugger!' muttered Taylor. The last thing he

wanted was this London mobster hanging around his patch. Of course he knew Rossi. He'd dealt with him several times, but not lately. He'd find out where he was hanging out, tell Freeman and get him off his back. He downed his drink and left the bar.

Doug grinned at Charlie. 'That put a fire cracker up his arse. He's bound to know Rossi. If there is anything crooked going on, you can bet your bottom dollar that Sonny Taylor is there at the bottom of it. He'll find out just to get shot of us.' He picked up his glass of beer and chuckled before drinking it down. 'All we have to do is wait.'

Meanwhile, Maggie had arranged with her mother to come around to her flat after the Bricklayer's Arms had closed on Sunday lunchtime. They would have something to eat, then go to the concert at the Guildhall.

Her mother had been delighted with the invitation.

'Mum!' She greeted her with a hug when eventually she arrived at the door. 'Come in,' she urged.

Moira looked around. 'My, but this is looking even nicer,' she said with a smile. 'No wonder you're happy here, so would I be.'

They sat down to some cold tinned ham that Steve had brought, boiled potatoes and a salad.

'So tell me about this concert,' said Moira.

'I'm not too sure,' explained Maggie. 'I know there's a choir, but Joshua didn't tell me too much about it,' she added.

Something in her daughter's voice made Moira look sharply at her.

'Corporal Lewis, the son of a preacher. The man I met at a dance. I told you about him.'

Maggie saw the look of consternation on her mother's face, but was relieved that she didn't question her further.

After finishing their meal, the two women washed up the dirty dishes and made their way to the Civic Centre and the Guildhall. They were sitting very near to the stage and Maggie was thrilled to see Joshua walk towards the piano.

She pointed him out to Moira.

Moira studied the tall soldier. His skin was the colour of ebony, his large, deep brown eyes shone. She noted his proud stature. His uniform was pristine as were those of the other choir members. She watched as he caught sight of Maggie in the audience and saw his broad grin. She felt her insides tighten with apprehension as she turned towards her daughter and saw the look of affection and the warm smile on her face.

But all was forgotten as the concert began. The master of ceremonies told the audience that it was a performance of American music. First of all the choir sang, accompanied only by the piano, a selection of popular songs: 'I Wish I Was in Dixie', the marching song of the Confederate Army, followed by a selection of Irving Berlin tunes. Then Joshua played George Gershwin's 'Rhapsody in Blue'.

Maggie sat spellbound, as did the whole audience, by his expertise and sensitive interpretation of the music. The applause was loud and long as he took a bow. Then a quartet took the stage: a drummer, a man with a trumpet, another with a double bass and the last one with a clarinet. They gave a lively performance of traditional jazz, and Maggie began to understand Joshua's kind of music.

Even the conservative Brits' feet were stomping to the music.

Amidst generous applause, the quartet left the stage and Joshua rose from his piano stool to join the choir who had returned. Moments later, beautiful voices in the closest harmony filled the hall, as they sang several negro spirituals. There was no accompanying music, and indeed it wasn't needed.

The choir's repertoire gave great pleasure; everyone listened intently to the words of the spirituals, sung from the soul of every man. Joshua stepped forward to sing a solo and Maggie's heart filled with pride as she listened to his low rich voice, singing 'Nobody Knows the Trouble I've Seen'. And finally the choir ended with 'Where Were You When They Crucified My Lord?'. It was a most moving experience, which surprised Moira, but not Maggie, who'd heard it before.

She turned to her mother and with shining eyes asked, 'Did you enjoy the concert? Didn't Joshua do well? Wasn't the singing just wonderful?'

'Indeed it was, darlin'. Indeed it was.'

Outside, they had started to walk away when Maggie heard her name called. She looked around and saw her friend coming towards her.

'I'm real glad you came,' he said.

'Joshua, I'd like you to meet my mother.'

Moira felt her hand held in a firm grip.

'Howdy, ma'am. I'm very happy to meet you. I sure hope you enjoyed the concert.'

She found herself smiling at him. 'Yes, thank you, corporal. I did. Very much. Such beautiful music and the words were very touching.'

'The jazz was great,' said Maggie with twinkling eyes.

With a slow smile he said, 'We weren't too sure if you reserved British were ready for that!' Turning to Moira he said, 'I have to get back to camp or I'd invite you ladies to tea somewhere.'

'That's all right,' said Moira hastily. 'I've got to get home.' She walked away leaving Maggie and Joshua together.

'Your mother's a pretty woman,' he said. 'Now I know where you get your good looks from.'

Maggie laughed. 'I'll tell her,' she said. 'She'll be flattered.'

'Have you heard from Rossi?' he asked.

Shaking her head, Maggie said, 'No. He hasn't been near.'

'What time do you finish work tomorrow?' he asked.

'I'm on until two in the afternoon.'

'I may be off for a couple of hours. May I come and see you?'

'Of course you can. Look, I must go, I'm going to walk Mother home.'

'Until tomorrow,' he said with a broad grin and a wave.

As Maggie walked towards Moira, she wondered just what her mother was thinking as she saw the thoughtful expression on her face. She tucked her arm through hers and they set off towards the docks.

'He seems a nice young man,' said Moira carefully.

'Joshua is different somehow, Mum. He's kind, considerate, but more than that; thoughtful, a man of principles. And a brilliant musician, as you saw for yourself.'

'You sound as if you know him well.'

'He's just a friend, that's all.'

'Your father would go mad if he knew.'

'I don't care what Dad thinks, Mum.'

'What about the sergeant you were seeing?' asked Moira.

Maggie could feel the tension mounting inside her. As much as she loved her mother, at this moment she felt like a child, trying to explain away some misdemeanour or other. 'I have been seeing him too, but as a matter of fact that's about to finish. I've decided I don't want to see him any more.'

'Take care, Maggie,' warned Moira. 'These men are all just passing through, knowing they're going off to war. It's an emotional time, be very careful in your dealings with them. Men were never very good at coping with rejection.'

'I know,' said Maggie, secretly wondering just what Steve's reaction would be. He certainly wouldn't like it when she eventually faced him, bringing their relationship to an end. But she'd had enough.

At Holy Rood, they parted and went their different ways.

Giving her mother a hug, Maggie said, 'You take care now.'

Moira held Maggie's face between her hands and stared intently at her. '*You* be careful, darlin'.'

As she walked towards College Street, Moira's heart was heavy. Joshua Lewis was probably everything that Maggie said he was, but she could see something else there. Something that Maggie seemed unaware of ... for the moment anyway. She prayed that she was wrong. But in her heart she knew she wasn't.

It had taken Sonny Taylor all weekend to discover that Rossi was away in Norfolk on army business and no one seemed to know when he would be returning. On Monday lunchtime he made his way to the Horse and Groom to pass his information on. He was worried that if Doug Freeman hung around for too long, he'd discover that he'd put a lot of stuff Jack Evans's way.

Doug Freeman dismissed Sonny once he'd given him the news, telling him to let him know when the American returned. He glared at Charlie. 'I'm not hanging around for that bastard,' he said. 'I'll get back to the Smoke. You can wait here until he gets back. Have a good sniff about the place, see what's going on.' From his pocket he took out a piece of paper and read it. As the barman called time he said, 'Before I go back I think we'll pay a visit to the girlfriend. See what she knows. Come on!'

When Maggie answered the knock on her door, she was surprised to see two men standing there.

As they pushed their way past her, she recognized them from the club in London and felt the chill of fear run through her.

'How dare you force your way into my home!' she demanded. 'What do you want?'

Doug looked her up and down. The girl was a looker all right. Good figure, lovely eyes – and that hair. If he had her working his patch in London she would be worth a lot of money to him. He glared at her.

'I'm looking for your Yankee boyfriend,' he said.

'I don't know where he is,' she said, staring back at him despite her fear. 'He hasn't been around for a couple of days.'

'In that case I know more than you do, girl. He's away in Norfolk, but I want to know the minute he's back. You tell him to give me a call. Understand?'

'If he wants to see you, I'm sure he'll get in touch,' she retorted.

Freeman caught her swiftly by the throat and squeezed. 'Now you listen to me, missy. Don't give me any of your lip or I'll have to teach you a lesson and I promise you, you wouldn't like it, would she Charlie?'

Charlie gave a wicked leer. 'No, love. Take it from me, you wouldn't enjoy it a bit?'

Doug released her and she staggered backwards against the wall. 'I don't know anything about his dealings with you,' she said, hoarsely, holding her sore neck. 'They're nothing to do with me and I don't want to be involved.'

She looked into the steely eyes of the Londoner and froze at the coldness reflected there. She could feel her legs trembling and shifted her position, terrified they would give way beneath her.

'But you are involved, my dear.' He took a step towards her and she stiffened, pushing herself against the wall for support. 'You tell him to pick up the phone the minute he gets back or I'll have to come after him.' He wrote quickly on a scrap of paper. 'You give this to him, then he can't give me any excuse about losing the number.'

They both walked towards the door. There he turned. 'I know you won't forget to pass on my message.' He smiled at her, but his eyes remained cold. He opened the door and the two men left.

Maggie slid down the wall until she was sitting on the floor, she started to shake. She put her hands to her head and began to sob with relief. Never had she been more terrified in her entire life. She tried to swallow what little spittle she had in her mouth, but her throat hurt. She rubbed it gently and was startled when there was another knock on the door.

She shrank back against the wall, terrified that the two men had returned. She remained still, hardly daring to breathe. There was a further knock, then silence. She froze as the letterbox opened.

'Maggie! Are you there?'

She looked at the open space and saw the dark brown eyes of Joshua Lewis peering in.

'Joshua!' With a cry of relief, she staggered to her feet and opened the door.

He took one look at her white face, the bruises deepening on her neck, the fear in her eyes and stepped inside the hallway. 'Maggie! What on earth has happened?'

'Oh Joshua. Thank God you're here.' She collapsed into his arms.

He quickly closed the door and, picking her up, carried her into the sitting room. He put her gently down on the settee, holding her close, comforting her as she wept in his arms. He didn't question her, just held her until her racking sobs had stopped.

He handed her a clean handkerchief and said, 'You'd better tell me what's been going on here.'

As she told him of the visitation of the two villains, she saw the anger in his eyes, but he made no comment until she'd finished.

'My poor Maggie,' he said when she had. 'You must have been terrified. You don't think they're liable to return, do you?'

She shook her head. 'No. They just want me to give Steve a message. If he doesn't get in touch with them, then I don't know what'll happen.' She paused. 'No, that's wrong. I do know what will happen, he said he'd go looking for him. He gave me his number. I was scared,' she admitted. 'This man meant business.'

'And so do I,' he said. 'I'll see that you're not involved in this.'

The harsh tone of his voice surprised her. 'I don't want you getting into trouble, Joshua. This mess is mine, not yours.'

'Wrong, Maggie. This mess is Steve Rossi's alone and I'm going to see that he sorts it out. Trust me.' He grinned. 'After all, I am the son of a preacher!'

Despite her bad experience, she couldn't help smiling. 'But what are you going to do?'

He put a finger on her lips. 'Hush now, no questions. Where's that telephone number? I want to write it down.'

She showed him and watched whilst he copied it into a small notebook. 'Look, I can't stop any longer, I have to get back to camp, but I don't want to leave you alone.'

Maggie shook her head. 'No, I'm all right, honestly,' she assured him. 'Ivy will be home later. I was shaken, but it's not me they want. And besides, this is my home. I'm not going to leave it just because Sergeant Rossi is in trouble! As you said, it's his mess.'

He stared intently at her. 'Are you sure now?'

'Yes, I'm quite sure.' By now she was angry that once again the staff sergeant had involved her and her anger overcame her nerves.

Joshua squeezed her hand. 'I'll see you real soon,' he said. 'But don't you worry none. I'm going to take care of everything. OK?'

Maggie nodded. 'But please don't get into trouble,' she pleaded.

He caught hold of her shoulders and gazed into her eyes. 'Don't you worry about me. I promise to take care.' He held her close for a moment. 'Are you sure you'll be fine? I hate to leave you like this.'

'You go on,' she urged.

And reluctantly he left her.

As Joshua walked down the road, he was seething with anger. God dammit! He wasn't going to let that Rossi get away with causing

Maggie so much trouble. He pictured the angry fingermarks on Maggie's neck and knew if he met the sergeant at this moment... He took a deep breath and tried to calm down. He knew by now that he was in love with Maggie. In fact if he was honest, he had been for quite a while. He admired her spunky nature, her anger at the way some folk saw him. But what was the use? They were worlds apart. He certainly couldn't let her know how he felt, but he would do his best to protect her.

Once Joshua had left, Maggie firmly locked the door. Not that she was expecting the two men to return, now that they had delivered their message, but she felt more secure. So much for wanting her independence! It had brought her nothing but trouble.

But when she went to the toilet and saw the tell-tale smear of blood on the paper she breathed a sigh of relief. At least one problem was solved.

Chapter Fifteen

Joshua Lewis walked back to the 14th Port headquarters at Hoglands Park. He showed his pass and, strolling past several Nissen huts, made for Steve's office where his friend Ezra worked as a clerk.

Joshua was relieved to find his friend alone.

'Hey!' said Ezra. 'What you doin' here? What's happenin', man?'

'Do you still have copies of those phoney stock invoices Rossi had you make up?'

His friend looked concerned and lowered his voice. 'Yeah. I've hidden them back at camp. I kept them just in case he got caught and tried to put the blame on me. They've got his signature on and he can't squeeze out of that. I ain't anyone's fall guy.'

Joshua grinned broadly. 'Looks like we'll be able to fix him for good. Meet me tonight back in the canteen, then we can make a plan.'

Ezra frowned. 'I sure hope you knows what you're doing. These boys don't take kindly to a nigger putting their white boys behind the eight ball.'

'Trust me,' said Joshua. 'This time we've got Rossi by the short and curlies.'

With a slow smile Ezra said, 'Man I'd give a month's pay to see that. He really gets to me. I hate the bastard.'

Joshua leaned closer. 'It won't cost you a dime, buddy, I promise. See you soon.' He made his way to the gate with a satisfied smile.

Two days later, Steve Rossi returned to Southampton. The first thing he did was call Doug Freeman to apologize for the delay.

'I heard you was in Norfolk,' said the racketeer.

'How the hell did you find that out?'

'Listen, Rossi, when some geezer has my dosh and don't deliver, I make it my business to find out. Now what have you got to say? When do I get my goods?'

'I can't tell you,' said Steve.

He held the receiver away from his ear as Freeman let out a string of expletives. After the tirade had ended, he said, 'Hold your fire! I only just got back in the office ten minutes ago. As soon as I know when the next shipment is, the deal still stands. OK?'

Freeman said, 'This is your last chance, Rossi. I hope you know that?'

'Yes, yes,' Steve assured him. 'I won't let you down. I'll call you tomorrow.'

'If you don't, then my boys will come after you and this time you won't get away.'

'There's no need to talk like that, Mr Freeman. I couldn't help it before, it was army business. I had to follow orders. I'll call you tomorrow, you have my word.'

He replaced the receiver just a second before Ezra, in the outer office, replaced his. He sat back in his chair and chuckled. So ... the game was still on. He'd tell Joshua what he'd heard, tonight, when he returned to camp. It was only a matter of time now.

Steve summoned his clerk. 'Get me the latest list of shipping arrivals,' he demanded, 'then go and get me a pot of coffee.'

'Yes, sir, sergeant!'

Rossi looked at him sharply.

'I'm on my way.' Ezra went for the list and handed it to his superior then made his way to the canteen. He smirked to himself. You stinkin' son of a bitch, you're going to get yours real soon.

Steve was studying the list. Damn! It would be another ten days before there was another shipment from the States. Freeman wasn't going to like that, but there was nothing he could do about it. He'd look at the manifest and see just what he could deliver to him before he called him tomorrow. That ought to sweeten the pill a little.

But he was really worried. To take stuff out of camp in small doses was fine, he could easily cover the shortages, but he was putting himself in a hell of a position by taking a whole load at once. It was only fear of Freeman that made him take such a chance.

He leaned back in his chair and lit a Lucky Strike from a pack of cigarettes. Later he'd go and see Maggie. He wondered if she'd heard about his run-in with Lewis. If she had she wouldn't be very happy. Well that was tough. She was his girl and it was time she realized that. He hoped she wasn't going to tell him she was carrying his child. He had enough problems as it was!

But Maggie wasn't at home when he called. She was out shopping with Ivy, on their day off. Her friend suggested, to cheer herself up and celebrate the fact that she wasn't pregnant, she should buy herself a dress and dig into her precious coupons.

They first went to C & A Modes in Above Bar, but couldn't find anything they liked, so made their way to Van Allen's. There, Maggie tried on one of several dresses that had a little more style. She turned to her friend. 'These Utility dresses aren't bad, but look at these seams. There's hardly anything there!'

'Of course not, silly. That's why they're Utility!'

Maggie eventually chose a pale green button-through dress with inverted pleats. She stood and posed in front of the mirror. 'What do you think?' she asked.

Ivy stood back. 'Turn round ... yes, the colour's just right for you, it looks really nice – take it.'

Maggie fished in her handbag for her clothing coupon book and handed it over. 'That's seven coupons down the drain,' she complained.

'Never mind. You'll feel nice when you wear it. A new dress always cheers a woman up.'

As they walked through the town, the two of them chatted away happily. The threat of air raids had now seemingly passed. In certain parts of the town, the blackout had been relaxed. Normal curtains were now allowed, but they had to be pulled at night. Fire watching was abolished except in London and the Home Guard had been partially stood down. Southampton was still full of troops being shipped out as before, and the wounded continued to return, German prisoners still arrived, but somehow the spirit of the town and the people began to lift.

They finished the afternoon with a cup of tea and a trip to the pictures.

It was well into the evening when Maggie arrived back at Bugle Street. She was just sitting down to a meal of Spam and chips alone, as Ivy had gone to meet some friends, when there was a knock on her front door. She froze. Ever since the two men had forced their way into the flat, she was nervous whenever anyone called. The milkman had to knock several times before she would answer, and she would do so only when he proclaimed his identity.

215

She walked to the door. 'Who is it?' she enquired.

'Hi, honey! It's me, Steve.'

This was an unexpected surprise and one she didn't relish. She unbolted the door and let him in.

'What the hell is going on? It's like Fort Knox here,' he said as he stepped towards her to take her into his arms.

She backed off, away from his reach. 'It's been like that ever since I had a visit from your two London mobsters.'

She saw the shock reflected in his eyes.

'They came here? What did they want?'

'They came here looking for you,' she accused. She glared at him. All the horror of that time was now coming out as anger against the man whom she held responsible for her traumatic experience. 'You could have got me killed, you bastard!'

'Jeez, Maggie. I can't tell you how sorry I am. Come here.'

'Don't you touch me! I don't want any more to do with you, *Sergeant* Rossi. You lied to me all along. You used my place to store your stuff and that's twice your gangsters have come here. As far as I'm concerned you can go to hell!'

'Now Maggie, calm down. This can all be sorted out.'

'He wants you to ring him as soon as you return.'

'I've already done that.'

'You would say that, wouldn't you. I don't believe you.'

'I promise you, honey. It's all straightened out. Honest.'

Her eyes blazed with anger as she faced him. 'I don't give a damn. You and me are finished as of now. I don't want to see you any more. Understand? I want you out of my life.'

He grabbed her arms in a vice-like grip. 'I suppose you'd rather have the company of that nigger!'

She was so incensed that she was beyond reason. 'As a matter of fact, he's more of a man that you'll ever be!' She saw stars as Steve slapped her around the face, sending her reeling.

He stood over her, his face pinched and white with rage. 'You dare to say that to me.'

She was still stunned and sat holding her burning cheek. But she showed no fear, although inside she was shaking. 'Get out!'

He hauled her to her feet. 'You listen to me and listen good. You're my girl and no one else is going to have you. You'd better understand that or no other man will want to look at you ever.'

Maggie was so scared now that she didn't reply. Why oh why had Ivy chosen this particular evening to go out!

He grabbed her arm. 'Now stop this nonsense and make me a cup of coffee and then we'll go to bed.'

'You expect me to make love to you after this? I don't believe it! Well anyway, you can't.'

He looked at her and laughed harshly. 'Why not?'

'Because, you'll be relieved to know, my period has started. And besides, Ivy is sharing the flat with me now.'

'Since when?'

'That's none of your business.'

'Well that shouldn't make a difference. She can make herself scarce when we want to be alone, and now our other problem is solved, we'll be careful it doesn't happen again.'

She looked at him with distaste as she said, 'And that's just about all it ever really meant: a small problem. I'm right, aren't I?'

'Yes, since you asked.'

'You are such a cold-blooded bastard! How could I ever have been fooled by you?'

He leered at her. 'You are such an innocent, honey. You were so easy to convince.'

'Well you can damn well go and find some other poor mut, I don't want you any more!'

He grabbed her again and pulled her close, his jaw taut, eyes bright with anger.

'You still seeing that Lewis?'

'No,' she lied.

'I don't believe you!' He caught hold of her and held her whilst his mouth bruised hers.

She tried to push him away, but his brute strength defeated her.

When at last he let her go, she glared at him. Through gritted teeth she said, 'I hate you. You are despicable.'

He grinned at her. 'You could have enjoyed it if you wanted to. You always did in the past. You couldn't get enough, as I recall.'

She was so enraged that she hit out at him, but he caught hold of her wrist. 'That's what was missing in our lovemaking. A bit of anger. Willing is great for a while, but eventually it becomes boring, like making love in the same position.'

218

'Have you finished?' she asked coldly.

'Yes, thanks, honey.' Looking at his watch he said, 'I'll be off now. But I'll be back another time.'

With great relief, she heard him shut the front door behind him and ran down the hall to bolt the door. She walked slowly back into the kitchen where, with trembling fingers, she automatically put the kettle on. Typically British, she thought bitterly. Whenever there's a crisis, reach for the bloody kettle. But she wanted to reach for Steve Rossi. Then the tears began to fall. If only Joshua were here now to comfort her. She covered her face with her hands and cried, 'Joshua! Where are you? I need you.'

Sitting at the table she pictured his face in her mind. His smile, the way his eyes twinkled when he teased her. The way he'd comforted her the other day. The feel of his arms around her ... and suddenly she knew it was him she wanted. He was a man worth loving, not a waster like Steve Rossi.

If only she had listened to him in the beginning, none of this would have happened. But how was she to know? And now, she was wiser, but faced with the impossible. Joshua was just a friend and how could he be anything more? Couldn't she just picture the hullabaloo in her family if she told them she was in love with this Southerner.

Why did there have to be wars, she anguished. Without them, people could just get on with their lives and all these complications wouldn't arise. Her father wouldn't be mixed up with the black market, her mother would be happy, she wouldn't have met Steve Rossi ... or Joshua. She stopped her inner raging. She was glad she knew Joshua Lewis. That she wouldn't have missed for anything.

But life was not that simple, and what the hell was she going to do when Steve called again? She didn't want him to touch her. She couldn't bear the thought of him making love to her, but he'd frightened her tonight. She looked at the bruises beginning to show on her arms where he gripped her so tightly. How was she going to make a clean break? She didn't want to tell Joshua of her fears in case he went after Steve. She couldn't bear to think of him being hurt if he did. God! What a mess!

When Maggie clocked on at the factory the following morning, she encountered Bill, the foreman, who took one look at her and said, 'Good God, girl, what's the matter? You look like hell.'

She didn't answer with her usual witty remarks, but said, 'Nothing. I just didn't sleep very well, that's all,' and walked to her machine, somewhat stiffly.

Knowing her as he did, Bill kept an eye on her during the morning, then later walked over to her, indicating to her to shut down the machine and go to his office. Once inside he told her to sit down.

'Now, are you going to tell me what's been going on?' he demanded.

She looked startled. 'I don't know what you mean.'

'How did you get those bruises, Maggie?' he

asked, pointing to her arms.

She cursed inwardly. It had become so warm that, without thinking, she'd pushed up the sleeves of her dungarees.

'Your Yankee boyfriend do that, did he?'

She felt the tears well up in her eyes and didn't answer.

Bill leaned forward. 'Listen girl,' he said. 'If you're in some kind of trouble, you'll feel better getting it off your chest. Anything you say to me remains within these walls. OK?'

It was a relief to tell him what had happened, but she didn't mention the London mob, the black market, or Joshua. Only that she wanted to end their relationship.

Bill was furious. 'He had no right to treat you like that. What are you going to do about it?'

'Nothing.'

'You could have him up for assault. If you went to the police, they would arrest him.'

'My dad would love that!'

'You can't let him get away with it, Maggie.'

'Look, Bill,' she said, 'I don't want any publicity about this. If I make a complaint I'd have to go to court. I don't believe in washing my dirty linen in public. It won't happen again, I'll make sure of that.'

'Does he have a key to your place?'

'No, I wouldn't give him one.'

He looked relieved. 'Will he come back?'

'Oh yes, he'll be back at some time. There's no doubt about it.'

'Can't you move out for a bit?'

Maggie's eyes flashed with anger. 'Why the hell

221

should I? It's my first home.'

'You going there straight away when you finish your shift?'

She nodded.

'I'll walk with you,' he said. 'See you safely inside.'

She was touched by his concern. 'There really is no need. After all, Ivy is staying with me, so I'm not exactly alone, but thanks anyway. You're a marvel.'

'Get out of here!' he said, but the smile on his lips belied the angry tone of his voice.

As it happened, when Maggie walked out of the factory gate, Joshua was waiting.

Bill, who was standing in the office doorway, saw Maggie rush over to the coloured soldier – and hug him. 'Bloody hell!' the foreman loudly exclaimed.

Maggie beckoned him over. 'Bill, this is my good friend, Joshua. Joshua this is my boss, Bill, who offered to walk me home.'

'Is something wrong?' he asked anxiously. 'Only I heard that Rossi was back.'

'He came round last night,' she told him. 'It wasn't very pleasant.'

Turning to Bill, Joshua said, 'Are you the cavalry, sir, coming to the rescue?'

'Something like that. But Maggie said she was fine on her own.'

'That's real good of you, sir, but if it's all the same to you, I'll take care of her. That's why I'm here.'

Bill looked at her and raised his eyebrows.

She kissed his cheek. 'I'll be quite safe now, honestly.'

The foreman didn't feel it was his place to interfere any further, but he looked at Joshua. 'You take good care of her, mind, or you'll have me to deal with.'

To his surprise, the GI shook him by the hand. 'You're a good man. Thank you. I'll look after her, you have my word.'

And for some reason, Bill believed him. He watched them walk away together and saw the look of affection pass between them. He shook his head. Young Maggie's troubles were far from over, he was thinking.

Joshua waited until they were inside the flat before asking Maggie what had transpired the previous night and was horrified at what she told him. 'He had no right to treat you that way!' His brown eyes seemed enormous when he was angry.

'I don't want you rushing off and getting into more trouble,' she pleaded. 'It was bad enough the last time.'

'Steve Rossi will be out of your life for good soon enough,' he said.

'What do you mean?' Now she was really worried.

'The less you know the better,' he told her. 'Don't you worry none. Everything will soon be ready and all done legally. But Steve Rossi's days are numbered. Soon he'll be Stateside and out of everyone's hair.'

'You're not going to get into any kind of

223

trouble, are you?'

'No way. And I'll see he doesn't bother you again.'

'Oh Joshua, I'm so worried that you'll do something silly.'

He held her hands. 'I promise that I won't. Come and sit down. You look so pale, you should have someone taking care of you.'

She sat beside him. 'You're such a kind man. You'll make someone a wonderful husband one day.'

He chuckled with delight. 'Sure, I can cook, clean... I've had enough experience in the army, that's for sure.' He put a comforting arm around her.

She gazed at him and saw the tenderness in his eyes. 'Have you ever been in love?' she asked.

His gaze didn't flinch. 'Oh yes, just once.'

She felt her heart sink at his words. She realized she loved this man, but until he told her he'd loved another, she hadn't realized the depth of her feeling for him.

'Did you ask her to marry you?'

He shook his head. 'No. I wanted to be with her for the rest of my life, but it wasn't to be.'

This was a devastating thing to be told, but Maggie felt a glimmer of hope. He had said before that he didn't have anyone waiting for him at home, so where was this woman?'

'I wish you could find someone, Maggie. Someone worthy of you, not a man like Rossi.'

This was not what she wanted to hear. She longed for Joshua to want her, not want her to find someone suitable!

She let out a deep sigh. 'Well ... he was a big mistake. But I won't make the same one twice.'

'Look, you should try and rest. How about I go out and buy some fish and chips for lunch. We can sit here and have a picnic.'

'What, and put grease all over everywhere? You go to the shop and I'll warm some plates.'

'What about Ivy? Will she want some?'

'No, she's working. We're on different shifts.'

As Maggie busied herself she thought, well, at least she could spend some time alone with Joshua, get to know him even better, and she felt that every moment was precious.

Soon after, they were settled at the table and he was telling her more about his family, making her laugh over his childhood memories. It sounded as if his early years were full of happiness, but she knew from other things he'd said on previous occasions that it hadn't been easy. How much she admired his optimistic attitude towards life.

As she listened, she watched the way his mouth turned up at the corners when he was amused, the way his eyes twinkled when he laughed. She longed to stretch out and caress his face, to tell him of her feelings. She was very curious about the person he'd wanted to marry. 'Why didn't it work out with this woman you wanted to spend the rest of your life with?' she asked.

'There were too many complications,' he said. 'I really don't want to talk about it. Let's leave it at that.'

His firm tone convinced her it would be unwise to press the subject and she didn't question him further.

225

After he left Maggie, Joshua walked purposefully towards Hoglands Park. He had a personal score to settle. He showed his pass to the sentry on guard at the 14th Port headquarters and walked swiftly to Steve's office. Opening the door to the outer office he saw Ezra sitting at his desk, typing. He put a finger to his lips and whispered, 'Is Rossi in there?'

Ezra nodded. 'Ain't nobody there but him.'

'Then I suggest you disappear for twenty minutes. You know nothing about my visit. Understand?'

Ezra hurriedly got to his feet. 'Me, I'm off to the john. I feel an attack of the shits coming on, man. You take care now, you hear?'

Joshua locked the main door, then walking quickly he threw open the door to the other room.

Steve Rossi was standing in front of a filing cabinet and looked up in surprise as Joshua burst in. 'What the—?

Grabbing him by the front of his shirt, Joshua pushed him up against the wall. 'I told you, Rossi, if you ever harmed Maggie I'd come after you.' He brought his knee swiftly up to Rossi's groin.

The Italian doubled over in pain, but Joshua forced him upright and punched him in the stomach. As his adversary slumped to the floor, he said, 'You go near Maggie again and the brothers and I will come looking for you. Understand?'

Steve was writhing on the ground unable to reply.

Joshua hauled on the front of him again until he

226

was looking at him. 'Understand?'

'Yeah, I understand,' the other man gasped.

Joshua looked at him with disgust, then left the building.

Outside he saw Ezra leaning against a tree. 'I suggest you spend a long time in the john, my friend,' he advised. 'I'll see you later.' He walked out of the camp.

Steve Rossi pulled himself up off the floor and sat in his chair behind the desk. His guts ached and he wouldn't want a woman for days. He gingerly touched his private parts. 'Bastard!' he muttered. With this deal coming up with Freeman, this was not the time to make waves... But after. After, he'd pay both Maggie and that nigger back. He rang for his clerk – but there was no answer.

Chapter Sixteen

The following day, Maggie, ruminating over past events, began to wonder just what Joshua was up to regarding Steve Rossi. He had seemed so certain that Steve would soon be gone, and he had said he would see that the Italian didn't bother her again in the meantime. She fretted that Joshua would get himself into trouble; yet he wasn't a man to go looking for it, she wouldn't have thought. She hadn't been able to talk to Ivy about her worries, as by the time her friend arrived home the night before, Maggie had been asleep.

At lunchtime in the factory, Bill caught up with her in the canteen.

'You all right?' he asked, sitting beside her.

'Yes thanks. And thank you for your kindness yesterday, I really did appreciate it.'

He dismissed her sentiments. 'Think nothing of it,' he said. 'That darkie ... a good friend, is he?'

'Yes, Bill. And that's all he is.' She replied tartly.

He gently caught hold of her arm. 'Don't get the wrong idea, girl. It's not my business, but I'd hate to see you jumping from the frying pan into the fire – that's all.' He rose from the bench and left her.

She knew he meant well, but of course she recognized that, as he saw it, he was right. Black and white didn't mix. But in wartime things change. She didn't want to lose Joshua's friendship just because of his colour.

A further week passed and Steve Rossi was getting edgy. In three days' time, the next shipment from the States was due to dock and he knew that his survival hinged on his getting the goods to Doug Freeman. No matter what chance he had to take, he had to deliver. He picked up the telephone and dialled.

Ezra, who had been monitoring all his calls, listened in. He noted down the number Steve gave the operator, then made notes of the time and place for the exchange, slipped the paper into his pocket and carried on with his work.

Later, he and Joshua approached the office of

the commanding officer and asked to see him urgently.

Standing to attention, Joshua spoke. 'Sir. What I have to say to you could land me in a deal of trouble, but I only have the good name of the United States Army in mind. I would like you to remember that.'

The CO frowned, put down his pen and said, 'Carry on, corporal. And this had better be good.'

In the East End of London, Doug Freeman was making his plans. The furniture van was prepared and his band of villains ready to roll. He looked at Charlie. 'I'm coming with you,' he said. 'I still don't trust that creep. I want to be there myself to see that he delivers everything he promised. If he tries to screw me...' He drew his finger across his throat.

'He wouldn't dare try anything, guv. After all, he did call, and the haul sounds very good. It should make a pretty penny on the black market. No, I don't think you have a thing to worry about.'

At the dockside in Southampton the cargo was being offloaded, put on forklift trucks, then moved onto lorries. Steve was checking every item, every crate, his stomach churning, knowing he was taking a huge chance, but knowing also that he had no choice.

Joshua Lewis was on duty with some of his company, helping as usual. He kept clear of Rossi, not wanting to interfere and cause any friction; trying to behave naturally. He had no idea what was going to happen. As the CO had told him,

'It's a need-to-know basis. If you don't know, you can't spook Rossi.'

When the commanding officer first learned of the duplicity of his staff sergeant, he was astonished. Then when Ezra showed him the copies of the false invoices he was furious at the scale of the thefts.

'This bastard has cost the US Government thousands of dollars!' he roared.

But when Joshua explained that Rossi was involved with Doug Freeman, a London gangster, things became really serious. Ezra and Joshua were made to give statements, but time was short, with only a few days to formulate a plan of action.

Rossi chewed vigorously on his gum, trying to calm his nerves. Most of the lorries had been loaded and sent to the camp. On one side of the dock stood his stash of contraband, waiting for the final lorryload. He glared across in the direction of Lewis who was supervising his men. Any other time he'd sort him out, but this was not the time or the place. Too much was riding on him. But after he'd got this shipment to Freeman, then he would have time to get even.

The penultimate lorry was on its way and the final one waited to be loaded. When it was finished, Steve dismissed the men and the driver, telling him to take his jeep back to headquarters, that he'd drive the vehicle himself.

The soldier didn't argue, and just handed over the keys.

Steve waited until the coast was clear, climbed

into the driving cab and made his way to Hill Lane, a quiet residential area. It had been difficult to decide where was the safest place for the hand-over. Anything near the docks would have caused some interest. All around the town, troops were parked waiting to board troop ships, heading for France. But in a quiet road off Hill Lane no one would take any notice of a furniture van. The local residents would just think that someone was moving out, or in.

He drove carefully towards Southampton Common, until he came to the cemetery, then turned left into Wilton Road, and eventually left again into Bridlington Avenue. Ahead of him, halfway down the road, he saw the furniture van parked. He slowed the army lorry and brought it to a standstill behind the waiting vehicle. He switched off the engine, opened the door and climbed down.

Steve was surprised when Doug Freeman alighted from the passenger seat of the furniture lorry and walked towards him.

'So you made it this time!'

'I told you I would. Now can we please get this stuff moved as quickly as possible?'

Freeman put his fingers in his mouth and whistled. The back of the vehicle opened and several of his men jumped out. They made their way to Steve's army lorry, and started to offload the gear. Freeman watched very carefully.

'You don't know how lucky you are that you came across this time, son. It looks like you'll live to be an old man after all.'

His nerves taut to breaking point, Steve

snapped, 'You got the stuff didn't you? So stop bellyaching!'

Freeman grabbed his jacket. 'You use a little more respect when you talk to me. You may think you're tough, but slick bastards like you are a dime a dozen. You think you're so bloody clever, but you're just an amateur. You'll make a mistake in the end and then you'll be finished, but me, I'll go on for years ... because I'm a professional.'

Steve shook off his hold. 'I won't have any more stuff for you,' he said. 'From now on I'll have to watch my step very carefully.' He stared at Freeman with an expression of arrogance. 'I'm no amateur,' he said. 'I've been pulling this sort of caper since I was fourteen.'

Doug gave an evil grin. 'Believe me, you'll end up behind bars. I know your type. That cocky attitude only leads to trouble. It makes you over-confident, you take chances and that's dangerous.'

The two men watched the rest of the unloading in hostile silence.

As the last crate was exchanged, the men moved a wardrobe and chest of drawers to the front, covering up the stolen loot. Doug turned to Steve and said, 'I'll be seeing you.'

'No, Freeman, you won't. This is my last business deal with you. Find another source!' He walked to the front of the army lorry and opened the door - then all hell broke loose.

From surrounding gardens uniform police appeared; from others, American military police rushed forward, revolvers at the ready. Police cars screeched to a stop at either end of the road, blocking off any getaway.

Freeman was held by two constables. Others swarmed all over the furniture van, pulling out the men inside. Rossi was held by military police. A constable came out of the back of the furniture van carrying three sawn-off shotguns. 'They came tooled up!' he proclaimed.

As the police put the handcuffs on Doug Freeman, he looked over at Rossi, his face flushed with anger.

'Fucking amateur!' he yelled. 'Didn't I tell you?'

The raid made the headlines in the *Southern Daily Echo* the following day: *Black Market Ring Foiled. London Villain Caught.*

Maggie read it, her fingers trembling as she held the paper. She felt her blood run cold as she read the track record of Doug Freeman. To think that this man had been in her home, threatening her, holding her by the throat. It made her feel sick. Then she saw Steve's name and at last realized just what Joshua had been referring to. What had he to do with all this, she wondered. But with a feeling of relief, she now knew for certain that Steve would not be bothering her again. She showed the paper to Ivy.

'Bloody hell!' she said, when she'd read it. 'And to think I told you to marry him. Well I don't know about you, Mags, but from now on, I'm all for a quiet life!'

Maggie grinned to herself, knowing her friend of old. A quiet life would drive Ivy mad. She had already started to go to dances again, visiting her old haunts, looking for excitement. But Maggie was relieved. Steve's violence had shaken her, and although she'd remained in her flat, albeit securely locked in and with her pal sleeping there, she'd been terrified of his return.

The following day she went to visit her mother, insisting as soon as the pub was closed that they go out and look around the shops, perhaps stop for tea somewhere.

When she saw her father it struck her that he'd aged suddenly. When she worked in the bar on a Friday evening, she scarcely looked at him, but tried to keep herself to herself in the confines of the small space behind the counter.

He barely answered her when she said hello, and she supposed that he blamed her still for his wife's unhappiness. And to some extent she was responsible, she couldn't deny it. If he'd been different, in time he and Moira should have grown even closer. Except of course for his dodgy dealings. She knew that Sonny Taylor was still keeping him supplied, and that didn't help his relationship with Moira. But she wasn't going to fret over him. Today was for her mother.

'Did you read last night's paper?' asked Moira as they walked.

'Yes,' said Maggie.

'Didn't you tell me your boyfriend's name was Steve Rossi, a staff sergeant?'

Maggie pursed her lips and cursed her mother's excellent memory. 'Yes, that's right'

'The same one mentioned in the *Southern Daily Echo?*'

'I'm afraid so.'

'Mm. Just as well that you got out when you

did, darlin', otherwise you might have been caught up in that mess. That would have been dreadful.'

Maggie breathed a sigh of relief. Thank God her mother didn't know how close she'd come to being involved.

The afternoon was enjoyable for both women. Their relationship was very special. They shared the same sense of humour, and when Maggie had lived at home they had often giggled together like children over silly things. Jack could never understand them.

As they sat in Tyrell and Greens, having tea, Moira looked happier. 'It always does me good to have you around. I enjoy our Friday nights in the bar, and the odd coffee we have together in the town, but today, I don't think I've laughed so much in weeks.' She sighed softly. 'It would be nice if we could go away on a holiday together, just the two of us,' she said wistfully.

'Why can't we?'

'You couldn't get time off from work and I certainly wouldn't leave your father alone to run the pub! Surely the war can't go on for much longer? I know our boys had a bad time at Arnhem, but they seem to be doing better in Italy. How much longer can both sides continue? So many deaths. That lovely Guy Gibson shot down. It's such a waste.'

'All because of that power hungry paperhanger,' said Maggie. 'Well if there is a God, he surely won't let him win.'

Moira looked askance. 'What do you mean, *if* there is a God! Of course there is. You'd better not

235

let Joshua hear you say such a thing.'

'Joshua?'

'Yes. Now there is a man with a belief.'

Maggie hid a smile. 'He's bound to, his father's a preacher, but what makes you so sure? You only exchanged a few words at the concert.'

Moira's expression softened. 'You only had to look at his face as he sang those negro spirituals,' she said. 'The words came from the heart. It's a pity he's–' She stopped.

'That he's black?'

Her mother looked embarrassed. 'Well I can't pretend. He seems a really nice young man, but, Maggie, there's no future for the two of you.'

'I know that! I've told you, it's purely friendship.'

'I'm not sure that's how he sees it.'

'He's never touched me, or even tried to,' Maggie protested.

'I didn't say he had, but the way he looks at you, my dear. I'm surprised you haven't noticed.'

Maggie was quite thrown by her mother's words. 'I'm sure you're mistaken, Mum.'

'I hope so, darlin', I certainly hope so. Well, I'd better make tracks for home. Come on, we'll walk to Holy Rood together ... that's if you're going home?'

'Yes, I am. I want to have a bath and wash my hair.'

As they parted, Moira kissed her daughter. 'I've had a lovely time,' she said. 'You could always come home one day and let me cook you a meal.'

Maggie hesitated. 'I'm not sure that Dad would approve. He can hardly bear the sight of me, and

236

the idea of sitting at a table sharing a meal with him ... well!'

'Think about it.'

Maggie said she would and they parted company. As she walked home, she couldn't get her mother's observations about Joshua out of her mind. Ivy had made a similar remark. She doubted that he would feel the same way as she did. He'd never said anything to make her think he did, except that he worried over her when she was going out with Steve.

If only what they said was true. But if it was ... where would they go from there? She really did like him. She liked his mind too. He stimulated hers with his conversation. They argued over so many different things, especially music. He'd changed her way of thinking. He'd opened her mind to so much and he soothed her soul. She felt, if only things were different, they could be happy together.

As she entered the front door, she could hear the sound of voices. There in the kitchen were Ivy and Joshua, chatting away.

'Hey Mags,' called Ivy, 'come and see who's here, and he's brought some food with him.'

Joshua looked up. 'Hello, Maggie,' he said softly.

For the first time in his company, she felt embarrassed. 'Hello. I want to talk to you. Just exactly what did you have to do with that raid the other day?'

He gave an impish grin. 'I told you Rossi was on his way, didn't I?' He then proceeded to fill in all the details leading to the arrests. 'The army wasn't too happy having to liaise with the Hamp-

237

shire police, they like to handle army matters internally, but when they heard about the guy from London, they had no choice.'

'Where's Steve now?'

'In the pokey where he belongs! He'll go before a military court, be sentenced, then do time in a military prison. And after, he'll be shipped home in disgrace.'

'How are the mighty fallen!' quipped Ivy.

'What a fool,' said Maggie. 'He was such a bright man.'

'And a violent one – or had you forgotten?' asked Joshua, sharply.

'I'll never forget anything about Steve Rossi,' she said angrily. 'How could I have been such a fool! I should have known better.'

'Don't be so hard on yourself. Rossi could be charming, and convincing. But at least now he won't be bothering you again.'

She looked at him, a frown furrowing her brow. 'You took such a chance going to see your commanding officer.'

He smiled. 'I had the proof; besides, I had to do something. I was worried about you. Rossi wouldn't have left you alone, especially when he learned of our friendship. That really stuck in his craw. I was concerned for your safety, Maggie.'

'But you put your career on the line for me.'

'That's not how I saw it,' he said softly.

'But won't there be trouble for you from his friends?'

'Rossi didn't have any friends! There's no one going to come after me just because he got caught with his hand in the cookie jar. And at least we were able to keep your name out of it.'

She looked horrified. 'What do you mean?'

'Had the police known you had a visit from Freeman, then you'd be called to give evidence.'

'Oh my God! That would be awful.'

'As it was, they caught the two of them red-handed and that was good enough to charge them.' Seeing the expression on her face he said, 'Now you need to forget all this and put it behind you. Get on with your life. Just be a little less trusting, next time.'

'Next time! There won't be a next time.'

Joshua burst out laughing. 'Don't be silly. A girl with your looks will always have men after her. Just take care, is all.'

'I got myself into this mess. I was in too much of a hurry to be a woman. I let my curiosity get the better of me. Well, now I know about sex.' Her eyes flashed with anger and indignation. 'And I don't need any man!' She saw the hurt look on his face. 'I don't mean a friend like you, Joshua. I mean a committed relationship. Look at my mother's marriage; she's not a happy woman. And Ivy's separated.'

'For goodness' sake, Maggie, don't let your experience with Rossi make you bitter. That's a wasted emotion. As for marriage, with the right partner, it's wonderful. My parents have no regrets, that's for sure. When you fall in love, you'll think differently, I promise.' He caught hold of her hand. 'How about we celebrate? Let's go dancing. There's a dance on tonight at the Guildhall,' he said, changing the subject. 'What do you say? Let's put all this mess behind us and have a good time.'

'Go on, Maggie,' urged Ivy. 'It'll do you good.'

And she agreed.

The Guildhall was quieter than usual, which pleased Maggie because there was more room to dance. As Joshua led her onto the floor when the strains of the waltz came over the microphone, she felt as if she'd come home. Within his arms, she relaxed and moved in unison with him to the music. His face was against hers. The warmth from his skin, the feel of his arms around her, made her wish the music would go on for ever. She felt safe, cosseted ... loved? She looked up at him and as he gazed back at her, she recognized the expression in his dark eyes.

But she was confused. She'd always known she didn't love Steve, had failed to realize how deeply she cared for Joshua. Now she thought she saw something special in the way he looked at her, but she'd been wrong so many times ... and what about the other woman? The one Joshua had loved so much?

The music stopped, but he just held her close until the next number started. He didn't speak, just clasped her to him.

When the dance was finished, he led her away from the floor and, seating her at a table, asked, 'What would you like to drink?' As he walked to the bar she watched him. He didn't swagger as Steve used to do, his walk was one of elegance, stature, pride. And she realized here was a man who was happy with who he was. She envied him his composure, his certainty.

He smiled at her as he put the drinks on the table and sat beside her.

Thinking of the expression she'd seen in his eyes, she asked, 'Why did you bring me here with you tonight? What was the real reason?'

'I just wanted to hold you in my arms,' he said, simply and honestly.

Her breath caught in her throat. Could it really be that he thought as much of her as she did of him?

'But apart from the time you found me after those men from London had called at the flat, and you comforted me, you've never given any hint...' She was lost for words. 'What are you saying?' she asked. 'I've made so many mistakes in the past...'

Putting his arm around her shoulders, he said, 'I'm in love with you, Maggie.'

'You are?'

His eyes twinkled as he said, 'You find that so very strange?'

'But what about the other woman, the one you wanted to spend the rest of your life with?' She had to know.

He gently stroked her cheek. 'Her name is Maggie Evans.'

'But why have you never said anything? How was I to know?'

'Steve Rossi was always in the way.'

She caught hold of his hand. 'Oh Joshua.' She brushed the back of it with her lips. 'You've never even kissed me.'

'You have no idea the many times I've wanted to.'

241

She looked around. They were surrounded by people. 'I want you to kiss me too. Let's get out of here.'

They left the Guildhall and made their way to the park.

Once alone, Joshua took her into his arms.

She relaxed as his mouth covered hers, let herself respond to the gentle urgency of his tender kisses; felt his strong arms about her, the caresses of his hands on her back. It was a long time before he released her.

In the low light reflected from the moon, he looked into her eyes and whispered, 'I love you, Maggie.'

'And I love you,' she responded. She smoothed his cheek and gazed longingly at him. 'What fools we've been ... or at least I have.'

He put his finger over her lips. 'Hush now. Better late than never, as they say.'

'But we've wasted so much time and you could be shipped out.'

He held her close and buried her head in his chest, stroking her hair. 'That doesn't seem likely just yet. They need us to work in the docks.' He tipped her chin upwards. 'We'll spend every moment we can together and make up for lost time. What do you say?'

'I'd like that. Let's go home. At least there we can be in comfort.' She gave a cheeky grin. 'And you can tell me exactly when you discovered that you loved me.'

He burst out laughing. 'Oh the vanity of women.'

'Not at all.' She reached up and kissed him. 'I

just can't believe that you feel this way and I want to know everything. How, where, when and why!' There was a momentary anxious look in her eyes. 'I can't quite make sense of it, you see.'

He pulled her to him. 'Believe it!' He lowered his lips to hers once again, his kisses ardent and demanding. When he released her he asked, 'Does that help to convince you?'

'Oh, yes,' she said in a soft voice. 'But I may need some further convincing.'

She heard him chuckle softly. 'It'll be my pleasure.'

They walked back to Bugle Street, hand in hand.

When they arrived at the flat, Maggie put the key in the door and opened it. Ivy came rushing forward. 'Thank God you're home,' she gasped. 'Your father has been arrested!'

Chapter Seventeen

The success of the raid and the capture of Doug Freeman had fired the enthusiasm of the Chief Constable who had gathered together all his senior officers.

'The other day was a good result,' he said with a satisfied smile. 'Now we must continue with our fight against these criminals. Strike while the iron's hot! I want more men on the beat. Question your narks, find out who's doing business with who. I want an end to this racketeering.'

When it was known that Sonny Taylor had been talking to Doug Freeman in the Horse and Groom earlier that month, a tight watch had been put on the spiv. Taylor had been panicked by Freeman's arrest and had hastened to his hideaway, in a bid to get rid of his goods. The police had followed him to his lock-up garage and arrested him.

When, in the interview room, he'd been charged, he sang like the proverbial canary. He named all his customers in the hopes that he'd get a lighter sentence for helping the police with their enquiries.

Later that evening, two detectives made their way to the Bricklayer's Arms, with a search warrant.

Jack Evans was cleaning out the beer pumps when he heard an urgent knocking on the side door. He cursed to himself. 'Can't the buggers wait,' he muttered. 'It's only ten minutes to opening time!' He was shocked when he opened the door to see two plain-clothed officers of the law standing there.

They pushed past him into the narrow hallway, one of them waving the warrant under his nose. The older one looked at him grimly. 'We hear you've been a naughty boy, Jack,' he said.

The landlord's face turned pale. 'What the bleedin' hell you talking about?'

'We've just arrested Sonny Taylor,' said the other. 'I believe you're one of his customers.' He turned to the door of the front room and tried the handle. It was locked. 'Open up, Jack,' he commanded, 'and don't give us any trouble, there's a good chap.'

At that moment Moira appeared from the direction of the kitchen. 'What's going on?' She stopped in her tracks as she saw the two men and the look on her husband's face.

'Unlock the door, Jack. Don't mess me about,' said the detective.

Putting his hand in his pocket, Jack Evans reluctantly put the key in the lock and turned it. The officer was the first to enter the room. Looking around he said, 'Well, well. Nice little haul you've got here. The Chief Constable will be pleased.'

Moira had followed them. She stood horrified at the sight of the cases of liquor, tinned Spam, fruit, nylon stockings, cartons of cigarettes, medical supplies and American army bed rolls. 'Jesus, Mary and Joseph,' she said, crossing herself. She looked at Jack in disbelief. 'You bloody fool!'

The senior detective said to her, 'We'll be taking your husband in for questioning. There'll be a police car along soon to take this stuff away. It'll be used in evidence.'

'What'll happen to my husband?' she asked.

He gave her a sardonic smile. 'I'm sure you must know the answer to that, love. Just take a look around you. You'll be wanted for questioning later too, Mrs Evans.'

She looked at him with a horrified expression, but didn't say a word.

Jack turned to his wife, a haunted look on his

face. 'I'm sorry, Moira,' he said in all but a whisper.

She glared at him. 'I hope you're satisfied!' She watched as they took him away in handcuffs.

By now, several of the locals had gathered. Grace Clarke came over to her and said, 'I'm sorry your man's in trouble. What are you going to do?'

Her mouth in a tight line, Moira said, 'I'm going to open the bar while I still have a business to run.'

'Where's Maggie?' asked Grace.

'She's at home and I don't want her bothered. She's got her own life to run.'

'But she'd want to know,' insisted Grace. 'She'd be furious if you didn't tell her, you know she would. You need her here now. You can't face this alone.'

Moira hesitated. 'Perhaps you're right. Would you pop round to her flat and put a note in the door for me?'

'Of course I will, and when I come back, I'll help you serve in the bar. You can't run the pub on your own. You want any barrels changing, my Nobby can do it.'

'Thanks, Grace, you're a good friend.'

It was almost closing time when Maggie hurried into the Bricklayer's Arms with Joshua. She went behind the bar and hugged her mother. 'I've only just heard, I came as soon as I could. Are you all right?' she asked anxiously.

'To be honest, darlin', I'm damned if I know. I've been serving all night like a zombie. Thank

246

God for Grace and Nobby. They've both been helping.'

Maggie turned to the couple and thanked them. Nobby drew her aside. 'Listen, Maggie,' he said. 'The brewers will probably take your old man's licence away. You need to go and see them if you want to keep this place on.'

She smiled at him. 'I've already decided to do so, in the morning. I'm going to ask them to transfer the licence to my mother or me. Do you think they will?'

'I don't know about your mother, they may think she knew all about what was going on. But you, that's different. These days, with so many men away at war, it has been known for a woman to hold a licence. After all, you've worked in the bar for long enough, you grew up in this place, you know the ropes. Just let them see you mean business, that you have the Bricklayer's and the brewers' best interests at heart. They can only say yes or no.'

'Thanks, Nobby. I'll talk it over later with my mother, and thank you both for helping her. I won't forget that.'

'Your father's an idiot,' he said. 'He's got a good business here.'

'I know,' she agreed. 'We both tried to talk to him, but you know Dad.'

'That I do. Stubborn as a mule. You all right now? Anything I can do?'

'No thanks. I'll see you tomorrow.' She looked at her watch and turning she rang the brass bell. 'Time, ladies and gentlemen – please!' she called, looking at Moira. 'Don't you worry,

Mum,' she said, 'we'll manage.'

When the customers had left, Maggie locked the door. 'You go and make a pot of tea, Mum. Me and Joshua will clear up.'

Moira looked at him. 'I'm so sorry,' she said, 'I haven't said hello. You must think me very rude.'

'Not at all, ma'am. You've got a lot on your mind, but I sure would enjoy a cup of tea.'

She smiled at him and left the bar.

He walked over to the tables and started clearing the dirty glasses. 'Your poor mother looks exhausted,' he said. 'I'm really sorry about your dad.'

'I should never have left home!' declared Maggie angrily. 'It was the biggest mistake of my life.'

'Ask yourself honestly, would it have made any difference to this outcome? Could you have stopped your father in his dealings?'

She looked thoughtful. 'No ... I tried often enough.'

'Then stop blaming yourself. But now you do have a problem, so what's the next move?'

'I'll go and see the brewers tomorrow, I'll ring them in the morning and make an appointment. I need to talk to Mum about the licence.' She looked around the dingy bar. 'This place could do with a facelift,' she said. 'If we could get the licence, I'd like to paint the bar a brighter colour. The walls are covered in nicotine and beer stains.'

'That would be a good move.'

'But hardly possible. I could never close the bar for two days, could I?'

Joshua studied the area. 'You could close it for a morning, that would be long enough.'

'What are you talking about?'

'If you got the licence, I could get some of my friends to come in overnight and paint it. I could arrange for all-night passes, maybe even get the paint. The final touches could be finished in the morning. How does that sound to you?'

She walked over to him and put her arms around him. 'Joshua Lewis. Why is it that you always seem to be around when I'm in trouble?'

He smiled down at her. 'Maybe I'm your guardian angel?'

'After the way you kissed me tonight, I don't see you as angelic.'

He kissed the tip of her nose. 'Me neither. Come on, let's get this place cleaned up.'

A little later, Moira called from the kitchen. 'The tea's made!'

They walked hand in hand out of the bar.

Joshua didn't linger for very long. He had to return to his base, for one thing, and he knew the two women needed to talk, but he was worried for Maggie's sake.

At the front door he took her into his arms. 'You know, honey, I'm around if you need me, don't you?'

She smiled up at him. 'You don't know just how much of a comfort that is at this time.'

He tilted her chin and looked deep into her eyes. 'I love you, Maggie, and don't you forget it.' He kissed her longingly, then opened the door and left.

Maggie returned to the kitchen. 'I'll stay with

you tonight, Mum. I don't expect you feel like being alone.'

'Ah, you're a good girl, darlin', so you are. I could do with the company that's a fact.'

'We need to see the brewery, Mum. Ask about having the licence in one of our names. What do you think?'

A frown creased her mother's brow. 'The detective said that they want to question me. If I'm under suspicion, the brewers wouldn't consider giving me the licence. But you wouldn't know anything about your father's dealings.'

'But I did. We both did.'

'But they don't know that! No, you be the innocent party here.' She thought for a moment. 'No. It's you that must take it ... if they agree.' She shook her head, her expression one of great sadness. 'You should have seen your father when they took him away. He looked a broken man.'

Maggie's lips pursed in a straight line. 'And so he should! Didn't we warn him often enough?'

'We did that, but we all have our weaknesses, you know. I'll go along tomorrow and see him.'

'What, and listen to his excuses? He'll tell you he did it for you. Stuff and nonsense! He did it for himself. Well, you may be able to forgive him, but I don't think I ever will. Come on, Mum. Let's get to bed, we've a lot to see to tomorrow.'

The following morning, Maggie rang the head office of the brewers and arranged to see them later that afternoon. She rang the factory also and spoke to the foreman, explaining her situation,

250

and was given the week off to sort out her problems.

Later that afternoon, she sat in the reception area of the brewery, waiting to see the managing director, trying to run over in her mind just what to say. She'd slipped back to her flat and changed into a grey costume and a clean, crisp, white blouse, hoping she looked businesslike. Taking a deep breath, she followed the receptionist who had come for her.

Albert Watkins, a middle-aged man with a bald head and bluff exterior, looked at Maggie as she walked into his office. 'Please sit down, Miss Evans,' he said. 'Now, what can I do for you?'

'My father is the tenant of the Bricklayer's Arms in College Street. You may not yet be aware of the fact but he was arrested by the police last night,' she began.

The man looked surprised. 'No indeed, I know nothing about this,' he said, his brow furrowing.

'Unfortunately it's true. He was involved in the black market, I'm sorry to have to tell you.'

'I'm sorry too, Miss Evans. Your father has been a tenant for a number of years at the Bricklayer's Arms.'

'Eleven,' said Maggie. She sat upright in the chair and looked Mr Watkins straight in the eye. 'I know this will reflect badly on the brewery and I apologize for that, but I'm here to ask you to transfer the licence to me. I can promise you that if you were to do so, the brewery would be assured of my loyalty. The business is a good one and, in my hands, it will do even better. After all, I was brought up in the public house. I know

251

how to run the bar, how to please the customers. I know I could succeed.'

He looked at her with an expression of curiosity. 'Why would you want to take such a thing on, at your age?' he asked. 'After all, I would have thought a young woman such as yourself would have other things to occupy her.'

'I want to secure my future and safeguard my mother's,' she said.

'Ah, I see. Well it's very commendable of you to be so concerned about your mother, in the circumstances.'

'She's a good, hardworking woman,' said Maggie evenly. 'She's an asset to the Bricklayer's Arms. The regulars all know her, and the other customers are charmed by her.' She smiled at him. 'She's Irish, you know. They have a way with them.'

He smiled back at her. 'You have quite a way with you too. But tell me, aren't you already employed?'

'Yes, I'm doing my bit for the war effort. I work in a munitions factory in Southampton.'

'Then how can you do that and run a business?'

'It's not a problem, Mr Watkins. I can always work an early shift. We can employ a barmaid to help in the morning if it's necessary. I of course will be there myself for the evenings when we're busiest. I know how to change a barrel, clean the pumps, clean the cellar. I've learnt a lot in eleven years,' she said with a note of defiance in her voice.

Mr Watkins's eyes twinkled. 'I'm sure you have.

252

I will have to put this to my board, you under-stand?'

'Yes of course.'

'I'll let you know in about a week's time. But thank you for coming to see me so promptly. It couldn't have been easy for you.'

His kindness and understanding was almost her undoing. She fought back the emotions that threatened to overwhelm her and rose from her seat, held out her hand and said, 'Thank you for your time. I hope you can convince your board that I will do a good job for them.'

'I'll let you know,' he said. 'Good day, Miss Evans.'

Maggie made her way to her flat, knowing that Ivy was on a late shift. Fortunately her friend was there. 'Ivy, I need to ask you a favour.'

'First tell me what happened to your father.'

'They are holding him until this morning when he goes before the magistrate to be charged. I doubt they'll let him out on bail.'

'Oh, Maggie, I'm so sorry. What can I do to help?'

'This morning I went to the brewers' hoping they'll give me the licence. Meantime I'm staying with Mum. If I get it, I won't need the flat.'

'And if you don't, then I suppose you and your mother will need this place?'

'I'm afraid so. I'm really sorry to mess you about, but I wondered if you would stay on until we get it sorted?'

Ivy put an arm around her. 'Of course. And if it all turns out well, I'll take the flat over.'

'That would be great. At least one problem would be solved, either way.'

Ivy walked into the kitchen. 'I'll make us a cup of tea whilst you pack a few things. I'm sure everything will be fine. After all, so many blokes are away at the war, and you do know the business.'

She walked back into the room. 'Imagine you, a pub landlady!'

Maggie smiled. 'Don't count your chickens.' The smile faded. 'God, I hope it works out that way, for Mum's sake.'

Whilst Maggie was sorting things out with Ivy, Moira went to the local police station to see her husband.

She was shown into an interview room, given a cup of tea and told to wait. Five minutes later, Jack was shown into the room.

He sat opposite her and, taking her hands in his, he said, 'I'm sorry I've got you into this mess. But I told them you knew nothing about it, only that I kept some stuff in the room. You must say the same.'

She shook her head slowly. 'Was it worth it, Jack?'

'It seemed like it at the time,' he said.

'So what's happened?'

'They charged me this morning and I'm on remand. They're taking me to Winchester prison later today. But I'm worried about you and the pub.'

'It's a bit bloody late for that, isn't it?' she snapped.

254

He lowered his head. 'Yes. I'm sorry.'

'Our Maggie went to see the brewers today. She asked if they would let her take over the licence.'

'Did she!'

'What else did you expect? Someone has to do something. Thank God for her, I say, and you might think a bit more kindly of her too! I have to get back. I'll ask when I can come and visit you in Winchester.'

Later in the afternoon, Maggie arrived at the Bricklayer's Arms in a taxi, with a couple of suitcases.

'What's all this?' asked Moira.

'I'm moving back in,' she said.

'But your flat...'

'Ivy's going to take it over.'

Moira's eyes lit up. 'That's splendid. But what happens if we lose the pub, where will we live?'

'We move back to the flat. Ivy and I have it all arranged.'

Putting her arms around Maggie, Moira said, 'Whatever would I do without you?'

She held her mother at arm's length. 'Remember when I was small, that teacher kept picking on me at school, making my life hell?'

Moira smiled at the memory. 'Yes.'

'What did you do?'

'I went and sorted her out. I complained to the headmistress.'

'There you go, now it's my turn to take care of you. Any news of Dad?'

'I went to see him while you were at the

brewers. He's been charged and now has to wait for his case to come up in court.'

'Well, that ought to give him some time to think about his mistakes!'

'Oh, Maggie. Don't be so hard on him. He's in a sorry state.'

'Hard! He put your livelihood in jeopardy. What did he care?'

'We all make mistakes, Maggie. You'll make a few in your lifetime. Some can be forgiven, a few never can. But only you know which they are.'

Maggie was filled with guilt. How right her mother was. Hadn't she just made a disastrous mistake with Steve Rossi? Turning to Moira she said, 'You're right. Who am I to judge?'

Her mother looked at her and said, 'I do believe you've grown up whilst you've been away. Before, you would have never been so philosophical, just angry. We'll just have to keep our fingers crossed and hope that the brewers see you as a good tenant. It's all in the lap of the gods, darlin'. Come on, let's get something to eat before we get the bar ready for opening.'

It was a busy night. All the regulars dropped in at some time or other, to tell the two women how sorry they were to see them in this position and hoped that all would work out for them.

Joshua arrived with several of his friends, introducing them to Maggie and her mother. They were a jolly crowd, mixing well with the locals, taking their goodnatured ribbing about their country and their colour. Joshua played the piano and all the customers sang together. The pub almost had an air of celebration about it, which was strange in a way, Maggie thought, with her father languishing in a prison cell.

When the bar closed, Joshua stayed behind to help with the clearing up, making sure the outside gents' toilet was locked, and the cellar, sweeping the floor and emptying the ashtrays.

'You'd make a good landlord yourself,' remarked Moira.

He looked at her in surprise. 'Gee, do you think so?'

'What are you going to do when you leave the army?' she asked.

'Me, Mrs Evans? I'm a jazz musician. I'll just go where the music is.'

'Well that sounds hopeful. Music is important, everyone can always do with a cheery tune.'

'He plays jazz, Mum. A cheery tune isn't quite how I'd describe it!' grinned Maggie.

'I can do those too,' he quipped. 'I did tonight, didn't I?'

'Yes, I suppose you did.'

Moira said goodnight and left the two of them together.

'I like your friends,' said Maggie, now held in Joshua's warm embrace.

'I'm glad,' he said, 'because they are the ones who'll be coming to paint up this place when you hear from the brewery.'

'You're jumping the gun a bit, aren't you?' she said.

'No, Maggie. I'm sure when you went to their offices, the man there was impressed by you. How could he not be?'

She kissed him. 'You have such a way with

words,' she said.

'That's because I read so much,' he laughed. He gazed at her and said, 'It's so good to feel you so close to me. I don't want to let you go.' He kissed her forehead, her eyes, her neck and her mouth.

She returned his kisses eagerly, responding to the growing passion between them.

He reluctantly released her. 'I must get back, much as I'd like to stay. I'm on duty tomorrow, but I'll call you. Give me the telephone number.'

She wrote it on a piece of paper and put it in the top pocket of his uniform. At the door he took her into his arms and kissed her again.

'If I don't go now I'll be AWOL,' he said as he opened the door. He caught hold of her hands and said, 'Remember that I love you. I'll see you real soon.' Then he walked away into the dark.

As they sat together in the kitchen having a cup of Ovaltine, Moira said to Maggie, 'That Joshua's a nice fellow. He thinks a lot of you, doesn't he?'

'Yes, Mum, he does and I feel the same way about him.' She saw the worried expression on Moira's face. 'I know it may seem wrong to you and other people, but we love one another.' She tried to explain. 'Joshua is a very special person. I don't suppose I'll ever meet another man like him. His colour is unimportant to me. It's what's inside that counts.'

'But it's what's outside that people see, darlin', and they can be so cruel.'

'I've already learned that, Mother! It makes no difference.'

'You have the same stubbornness as your father. Just think about it will you, please? It's not that I don't like the lad, it's you I'm concerned about. There is no happy ending here. Surely you can see that?'

'I'm content to take what is given to me, for as long as it lasts,' said Maggie. She put her hand over her mother's. 'I know it will end in tears. Joshua will eventually be posted and we probably will never meet again, but don't you see, until that happens, we want to be together.'

'Well, Maggie, you're old enough to make up your own mind about such things, and I'll always be here to pick up the pieces. That's what mothers are for.'

Maggie leaned forward and kissed her cheek. 'I really love you,' she said.

In the military prison in Southampton, Steve Rossi paced up and down his cell. He hated being cooped up like this. All the years of his youth in New York, taking his chances with the law, he'd only ever spent one night behind bars, until his father bailed him out the following morning. It was driving him crazy.

He was angry at being caught, furious with Doug Freeman for pushing him into making a mistake, but worse, eating away at him, was the relationship between Maggie and Joshua Lewis. Although Maggie had sworn that the two of them had never been lovers, he didn't believe her. The thought of those black hands touching her body, *his* girl's body, gnawed at him every hour of the day. He wanted to get his revenge on

259

both of them. If only he could get out of this stockade. There must be a way, a moment when the guards were careless. So far there had been no chance, but he'd remain alert. His moment would come and he'd be ready.

Chapter Eighteen

The following week seemed endless, waiting to hear from the brewers. Maggie and Moira spent every spare moment, when the pub was closed, cleaning: washing walls; scrubbing floors, windows and window frames; trying to get the grime out of the benches and tables in preparation for the redecorating, in case she was successful in her bid to take over the licence.

Ivy, too, had come along to help when she wasn't working, and had been roped in from time to time to serve behind the bar, much to the locals' amusement. Ivy with her cheek and ready wit had livened up the atmosphere considerably. It had also been therapeutic for her, helping her to get over her broken marriage and the loss of Bob Hanson.

She'd written to Len weeks ago to verify the end of their relationship and in return had received a letter from him full of vitriolic rhetoric. She'd torn it up, burnt it in the fire and forgotten about him, saying to Maggie, 'He's in the past. Now I have to make a new future for myself.'

Maggie had admired the determination and resilience shown by her friend and wondered just how she herself was going to cope when the day came for Joshua's departure, when he would leave Southampton ... and her.

He was now a regular in the pub, coming around when he wasn't on duty, helping out whenever he could, even washing the glasses when required. The locals were getting used to him, most of them accepting him into their midst.

Moira, too, could at last see the hidden depths to this man, through her various conversations with him, and could well understand why Maggie felt the way she did; yet still, deep inside, she worried about the consequences of their friendship.

Finally the letter from the brewers arrived and Maggie picked it up and took it into the kitchen, her fingers trembling as she held the unopened envelope.

'It's here,' she said to Moira who was clearing away the breakfast dishes.

'Oh my God!' Moira's eyes grew wide. 'Well, are you going to read it or are you waiting for me to have a heart attack with worry!'

Sitting down at the table, Maggie tore open the envelope, removed the letter and read it. She looked up at her mother without saying a word.

'I knew it!' exclaimed Moira. 'We're out on the street. We'll have to move, I'll have to find a job.'

Maggie grinned broadly. 'You can go if you really want to, but me, I'm staying – if only to see my name over the door!' She held out the letter to her mother.

Moira snatched it out of her fingers and quickly read it ... then threw the paper into the air with a whoop of joy and, pulling Maggie out of her seat, danced around the room with her. They both eventually collapsed into chairs, breathless and excited.

'My darlin' child,' she said. 'You're a marvel. Dear Lord, what a relief, I was dreading having to move. If that had happened I honestly don't think I could ever have forgiven your father!'

With an expression of amusement Maggie remarked, 'I wonder what he'll have to say about it?'

There was a momentary flash of anger in Moira's eyes as she said, 'He's in no position to say anything. And I'll be honest, it will give me a certain amount of satisfaction to tell him of your success.' She looked at her daughter and asked, 'Will you have him back after he's served his time?'

Maggie hesitated. 'I've not given the matter any thought. In any case he hasn't been tried yet, so we don't know what's going to happen to him.'

'Of course we do! He'll do time! What we don't know is how long.'

'Let's wait and see, shall we,' said Maggie. 'He may not be able to accept that now I'm the landlady. You know how stubborn he is. It's a situation maybe he couldn't cope with. Anyway we have much more important things to think about at this moment. I'll call Joshua at the camp. Now we can get on with brightening up the place.'

Joshua, true to his word, arranged for a working party of three of his buddies to come along a couple of nights later, loaded down with paint, brushes and ladders. As soon as closing time was called, they set about their task with a vengeance.

With pots of cream-coloured paint, supplied by Joshua, the men began. There was much hilarity exchanged between them as they worked. As one of them said to Maggie, 'This is much better than doing army chores with a bad-tempered sergeant watching over you.'

The two women made numerous pots of tea and sandwiches to keep them going, but at one o'clock in the morning, Joshua walked over to them both. Putting an arm around Maggie's shoulders he said, 'You and your mother should go to bed. You have to go to work and Moira has to get the bar ready for opening tonight.' He tilted her chin and kissed her slowly. 'I'll see that everything's all right. And ... I'll be here when you wake up.'

She put her arms around his neck and looked up at him, the love she felt for him shining out for everyone to see. 'Don't work too hard,' she said and kissed him goodnight.

The following morning, Maggie was awakened by the smell of bacon wafting up the stairs. Feeling ravenous, she quickly washed and dressed, putting on her dungarees ready for the factory, and ran down to the kitchen. There, Joshua and her mother were cooking eggs and bacon and making toast. The boys who'd been working in the bar were sitting around the table, stuffing themselves.

'Hi, Maggie, come on in and get something to eat.'

She looked at her mother, who grinned at her. 'Not only do we have a workforce, but they brought their own food with them. Sit down, darlin', or you'll be late for work.'

One of the boys poured her a cup of tea, saying with a wide grin, 'I'm getting real worried, Maggie, honey. I'm actually beginning to like this stuff!'

She laughed at the look of mock horror on his face. 'I can't begin to thank you all enough,' she said.

'Any time, Maggie. Anyway we're not quite finished, there's just a few little touches, that's all. By lunchtime, we'll be gone.'

'I can't wait to see it.'

She made to get up from the table, but Joshua was behind her and put his hand on her shoulder, saying, 'Now you just finish your breakfast or there'll be no time before you go to work.' He kissed the top of her head and sat beside her.

She looked at him and said, 'You look tired.' She looked around at the others. 'You all look as fresh as daisies!'

Joshua laughed. 'It's because I had to keep this lot working.'

'Yeah,' said another. 'He wouldn't let us rest for a moment. A hard man, this Corporal Lewis is.

God knows what he'll be like as a sergeant!'

She looked at Joshua with an expression of surprise. 'A sergeant?'

He looked a mite embarrassed. 'I've been promoted.'

'That's just great,' she said, thrilled for him.

'The army's rewarding him for getting that Rossi put away,' said one of the men.

'Maggie's not interested in hearing about that,' he said quickly. Seeing she'd finished her breakfast he said, 'Come with me and take a look at the bar.'

She followed him. As she stepped into the room from the hallway she gasped in surprise. It didn't look the same place at all. Everything was pristine and clean. The walls were light and bright, the window frames had been painted and the ceiling was now white, all traces of nicotine removed. It made the area seem much bigger. They had even put a fresh coat of varnish on the bar.

She turned to him. 'Oh, Joshua, thank you so much.' She flung her arms around him and rained kisses on him.

He held her at bay after a moment. 'Hey, you're not playing fair,' he said. 'You smother me with kisses and then you take off for work.'

She ran a finger over his mouth. 'Well, it wouldn't make much difference would it?' she said archly. 'You are always in such control of your feelings.'

He gazed down into her eyes. 'You think that's easy for me?' he quietly asked.

'I don't really know. You tell me.'

He held her close and caressed her cheek. 'I want you more than anything in this world,' he said. 'I long to take you into my arms and make love to you. The thought of it keeps me awake at night.'

'Don't you realize that I feel the same?'

His searching gaze looked deep into her eyes as if he needed confirmation. 'Honestly? Do you really want me too?'

She caught hold of his hand and placed it on her breast. 'So badly, that I ache to be in your arms.' As he went to protest she shushed him.

'We'll just have to wait for the right time. I must fly or I'll be late for work.' She walked back to the kitchen and said, 'I don't know how to thank you, boys, you've done a grand job. The next time you come in, the first drink is on the house.'

They all cheered. And Moira smiled.

'I'll see you later, Mum,' said Maggie as she kissed her on the cheek and left for work.

When she returned later that day, it was to see the front of the Bricklayer's Arms covered in bunting and a large notice which read, *Under New Management*. She chuckled with glee, and entered the side door.

Moira greeted her as she walked into the kitchen. 'Did you like the flags?'

Maggie hugged her mother. 'It all looks so good. I hope we have a good night.'

'To be sure,' said Moira, 'there'll be no spare room. Word has got about that you now have the licence and everyone's coming.' She looked at

Maggie. 'That Joshua has been wonderful. I can see why you think so much of him.'

'I'm glad you understand. It means a great deal to me.'

That night, the bar of the Bricklayer's Arms was packed to capacity. Ivy, who had come to join in the celebrations, was roped in to help behind the bar, and the place buzzed. The pianist had been hired and the pub rang with the sound of voices. 'Roll me over in the clover, roll me over lay me down and do it again', sang the locals, much to Maggie's amusement.

Joshua arrived at nine o'clock and was greeted warmly by the customers, who knew that he and his men had done all the hard work and, being concerned for the welfare of Maggie and her mother, were grateful to the GI for his help. They all wanted to ply him with drinks. He accepted one or two, buying drinks back for the locals, which went down well with the men.

They tried to teach him how to play darts, and there was much joshing and teasing until he got his eye in and started hitting the right spot on the dart board.

Nobby Clarke, who was his partner, was highly delighted. 'You'd better join the darts team, lad. With a bit of practice you'd be quite useful.'

At last, closing time arrived and Maggie rang the bell. She and Ivy, Moira and Joshua cleared up the mess. Ivy called a taxi and went home, and Moira made some Ovaltine and wished Maggie and Joshua goodnight, going upstairs to her room and leaving them alone in the kitchen.

'I was real proud of you tonight,' he said, pulling Maggie onto his knee. 'You'll make a good landlady.'

'I'm glad for Mum's sake,' she said. 'At least I've secured a future for her.' She gazed at Joshua, her expression one of uncertainty. 'But I'm wondering about mine.'

'What do you mean?'

'When you eventually leave.' Tears welled in her eyes. 'I can't bear the thought of you going away.'

'Neither can I, darling. I don't want to leave you, ever.'

'Oh, Joshua. What are we going to do?'

'We could always get married.'

His proposal took her by surprise. 'Do you really mean that?'

'Of course I do. I'm in love with you, Maggie. If I get shipped out I don't want to have to say goodbye and never see you again ... but it wouldn't be easy. You know how people react to mixed marriages. There would be great opposition. I don't know how your mother would feel about it, or your father.'

Maggie closed her eyes in despair. 'My father would go mad! Mother, maybe not, I don't know. But what about your own family?'

'My father's a pretty broadminded guy, but this might throw him. Remember where I come from.' He stroked her hair. 'Why are we worrying about other people? It's how we feel that's important. We love each other, but you have to really think about the consequences. It won't be a piece of cake.'

She leaned forward and kissed him. 'I don't care! I love you, Joshua. I don't want to lose you.'

He cupped her face in his hands and kissed her passionately. 'You'll never do that, I promise, but I think we need to tread carefully.'

'What do you mean?'

'Let's keep this to ourselves for a while, get people used to seeing us together. Then, when the time is right, I'll go to the captain and get the necessary details and documentation.'

He frowned and Maggie asked, 'What is it?'

He let out a sigh. 'Getting permission ordinarily isn't that simple, but with us, it's going to be more difficult.' Then he smiled at her. 'As long as we love each other enough, then we'll face such things when the time comes.'

'What will we do when the war is over? Where will we live?'

'Hey, slow down. Let's wait. No one knows how long the war is going to last. When it's over, then we'll make plans. OK?'

She entwined her arms around his neck. 'Whatever you say, sergeant.'

As she climbed into bed that night, Maggie was filled with happiness. Yes, Joshua might be shipped out eventually, but at least she knew that in the end they'd be together. She desperately wanted to share her joy with her mother, but realized the wisdom of the man she loved. In time, the sight of them together would become accepted, and hopefully that would make things easier ... except for her father. That would be a huge problem to face.

Moira walked towards the prison gates, her pass clutched tightly in her hand, her heart racing. This was her first visit to Winchester Prison. She felt her stomach tighten as the prison gates clanged shut behind her. Handing over her pass, she was sent to the waiting room.

The room was full. The atmosphere was charged as she sat among women alone, others with children. There were one or two older men, maybe waiting to see a son, she guessed.

At two o'clock they were ushered across the cobblestone courtyard into a large room with tables and chairs. At one end were cubicles, and she wondered what they were for.

The woman sitting beside her saw her expression of curiosity and said, 'That's for the lifers.'

Moira nodded, then sat twiddling her gloves with a feeling of shame, not wanting to look at anyone.

There was a sound of footsteps as the assortment of men entered the room from within the prison. She looked up and saw Jack limping towards her. He looked pale and tense.

'You came then!'

'What's that supposed to mean?' she snapped, angered by his attitude. 'I wrote and told you that I would.'

'I'd have thought you'd have better things to do.' He glared at her, his lips drawn in a tight, bad-tempered line. 'Well, did she get the licence?'

Incensed by him, Moira said, 'Yes of course she

did. The brewers could see that she was trust-worthy and competent. They're not fools!'

'Not like me, is that what you mean?'

'You've changed your bloody tune, haven't you? Last time I saw you, you were full of apologies for all the trouble you caused.'

'Well I hadn't been banged up in this hellhole then.'

Moira sat bolt upright, her back stiff with anger. 'Now you listen to me, Jack Evans. You're here because you did wrong. No one asked you to get mixed up with Sonny Taylor, and if you'd listened to me and our Maggie, you wouldn't be here now. You'd still have a pub to run!'

'Oh yes, it was all my fault.'

Moira looked at him in amazement. 'If it wasn't down to you, I'd like to know just who you blame... And don't you dare say you did it for me, because as God is my judge, I wanted none of it.'

There was a sudden flush of guilt on his face. 'I know, I know,' he said, calming down as he took out a cigarette and lit it. 'When did Maggie officially take over?'

'Yesterday – and you wouldn't believe how busy we were.' Moira couldn't stem her enthusiasm. 'Some of Maggie's friends from the 552nd Port Company came and painted the bar. It looks lovely,' she said with a broad, beaming smile.

'That's the niggers' company! What the hell were they doing painting my pub?'

Moira cursed her runaway tongue. But she wasn't going to lie to him. He was going to have to know about Maggie and Joshua sooner or later. 'They were all charming young men. They worked hard, all through the night, to get it done. And it isn't *your* pub any longer!'

He let the jibe pass. 'But I don't understand. How did they come to be there?'

Taking a deep breath, Moira said, 'Maggie is friendly with one of the sergeants.'

'She's still going out with the Yank then?'

Moira was beginning to wish she'd left well alone, but now was the opportunity to put things straight. She'd seen the love shared between Maggie and Joshua, and if necessary she'd stand by her daughter against anyone, as long as she was happy.

'This is a different GI,' she said, 'the son of a preacher, a nice lad.'

Jack's eyes narrowed. 'Are you telling me that my daughter is going out with a darkie?'

'Yes.'

'Well, she's no daughter of mine. I'd be ashamed to own her!'

'Strange that, isn't it Jack? I've never heard Maggie say she was ashamed of her father being a gaol bird!' She stood up. 'If you feel like that when you've served your time, I assume you'll be making your own arrangements. You certainly won't want to come and live with us if you feel that way about Maggie. And after all, she is the licensee.' She walked out of the room before he could answer, leaving him sitting there, open-mouthed.

Moira walked to the station, seething with rage. How dare he talk like that about his own daughter – the girl who stepped in and saved the day and her future. As far as Jack was concerned, she could have been out on the street with no place to go, all because of his lust for money. Joshua Lewis was more of a man than her husband could ever be, and as far as she was concerned, Jack Evans could go to hell! Maggie was the one she worried about. And if she was forced to choose between them, it would be no contest.

Chapter Nineteen

The following weeks went by quickly enough. The pub was doing well, the brewers were pleased and Joshua Lewis was now firmly established as the man in Maggie's life.

Working at the Bricklayer's Arms and the factory didn't give Maggie much free time, so Ivy came to serve in the bar some evenings, to help Moira and to allow Maggie a night off to spend with Joshua.

One evening when he called to take her out, Moira was in a state because a close friend of hers had had an accident and she had offered to go and stay the night.

Maggie quickly changed her plans and stepped in. With Ivy's help, she ran the bar until closing time. She'd insisted that Joshua go and spend the evening with his friends instead of hanging around, wasting his free time. So he went, returning to help them just before closing time.

'I'll get us some sandwiches,' Maggie said to him when they were alone at last. 'Come through to the kitchen.'

As she cut the bread, he stood behind her, his hands round her waist, kissing the back of her neck, caressing her bosom.

'Stop it, I'll cut myself,' she protested.

'For goodness' sake, put the darned knife down will you! I haven't seen you for thirty-six hours.'

She did so and turned to face him. 'I'm sorry about–' she began, but she could say no more as he covered her mouth with his own, kissing her ardently, caressing her softly, until she returned his passion with hers.

When at last he released her, she said, 'About tonight, I'm sorry everything was messed up. What time do you have to be back at the base? How long do we have?'

He gazed into her eyes. 'We don't have any rush, honey. I've got an all-night pass.'

'You do?'

'Mm. So we don't have to worry. We even have time for those darned sandwiches, if you really insist.'

'But I thought you'd be hungry,' she said, giving a mischievous grin.

'I'm sure hungry, but it ain't for food.'

She gently put her finger to his lips, and cried out as he pretended to bite on it. 'You know, darling, I've got an all-night pass too. Mum is away.'

'Are you trying to lead me astray, young lady?'

'Yes please,' she said, 'this is the opportunity

we've been waiting for. It would be a pity to waste it.' Taking him by the hand she led him upstairs to her bedroom, closing the door behind them.

He took her into his arms. 'I really do love you, Maggie,' he whispered against her hair.

'I know, and I love you too.' She reached up and kissed him eagerly.

'I've waited so long for this moment,' said Joshua. 'Dreamed of holding you close, making love to you.'

She stepped out of his embrace and unbuttoned her dress, letting it slip to the ground. He helped her remove her underwear until she stood naked before him.

He smoothed her soft skin, as he gazed at her.

'You are so beautiful,' he said, as he kissed her shoulders, her neck, her ears, her mouth.

She undid his tie and cast it aside. He took off his shirt, trousers, his olive green singlet, his socks and lastly his underpants. Maggie looked at his fine frame standing before her and thought he should be cast in bronze, he was so perfect a picture of manhood.

They lay on the bed, close together, exchanging embraces, discovering the delights of each other's body, both wanting the night to be memorable.

Joshua was a gentle, thoughtful lover, whispering in his deep voice, telling the woman in his arms how much she meant to him, how much he desired her.

'I'll always take care of you, darling,' he said. 'We'll have a great future together. We'll be real

275

happy, just like my parents, you'll see.'

Maggie caressed his broad shoulders, kissing him with a passion that showed just how much she wanted him. 'I love you more than anything else in the world,' she whispered. 'Nothing is going to keep us apart'

Joshua insisted on wearing a condom to protect her, saying, 'The last thing we need is for you to become pregnant before we get married. There'll be plenty of time for a family after.'

'Mrs Maggie Lewis,' she said. 'I like the sound of that.'

He caressed and kissed her, teased her, until the longing for him to take her was almost unbearable. But as she felt him inside her at last, she wanted desperately to have his baby, to have something that was part of him, of their love for one another, but she realized the wisdom of his words. One day she would hold his child. And she was content to wait.

At long last they slept, entwined in each other's arms, content in their love for one another.

When her mother returned to the pub the next day, Joshua had already left. Maggie made Moira a cup of tea and asked after her friend.

'Poor soul,' she said. 'She slipped and broke her ankle. Her daughter couldn't get down from Cheltenham until today. She's taking Elsie home with her until it's better, so that's a relief. I'm sorry I mucked up your night out with Joshua.'

Maggie felt the colour rise in her cheeks. 'It was all right, I didn't mind. He went out with some of his mates, but he came back before closing time to help us.' She looked straight at her mother. 'He stayed the night.'

'I see,' said Moira. 'It's that serious then?'

'Yes, Mum. Joshua has asked me to marry him and I've said yes.' At the look of consternation on her mother's face, Maggie said, 'If I can't have him, I don't want anyone.' She waited, tense with nerves. She would marry him, but she really wanted Moira's blessing.

Her mother stretched out her hand and took Maggie's in hers. 'If you feel that strongly about him, then no one has the right to interfere.'

Maggie flung her arms around her. 'Oh thank you, Mum. I don't care about Dad, but I really wanted you to understand. We know there will be problems, but we're prepared for that. For the moment, though, we'll keep the fact that we intend to marry to ourselves. We want people to get used to us being together.'

Moira thought that was a good idea. 'When you can pick the day is the time to make it public,' she suggested. Then she added, after a moment's hesitation, 'If you're going to marry the boy, then I suppose it's all right for him to stay at night, when he can. After all, you're more or less engaged.'

Maggie was taken aback by her mother's liberal view, but then she'd always been somewhat different from most women. Still, knowing how strongly held were her views, about the two different cultures mixing, Maggie admired her change of heart. It just proved to her the strength of a mother's love.

Although Maggie and Joshua were happy in their love for each other, it was not without its down side. Their relationship, now out in the open, caused a great deal of gossip. People took sides. Angry words were exchanged in private ... and in public. Human nature being what it was, those who wanted Maggie's happiness gave her no trouble, but for others the relationship was distasteful, and these people made their feelings known to all and sundry. One or two spoke out to Maggie herself.

'How can you bring yourself to consort with a black man?' one of the men asked one day when the bar was quiet. 'If you were my daughter I'd take my belt to you!'

Maggie's nostrils flared. 'Well I'm not your daughter and I'll thank you to mind your own business!' she retorted.

Another spoke up: 'It's not right. What's wrong with your own kind?'

'Now you listen to me,' said Maggie. 'I don't tell you how to run your life, don't you dare try and interfere with mine.'

Later that night a group of women sat in the corner of the bar, talking in low voices. 'Well I think it's bloody disgusting!' said one. She grimaced. 'Imagine those black hands touching you. Ugh! It makes me shudder.'

Another, called Edie, grinned slyly. 'You know what they say, don't you? Black men are very well endowed.' The others looked at her with interest. She leaned closer. 'I was told that a nigger's dick is usually huge.'

They turned and looked at Maggie, each

thinking her own dirty thoughts. One turned back to the woman. 'Ask her if it's true. Go on. It's your turn to get the drinks in anyway. Ask her. I dare you!'

Edie glared at the faces all turned towards her.

'Or are you all mouth?' taunted her friend.

Picking up the empty glasses, Edie strode over to the bar and asked Maggie for four halves of bitter. When she returned with the full glasses, the woman asked quietly, 'Could you settle an argument for us?'

Maggie, completely unaware, smiled and said, 'If I can.'

Edie leaned over the counter and said, 'It's a bit personal. I don't want the men to hear.'

Maggie put her head close to the woman's.

'Well ... me and my friends have heard that the dick of a black man is really big. Is it true?'

Maggie's head shot back and she looked at her customer with a shocked expression, then with one of anger. 'Go and wash your mouth out,' she snapped, 'and at the same time, swill your filthy mind.' She glared at Edie, and over her head at the others, then she walked around the counter and crossed to the women who were sitting at the table smirking, waiting for an answer.

'It seems, ladies, and I use the term loosely, that you're interested in my sex life! Well it's none of your business and I'll thank you to keep your dirty little minds to yourselves.'

'Now look here,' said one, 'that's no way to talk to your customers.'

Maggie froze her with a look. 'You keep a civil tongue in your heads if you want to drink in my

279

pub or I'll bar the lot of you!' She stomped back behind the bar.

Nobby Clarke had overheard some of the exchange and said quietly to Maggie, 'That's all they've got to do, love, is gossip about someone. And after all, girl, you must expect it.'

She pressed her lips together stubbornly. 'It's still nobody's business but mine.'

He gave a sardonic grin. 'Come on, Maggie, you know better than that. In a local pub everyone knows everyone else's business and has an opinion about it. You must expect the flak.'

She walked away to serve another customer. Nobby was right of course, but such smutty talk made her relationship with Joshua sound sordid ... and it wasn't.

Strangely, most of the men seemed to accept the American more easily than the women. They saw in him a man of pride and intelligence. He was easy to talk to and was, in their minds, a real man. They admired his skill at the piano, his sense of humour, and easily exchanged quips with him. In a male way, he got on well with them and they with him. In private, however, talking to their wives, now aware that the GI sometimes stayed the night, they didn't feel so at ease with the thought of him sharing a bed with Maggie.

Joshua was not unaware of the hostility of a few of the customers. With those, he kept himself to himself. It was Maggie that he was worried about, and the effect the gossip was having on her. But when he approached her on the subject, her stubborn chin stuck out.

'This is my pub! If they don't like it they can drink elsewhere! I'm not hiding our relationship. I'm not ashamed of it ... are you?'

He took her into his arms. 'Of course not, how could you even think so? I love you. But it breaks me up to see the looks some of them give you, and the way they whisper behind your back. All because of me.'

She gazed up at him and said softly, 'Joshua Lewis, you're worth more than any of them. No one is going to spoil what we have.' She pulled his face down to hers and kissed him passionately.

The winter of 1944 was a severe one, with a chronic shortage of coal. Maggie managed to get a supply of logs from a farmer who had felled some trees on his land. But the threat of war was still hanging over everyone when the Germans continued their raids over London with the new V2 rockets. Everyone in Southampton wondered if they too would be faced by these terrifying weapons. Fortunately they escaped them, apart from two attacks from the V1 flying bombs, popularly known as doodlebugs. Happily there were no fatalities, but everyone's heart was heavy when in late November one of the rockets scored a direct hit on a Woolworth's store in New Cross, killing 160 people.

Maggie was upset when she read the news and asked Joshua, rather scathingly, 'If there is a God, how can he let this happen?'

Seeing the anguish in her expression he put his arm around her and softly said, 'I don't know, honey, I haven't got all the answers. All I can tell you is that without my faith in the Lord, I wouldn't have survived all these years.'

She snuggled into him. 'Oh, Joshua. If only I could be as certain as you.'

'No one can make you believe, Maggie. It's something you feel in your heart. Even non-believers turn to God in times of trouble. Some of the most hardened soldiers start to pray as they go into battle. There must be something there.'

There was much excitement all round as Christmas approached. Joshua was able to help them out with some food, as whenever any troops were invited into a civilian's home, it was army policy to allow them to take goods with them.

Moira had managed to get enough ingredients together to make a cake, and between them all they decorated the bar with old paper chains from the loft and the pub looked very festive.

Joshua's company gave the local children a Christmas party and a bag of sweets each, saved from the soldiers' weekly ration. Gifts of Canadian apples arrived and even a few bananas. One of the white officers acted as Father Christmas, figuring the children would comment if Santa Claus had a black face.

Maggie had been invited along. She joined in all the games and watched with delight as Joshua played with the children, crawling around the floor with two little ones on his back, giving piggy-back rides to the bigger ones. They all loved it. She thought how wonderful it would be when he'd be able to hold their child in his arms.

They all sang nursery rhymes and played Piggy in the Middle and Blind Man's Buff, the children having a high old time with Joshua in the middle of the room, hands outstretched, trying to find a quarry.

In the military court, Steve Rossi stood before the panel of American officers and heard the sentence. He was to serve two years in an army prison, after which he would be shipped home, in disgrace.

He marched out of the courtroom with an arrogant glance at the men who had passed sentence on him, but inside he was seething, cursing beneath his breath.

During the forthcoming weeks in the prison, he watched every movement of all the departments, looking for a way out. He monitored the incoming army trucks bringing the food and medical supplies. The laundry from the nearby army camp was sent here to be washed by the inmates and at last, one day, he saw a possible way of escape. If he was very smart, he figured he could do it. But he would have to bide his time and pick the right moment. Timing was everything. Already, though, he was in the right place. He'd been given a job in the laundry.

Christmas Day was busy. The bar was open for a couple of hours, but closed for the evening. The pub was packed with locals, drinking and singing whilst the Christmas dinner was cooking. It was traditional to go to the pub in the morning, and no wife with any sense would plan to eat before closing time.

Nobby Clarke and his wife were in good form, Nobby playing darts with his mates, Grace singing at the top of her voice. He came over to the bar to order more beer and smiled at Maggie. 'You're doing a grand job here, girl. I take my hat off to you. Have you seen your father? What does he think about it all?'

Maggie shook her head. 'He doesn't approve of my association with Joshua, so there's no point my seeing him, I'd only have to listen to him going on about it.'

'What a pity,' said Nobby. 'That Joshua is a grand chap, even if he's black. But being a father myself...'

Maggie didn't take offence. 'I know. But I love him, you see, and love is colour-blind.'

'Yes, my dear, love is a very powerful emotion. It can be good and it can be destructive. You just take care, that's all.'

Ivy was in good spirits. As she was still living alone, without a steady boyfriend, she had been invited to stay on after closing time and partake of the Christmas dinner. She was invaluable behind the bar with her quick wit and speed at the beer pumps. The regulars liked her.

She beamed across at Maggie. 'This isn't a bad life, you know. When the war's over, I wouldn't mind a job as a barmaid. Plenty of company ... you meet lots of men.'

'I'd have thought you'd have had enough of them,' teased her friend.

'Don't be daft!' She sipped a gin and tonic

someone had bought her. 'You know me, Mags. I always like to have someone interested. In a bar I can flirt without getting too involved ... unless I want to.'

'And you want to.'

Ivy pulled a face. 'I miss the sex,' she confessed. 'Ever since Bob left, I've been a bloody saint. What I really need is a good seeing to.'

'Ivy! You're incorrigible.'

Her friend sidled up to her. 'Listen you. You're all right. You get plenty of it with Joshua.' As Maggie blushed she continued. 'And I'm happy for you. Sex is healthy – but I'm getting very frustrated!'

Later, at closing time, Maggie saw Ivy enjoying herself under the mistletoe with several willing customers and smiled. She was such a character. But she was happy to see her bouncing back after her ordeal with her husband and her lover.

The Christmas dinner was a happy occasion. Moira had managed to buy a small turkey and Joshua had arrived that morning bearing gifts which were opened after they'd eaten and listened to the King's speech. He'd bought a scarf and some American chocolates for Moira, nylons for Ivy, who was delighted, and for Maggie, a gold locket on a chain.

She slipped it around her neck and smiled at her lover. 'I'll put a picture of you in it,' she told him. She had some snapshots taken during the summer. She could use one of those. She handed him a gift.

He opened it eagerly and was thrilled to find a

285

book about New Orleans and the jazz musicians that played there. There was also a record of Duke Ellington and his music.

His eyes shone with pleasure. 'I'll cherish these,' he said. His eyes twinkled as he held up the record. 'Maybe there's hope for you after all.'

'Maybe not,' she laughed. 'I still like Frank Sinatra. I haven't changed that much.'

He held her close to him. 'Wait until you come to a few clubdates with me when we're married,' he said. 'Then you'll hear real music.'

After the others had exchanged gifts, they sat and drank a cup of coffee before Ivy said, 'I'll wash up. It's the least I can do.'

Moira insisted she helped, leaving Joshua and Maggie alone to sit in the front room. As she explained to Ivy, 'He has to be on duty at five o'clock. It'll give them some time together.'

'It's been one of the nicest Christmases ever,' he said as Maggie snuggled down in his arms, fingering her locket.

'I'm so happy you enjoyed it,' she answered. Turning, she put an arm around his neck and kissed him. But there was a sudden sadness about her expression that he immediately noticed.

'What is it?'

She looked at him and said, 'I was only wondering where you'll be this time next year.'

'Come on, honey,' he said. 'Cheer up. By that time the war will be over, we'll probably be married and settled down somewhere.'

'I do hope so.' She looked at the clock on the

286

mantelpiece. 'You'd better be off,' she said reluctantly, 'or you'll be late back.'

Joshua went to the scullery and thanked the others for their gifts. He walked with Maggie to the front door, where he took her into his arms. 'This war can't last for ever, darling. We'll be together real soon, you'll see.'

She watched him walk down the street and waved as he turned the corner. Looking across at the houses opposite she could see all sorts of family gatherings through the windows and for once she thought of her father. She wondered what he was doing behind prison bars, and was filled with pity for him.

Chapter Twenty

In the laundry of the military prison Steve Rossi wiped the sweat away from his forehead. His singlet was soaked with perspiration too. The steam from the presses that ironed the damp sheets filled the air, making it like a Turkish bath. He hated it here. Fastidious about his appearance, he knew he reeked of sweat. He was allowed to shower at night, but every day was the same.

Gone were his dreams of a big business, of being able to show his father just what a successful man he was. He would be sent home in disgrace ... a failure. His hot temper had already got him into trouble, adding more months to his

287

sentence, but he had a plan. He had no intention of staying in this hellhole for very much longer.

Every day a big army truck arrived with the dirty laundry from several of the army camps nearby, taking with them on the return journey the clean linen, stacked in large wicker trolleys. He intended that one of the trucks would take him out in the back of it, as soon as the opportunity presented itself.

He smirked to himself as he pressed yet another sheet and folded it. He'd got it all worked out, and when he was free he'd go looking for that bitch and her boyfriend. He was going to settle the score there all right. Maggie Evans was his. Wasn't he the one who took her lovely little cherry? He grinned with satisfaction at the memory. Well, he'd have her again. Christ! He hadn't had a woman since he'd been shut up inside this place and he ached for sex. Masturbation wasn't the same, not the same at all. He closed his eyes as he thought of the feel of her soft flesh, her open legs, and he felt the movement in his loins as he imagined himself thrusting deep inside her.

'Rossi!' one of the soldiers in charge called. 'Get on with your work!'

Steve cursed. The regime in here was harsh. Every morning they were on a parade ground, marching before breakfast, then they dispersed to do whatever job had been assigned. The army had no time for prisoners and worked them until they crawled into their bunks at night, exhausted. That way, they figured there would be less trouble. Well that was fine with him. He was fit and he was tough, but soon they'd have one less to think about.

Jack Evans sat in his cell, alone, after dinner on Christmas Day, wondering what was going on at the Bricklayer's Arms. He remembered previous Christmases. The bar would be packed as usual, plenty of singing, plenty of beer, an entirely different atmosphere than inside this God-forsaken place.

He admitted to himself, as he smoked a cigarette, that his incarceration had been his own fault. He realized how badly he'd let Moira down and how grateful he should be to Maggie. And he was now scared that when at last he was free he'd have nowhere to go.

Moira was still angry with him. She'd come to see him just before Christmas, but she'd been so cold towards him that it was like talking to a stranger. He longed to tell her how sorry he was and make things right, but he realized that things between them would never be the same.

Deep down he was proud of Maggie, the way she'd stepped in and taken over the licence, and cursed his own foolishness – on occasion. And as the days passed he became more and more depressed. Life inside His Majesty's Prison was no life at all. There were some very dangerous people here; people doing life for murder, for grievous bodily harm; and sexual offenders, as well as petty criminals.

He'd learned very quickly to keep his head down and stay out of trouble. Thankfully his age and disability kept him safe from sexual advances, but many of the young men were in real danger. The screws turned a blind eye to so much, to keep the place peaceful. It was like sitting on the edge of a volcano, waiting for it to erupt.

Only the other day a couple of the old queens had a fight over a new inmate, a pretty boy of twenty. He'd never forget the look of terror in the lad's eyes as he stood, pressed against the wall, petrified. It was at such times he realized just how much he'd thrown away.

He tried to come to terms with Maggie and her boyfriend, knowing if he was ever to return to his home, he'd have to accept whatever the situation was, but for him that was very difficult. In his eyes, people should stick to their own kind. Not just their own racial kind, either; Catholics should marry Catholics, Jews should stick with Jews. The basic cultural differences only led to trouble. That was the way he'd been brought up. He blamed the war. Without all these foreigners around, life would not be so complicated. Wives wouldn't be lonely without their menfolk around, wouldn't be tempted into having a fling. Without the war ... he wouldn't be here sitting in this cold cell, wasting his life.

A few days later, he was surprised to be told he had a visitor, and even more surprised to see Maggie sitting waiting for him. He sat opposite her, embarrassed that she should see him in his prison clothes, wondering what she was thinking.

Maggie had made the decision to see her father after Christmas Day. Although she couldn't forgive him for letting her mother down, she remembered the good times, when she was a child, when he was a happy man and when she was close to him, and she felt a little guilty that she'd stayed away. She'd talked to Joshua about it and he'd persuaded her that it was the time to forgive and forget.

As he'd said, 'Bitterness only festers inside, it's like something bad that grows and grows until it seeps into your soul. We all need forgiveness for something at some time in our lives.'

And so she was here; but she was really nervous. She knew well his bigoted attitude, and now that she and Joshua planned to marry in the future, she was more than a little concerned about Jack's reaction.

'Hello, Dad,' she said, shocked by his prison pallor. 'How are you?'

'Not so bad,' he said. 'Congratulations on getting the licence. Your mum tells me the pub is doing well.'

'Yes, it is.' How stilted their conversation was, she thought, but it wasn't easy for either of them to act naturally.

'I believe your friend had the place painted up.'

'Yes, and they made a very good job of it.' She saw the tightening of his jaw as he spoke and, knowing him as well as she did, realized he would find this a difficult thing to accept, knowing who the workforce had been.

'My friend Joshua arranged for them to do it, he supplied the paint too, so it didn't cost a penny.' At least that ought to please him!

'So, who is this Joshua chap?'

'He's a sergeant in the US Army.'

There was a bitter twist to his mouth as he said, 'You seem to go in for sergeants, don't you?'

Maggie could feel her anger beginning to rise inside. Her father always seemed to have this effect on her ... nothing had changed. But she was determined to stand her ground.

'Joshua Lewis is a fine man,' she said determinedly. 'I don't expect you to like him, because of his colour, and that's a shame, because he's intelligent, talented, and he loves me.' She saw the narrowing of Jack's mouth, but ignored it. 'We plan to get married sometime in the future.'

'You what!' he yelled. The people around them turned and stared at the loud remark.

'You heard me, Dad. We're in love. Do you remember what that was like? Did you ever love my mother?'

This completely shook him. 'Of course I did! What sort of a question is that?'

'Then if you did, try and remember just how it felt.' She saw the look of embarrassment on his face and hoped for once she'd be able to get through to him. 'We want to spend the rest of our lives together.'

'But Maggie, the man's black.'

'I know that, Dad. And I know that things won't be easy for us, but we're prepared to face all that – even if it's against my own father's wishes.'

Jack looked at the stubborn expression on his daughter's face and knew whatever he said wouldn't change a thing. 'I can't help the way I feel, Maggie. And if you insist on this, you'll find life far more difficult than you can possibly imagine.'

'I've already had to cope with prejudice, Dad. Joshua has had to cope with it all his life, but he's a lovely man. I don't want anyone else.'

He shook his head. 'I don't know what to say. I just can't bear the idea – not my own daughter.' He took a cigarette out of a packet and lit it.

Maggie changed the subject. 'When does your case come up? Have you heard?'

'In a couple of weeks' time, so I'm told.'

'Is it awful in here?' she asked.

'Pretty grim, but let's face it, it's my own fault.' He looked somewhat shamefaced as he said, 'I'm sorry I let you and your mother down. If I hadn't, your life wouldn't be in the mess it is.'

He cheeks flamed with anger. 'You haven't understood a word I've said, have you! I love this man and, like it or not, I'm going to marry him and you'd better get used to the idea, Dad.'

He didn't answer.

She rose from her chair. 'There really isn't any more to be said, is there?' She waited but there was silence.

She turned and walked away.

On the journey home, Maggie wondered just what would happen when her father had served his time. She couldn't see him without a home, which meant that there would be trouble on his return. Well, she just wouldn't have it. She was the landlady now, she'd chosen Joshua as her man and her father would have to behave – or else!

She tried to talk it over with her mother when

293

she arrived home.

Moira was furious at his attitude. 'I can't forget that, without you, I could be homeless and penniless. I'm glad that he realizes his mistake, and I'm sorry that he's where he is. It terrifies me when I go there, and it must be a thousand times worse for him. But the least he could do is to see your side of things. That is typical of Jack Evans, though.'

Maggie put her arm around her mother. 'Yes, I'm afraid it is. But when eventually he's free, this is his home. I can't turn my own father away, can I?'

'Sure and where else would the silly sod go,' conceded Moira.

But Maggie knew that when that time came, things would not be easy. Apart from her own situation, there were too many recriminations left in the air. Moira still felt bitter and some of the customers, too, felt angry towards Jack. Oh well, thought Maggie. That would give them something else to chew over for a change! She was fed up with being the subject of their gossiping.

In the military prison where Steve Rossi was incarcerated it had been a busy afternoon with extra work for everyone as two companies had been out on manoeuvres and the battle fatigues, covered in mud, had to be washed. This had entailed the use of two army trucks to bring in the laundry. One of the washing machines had broken down and everyone was working under pressure to get it all finished.

During the rush and confusion to load the lorries, Rossi had hidden at the back of one of them, inside a wicker basket where he'd piled clean linen on top of himself. He held his breath hoping he wouldn't be discovered.

Eventually, to his great relief, he heard the engine start and felt the vehicle move away. It paused at the base entrance gates and a sentry peered inside the truck. Steve let out a sigh of relief as he heard the order to proceed.

It was Friday night and pay day. The Bricklayer's Arms had been busy as usual. The locals still milled around outside after closing time, chatting, whilst in the bar Maggie and her mother cleared the glasses and swept the floor.

Outside in an alleyway hid Steve Rossi, cursing to himself about the small groups of men, laughing and talking, wanting them to go home so he could try and find a way to enter the pub unobserved.

Eventually, one by one, they wandered off and Steve emerged from the dark into the empty street. He tried the doors to the pub but they were securely locked, then wandered along to the gate that led to the gents' toilet. The gate was open. He walked up the alleyway and into the toilet. He stood in front of one of the urinals and relieved himself, looking around to see if there was a back way out. Then he heard footsteps and quickly hid himself in a cubicle, closing the door to.

Maggie made her way to the toilets to put out the lights before she locked the gate. She turned up her nose at the smell of stale vomit and looked around to see where it came from. 'Damn,' she muttered. She'd best go and get a bucket of disinfectant and swill it away now, or by the morning it would be hard to shift. She turned away and was about to walk outside when she was grabbed from behind, a hand over her mouth to stop her screaming. She stiffened with terror as she heard the familiar voice.

'Hello, honey. How you doing? I bet you thought you'd seen the last of me.'

Steve spun her round and grinned broadly as he saw the fear reflected in her eyes. 'Not happy to see me? Now that is a disappointment. Well, baby, I'm sure glad to see you. I haven't held a woman in my arms for far too long.' He grabbed hold of a handful of her hair, trapping her head with his grasp and covered her mouth with his, kissing her roughly, his tongue making her choke.

Recovering from her shock, Maggie tried to push him away with all her might, but he still held her tightly.

'What are you doing here?' she asked. 'I thought they had you safely behind bars – where you deserve to be.'

His cruel laugh echoed around the empty room. 'My God you're a spunky broad, I'll say that for you.' Then the expression on his face changed as he glared at her. 'All the time I've been inside, I've thought of you.' He ran his hand over her breast, pulling her close with his other arm. As she struggled he put his hand between her legs. 'I remember this very well,' he said.

Maggie started to pound him with her fists, but he caught them in one hand and gripped them tightly behind her back, pushing her against a urinal. With his other hand he pulled up her skirt. 'Remember how good we used to be together, honey? Well, tonight will be the best ever. You'll be able to tell that black son of a bitch all about it. He won't want you then.'

Maggie went berserk, kicking out and catching Rossi in the shins. He yelled at the pain and let her go. She made for the door, but was dragged back inside and thrown to the floor.

She felt the cold of the tiles as she lay there, momentarily stunned as her head hit a corner of a basin. She felt Steve tearing at her skirt and knickers, then he was astride her. She fought to gather her senses and lashed out at him, her nails to his face, screaming for help. He hit her and she was silenced, but she continued to struggle, determined that this piece of dirt was not going to rape her. Steve Rossi's strength overwhelmed her and she felt helpless as he gripped her flailing arms in one hand and undid his trousers with the other. He took out his swollen member and leered at her. 'Is this as big as that buck nigger's?' he asked.

'Get off me, you crazy bastard,' she yelled. 'I'll kill you before I let you touch me again.'

He laughed loudly. 'And how are you going to do that? Look at you, you can't move.'

And he was right. Maggie felt the helplessness of her situation. He had her body pinned down beneath him, her arms held above her head in one hand. Every time she tried to move he had her trapped between his knees. Quickly she sat up and sank her teeth into his chin, biting as hard as she could.

With a yelp of pain, Rossi let her go and she pushed him off her and got to her feet. She turned to run but he grabbed her around her ankle. She screamed as loudly as she could, but Steve was relentless. He caught her round the knees and pulled her to the ground.

'What the bloody hell's going on?' asked a voice from outside.

Maggie nearly collapsed with relief as Nobby Clarke stood in the doorway.

He quickly took in the situation before him and, swiftly hauling Maggie to her feet, pushed her outside. Then he grabbed hold of Steve Rossi, heaving him up from the floor and landing a punch any boxer would have been proud of, right on the point of the American's chin. Rossi sank to his knees, unconscious.

Maggie threw her arms around Nobby's neck and sobbed with relief. He extricated himself from her grasp and said sharply, 'Listen to me! Go and call the police. Don't hang about. I don't know just how long this bugger will be out for.' He pushed her towards the gate. 'Go! Now!'

Maggie ran for all she was worth and dialled 999.

Later, she, Moira and Nobby sat in the bar drinking a glass of brandy each. 'I keep it for medicinal purposes,' Moira explained.

'How can I ever thank you, Nobby?' Maggie asked in a trembling voice.

'Well, you could always say I wasn't looking well, about once a week, and give me a glass of this stuff,' he said, shrugging off her thanks.

Maggie, still shaken by her ordeal said, 'If you hadn't come along...'

'Now you listen to me, girl. Wondering what might have happened is the worst thing you can do. I got there in time, that's the thing to remember.' He turned to Moira. 'It was quite by chance that I stepped outside to let the cat out and saw the gate to the gents' toilet still open. I thought that was unusual, Maggie is always so careful to lock up. I walked over and that's when I heard her screaming.' He looked across at her. 'You've got a fine pair of lungs on you, my dear.'

She gave a wry smile. 'You did look funny, Nobby, when the police arrived. Sitting on Steve Rossi like that.'

'Well, love, I wasn't sure how long it would take for him to come round. I wasn't taking any chances. Best be off home. My Grace will be thinking I've run off with a blonde.'

Maggie let him out of the side door. She hugged him and kissed his cheek. 'Thanks,' she said.

He patted her shoulder. 'At least he's safely locked up. The army will take him out of the local cells tomorrow. They won't like the idea that he escaped, they'll watch him like a hawk in future. Now you go and get a good night's sleep.'

She watched him walk away, thankful that she had such good neighbours. But the experience had shaken her and her hands were trembling as she locked the door. Much as she tried she couldn't help wondering what Steve would have done if Nobby hadn't intervened. Would she still be alive?

That night she had nightmares.

Joshua was furious when he heard all about it the next day. Maggie had never seen him so angry and it surprised her. 'It's all over,' she said, trying to calm him.

'That scum!' he cried. 'How dare he try to touch you! What right has he to behave in such a way?'

She laid a hand on his arm. 'For heaven's sake, calm down. Nobby arrived in time to save me.'

Joshua gathered her into his arms and, holding her tightly, kissed the top of her head and said, 'If anything bad happened to you, I don't know what I'd do. You should have someone here all the time to protect you from this kind of thing. I want to be here to look after you.'

She snuggled against him. 'I know, I know, but you can't be.'

He led her over to the settee and they sat down. Putting his arm around her he said, 'The sooner we get married the better. Tomorrow I'm going to see the officer in charge.'

She looked up at him and said, 'Even if we'd been married you might not have been here.'

'I know that, but I don't want us to wait any longer. Let's not waste any more time. The sooner you're my wife the better.'

That night in bed, they made love, but this time without any means of protection. They both wanted to be close to one another, to be truly as one. 'I'll never let anyone hurt you again,' Joshua promised as they lay in each other's arms. 'You'll always be safe as long as I'm around.'

Maggie was so happy. It didn't matter what the future held; as long as Joshua was beside her, she could stand up to anything. She would be with the man she loved and the rest of the world could go to hell!

Joshua, too, knew the way ahead would be hard. The first thing he would have to do tomorrow was write to his father and try and explain how it was that he intended to spend the rest of his life with a white woman. In the depths of Mississippi, that would be an unthinkable thing, but he had faith in his father's understanding; he only hoped that he could come to terms with such a situation. He knew also that Maggie's father would find it difficult to accept. Already their problems had begun.

Chapter Twenty-One

When Ivy came around to the pub the following afternoon to visit, she was appalled at Maggie's news.

'You're going to *marry* Joshua? But you can't!'

Surprised at her friend's attitude she asked, 'Why not?'

Ivy looked at her accusingly. 'I can't believe you have to ask. I thought you were just having an affair. You can't marry a darkie!'

Maggie felt the blood drain from her face, but then the rage that surged through her flushed her cheeks. Her eyes flashed with anger. 'How dare you sit in judgement on me. You, the woman who got engaged whilst you were still married to another man!'

Ivy looked embarrassed; nevertheless, she returned Maggie's angry gaze. 'That was different.'

'You're damned right it was different! For one thing it was illegal, and for another you lied to both men. Joshua and I are free to make up our own minds, and no one gets hurt.'

'Oh come on, Maggie. Grow up. No one gets hurt, I can't believe you're that stupid.'

'What do you mean?'

'How does your mother feel about her daughter marrying a black man? And as for your father, he'll have a fit! And how about Joshua's parents? How will they feel?'

'I don't know about Dad, although I can imagine. Mum knows, and she's accepted that we love one another. As for his family, Joshua is writing to them.'

'He's from the Deep South remember. Think about it ... the Ku Klux Klan! It's for real that, not just like in a film. You couldn't live there. They'd kill you both.'

'We haven't made any plans yet. We'll probably stay in England.'

Ivy shook her head sadly. 'And who would employ him?'

'He's a musician. He'll always find work.'

'If he stays here, he'll have a hell of a life if you get married ... and so will you.'

'We don't care!' said Maggie, defiantly.

'Brave words - but very foolish ones.' Ivy put an arm around her friend's shoulder. 'Listen to me, Maggie. You're like the sister I never had. I understand you love him and he loves you, but this is wartime, all sorts of madness exists. Afterwards, though, when everything returns to normal ... think about it. People will stare at you both wherever you go, they'll gossip, taunt you. Insult you.'

Maggie would not be deterred. 'What you fail to understand, Ivy, is that none of that matters. I would rather put up with all that prejudice than lose the man I love. Life without him would be meaningless.'

'And what if you have children? What sort of a life will they have?' Ivy was relentless.

Maggie closed her eyes to shut out the angry words she'd heard from others when they'd seen a woman with a coloured child in a pram. She could hear them now. 'Harlot! Nigger lover!' But she would be a married woman. Yet she knew that there was a strong element of truth in her friend's words.

She gave Ivy a piercing stare. 'We'll bring them up to realize how much they are loved, and teach them about the ignorance of others. They'll know what a wonderful man their father is, and in time others will know that too... I'll make bloody sure they do!'

Ivy looked at her friend for a moment, then she went and put her arms around her. 'I'm sure you will. You have more courage than I do, love. But if you feel that strongly, no one's going to change your mind. And you're right, it's not my place to have a go at you, after all you stuck by me when I needed you, and I'll do the same.'

Maggie hugged her. 'There you are, you see. In time others will accept us as a couple too, and if they don't, it's their loss, not ours.'

'Your father will be the one you have to worry most about,' said Ivy.

'Well he's just been sent down for six months. At the end of that time he'll be so glad to come home, he'll be more reasonable. By then I'll be married anyway.'

To add to her problems, Maggie had to go to the police station to give a statement about Steve Rossi. The local police knew her through her father being in the pub business. Many of them had stood in the hallway of the Bricklayer's Arms, drinking beer; had seen her grow up; and they were aware of her relationship with a coloured soldier. They were less than understanding.

The sergeant who took her statement was scathing. 'You young girls look for trouble, mixing with the GIs,' he said shortly. 'They all look the same in their uniforms, you have no idea what sort of men they are, yet you lead them on!'

Maggie's cheeks flamed with indignation. 'I didn't lead him on, I had no idea he was there. I didn't deserve to be nearly raped!'

'But you'd had a relationship with this man before, hadn't you?'

She couldn't deny it.

'I don't know what the world's coming to. Before the war most women were content to save themselves for the man they married. But nowadays, they give themselves to anybody!'

'That's not true, and you have no right to talk to me like this. I came to give a statement about a man who attacked me, not to get a lecture on my morals.'

He pushed a pad and pen over to her and coldly said, 'Write down exactly what happened, from beginning to end.' He rose from his chair. 'I'll be back later.'

Maggie watched him go, filled with anger at his righteous attitude. And he was the type she would have to face up to when she married Joshua. It made her furious that so many could be so bigoted.

She wrote out her statement, finding it very difficult reliving those terrible moments, knowing that others would read it and know of her humiliation. When she'd finished, she signed it in front of the sergeant and left.

On her way home she walked through the rose garden in front of the Civic Centre. The beds were devoid of flowers at this time of year and the fountain wasn't flowing. Come the spring, the parks would be full of colour, but now most of the trees were bare, standing like sentinels over the parkland.

She hated the winter and longed to see the growth of spring. It was like a renewal of life as the daffodils bloomed and the trees were covered with cherry blossom. Now, in the month of

January, there was little to cheer her. But as she stopped at the newsagent to buy a paper and saw the shocking pictures of the skeletal figures of the prisoners of Auschwitz, she counted her blessings.

Joshua had at last heard from his father. The pastor had been shaken by his son's plans, and pointed out that there would be no life for them in Mississippi, but he hoped that if they were to marry and stay in England, they would face a better future. He wrote:

My son, knowing you as I do, you must have found a wonderful woman to make you so determined to go down this path. One hopes and prays that as the years pass, all races can live happily together. My prayers will be with you, and my blessings on your union.

Joshua smiled softly. He could almost hear his father's voice as he read the words. He was a man ahead of his time. One day in the future it would be nice for them all to meet up, perhaps with their own children. He would show the letter to Maggie. At least they had most of their family on their side. If only Maggie's father would accept them, it would make them really happy.

He had confided his plans to Ezra, who had looked at him with eyes wide with astonishment. 'You're going to marry Maggie! Have you gone crazy, man? For Christ's sake, remember where you come from. At home we don't have the freedom we have here, as well you know. You think it will be any better in England, once the war is over? Take a look in the mirror, Joshua. You're still as black as the day you were born and that's what these limeys will see. The colour of your skin. Black and white don't mix, man. Maggie too would have a real hard time.'

'You forget, my friend, my world is music. There, there is no colour bar. With music, your talent is what counts. I can get work in London. We'll be just fine, you'll see.'

Joshua sat in a chair in front of his commanding officer's desk.

'Sergeant Lewis, you've applied to marry an English girl.'

'Yes, sir. That's right.'

'As you know, sergeant, the army is especially concerned about the GIs who apply to us to marry. In wartime things are so different. Once the soldiers return home and settle down, we are worried that when things are normal, the men may decide that it's all been a huge mistake. They catch up with the girls they left behind, then we have unhappy war brides left in a foreign country. It's not a situation that we relish. Apart from which, there is still a war raging in Europe. What happens if you are sent there and killed? Would it be fair on your bride? She'd be a widow before she had a chance to be a wife. These things happen, after all.'

'I do realize the difficulties, sir. But my girl and I love one another.'

The officer smiled kindly. 'If I had a dollar for every time some GI told me that, I'd be a rich man.' He became serious. 'I don't need to tell you of the particular difficulty in your case, Lewis.'

'No, sir. Maggie and I have talked long and hard about the future. We know it won't be easy, but we want to be together for the rest of our lives.'

'And nothing I can say will dissuade you?'

'No, sir.'

'Then we'd better make an appointment for her to come and see me.'

Joshua left the office with a wry smile. The appointment wasn't for another three weeks: no doubt giving him time to change his mind.

Later that evening, after the bar was closed, he and Maggie sat talking about the forthcoming interview.

'I don't care what he says,' she said firmly. 'Nothing is going to change my mind.'

He kissed the tip of her nose. 'That's my girl.' He took his father's letter from his pocket and handed it to her.

When she'd read it, tears brimmed in her eyes. 'What a lovely man. If only my father could think like him.'

Joshua held her close. 'We'll meet the obstacle of your father when the time comes,' he said.

Looking at the letter again she said, 'Your father thinks we should stay in England, rather than go to the States.'

'He's probably right, although New York is pretty cosmopolitan.' He put his arm around her. 'In any case, you would probably feel happier being near your mother. London isn't too far away.'

'Will it be easy for you to find work?'

He chuckled. 'Sure will. Even now there's plenty of clubs with small dance floors needing musicians, and when the war is over, the big bands will come back into their own. Listen, honey, a good pianist can always find work. And in time, I'd like to form my own jazz band. Given the right breaks, who knows, I may make a name for myself.'

'Well if the performance of your group at the Guildhall is anything to go by,' she smiled at him, 'I can see your name in lights!'

'I've been trying to think of a name for a small band. How about "The Cool Cats"?'

She looked a little puzzled.

Joshua burst out laughing. 'I'm going to have to teach you American, honey. If you're hep, you're cool. A real cool cat.'

'Like a smart cookie, do you mean?'

'My oh my, you're learning already.'

'Well I know the pavement is the sidewalk, a vest is a waistcoat and a lift is an elevator. And we go to the movies not the pictures!'

He gazed at her in delight. 'I knew you were a bright girl, but maybe you'd better start teaching me the English way of speaking, if we're going to stay here after all.'

She kissed him soundly. 'Never. I don't want to change you in any way, I love you the way you are.'

Maggie related the conversation to her mother

309

the next morning over the breakfast table.

'Well there's no doubt about it,' said Moira, 'Joshua is a talented musician. And I can't tell you how pleased I am that you won't be far away. But what'll happen about the pub?'

'Now don't you worry. I'll definitely keep it on until the war ends. I can come down maybe three days a week, after all it doesn't take long on the train from London. You can look after it the rest of the time. Hopefully, Joshua will be busy. I'll need something to keep me occupied.' She gave her mother a searching look and asked, 'Were you deeply in love with Dad?'

Moira thought for a moment. 'If I'm honest I suppose I wasn't. I was fond of him, I admired him.' At the look of surprise on her daughter's face she said, 'Your father has been a brave man in his day. He met with prejudice himself, you know. He was taunted at school about his limp. Adults weren't much better, at times, but he rose above it. And he was kind.'

'You married him because he was kind!'

Moira laughed. 'Don't be daft ... he was a good kisser!'

They both dissolved into laughter.

'Oh, Mum. You really are the end.'

Her eyes still full of merriment, Moira said, 'Listen, your father in his youth was a lot of fun. We had a good time together. It's only as the years passed he became bitter.' The expression in her eyes softened. 'We used to be very happy.'

'Maybe you will be again,' said Maggie quietly. 'He made a terrible mistake, but I'm sure he's learned his lesson.'

Moira nodded. 'Yes. Yes, he has. And who knows, being inside may have made him realize what a good home and family he has.'

'I do hope so,' said Maggie, but in truth she didn't think he would change his outlook regarding her marriage to Joshua.

Chapter Twenty-Two

Whilst working at her machine in the factory the following morning, Maggie wondered just how long it would be before she and Joshua could name the day. She was anxious now to get on with the wedding. She didn't want a big one, just a small gathering at the registrar's office and a modest reception for her close friends and Joshua's.

She thought she'd better think about what she would wear. A simple dress, and a hat, she should have enough coupons for that. Ivy and one of Joshua's friends could be the witnesses. At least her mother would be there; but who could she ask to give her away in the absence of her father? There was only one man: Nobby Clarke. She'd have to ask him.

But when Joshua walked into the Bricklayer's Arms that night, Maggie knew something was wrong. His usual smiling countenance was set in grim lines. He asked her to step out from behind the bar and talk to him. She led him to the kitchen, her heart beating wildly.

He sat her down at the table, seating himself opposite, taking both her hands in his.

'What is it?' she asked.

'My company is being shipped out,' he said quietly.

Maggie felt as if her stomach had been gripped by an iron fist. 'Oh no! When?'

'The day after tomorrow.'

She felt the blood drain from her face and a feeling of nausea sweep over her. Joshua rushed to the scullery to fetch her a glass of water.

'Drink this,' he said.

When she'd recovered she asked, 'Where are they sending you?'

'To Germany. We're to join the US Ninth Army.'

Maggie knew that the fighting in Germany was fierce. The British and Canadian troops were fighting around Reichswald; the Germans were in disarray, drafting women into the army to bolster their forces. And now he was to be part of all this. She closed her eyes in despair.

Joshua rose from his seat and came around the table to her, taking her into his arms. 'We always knew it was possible, honey,' he said.

She sobbed against his shoulder. 'I know. I know. But we were so close to getting married. I've been thinking about it all day ... even what I was going to wear, who would give me away. Oh, darling, war is so cruel.'

He tipped her chin upwards and looked into her tear-filled eyes. 'But for the war, we would never have met, and that's something I wouldn't have missed for the world.'

She clung tightly to him. 'You will write to me, won't you? I need to know you're alive.'

'Honey, I'll write every second I get. But don't worry if the mail takes a long time to get through.' He kissed her eyes, her cheeks, her lips. ' I love you more than you'll ever know.'

'Will I see you before you go?'

He held her tighter. 'No, Maggie. I have to get back to camp now. I shouldn't really be here. All leave has been cancelled.'

She looked at him in horror. 'This is our last time together?'

He nodded. 'I'm afraid so.'

She looked into his large brown eyes and saw the anguish reflected in them. He kissed her again and she could feel the longing in him. 'I'm going to miss you so much,' she said. She caressed his face, wondering if she would ever see him again, feel his strong arms around her. If he was killed in action, she didn't know how she'd survive.

He cupped her face in his hands. 'I *am* coming back, Maggie. We *will* get married. I promise. I love you, honey,' he whispered. 'Always remember that. These past months have been the happiest time of my whole life, and we are going to grow old together.' There was a note of disappointment in his voice as he said, 'I was going to buy you an engagement ring this week; now I won't have time.'

'I don't need a ring. I'm already married to you in my heart, and I'll be here, waiting for the day you return, no matter how long that takes. I love

313

you too, darling, and I'm going to miss you terribly,' she said. 'Please keep safe.'

They clasped each other in one last desperate embrace, then walked to the door together.

He caught hold of her shoulders and gazed into her eyes. In his deep mellow voice he said, 'Let me look at you, Maggie.' He stroked her hair, her face; he took her in his arms and kissed her longingly, held her close for a moment, then he opened the door.

Outside a jeep was waiting. He climbed in and waved to her as the driver drew away. But there was no smile on his face, only an expression of great sadness.

As she watched the vehicle depart, she fingered the locket around her neck, lifted it to her lips and kissed it.

Moira popped her head around the bar door and asked, 'Has Joshua gone?'

Maggie was unable to do anything but nod.

Her mother closed the door behind her and stepped into the narrow hallway. 'Maggie, love. What is it? What's happened?'

'He's being shipped out. He came to say goodbye.'

Moira drew her into her arms and held her. 'Oh, Maggie, darlin', I'm so sorry.'

'Can you manage on your own, Mum? I can't face anyone tonight.'

'Of course I can. Anyway, Nobby's in the bar. If I get a rush on, he'll give me a hand. You go and have a lie down. I'll come up in a while.'

'I just need to be alone, Mum.'

'I understand. Away you go.'

Moira returned to the bar and served her customers automatically, her thoughts full of Maggie. She knew how distressed she would be. All the wedding plans ruined. If nothing else, however, this would be a true test of their love for one another.

Maggie lay on top of her bed, staring wide-eyed into space. Joshua had gone. She'd got so used to seeing him, of his being such an important part of her life. She tried to fill her mind with all the happy times they'd spent together; with the sound of his deep soft voice as he read poetry to her, his twinkling eyes when he teased her, as he so often did. She willed herself to remember the love they shared, his outlook on life, the tolerance he'd shown when people had been vindictive towards him, the plans they had for their future. But the realization that he was going away to a battle zone swept over her and she sobbed. 'God, if you really do exist, keep this wonderful man safe,' she prayed. And smiled to herself through her tears, remembering how Joshua had said that in times of need, people turn to the Lord. Who else could she ask to protect him, except a superior being?

When Moira crept upstairs some time later, Maggie had fallen asleep. Her cheeks were still wet with the tears she'd shed. Her mother covered her with a blanket and slipped quietly out, leaving the door open a little, as she had done when her daughter was a child.

Two months passed and Maggie read every newspaper to try and keep track of her man. The last newspaper article told her his company was just outside Mönchen-Gladbach and Germany was now recruiting boys of sixteen. Surely the war couldn't last for much longer?

She'd had one letter from him soon after he'd landed on foreign soil, telling her that he was safe and that he loved her, but with the censorship he was unable to say more. And she'd heard again, two weeks later. He was well, missing her terribly, and she wasn't to worry, but she'd heard nothing since. The letters were beneath her pillow and she read them every night, clasping them to her in the knowledge that these pieces of paper had been in his hands.

One morning a few days later she visited the doctor who told her she was almost three months' pregnant. By his calculations, her baby would be due around the middle of September. She left the surgery and walked home through the park. She looked at the daffodils, their bright golden trumpets swaying in the breeze, the crocuses peering out of clumps of grass, the sweep of the cherry trees. All around her was new life, and growing inside her was Joshua's child. She couldn't wait to tell her mother.

Moira was sitting in the kitchen after closing time having a sandwich and a cup of tea when Maggie arrived. She kissed her mother on the cheek, fetched a cup and saucer from the scullery, poured a cup of tea, then sat down. She looked across the table at Moira. 'Mum, I've got something to tell you,' she began.

'When is it due?' asked Moira.

Maggie looked at her in astonishment. 'How did you know?'

'I can spot a pregnant woman a mile away,' she said, as she put her arms around her. 'But I'm afraid you're going to be hurt, being unmarried. You know what people are.'

'I don't care. When Joshua comes home, we'll get married. They can say what they like!'

Seeing the determination in Maggie's eyes, Moira admired her spirit. It reminded her of the time when, as a child, Maggie had climbed a tree, terrified at its height but determined to get as near to the top as possible. She'd made it, with a little help from her father. Now she was going to need all the help she could get.

'*We* won't let them say anything,' said Moira with a smile.

'Oh, Mum. I knew you wouldn't let me down.'

But Moira's brow furrowed with concern. 'What about your father, Maggie? You say he's coming back home when they let him out – what about him?'

'I'll tell Dad myself. He has a right to know.'

Moira shook her head. 'Well, that won't be easy. You know how he feels about...'

'Negroes! I'm not ashamed of my child's father and neither will his baby be.'

'Would you like me to come to the prison with you?' ventured Moira.

'No thanks, Mum. This is something I have to do for myself.'

The following day Maggie sat in the bare room in Winchester Prison, waiting with the other visitors.

The prisoners were allowed in and she saw the smile on her father's face as he walked towards her. He leaned across the table and kissed her cheek. 'Hello, Maggie, love. How are you?'

'Fine, Dad. You're looking better.'

He beamed happily at her. 'Of course I am. I only have another three weeks in here now, with my time off for good behaviour, then I'm a free man again.' He looked fondly at her. 'I can't tell you how much I'm looking forward to walking out of this place. I can already taste the pint of beer I'm going to have when I get back to the Bricklayer's Arms. How's business?'

'Dad, I've got something to tell you and I'm afraid you're not going to like it.'

His smile faded. 'What? You haven't lost the licence have you?'

Despite the seriousness of the situation, Maggie couldn't help smiling. 'No, that's secure. The business is doing well and the brewers are pleased with me.'

'Then what is it?'

'I'm going to have a baby.'

The shock which registered on her father's face shook her. He looked blankly at her as if he couldn't believe what she'd told him. He leaned forward with his elbows on the table and held his head with his hands.

She sat still and silent, wondering what he was going to say.

Eventually he looked at her. 'I was so very much afraid this would happen. Oh, Maggie, how could you?'

If he'd raged at her it would have been easier to

318

cope with, but the sadness in his eyes and the disappointment in his voice hurt her deeply.

'I really love him, Dad. And when he comes home, we'll get married. We'd have done so before if Joshua hadn't been sent abroad.'

'The father is the coloured boy then?'

'Of course! Who else would it be?' she asked shortly.

Jack didn't answer.

'He was shipped to Germany a few weeks ago.'

There was a flash of the old Jack as he said, 'Gone off and left you in trouble has he?'

'No, Dad, it wasn't like that at all. He doesn't know about the child. He loves me. He's going to return to England after the war.'

'And live off you and the pub, no doubt!'

She fought to keep the anger from her voice. 'Not at all. He's going to work in London. He's a very talented pianist.'

'Well there's lots of them around,' he said. 'We never have trouble getting them to play in the bar.'

'He's not that kind of pianist. He's a proper musician, he plays jazz. One day he's going to have his own band. He is a lovely man, Dad. I wish you could have met him, His father is a pastor in Mississippi. He taught Joshua so much. He loves books, he's kind and gentle and he wanted the best for me.' She hesitated then said, 'I have some photos here if you'd like to see them.' She took the snapshots out of her bag and handed them to Jack.

She watched his expression as he looked at

them. He couldn't hide the distaste he felt. He looked up and said, 'You may well have loved each other but this still doesn't look right to me. I'm sorry, Maggie, but I have to be honest.'

She shrugged. 'What you think about Joshua doesn't matter. What I want to know is, how will you treat my baby when it's born? He'll be coloured too ... and your grandchild.'

He looked surprised. 'Of course it will be.' He looked back at the snaps then at Maggie. 'I don't know ... I honestly don't know.' He saw the disappointment in her expression. 'I can't lie, Maggie, and as you well know, I always speak my mind.'

'That's very true.'

'All I know is how I felt when I saw young girls pushing prams with their Yankee bastards in them. And now my own daughter will be doing the same.' He saw her wince at his words. 'You'd better get used to such remarks, my girl, you'll hear plenty of them in the future.'

'I know it wasn't what you wanted for me, Dad, but there you are. I'm proud to be carrying Joshua's child. And he will come back – and we will be married.'

'What about your mother? How does she feel about all this?'

'She's upset, I won't deny it, but she's behind me.' She appealed to him once more. 'Mum told me that at school, and even after, people used to taunt you about being a cripple.' She saw him blanch. 'I would have thought that you of all people would have understood.'

'But this is quite different, Maggie.'

She gave him a hard look. 'Is it? That's not the way I see it...' She realized there was no more to be said on the subject, and to lighten the conversation said, 'I'll see you back at the pub when you get out. I'll have a pint pulled for you.'

'It had better be clear or I'll complain to the landlady.'

'You won't have any need for complaints ... and I hope I'll be able to say the same about you.'

'What do you mean?'

'You almost lost us the pub. Well, we – Mum and me – are ready to put that in the past. I expect the same consideration from you about my situation. Think about it.'

'Yes, I will.'

She kissed his cheek and left the prison. As she sat on the train she was still angry with her father. But he'd have to toe the line. Her baby came before anyone.

Alone in his cell, Jack Evans sat on his bunk smoking a cigarette, arguing with his conscience. He was too old to change the way he felt. But in his heart he was worried as to how he would feel when he first looked at his grandchild. He prayed that he would be able to accept it. He loved Maggie and was proud of her. She had looked so unhappy today, and he supposed if she truly loved this fellow, she had reason to be so. But he was afraid that when the baby was born, he'd hate it! And that would break her heart.

He stubbed his cigarette out and listened to the sounds of the prison: the clatter of footsteps, the voices raised in anger, the rattle of the keys. He supposed if he really thought about it, here he'd learned to keep his mouth shut to stay out of trouble. Well, he'd just have to do the same when he got home. But would he be able to, feeling as he did?

Chapter Twenty-Three

Sergeant Joshua Lewis sat, holed up in a half-ruined building, with his men. There was a lull in the fighting and they took time out to rest. Sitting with his back against the wall, near an open window, his rifle at the ready, he took a cigarette from a pack in his pocket and lit one. He tipped his steel helmet to the back of his head and wiped the sweat and dust from his brow. It had been a hard day's fighting. His company and others had followed the tanks into this small German town before peeling off into buildings along the way, searching out the enemy troops hiding there.

He took a snapshot of Maggie out of his jacket and gazed at it. How happy she looked. It had been taken in the park in Southampton last summer. God how he missed her. He hoped like hell she'd received his last letter. It was important for him to let her know he was still alive. He put the picture away as he saw the officer in charge making his way towards him.

'Sergeant. You OK?'

'Yes, sir.'

'Did you lose any men today?'

'Two, sir.'

The lieutenant looked weary. 'We have to make a concerted effort to clear these streets.' He looked at his watch. 'In ten minutes, take your men over there.' He pointed to a house opposite. 'In the next street there's a machine gun post, it's playing havoc with the troops. We can't move from our present position. They've got us pinned down. I want you to wipe it out. My boys will give you cover. OK?'

'Yes, sir.'

The man turned away, heading for the exit. 'Good luck, sergeant.'

Joshua gathered his men together and gave them their orders. 'You three go first, make for the doorway. If it's clear, signal me. We'll give you covering fire.'

He counted down the seconds. Five, four, three, two, one – go!

The sound of rifle fire filled the air as the men ran in a zigzag towards the building. A sniper was seen in an upstairs window and shot, his body plummeting down to the road below. After a few minutes, and more sounds of firing within the building, Joshua got the signal to proceed.

In small groups he and his men managed to cross the road safely. The house was now empty of live opposition, but as they went upstairs, climbing over dead bodies, they could see, in the opposite building, the position of the machine gun, placed on a small balcony, manned by two German soldiers. It could cover three directions, holding up any further advance.

He eyed the situation carefully. There was one

blind side; if he and his men could manage to enter the house from the back, they had a chance, but they had no way of knowing if there were any more enemy soldiers in the building. He felt it was more than likely.

Stealthily, they crept out of the house, crossed the alleyway and made it to a wall beside the building. They listened but could only hear gunfire in the distance. He knew the rest of the troops were waiting for him to destroy the machine gun position before they moved in. He looked at the others and, taking a grenade from his belt, said, 'Right! Let's do it.'

On the lower floor they eliminated two of the enemy, then another appeared at the top of the stairs. One of the men shot him, then yet another arrived, crouched low. He aimed his rifle and Joshua heard the cry of pain as one of his men was hit, before the German went down in a hail of bullets.

Joshua leapt up the stairs two at a time and, pulling the pin from the grenade, threw it into the front room, ducking down behind a wall to escape the blast. Guns at the ready, his men entered the room, firing their rifles. The machine gun was in pieces, as were the German soldiers. He looked out of the window and waved to the officer in the distance, waiting to advance. The building was secure.

He and his troops went down into the street below and crouched behind any cover they could find, waiting for the rest of the company to move forward.

'Good work!' said the officer as he passed.

'Let's start on the next street ... and keep your head down.'

One of the men quipped, 'He's a crazy man if he thinks I'm putting my head above the parapet!'

They moved forward again, from house to house, ducking and diving, firing at any of the opposing army who had lingered, moving along the street until it all seemed clear. Then they took a rest.

'Jeez,' said a voice from the rear, 'that was real hairy and I want my momma!'

There was a sound of laughter as the man who'd spoken was huge. 'No momma ever gave birth to you, Samuel. You'd have killed her. I reckon you was regular army issue.'

The call came for them to advance. They moved down to the end of the street. The tank in front turned the corner. As it did so, Joshua heard the whine of a shell, then there was a massive explosion as the tank in front of him was blown up.

He felt a searing pain in his shoulder as he was lifted from the ground by the blast – then everything turned black.

Men scurried forward, keeping low, pulling the injured away from the burning tank. There were moans from the injured. One of the men cursed. 'That son of a bitch has got the sarge!' There was a burst of gunfire and loud calls of 'medic'.

Ezra came running over as Joshua, sheltered by a wall, was attended to by a medical orderly.

'Is he alive?' asked Ezra.

'Yeah, but his shoulder's a mess. He took some

shrapnel in it by the look of it, and he's been hit in the head.'

'Is he gonna make it?'

'Difficult to say, buddy. We need to get him to the field hospital pretty quick. I'll just give him a shot of morphine.'

Ezra looked at the men standing around. 'Well, we ain't leaving him behind. Get the frigging meat wagon over here!'

They stood and watched in silence as Joshua was put on a stretcher and into the ambulance.

At the military hospital, behind the lines, Joshua Lewis waited on a stretcher along with the other wounded. He came to for just a moment, and tensed as he felt the pain from his wounds, then he lapsed into unconsciousness.

His stretcher was lifted and he was taken into the surgery. The surgeon looked at his shoulder after the nurse removed the dressing. 'This looks a bit of a mess. We'll know just how bad when we take a look inside. He's also got a piece of shrapnel lodged in his skull. Let's hope it isn't a big piece. Right, let's get on with it.'

Several hours later, Joshua regained consciousness. He could see that his shoulder was heavily bandaged. He put a hand to his aching head and felt the bandages there too. He tried to move, but found it too painful. He looked around, puzzled. Where the hell was he?

A nurse came over to his side and put a thermometer in his mouth. 'Back in the land of the living I see, soldier. How are you feeling?'

'A bit woozy. Where am I?'

'You're in a field hospital. You were caught in an explosion.'

'I was? Where?'

The nurse smiled and said, 'Don't talk, sergeant. You might swallow that.' She held his wrist and took his pulse.

When she'd removed the thermometer, he said, 'I don't remember anything. Nothing at all.'

She patted his arm reassuringly. 'That's all right, nothing to worry about. It's quite normal. No doubt after a good sleep you'll feel better. The doctor will come and see you later today. You try and get some rest now.'

He watched her walk away. She called him sergeant. How strange...

It was early evening before he was seen by the surgeon.

'Hello, Sergeant Lewis, and how are you?' He picked up the chart at the end of the bed and studied it.

'A little sore, doc.' He looked anxiously at the man. 'I don't seem to be able to remember anything.'

The doctor frowned. 'Do you remember your name?'

'No, sir. But you called me Sergeant Lewis.'

The doctor sat on the edge of his bed. 'What month is it?'

Joshua shook his head.

'Who is the president of the United States?'

Joshua looked blankly at him. Suddenly fearful, he asked, 'What's happening to me?'

'You were caught in an explosion, it seems. You took a piece of shrapnel in your shoulder. It went in at an angle and tore one of your ligaments pretty bad, but I patched it up real well, if I say so myself. We've cleaned out where the ball goes into the socket of your shoulder, explored the joint, repaired the ligament, but there's been a lot of internal bruising of the muscles, which will take time to heal. Apart from that you caught some more shrapnel in your skull.' Seeing the look of anxiety on the face of his patient, he tried to reassure him. 'You've been a very lucky man. It didn't go deep enough to cause you any real danger ... but it is probably the reason for your memory loss.'

Joshua's eyes widened. 'Will my memory come back?'

'Most probably, in time. But I can tell you that you are Sergeant Joshua Lewis. That at least is a starting point. We have informed the authorities of your whereabouts. They'll get in touch with your next of kin – then we can fill in the blanks about your background.' He rose from the bed. 'Try not to worry. I know that's difficult, but if you do, you could impede your recovery. I'll see you tomorrow.' He turned to the nurse. 'See that the patient is put on a light diet for twenty-four hours.' He turned to Joshua. 'In a few days we'll have you back in England in a hospital there. Your war is over for a while, son.'

Joshua lay back against his pillows. He had a name, it seemed, but it didn't sound in the least bit familiar. He felt a rising tide of panic inside and tried to control it. He was a man from ...

328

where? He was obviously in the army. Had been in the fighting, but that was all.

He looked around the ward with its stark iron beds, all filled with men with a variety of injuries. Several, it was obvious to see, were in a worse state than he was. The doctor said he'd been lucky, and compared with one or two men in beds nearby he could see the truth of the remark, but at least they all probably knew who they were.

His head was throbbing. He closed his eyes and tried to sleep, to blot out the fears that were filling his mind. What if he never regained his memory? What then?

In Southampton, Jack Evans made his way along College Street carrying a small suitcase. When he arrived at the side door of the Bricklayer's Arms, he hesitated. The pub was closed at this hour of the afternoon; he knew the side door would be open, as usual, but should he knock? Taking a deep breath, he opened the door, closing it behind him, and walked down the narrow corridor towards the kitchen, calling as he went: 'Moira! Anyone at home?'

Moira looked up from her newspaper as she recognized the voice of her husband. 'I'm here, Jack.' She rose from her chair and went into the scullery to put on the kettle. When she returned she saw him, standing just inside the door, with a look of uncertainty on his face. He looked like a lost child, and she felt pity for him. It couldn't have been easy for him, coming home after what he'd done. She walked over to him and kissed him briefly on the cheek and saw his expression of relief at her greeting.

'Sit down,' she said. 'I've put the kettle on. How are you, Jack?' He looked pale and drawn.

'I'm fine,' he said quietly, still unsure of his ground. 'Where's Maggie?'

'Working. She'll be back at eight o'clock. They asked her to work the later shift. She only works the early one usually, so that she's home to run the bar in the evening, but Tuesday's normally quiet, until later.' She returned to the scullery and came back with a tray of tea.

They sat at the table together. 'How is she?' he asked.

'Fine. She told you about the baby?' Moira asked as she poured the tea.

He nodded. 'It came as a bit of a shock, I must admit.'

'He's a nice boy, Jack. He thinks the world of her, and she of him.'

He sipped his tea slowly. 'How could you let her go out with a darkie?' He looked accusingly at her.

'You think you could have stopped her?'

'I'd have had a bloody good try!'

She gave him a scornful look. 'Remember the last time you tried to put your foot down? She left home. If you hadn't interfered she might not have met him!'

He looked appalled. 'Are you trying to say it was my fault?'

She shook her head wearily and sighed. 'No, it wasn't anyone's fault. I'm just worried about the future ... when the child is born.' She stared hard

330

at him. 'She's going to need our support, Jack, whether Joshua comes back or not. Can you give it to her, feeling the way you do about coloured folk?'

He looked away. 'To be honest, I don't know. I hope so.'

Moira's temper flared immediately. 'Now you listen to me, Jack Evans. After what you put us through, you'll have to do better than hope so! Maggie saved this place ... and your neck.'

'What do you mean?'

She glared angrily at him. 'You've got a home to come back to, haven't you? You owe her - and don't you forget it!'

He looked shaken at her outburst, and ashamed. 'I know what I did was wrong.'

All the anger and frustration she had been harbouring inside her these past months came to the surface in a rush. 'Wrong! I'll say you did wrong. As far as you were concerned, I could have been out in the street without anywhere to live. Penniless. Did you bloody care? Did you hell!'

'Oh, Moira. Don't you think I know all this? Christ! I've had a long time to think about it. Believe me I've paid for my mistake. I can only tell you how very sorry I am. You didn't deserve to be treated like that.'

'No I bloody well didn't.' Her eyes flashed with anger as she stared at him with a long accusing look. 'You say you're sorry. Right, now is the time to prove it. Maggie needs both of us. You let her down once more and you and I are finished for good. Understand?'

He knew that she meant every word. 'I understand. Don't you think I'm worried about her as well? She's my daughter too.'

'Then be a father to her, that's all I'm saying.' She rose from her seat. 'I'll get you something to eat.'

He lit a cigarette and drew deeply on it. It would be a very long time before Moira forgave him, if she ever did, he thought. And because he really loved her, for all his thoughtless ways, it hurt. Well it was payback time for him, his chance to prove he was sorry for his misdeeds. Would things ever be right between them? Only time would tell, but he'd have to step carefully.

By the time Maggie returned home, Jack had taken his things upstairs and put them away ... in the spare room. He had hoped that Moira would have taken him back into their bed, but she'd made it very clear where he was to sleep. He had a bath and a shave, changed his clothes, and for the first time in months he felt like a human being. He was sitting in the kitchen by the fire, reading the newspaper, when his daughter walked in.

'Dad. How are you?' She walked over to him and kissed him. At least she looked genuinely pleased to see him.

She was still in her dungarees, with her turban around her hair. 'I'll go and have a bath and then I'll take you into the bar and pour you that pint I promised.'

He looked hesitant. Moira was working in the bar, but he hadn't had the courage to step inside and see the locals.

She recognized his anxiety. 'There's no reason to hide away. Everyone knows you're coming home today. I won't be long and we'll go together.'

It was only then that he realized just how much his little girl had grown up. She was in charge, and to his chagrin, he didn't seem to mind. When at last she appeared in a clean jumper and pair of slacks, she grinned. 'Come along, you might as well get it over with.'

He followed her along the hallway and paused as she opened the door which led to behind the counter. 'Come on,' she said.

He stood in a corner behind the bar and looked around, feeling very conspicuous. Several regulars called over to him, and he greeted them in return. Moira was busy serving and ignored his presence. Maggie took a pint glass down from the shelf, walked to the pumps and with a grin in his direction, pulled him a pint of beer. She walked back to him and handed him the glass.

'There you are, Dad. That'll be the best pint you've ever tasted.'

He put the glass to his lips. 'Cheers!' he said and took a deep swig. The froth clung to his mouth and he licked it away with great relish. He held the glass up to the light and peered at the remains. 'Good and clear,' he remarked.

'What else did you expect?' said Maggie.

Nobby came into the bar at that moment and, walking over to the counter, shook him by the hand. 'Come on round this side, Jack, and I'll fill you in with all the local gossip.'

Nobby Clarke had always been a good mate and Jack felt at ease with him, and Nobby, being the man he was, didn't beat about the bush. 'Was it tough inside?' he asked.

And Jack told him.

He shook his head. 'You were a bloody fool. I credited you with more sense,' he said bluntly.

'I know,' admitted Jack. 'If I could only turn back the clock.'

Nobby looked across the room at the two women behind the bar and said quietly, 'I wonder if Maggie feels the same?'

Jack glanced sideways at him. 'What do you mean?'

With a sympathetic expression, he said, 'I know she's pregnant.'

Jack looked shocked. 'I didn't know it was common knowledge.'

'It isn't, but Moira confided in Grace, she was so worried. Let's face it, Jack, you weren't here – and if you had been I doubt she would have told you.'

A frown creased Jack's forehead. His feelings were well known. 'Well I know now. Not that I'm happy about it, of course.'

'What father would be? But I have to tell you that Joshua's a nice bloke, even if he is black. He's intelligent, well read, he made me feel quite ignorant beside him.'

'Really?'

'Oh, yes. Pity isn't it?'

At closing time, Jack helped them to tidy up the

334

bar. Maggie asked him to go and lock up the gents for her. Ever since her run-in with Steve Rossi, it was a job she could no longer do. She always got one of the locals to do it for her.

When the bar was finished she sat on a stool beside her father, Moira having gone to bed. 'I need your help, Dad,' she said.

Jack was thrilled to hear this as he had wondered what his place would be in this household now.

'I can't lift the barrels any more, it's dangerous for the baby, so will you take over the cellar?'

'Of course, love. I'd be happy to.'

'And if the brewers are agreeable, perhaps you'll help out in the bar too, give Mum and me a break. But I'll have to get permission first.'

He pursed his lips tightly, then said, 'I'm so sorry, Maggie, for all the trouble.'

She patted his knee. 'It's all in the past now, Dad.'

'I don't think your mother thinks so.'

'Just give her time, she'll come round,' she said. 'Come on, it's late, let's call it a day.'

Jack lay on the bed in his solitary state, tired from the emotions and traumas of the past few hours. But he felt at peace with himself. Maggie needed him and that made him feel good, and the fact that Nobby had spoken so highly of this Joshua pleased him too. Nobby was a canny man and a good judge of character. Knowing that the father of Maggie's unborn child was highly thought of helped him accept the situation a little better. But he knew his greatest test was yet to come.

335

Chapter Twenty-Four

A week later, Joshua was put on a troop ship and sent across the Channel to a hospital at Netley, just outside of Southampton. But of course in his present state of health it might as well have been Timbuctoo. Places meant nothing to him. He had an American accent and was in the US Army. But where was he born? He knew not.

There had been some snapshots in his uniform pocket that he'd studied carefully time and time again. One was of a family gathering with a minister, a lady who was probably his wife, two sons and a cheeky-looking girl holding a younger girl by the hand. He wasn't in the picture though. Was it his family? Perhaps he was behind the camera. Then there was a picture of this beautiful white girl; with laughing eyes and flowing hair. Who was she?

He kept flexing the fingers on his right hand. It bothered him that they were stiff because of the wound in his shoulder. But deep in the recess of his mind, it was more than that. It seemed vitally important to him that he should get back their natural dexterity.

When he questioned the doctor about the stiffness in his fingers, he was told that in time, he should get the full use of them. 'There was a lot of damage done, Sergeant Lewis. The surgeon did a good job when he operated, but the wound and interior bruising take a long time to heal. Soon we'll give you some physiotherapy treatment. That'll help.'

The following few days were a living nightmare for the injured man. The medical staff were kind and efficient, but he felt as if he was occupying a space in a crowded world of strangers, of which he had no part. He was an unknown quantity.

In the bathroom, he looked in the mirror and this stranger stared back at him. It was a terrifying experience. He touched his face, the man in the mirror did the same, so he knew it was him. But who was he? Had he been a nice person, was he a good man? So many questions ... and if his memory returned, would he be disappointed at what he discovered? He frowned. He could be anyone. A murderer for instance... No, he couldn't believe that; yet how was he to know?

He walked back to his bed, still delving mentally. Perhaps he had a wife and children. If so, they must be mad with worry. By now his head was throbbing and he lay on his bed and closed his eyes. Once the authorities contacted his next of kin, he'd know who he was of course, but he wasn't at all sure he was ready for such revelations.

Later in the week, one of the nurses helped him into a wheelchair and pushed him outside into the expansive grounds of the hospital. She settled him under a large cedar tree, wrapped a blanket around his shoulders to keep out the spring breeze and, putting the brake on the chair, said, 'There you are, Joshua. A change of scenery will do you good. Are you warm enough?'

'Yes, ma'am. I'm just fine.'

'I'll come back for you in an hour.'

Looking out over the lawns he gazed at the horizon and asked, 'Where is this place?'

'You're looking out over Southampton Water,' she said. 'We took over this hospital from the British. Before the war, ocean liners would pass by here on their way to the States. The ones you see now are bringing stores and troops back to the port. Not a bad view, eh?'

He smiled. 'I always did like being by the water,' he said.

'Did you now? I wonder why?'

He frowned. 'I don't remember.'

She patted his shoulder. 'You will, you'll see.'

Alone, Joshua sat back in the chair. It certainly was peaceful here. The sun was shining, the birds were singing and the scent of cedar wafted on the air. In the distance, he looked out over the water sparkling from the sun, and for just a moment a picture flashed into his head of a large paddle steamer ... a river boat. Then it was gone.

He sat very still and closed his eyes in the hope that it would return. There was nothing – but at least there had been something. He reached into the pocket of his pyjamas, took out the two pictures and looked at them again and again, but as before, they meant nothing to him. He looked at the picture of the girl and wished he could remember just who she was. She sure was pretty.

338

The war was over! On May 6th at 3 p.m. Maggie and her family sat and listened to Winston Churchill make his speech from 10 Downing Street. The official announcement had been a long time coming. In the morning edition of the *Daily Mirror*, Jane, the scantily clad character in the strip cartoon, had disrobed completely, as she'd promised to do, for peace.

Crowds massed in front of Buckingham Palace, chanting, 'We want the King.' He and his family appeared, waving to the crowds. Such was the enthusiasm, they came out onto the balcony eight times in all.

Moira, Jack and Maggie cheered and hugged each other. At last. No more fighting, no more terrible loss of life, and for Maggie, hope at last that she would hear from Joshua. She had no doubts whatever that he would keep his word and get in touch again. She had convinced herself that the reason she hadn't heard was because he must be a prisoner-of-war. She ran to collect the post every day, hoping for a letter. Now she wouldn't have to worry. Soon she would hear.

That evening, she and Ivy rushed off to the Civic Centre forecourt where there were great celebrations. People danced and sang, drank beer and made merry.

The pub was full to overflowing and nearly everyone had far too much to drink. And why not? There was so much to be grateful for.

'Thank God!' said Moira to Grace Clarke.

'Has Maggie had any news?' asked her friend.

Moira shook her head. 'Not lately. We just live in hopes. It's the not knowing that's driving her crazy.'

There were street parties during the following days. Houses were decorated in bunting and the morale of the locals was jubilant.

'At least your child will be born into a free world,' said Moira, as she sat with Maggie outside the pub at one of the trestle tables.

Looking around at the happy faces, Maggie couldn't help being infected with the jubilation. 'It's a wonderful time,' she said. And thought how nice it would be when eventually all the rationing would be lifted and everyone could get back to normality. She just wished that Joshua was here to join in the celebrations.

She had been making regular trips to the doctor and all was well with the baby. She had requested a home confinement and the doctor had said she was strong and healthy and he couldn't find any reason why she shouldn't. She had seen the midwife and made the arrangements. As she had said to her mother, 'I don't want to be in some strange hospital, alone. I want to be at home, with you to hold my hand.'

'I'll be happy to, darlin'. I can't wait to see my grandchild.'

Jack kept out of such discussions. But he was worried about Maggie. She was convinced that Joshua was in some prison camp, but he wondered, cynically, whether the boy had just forgotten about his time in England with her, as so many GIs would do as they prepared to return home to their families.

340

There had been great celebrations within the confines of Netley Hospital too. They were a little more tempered due to the condition of the patients, of course; nevertheless, they were very much appreciated. An army band visited the hospital to give a concert. Those who were well enough sat in rows of seats, others in wheelchairs, and some had their beds pushed into the hall.

As the music started, Joshua's feet began to tap and he automatically played every note of the music, using his knees as a keyboard, a thing that didn't escape the attention of the senior sister, who watched him for several minutes. She came to sit beside him.

'Great music, Joshua, isn't it?'

'Yes,' he replied. 'This is a Duke Ellington number. One of my favourites.'

She smiled to herself but made no comment. The following day she took him into a recreation room and sat him at a piano. Lifting the lid, she said, 'Try it!' and left him alone.

He looked a little nonplussed and nervous. The keyboard looked very familiar to him. He ran his fingers over the keys and picked out a bass note with his left hand, then a melody with his right. He suddenly felt alive. He closed his eyes and began to play, finding the slight stiffness in his right hand very frustrating when his fingers wouldn't do as he wanted. But for the first time since he'd arrived in hospital, he was a happy man.

Outside the door, the sister listened to the music and went to fetch the doctor.

A while later the door opened and Joshua looked up with a broad smile on his face. 'Hi, doc. What do you know. I can play piano!'

'And you like Duke Ellington. I'm a Tommy Dorsey man myself.'

'Well then you've got great taste. Have you ever heard Harry James, Benny Goodman or Louis Armstrong? And what about Count Basie?' He looked at the doctor in surprise. 'Hell, where did all that come from?'

The man looked at him and said, 'It's the beginning, sergeant, and an excellent sign. Carry on, but don't do too much.'

'Thanks, doc.' As he continued to play he found himself thinking of the girl with the laughing eyes.

The following day Joshua was sitting at the piano, perspiration beading his forehead as he practised. The left hand played the syncopated rhythm just fine, but the fingers on the right hand were still so stiff. He stopped and stretched them. His shoulder ached. But still he kept going until the senior sister came into the room and stopped him.

'Sergeant Lewis! That's enough.'

He sat up and rubbed his shoulder.

'There you go now! What's the point in us working hard to heal your injury if you go and undo it all? You're too impatient.' She sat alongside him on the stool and placed an arm around him.

'Look, sergeant, I know that discovering you can play has been a boon to you, but unless you listen to me, you'll do yourself untold damage. Your muscles aren't ready for all the pressure you're putting on them.'

He sighed. 'I guess I'm not a very patient man. But don't you see, this is the only thing that has made any sense since I came here.' He had a look of desperation. 'Until now, I've been a nobody with nothing. Just a name. At least I have this ... and that's all I have.'

'I know it's tough for you, Joshua, but at least you have something. And this is just the beginning. Other things will come back to you, given time.' She took a small rubber ball out of her pocket and said, 'Here, take yourself off for a walk around the grounds and keep squeezing this. Don't let me see you in here again before tomorrow! And then only for thirty minutes.'

He grinned broadly. 'They should have sent you to the front line, sister. You'd have put the fear of God up the Hun!'

'Enough of your cheek. Now get out of here!'

Joshua made his way out into the grounds, squeezing the rubber ball in his right hand as he walked.

He sat beneath the tall cedar tree, which was now a favourite spot of his, and started humming to himself. He felt that music was important to him, more than just being able to play a piano, but try as he might, he couldn't understand why. Where did he learn? Did he just play for pleasure? He didn't think so, but he didn't know why. Perhaps he was a professional.

Putting down the rubber ball, he held out his hand and flexed his fingers. There was no doubt that they were much better, but he was extremely worried that they wouldn't ever be dextrous enough to play properly. He supposed that when eventually he was released from here and sent home, he at least could earn a living.

The authorities would have been in touch with his next of kin - whoever that was - but this took time, he knew that. Especially now he'd been moved to a hospital in England, his papers would have to catch up with him. Even if they arrived with his home address, he'd be writing to perhaps a wife or a mother of whom he had no recollection. These problems weighed heavily with him.

Some of the troops that had recovered would soon be repatriated, and eventually the entire American staff would vacate the hospital; Joshua had elected to stay where he was until they did. Somehow he felt safer. Here, no one would come to visit him. He couldn't bear the idea of a stranger coming towards him, arms outstretched in welcome and him not knowing just who they were. And the doctors were in agreement, feeling that such an experience could be too traumatic for him to cope with at the moment.

Early in the month of August, Ivy's husband Len had returned to Southampton from the war overseas and pleaded with her to take him back. But she was very uncertain. As she said to Maggie, 'I know I was in the wrong, but he was having a good time too ... and I haven't forgotten the beating he gave me. Yet ... somehow the war has changed him.'

'In what way?' asked Maggie.

Ivy looked thoughtful. 'I don't know, he's more of a man now. More thoughtful, more inclined to think of me and not his mates and the boozer. Mind you, some of them were killed overseas.'

'What are you going to do?'

'I really don't know.' She looked at Maggie. 'I've got used to pleasing myself, not having to think about putting a meal on the table at a certain time, and all that. But...' She looked at her friend. 'I do get lonely, Mags.'

'I know what you mean,' said Maggie.

'Oh, I'm sorry, love. How stupid of me to run off at the mouth like that without thinking.'

'Come on, don't be silly. Life goes on,' Maggie reassured her. She sat up straighter in the chair, holding her back. 'I'll be glad when this is all over,' she said. 'This child is so heavy to cart about.'

'Do you want a boy or a girl?' asked Ivy.

'All I want is a healthy baby.'

Ivy looked at her, a soft expression in her eyes. 'You make me feel broody.'

'You! I didn't think of you wanting children. Well, not yet anyway.'

'To be honest,' confessed her friend, 'I feel it's time to settle down. But somehow I really don't see me spending the rest of my days with Len. Bob showed me that there are better men around... I'll just have to wait until I find one.'

Maggie gave her friend a cheeky grin. 'You won't ever be on the shelf, Ivy. Men have always gathered around you like bees round a honey pot.'

'Yes, and we know why! So I like a good time, but there's more to life. I want a home and kids, like everyone else.' She pulled a face. 'Christ! I must be getting old.'

'What, at twenty-four? Hardly.'

'My old gran thinks I'm definitely on the shelf now I don't have Len. She said as much the other day.' She chuckled. 'I told her, I don't mind, as long as someone takes me down now and then and gives me a dust!'

'What did she say to that?'

'She's a quaint old bird. She said, "Quite right girl, but don't wait too long or all the good uns will have gone." Cheeky sod.'

The following days seemed to drag to Maggie. She couldn't get comfortable at night, even with a small pillow beneath her bump as her mother had suggested. The baby seemed to have settled on a nerve, and to help the discomfort she walked around, lifting the weight with one hand.

'I'll be glad when this is all over,' she said to Moira as they sat in the kitchen one afternoon.

'The last few weeks are the worst,' explained her mother. 'I remember it well. But when you hold that child in your arms ... there is nothing like the thrill of it.'

'I wish Joshua were here,' said Maggie plaintively. 'I miss him so much.'

'Of course you do, darlin'. If he is a prisoner-of-war, it takes ages before everything is sorted and the men go home. You're bound to hear in time.'

Maggie squeezed her mother's hand. 'I know.'

But Moira was beginning to have her doubts. Perhaps Joshua had been killed in action. If he had, then his parents would have been notified, not Maggie. God! She hoped that wasn't the case. She'd seen the telegraph boy on his bike stop and knock on a couple of doors in this street, delivering the dreaded telegram in its orange envelope. The anguish the family suffered was heart-wrenching. But if Joshua had been killed, Maggie might never know, and that would be even worse!

A week later Maggie went into labour. It took them all by surprise as, according to the doctor's calculations, the baby wasn't due for another three weeks.

Both the doctor and the midwife were summoned and the long wait began. Moira stood at the top of the bed, bathing her daughter's forehead, holding her hand when she had a contraction, soothing her as the pains increased.

Downstairs Jack was pacing the kitchen as he'd done when Maggie had been born so many years before. He was surprised to realize he was as much concerned now as he'd been then. The cries of pain coming from the upstairs room went through him like a knife and he wanted to rush upstairs and comfort her, but he knew better than to do so.

'I can see the baby's head,' said the doctor. He looked up at his patient. 'It won't be long now.'

Moira wiped the sweat from Maggie's brow. 'It'll all be over soon,' she said.

'I didn't know it hurt so much,' complained Maggie.

Her mother smiled at her. 'You'll soon forget all about the pain.'

But she couldn't answer, as another contraction gripped her.

'Push, Maggie. Push!' encouraged the doctor.

With all her might she bore down, her voice loud with the effort.

'Once more,' he pleaded.

Her face puce, she did as she was asked. Then she rested, exhausted, perspiration trickling down her face.

The doctor looked at her. 'One more push ought to do it,' he urged.

And at last it was over.

Dr Pierson grinned at her. 'You have a fine son, Maggie. Congratulations!' He wrapped the child in a clean towel and handed it to her.

She took the small bundle from him and stared into the little puckered face of her newborn child. 'Little Joshua Lewis,' she said and looked up at her mother. 'What do you think of your grandchild?'

Moira peered at the baby. 'Ah. He's absolutely beautiful,' she said. 'I can see both you and Joshua in him.'

Downstairs, Jack Evans heard the baby's cry and was relieved. But at the same time he was terrified. Terrified of what he would think when first he saw the child.

When later he was called upstairs, he made his way with great trepidation. He entered the bedroom and, walking over to the bed, leaned forward and kissed Maggie's forehead. 'Are you all right, love?'

'Fine, Dad. Take a look at your grandchild.' She moved back the fold of the towel so he could see.

Taking a deep breath he leaned over the small bundle. The baby had a smooth skin the colour of caramel toffee. His little mouth was moving, and his fingers. Jack looked at him as he put out his own finger and the baby enclosed it in his tiny hand.

He looked at his daughter and smiled broadly. 'He's lovely. I'd forgotten how small a newborn baby is.' He gazed at Maggie and in a soft voice said, 'It takes me back a few years.' He looked down at the child again. Poor little chap, he thought. None of this was his fault, and he's going to have enough problems as he grows without my adding to them. With a proud note in his voice, he said, 'I am your grandfather.'

Moira came over to him and kissed him on the cheek. 'You'll have to move back into our room,' she said quietly. 'We'll need the spare room for a nursery.'

Later, when she was alone with her baby, Maggie looked at the tiny toes, the fingers, the little tongue, and thought what a miracle childbirth was. It seemed impossible that this beautiful living creature had been growing inside her for almost nine months. She kissed the top of the baby's head. 'You are my precious little miracle,' she whispered. 'How proud your father will be of you when he sees you.' But when would that be?

she wondered. She gazed once more at their child. 'We'll just have to be patient,' she said. 'I know he'll come back one day. I just *know* he will.' But deep down she was beginning to experience her first doubts.

Chapter Twenty-Five

Whilst Maggie was coming to terms with being a mother, Joshua was extremely frustrated. Now he was having more of these flashbacks, but they were always so fleeting, never tangible. On the wireless one day he heard a spiritual being sung by a choir and suddenly he visualized the minister in the snapshot, standing in front of an altar – then it was gone. He kept looking at his reflection, but still a stranger stared back. It was driving him crazy.

He had nightmares about an explosion. The scene was fragmented: a burning tank, soldiers, the sound of gunfire, the whine of a shell. He woke up always with a start, perspiration dripping off him.

The nursing staff and the doctors were all very supportive, explaining that this was a good sign, even if it was distressing.

'But they don't last long enough for me to grasp!' he exclaimed.

'One day they will,' he was told. And he held on to this thought. He hoped it would be soon, because the authorities were closer now to giving him all the information about his background. As the doctor explained, 'There are so many wounded and dying to trace. Some dead, with only their dog tags for the office to follow up. But you'll hear very soon and then you'll go home to your family.'

But what if he didn't remember before then? He'd be sent to a home, surrounded by strangers, all making a fuss – and he wouldn't know them. The very idea terrified him.

He walked along the corridor, making for the gardens. Through a window he looked out over the lawn. There in the distance was a girl in a floral dress, her auburn hair flowing in the breeze. He stopped. 'Maggie,' he murmured and started to run, down the corridor, out into the grounds. He didn't even feel the grass beneath his feet as he flew towards the figure. 'Maggie!' he called, but she didn't look round.

Breathless, he caught up with the young woman, grabbed her by the shoulders and turned her round to face him.

She let out a cry of fright. He looked at the features of a stranger and apologized profusely. 'Gee, ma'am. I'm real sorry. I thought you were someone I knew.'

'It's all right, soldier,' she said, somewhat nervously, and walked on.

He made his way to the water's edge and sat on the grass. He took the picture from his pocket and looked at the girl with the smiling eyes. 'Maggie,' he said softly. 'How could I ever forget you?'

He sat for a long time, alone, staring at the

picture, then at the other one. He closed his eyes, letting his mind roam freely. Images crowded in one after another, until his head throbbed and he felt sick. He tried to look out at the horizon, but his head spun and his vision blurred. He held his head with his hands and rocked back and forth with the pain.

A nurse came rushing over, took one look at his haggard face and called two orderlies who put him into a wheelchair and took him back to his bed.

The doctor came in and took his pulse. 'What happened, Joshua?'

'I started remembering, then this pain in my head.'

'You try and rest now. I'll give you some pain killers.'

'But what if I rest then I can't remember again?' There was a note of panic in his voice now.

'You will, I promise.'

The nurse took his temperature, it was up. 'Just try and keep calm,' she said.

Joshua tossed from side to side in his bed. How could he keep calm? Memories were crowding his brain until he thought it was going to burst. He lay back and closed his eyes after taking the pills with a sip of water, until the throbbing subsided into a dull ache and he recovered his equilibrium... He was so tired. His eyes gradually closed and he slept.

Later in the day, the doctor came back to see him. 'How are you feeling?'

'A bit woozy, but my head doesn't hurt so much.'

'I've got some news for you, sergeant. Your papers have come through, now I can put you in the picture about your family, your home.' He sat on the edge of the bed. 'Your father,' the doctor began...

'Is a pastor of the church in Mississippi. I have two brothers and two sisters ... and I have a girl. We're going to be married.' A frown furrowed his brow. 'But the rest is somewhat hazy.'

The doctor smiled. 'Well done, son. When did all this actually happen?'

'A while back... All because of a girl with red hair.'

'No wonder you're in a state. But I'm surprised you're taking it so calmly.'

'Believe me, sir, calm is the last thing I feel. I'm just so happy to know who I am. Before, I knew I was Joshua Lewis because you told me so, but it was just a label to me. Any name would have done. But now ... well, now it's different... I need to spend some time alone to collect my thoughts.'

'Who is the president of the United States?' the doctor asked suddenly.

With a grin, Joshua answered, 'Harry Truman.'

There was a look of satisfaction on the doctor's face. 'I'll need to give you a thorough examination later today, but now I suggest you just rest.'

'My family?' asked Joshua.

'They've been advised of your whereabouts, sergeant. Soon you'll be going home and then you'll be discharged from the army.'

Joshua asked, 'Any chance I could be discharged from here, sir?'

'I'd have to make enquiries about that. You may have to go back to the States.'

'There's someone in Southampton I have to see. It's real urgent.'

The doctor got to his feet. 'You aren't going anywhere for a couple of days. How's your head?'

'Throbbing,' he admitted.

'You need to take it easy. This has been very traumatic for you. Give yourself some time to come to terms with what's happened. We'll talk in the morning.'

He felt so unwell that, although he desperately wanted to see Maggie, Joshua knew he wasn't up to it. After all, he didn't want to collapse on her doorstep! But at least now he could lie back on his pillows and plan for the future ... if she still wanted him.

It worried him that as she hadn't heard from him for so long she might have changed her mind. She was probably thinking all sorts of things. Maybe that he didn't love her. What would he do if she didn't love him any more? These tortuous thoughts plagued him as he lay in his bed.

'Just one thing, doc.'

'What's that?'

'Have you got a mirror somewhere?'

The doctor looked puzzled and gazed around the ward. He went to a locker, took a shaving mirror from the top of it and handed it to his patient.

Joshua looked in it and with a broad grin said,

'Hey. I know this guy!'

The doctor burst out laughing and shook him by the hand. 'Congratulations sergeant. I'm glad it all worked out.'

'Thank you, sir. So am I.' He lay back on his pillows, clutching the mirror, his mind filled with an image of Maggie Evans.

Baby Joshua was now three weeks old and the pride of the family. Jack had become besotted with the child, cuddling him at every available moment. Talking to him, cooing.

Moira looked on and with a wry smile said to Maggie, 'He never spent this much time with you.'

'It doesn't matter. I'm just so happy to see it. Knowing how Dad felt, I was afraid he'd have nothing to do with his grandchild. And as he grows, he'll need a man's authority and guidance.'

With a sharp look at her daughter, Moira said, 'What do you mean?'

'Well, Mum, I've not heard a word from Joshua, and I'm afraid that something has happened to him, because I know if he was alive, he would have moved heaven and earth to get in touch.'

She looked so sad that Moira's heart ached for her. 'You don't know that, darlin'.'

'True, but I have to be prepared, just in case.' She forced a smile. 'At least I have his child.'

Moira gathered her into her arms and held her. But neither spoke, both too full of emotion for words.

Most of the regulars of the Bricklayer's Arms fussed over the baby, but there were a few who gathered in small groups to gossip about Maggie being unmarried, with a black bastard. They didn't voice their opinions in front of the family, however.

Maggie was nevertheless very aware of the veiled hostility, and completely ignored it, holding her head with pride. This child was hers and Joshua's. He was born out of love, the child of the man she'd wanted to share her life with. She had nothing to be ashamed of. Had Joshua not been shipped out, they would be a happy family, and as young Joshua grew, she would tell him what a fine man his father was, so that he would be proud too.

Already she would hold her baby close to her and tell him of his father's talent, his gentleness, and how much she loved him.

As she gazed at her child, she could see how much he took after his father. She drank in every detail, remembering how Joshua's eyes twinkled, his laugh, how he held her to him and made love to her. She was scared that the memories would fade in time, but she'd had a snapshot enlarged and framed. It stood beside her bed on the table. It was the last thing she looked at every night, before she slept.

Sometimes she dreamed of him. He was always somewhere trying to reach her, but something always seemed to stop him and she'd wake in the morning feeling bereft.

Her friend Ivy was a great comfort to her. She would hold the baby and play with it whilst she tried to cheer Maggie. 'You'll hear eventually. I know you will. That man loved you so much, nothing will keep him away.'

'But what if he's been killed?'

'I've always thought that when two people are really close, like you were, you'd know. You'd get the feeling that something was wrong.' She looked at Maggie. 'Has anything like that happened?'

Maggie shook her head. 'It's just the uncertainty, that's all.'

Ivy smiled at her. 'He'll come back to you ... and the baby. I know he will.'

Two days later, the doctor told Joshua he could go into Southampton. 'But I want you back tonight, just to check on your health. If you're all right by the end of the week, we'll see about getting you discharged. Then you'll be free to do what you want.'

'Thank you, sir. That sounds mighty good to me.'

He showered and dressed in his uniform, his fingers trembling with nerves as he tried to knot his tie. He caught a bus and headed for the town, looking around at the streets, buildings, for anything that he recognized. He knew his way to the Bricklayer's Arms, and that was the only thing that was really important.

Getting off the bus, he walked through the park, heading for College Street, remembering how he and Maggie had sat among the trees, talking, on many occasions. He smiled to himself as he recalled their conversations – her liking for

Frank Sinatra, his teasing her about her taste in music.

At the corner of Maggie's street, he paused and nervously lit a cigarette. His heart was pounding. Would she be pleased to see him? What if she wasn't in? He couldn't bear the suspense any longer. Tossing the cigarette into the gutter, he took a deep breath and walked towards the pub.

Jack Evans heard the knock on the side door as he walked towards the bar. He was very surprised when he opened the door to see a GI standing there.

'Hello, sir. Are you Mr Evans?'

'Yes, that's right.'

The soldier held out his hand. 'How do you do, sir. My name is Joshua Lewis, and I've come to see Maggie.'

'Bloody hell!'

Maggie pushed the back door open with her backside, her arms full, carrying a basket loaded with dry laundry and wooden pegs. She looked at the open doorway and the silhouette of the man standing there. She heard him mention her name. She dropped the basket and, with a cry, staggered against the wall, her face drained of colour. Then she ran past her startled father and hurled herself into the arms of the soldier.

Moira came running from the kitchen, alerted by the noise and saw the two in an embrace. Jack looked at her, astonishment written over his face. She took his hand. 'Come on, love,' she said. 'This is no place for us old ones.'

When at last Maggie was able to speak, she said, 'Oh, Joshua, darling, is it really you?'

He chuckled softly. 'If it isn't I'd like to know who you think you're kissing so passionately.'

She ushered him into the front room, once filled with contraband, now a cosy sitting room. 'Let me look at you,' she said, gazing at him, touching the face of the man she loved so much. 'I was beginning to think I'd never see you again.'

He drew her into his arms and held her to him. Then he looked into her eyes. 'No one is ever going to keep us apart. I love you, Maggie. More than you'll ever know.' He smothered her with kisses. 'You are just as beautiful as I remember.'

She led him to the settee. 'Where have you been? Why didn't you write?'

'I was in an explosion... I lost my memory for a time.'

She covered her mouth in horror. 'Oh darling, how dreadful. Are you all right now?'

He caressed her cheek. 'Now I'm with you.'

'Were you in hospital?'

He nodded. 'You wouldn't believe it, but I've been at the one in Netley.'

'For how long?'

'Since just before the end of the war.'

'Oh no!' Maggie looked desolate. 'To think you were so near for so long. That's really cruel.'

'But I'm here now,' he said softly. 'I have to go back this evening, and if I'm all right, they'll discharge me at the end of the week.'

She gazed at him and, with a note of uncertainty in her voice asked, 'And what then?'

He looked puzzled. 'And then I thought we'd arrange to get married as we planned ... if that's what you still want?'

She kissed him longingly. 'What else would I want, you goose.'

'Oh, Maggie. Coming here today I was real scared.'

'Why?'

'I was worried that you'd have changed your mind.'

She cupped his face in her hands. 'Joshua Lewis, you're the only man I want, and now I know you still want me, that's reason enough.' She gazed into his eyes and smiled softly. 'I do have another reason, and so do you:

He looked confused. 'My memory is still a bit hazy. Is there something I should remember?'

She took his hand. 'Come with me,' she said. 'There's someone I want you to meet.'

'I've already met your father,' he said hurriedly.

She walked to the back door and opened it.

He followed, now curious, searching his brain, wondering who it could be. Who had he forgotten?

She led him to a large perambulator, its hood down, a canopy keeping the sun off the occupant. She untied the canopy and put it back, revealing the baby, asleep in the pram.

'Joshua, meet your son.'

He looked at her, eyes wide with astonishment, then he gazed down at the baby. He bent closer and studied the child, smoothing his soft cheek. Then he looked at Maggie again. 'This beautiful creature is ours?'

'Yes, darling, he's almost a month old.'

She saw the tears in Joshua's eyes as he looked at the child. Then at her. 'I had no idea,' he said in a choked voice.

'I didn't know I was pregnant when you were shipped out.'

'Oh, Maggie ... you had to go through this all on your own.'

'No, Joshua. Mum and Dad were here. They took care of me.'

'Your father! And what does he have to say about all this?'

She chuckled. 'He's besotted with little Joshua.'

'You named him after me?'

'Who else would I name him after?'

He shook his head slowly as he gazed into the pram. There was a look of wonderment on his face. 'He's so perfect,' he said. Then, gently stroking her face, he added, 'And so are you.' He leaned forward and kissed her forehead. 'We're going to have a good life together, darling. When I get clear of the hospital and discharged from the army, I'll go up to London and look for a job.'

Maggie picked up the baby and looked at Joshua with an expression that was full of love. 'I don't mind what you do or where, as long as we're together.' She placed the baby in his arms.

He looked down at his son and said, 'You are such a lucky little fellow. Your mother is beautiful and your father is going to make good.' He kissed the baby and cradled him. When he could tear his gaze from his child, he looked up at Maggie and with a broad grin said, 'You don't know it yet, but you're marrying one hell of a guy! I'm gonna make it big one day, have my own band and who knows, maybe, eventually, my own jazz club. It may take a little time, but your husband is going to be a successful man. I'm gonna take real good care of you both.'

Maggie kissed him tenderly. 'I know,' she said. She had no fears about the future. She knew it wouldn't be easy, that there would be prejudice from some. But she knew that Joshua had the talent to overcome all this and she had his love, which would shelter her and their baby. 'Come on,' she said. 'Let's go inside, he's due a feed.'

The two of them walked into the kitchen. Moira leapt to her feet and hugged the American. 'Oh Joshua, love. I'm so glad you're all right.'

He smiled at her. 'Gee, it's good to see you.'

'And this is my father,' said Maggie. 'Although you did meet briefly.'

Jack got to his feet, looking first at the baby, then at the GI. He shook Joshua by the hand. 'Nice to meet you,' he said shortly.

Joshua looked into the other man's eyes. 'Whatever your reservations about me are, sir, I want you to know that I love Maggie with all my heart and my wish is to take care of her ... and my son. Ain't nobody gonna stop me.'

Jack was impressed by the young man's candour and recognized the challenge. 'Good, I'm very glad to hear it. Sit down ... Moira, put the kettle on for a cup of tea.'

Joshua looked across at Maggie and silently mouthed, 'No coffee?'

She chuckled to herself softly as she put a finger to her lips to silence him. Joshua would learn their quaint English ways in time,

362

including how a cup of tea was the answer to all problems. He had taught her so much and now she would be able to teach him. She could see it was going to be an interesting life.

The publishers hope that this book has given you enjoyable reading. Large Print Books are especially designed to be as easy to see and hold as possible. If you wish a complete list of our books please ask at your local library or write directly to:

Magna Large Print Books
Magna House, Long Preston,
Skipton, North Yorkshire.
BD23 4ND

This Large Print Book for the partially sighted, who cannot read normal print, is published under the auspices of

THE ULVERSCROFT FOUNDATION

THE ULVERSCROFT FOUNDATION

... we hope that you have enjoyed this Large Print Book. Please think for a moment about those people who have worse eyesight problems than you ... and are unable to even read or enjoy Large Print, without great difficulty.

You can help them by sending a donation, large or small to:

The Ulverscroft Foundation,
1, The Green, Bradgate Road,
Anstey, Leicestershire, LE7 7FU,
England.
or request a copy of our brochure for more details.

The Foundation will use all your help to assist those people who are handicapped by various sight problems and need special attention.

Thank you very much for your help.